A SUITABLE WIFE

THE FITZGERALDS OF DUBLIN BOOK TWO

LORNA PEEL

Chapter One

Dublin, Ireland. Monday, January 17th, 1881

Will helped Isobel out of the cab outside the Shelbourne Hotel on St Stephen's Green. He paid and tipped the cabman generously and they made their way carefully up the steps. A bellboy with a shovel – fighting a losing battle to keep the steps clear of snow – stood to one side to let them pass, and the liveried doorman touched his silk top hat with a white-gloved hand as they went into the foyer.

The heaviest snowstorm for years was wreaking havoc on Dublin and Will had considered cancelling the celebratory dinner but hadn't the heart to send a servant out in such atrocious weather. The deep snow had resulted in traffic chaos, the cabman had been forced to take a longer route to the hotel, and they were cold and late.

Will's oldest friend, Fred Simpson, and his wife Margaret were waiting near the reception desk and gave them relieved smiles as Will and Isobel stamped snow from their shoes. They were shown to a table in the hotel's dining room and they sat down. Although the large room was pleasantly warm, Isobel opted to unbutton but continue wearing her

striking new coat of black velvet leaves on a white velvet background with black velvet collar and cuffs and Margaret chose to keep her exquisite black velvet cloak around her shoulders for the time being.

"May we have a bottle of champagne?" Fred asked the waiter. "We will make our selections from the menu shortly."

"Very good, sir."

The waiter left them and Fred grinned around the table.

"It is the 17th of January. Doctors Fitzgerald and Simpson have been in general practice together for just over a month and in partnership for a week. We couldn't allow it to pass uncelebrated – despite the best efforts of the weather."

"No," Will agreed. "And I've never been for a meal here before. Have you?"

"I have," Margaret replied, glancing around the elegant room, where the murmur of conversation intermingled with the clinking of glassware and china. "But it was a birthday dinner a long time ago. Fred." She turned to her husband. "Isobel and I shouldn't really be drinking champagne."

"One glass won't do you expectant mothers any harm."

"No, I suppose not," she conceded.

"Could you ask for a jug of water as well, please, Fred?" Isobel asked. "I'm parched."

"Yes, of course. I hope this will be the first of many celebratory dinners."

"So do I," Isobel replied but didn't sound particularly enthusiastic as she tucked a wisp of her dark brown hair behind her right ear.

At almost three months pregnant, the new gold-coloured

evening dress she wore only emphasised how pale she looked and she was unusually quiet. While at four months pregnant, Margaret in mauve was positively blooming with colour in her cheeks following a weekend away in Co Wicklow. He and Isobel wouldn't stay out too late this evening. Reaching for her hand under the table, he gave it a little squeeze and she squeezed it in reply.

The waiter served the champagne and they made their orders from the menu before Fred raised his glass.

"I propose a toast – to Margaret and Isobel – and to the continued success of Doctors Simpson and Fitzgerald's medical practice."

"To Margaret, Isobel and the medical practice," they all chorused and sipped the excellent champagne.

"You're going to have to excuse me for a few minutes." Isobel got up and Will and Fred also got to their feet. "Could you come with me please, Margaret?"

"Of course," Margaret replied and the two women left the dining room.

"Will, is Isobel all right?" Fred asked as he and Will sat down again.

"She's tired," he explained. "I'm delighted she's pregnant but, ideally, it could have waited a few more months. She was prepared to come and live with me in Brown Street but then her mother gave us number 30 and all it entailed."

"I thought she was coping well with the servants?" Fred added.

"She is, but being mistress of number 30 is still a huge responsibility, as is trying to ensure we don't spend too much while you and I rebuild the practice."

"She must think this dinner is an enormous extravagance?"

Will opened his mouth to reply but heard Margaret's voice calling him.

"Will? Please, come quickly."

Turning in his seat, he saw Margaret at the entrance to the dining room beckoning him to come to her. Both he and Fred went to her and Will's heart turned over as tears rolled down her cheeks.

"Where is Isobel?" he demanded.

"In there." Margaret pointed to the ladies cloakroom.

Will pushed the door open and found Isobel sitting on the edge of an armchair just inside the door, her brown eyes wide with horror.

"Will, I'm bleeding. The baby—"

"We'll go straight home." He helped her up and out into the foyer. "Fred, find a cab."

"I'll ask the doorman to hail one for us," Margaret said and hurried away from them.

"Isobel's bleeding," he whispered to Fred. "We need to bring her home at once."

"Waiter." Extracting his wallet from the inside pocket of his tailcoat, Fred pulled out a banknote and handed it to the young man. "I'm afraid we must leave."

"Thank you, sir. Do you need any assistance?"

"No, thank you," Will replied, searching the foyer for Margaret's blonde head and spotting her at the revolving doors signalling for them to leave the hotel.

He and Fred guided Isobel outside, carefully down the steps, and into the waiting cab. Sitting beside her, he clasped her hands. They were freezing cold and he raised them to his mouth, gently blowing his warm breath onto her fingers.

"Number 30 Fitzwilliam Square, please," Fred told the

cabman before tipping the doorman, assisting Margaret into the cab, then getting in himself.

The cab, with the four of them squashed in the back, travelled excruciatingly slowly through deep snow to Fitzwilliam Square. When it stopped outside the Georgian townhouse, the cabman was asked to wait and they led Isobel inside.

"Some towels and warm water, please, Mrs Dillon," Will instructed the cook-housekeeper as she approached them with concern in the hall. "My wife is unwell."

Isobel was brought upstairs to the bedroom they shared on the second floor and Will lit all the gas lamps then the oil lamp on his bedside table. Mrs Dillon came in with an ewer of water, a basin and some towels draped over her arm and placed them on the marble-topped washstand. She and Will undressed Isobel, helped her into a nightdress and let down and plaited her hair while Fred pulled back the bedcovers and laid out the towels in the bed. Isobel was bleeding heavily and Will's heart plummeted.

"My wife has gone to wait in the morning room, would you please look in on her, Mrs Dillon?" Fred asked. "She may be a little upset. Oh, and please bring the cabman inside for a hot drink, he must be frozen."

"Yes, Dr Simpson," the housekeeper replied and left the bedroom.

Isobel was lifted into the huge double bed on top of the towels and the pillows arranged at her back.

"Let me examine her, Will," Fred offered.

"No—"

"I'm calmer than you are, so let me do it," Fred insisted softly. "Wait outside."

Will nodded and went onto the landing. *I'm delighted she's pregnant but, ideally, it could have waited a few more months.* Wincing at what he had told Fred, he pulled open his white bow tie and his collar before leaning on the banister rail and closing his eyes.

Feeling a hand on his shoulder, he jumped and turned around.

"You probably already know," Fred told him. "But Isobel is miscarrying. There is heavy vaginal bleeding with clotting, but it's not excessive and I'm afraid nature will just have to take its course. I'm so sorry, Will."

"Is she in pain?" he asked.

"She says there is cramping but nothing too extreme. I've helped her into her drawers and placed two small towels in the drawers to absorb the discharge."

"Thank you, Fred. Take Margaret home. This must be awful for her."

Fred nodded. "I'll take your surgery and house calls tomorrow. Be with Isobel."

"Yes. Thank you."

Fred squeezed his arm and went downstairs.

Will took a deep breath before opening the bedroom door. Isobel was lying back against the pillows but her face was turned away from the door.

Closing the door behind him, he went to the bed and sat down. Gently putting his arms around her, he held her, feeling her trembling.

"I'm sorry," she whispered.

"This is no-one's fault."

"But it must be my fault," she insisted. "Did Fred's father leave me damaged when he carried out the abortion?"

"I don't know," he replied helplessly and kissed her temple. "You wanted some water at the hotel, would you like some now?"

"Yes. But please hold me first."

"Of course I'll hold you. Fred is taking my surgery and house calls tomorrow. I'm staying here with you. Are you hungry at all?"

"No. Just very thirsty."

"I'll ask for some water."

He laid her back against the pillows and left the bedroom. Downstairs in the hall, he met Mrs Dillon.

"How is Mrs Fitzgerald?" the housekeeper asked anxiously.

"Please come into the morning room." He opened the door for her and they went into the large reception room at the front of the house. "My wife is having a miscarriage," he said, hearing his voice shake, and Mrs Dillon's face crumpled in sympathy. "She isn't in any pain but the process will take a day or two. After that…" He tailed off and sighed. "She will need time to recover, both physically and mentally. But now, she would like some water, please."

"Water? Is that all?"

"Yes. And Dr Simpson will be taking my surgery and house calls tomorrow, so I can be here."

Mrs Dillon nodded. "I'll bring up a jug of water. I am so sorry, Dr Fitzgerald."

"Thank you."

He went back upstairs and into the bedroom. Isobel was sitting up, her face in her hands. He sat on the bed and she clung to him, sobbing. He stroked her hair until she rested her forehead on his shoulder and he heard a knock at the door. He lifted her head, kissed her lips, and opened the door.

Mrs Dillon, with more towels of various sizes laid over her arm, was lifting a tray with a jug of water and a glass on it from a table on the landing. She had clearly discreetly waited for Isobel to stop crying before knocking.

"Thank you," he said, taking the tray from her, and watching as she draped the towels over his arm.

"If there is anything else you or Mrs Fitzgerald need, just ring."

"I will. Goodnight."

He closed the door and put the tray down on the bedside table. He poured a glass of water, sat on the bed again, and passed it to Isobel. She drank the water in three gulps, he took the glass from her and placed it back on the tray.

"I'm going to put some more towels under you and then I think we should try and sleep."

"Yes." She lifted herself, he laid the towels under her, then leant back against the pillows.

He got undressed and pulled on a nightshirt, extinguished the gas lamps and got into the bed. "If you are in any pain or if you feel the bleeding getting any heavier, wake me."

She nodded and he turned the oil lamp down before lying down and holding her hand. He listened until hers was the deep and slow breathing of an exhausted person fast asleep. But he couldn't sleep. This was two miscarriages now. Was she right? Had Duncan Simpson damaged her while carrying out her abortion? Would she never be able to carry a baby to full term? He lay staring up into the darkness and didn't fall asleep until dawn was breaking.

Isobel opened her eyes and ran her hands over her stomach. She was still cramping and could feel herself bleeding like a

very heavy monthly. Will was fast asleep and snoring a little so she didn't move. Two miscarriages. She blinked back tears. She'd so wanted a baby with Will and this pregnancy had been progressing positively – she'd almost reached the three-month mark.

"Isobel?"

Hearing Will's voice, she turned to him in the twilight. He looked as exhausted as she felt and more tears stung her eyes. This must be awful for him, he had been looking after her so well.

"I'm all right."

"Are you in any pain?"

"No, but I am hungry."

"Good." He raised himself up onto an elbow. "So am I."

"And I'd like to get up. I don't want to lie in bed all day."

"Well, if you're sure?" he said, sounding uncertain.

"I am. And please don't tell my mother?" she begged.

"Isobel, I'm going to have to tell her. I want her to be here with you tomorrow."

"Mother can fuss tomorrow," she said. "I want peace and quiet with you today."

He leant over and kissed her lips. "I need to examine you first."

He got out of bed, opened the curtains, then went out to the table on the landing where their water for washing and shaving was left for them. Carrying the two ewers into the bedroom, he closed the door with a foot before placing them on the washstand. He washed and dried his hands then pulled the bedcovers down.

He removed the soiled towels from her drawers before helping her to take the drawers off. Wrapping them in a large

towel, he placed it on the floor by the door. Lying down on the bed, she opened her legs and stared up at the ceiling as he examined her.

"Is your bleeding heavier than the last time?" he asked.

"It feels heavier. But I wasn't quite two months pregnant then."

"Yes." He straightened up, reached for a flannel, and began to clean her. "I can't see anything which would lead me to worry. Nature will just have to take its course."

"That's what Fred said."

After washing, shaving and dressing, Will helped her to wash and dress. She pinned up her hair, placed two more small towels in her drawers, then stood in front of the full-length wardrobe mirror smoothing her hands down the skirt of her new high-necked emerald green day dress.

From arriving in Dublin with nothing but the square-necked navy blue dress and black coat she was wearing, she now had five dresses, two coats and three hats to her name. Sadly, the gold-coloured evening dress would now be forever associated with the miscarriage. Perhaps she could bring it back to the dressmaker and have it altered in some way, as it would be a shame – and a waste – to never wear it again. But that is a decision for another day, she told herself, closing the wardrobe door.

Taking Will's arm, they went slowly down the stairs to the ground floor breakfast room overlooking the rear garden which they used as an everyday dining room.

"Mrs Fitzgerald?" Mrs Dillon followed them inside. "I was preparing a breakfast tray for Florrie to take up to you."

"Thank you, but I didn't want to lie in bed all day."

"My wife needs peace and quiet today, Mrs Dillon," Will

told her. "So, no callers, please." As he spoke, a bell jangled downstairs in the servants' hall and he sighed. "I'll see who that is."

He went out to the hall and Isobel sat down at the table, her stomach rumbling.

"Some porridge, toast and marmalade and coffee, Mrs Fitzgerald?" Mrs Dillon asked.

"Oh, yes, please." She gave the housekeeper a grateful smile as she heard Fred's voice in the hall. "I'm very hungry."

"That's good to hear."

"I'm afraid the bed is in rather a mess—" she began but Mrs Dillon held up a hand.

"Don't you worry about that, Mrs Fitzgerald. You just rest and recuperate."

Mrs Dillon left her and a couple of moments later both Will and Fred came into the breakfast room. The weather must be bitterly cold still as Fred was wearing a black woollen overcoat with a grey scarf wound around his neck almost covering his chin.

"I'm delighted to see you up and about." Fred bent and kissed her cheek and she smiled as his black moustache tickled her ear.

"Thank you for all you did last night, Fred."

"Not at all. I'm glad I was able to help."

"I hope Margaret wasn't too upset?" she asked.

"She was, a little, but she'll be very relieved when I tell her you are up and about and hungry."

"Fred." She clasped his hand. "The last thing I want is any awkwardness between Margaret and myself. I would be delighted if she would call here in the next few days. Will and I are going to have a very quiet day today."

"Of course."

"And perhaps we could attempt the celebratory dinner again soon, too?"

Fred gave her a grin. "When you're well enough, we'll all go to the Shelbourne again."

"Yes. Will you stay for some breakfast?"

"Thank you, but no. I simply called to see how you were. It has stopped snowing at last but it's deep and difficult to walk in so I'd better be on my way to the practice house."

"Thank you, Fred. Be careful."

Fred kissed her hand and Will followed him out of the room. A few minutes later Will returned with Florrie, one of their house-parlourmaids, and their breakfast.

Isobel soon finished a bowl of porridge, two triangular slices of toast and marmalade followed by a cup of coffee, and was sitting back satisfied in her chair when she heard her mother's angry voice in the hall.

"What do you mean, no callers today? Don't be ridiculous, girl, I'm her mother. Is she still at breakfast?"

Isobel exchanged a weary glance with Will and he swore under his breath as footsteps approached the breakfast room door and it opened.

"Mrs Henderson." Will got to his feet as her dark-haired mother came in wearing a russet-coloured dress and hat she favoured with a matching cloak.

"What is this nonsense, Isobel?" she demanded, pulling off her black gloves. "The maid said you were receiving no callers today?"

Will closed the door to the hall then held the chair next to Isobel's as Mrs Henderson sat down.

"I'm afraid we have some bad news," he said, returning

12

to his seat at the head of the table. "Isobel is losing the baby."

"Losing..?" Her mother frowned, struggling to grasp Will's meaning.

"I'm having a miscarriage, Mother," she said quietly.

Mrs Henderson clapped both her hands to her cheeks. "Oh, Isobel. Oh, why didn't you tell me at once? Why are you not in bed?"

"We were going to tell you later, Mother, and I wanted some peace and quiet today but not to lie in bed all day."

"Why did this happen, Will?"

"I'm afraid there is no answer to that," he replied. "It's just one of those things."

"I'm so sorry. I was so looking forward to being a grandmother."

"Would you like some coffee, Mother?" she asked, changing the subject and gesturing towards the coffee pot.

"No, thank you. As it has stopped snowing, I called to ask if you would like to visit the National Gallery this afternoon as I have never been, but it can wait."

"Perhaps next week?" she suggested.

"Oh, Isobel," Mrs Henderson whispered, her voice shaking.

"Don't cry, Mother, please," she said, fighting to keep her own voice steady. Or I will start again, she added silently.

Mrs Henderson pulled a handkerchief from a sleeve and dried her eyes. "Would you like me to stay with you?"

"I will be staying with Isobel today," Will told her. "But if you could stay with Isobel tomorrow, I would be very grateful."

"Yes, of course. But may I call this evening?"

"Yes, you may." Will nodded. "Shall I see you out?"

Her mother kissed her cheek before getting up and

leaving the room with Will following. He returned a few moments later, kissed the top of her head, and poured them some more coffee.

"How are you feeling?"

"Better. The porridge was delicious."

"Good."

They settled on the huge reddish-brown leather sofa in the morning room, fell asleep, and didn't wake until luncheon was announced at one o'clock. After some delicious thick vegetable soup and soda bread, she went upstairs to change the towels in her drawers. She then put on her beautiful black and white velvet coat and joined Will in the garden for some fresh air and to see the snow.

The steps down from the back door and a couple of yards of the path had been dug out but the remainder of the long and narrow garden which ran between the house and the mews was covered with at least five inches of snow. She hadn't seen so much snow since one severe winter in Co Galway when she and her elder brother, Alfie, her parents and the servants had been snowed in at Ballybeg Glebe House for three extremely long days.

Snow drifts had rendered the roads impassable and being cut off from, not just Ballybeg village, but also from his beloved church, her father's cruel and vindictive temper intensified. The Reverend Edmund Stevens took his frustration out on, not only his wife and children but also on the servants for the first and last time. As soon as the roads were passable, their cook-housekeeper and house-parlourmaid packed their bags and left. It was almost a month before they were replaced and, having inherited her mother's lack of culinary skills, the meals the two of them

struggled to produce simply served to infuriate him even more.

February 23rd would bring the first anniversary of his death. Were any of his former parishioners mourning him, she wondered because his widow and children most certainly were not. Crouching down on the path, she laid the palm of her right hand on the snow. It had an icy crust which even the warmth of her hand couldn't melt. Her father's heart had been frozen through and through and his grave in cold, damp peaty soil near the church door in Ballybeg Churchyard, and now likely covered with a deep blanket of snow, was a fitting resting place for him.

"Whenever there was snow at the Glebe House, my father never allowed Alfie and I to play in it," she told Will, straightening up and rubbing her hands together. "He wanted his precious garden to always appear pristine. But when it began to snow here, I was already visualising our child playing out here with us – throwing snowballs and building a snowman – things Alfie and I were forbidden to do. How silly of me."

"Remember what I said, Isobel," he said, raising her hands to his lips. "If it turns out that we can't have a child ourselves, we will adopt. We may not have made the child ourselves but we will have a child."

"But I wanted us to have a child we made. I wanted to have your child, Will."

"Isobel?" They turned around as Alfie stood at the back door wearing a black woollen overcoat similar to Fred's and a pale blue scarf wound around his neck. "No, don't step into the snow, there's enough room on the path for the three of us." Closing the door, he came down the steps. "I had lectures this

morning and Mother has just told me. Oh, Isobel." He kissed her cheek before hugging her. "I'm so sorry."

"Is Mother very upset?" she asked.

"Yes, she is. I've persuaded her to go and lie down. I have only one lecture tomorrow and it's first thing in the morning. Would you like me to call here afterwards and keep you company?"

"Well, I had already asked Mother, but if you could come as well and try and keep the conversation a little upbeat?"

Alfie smiled. "I'll try my best."

After her mother called that evening, Isobel and Will retired to bed early. Will examined her again and agreed with her that the rate of bleed was slowing. He kissed her lips then turned down the oil lamp and she fell into a deep sleep with her head resting on his chest.

In the morning, Will waited for the breakfast room door to close after Florrie before speaking.

"I need to go to Merrion Square and tell my parents," he said, pouring some milk onto his porridge then adding a little sugar. "I don't want them to hear it from anyone else. As Alfie and your mother will be here with you today, I'll go in time for luncheon so Mother and Father will both be there."

Isobel nodded and he squeezed her hand.

At the front door, he gently took her face in his hands and kissed her.

"I will be back as early as I can this evening," he promised.

"Don't rush back on my account. I'll ask Mother and Alfie to stay to dinner, too, if need be. I won't be on my own. Don't do anything to jeopardise the practice."

"I won't." He kissed her again and opened the door, peering up at the dark clouds. It was blowing a gale and he sighed as if on cue it began to snow. "See you this evening."

Eva Bannister, practice secretary for the past twenty years, gave him a sympathetic smile as he hurried into the practice house on Merrion Street Upper. He shook the snow off his hat and overcoat before passing them to her to hang up on the coat stand in the office.

"I am so sorry, Dr Fitzgerald."

"Thank you, Eva," he replied simply and went upstairs.

"Will?" Fred looked out from his surgery and Will followed him inside. "How is Isobel?"

"Bearing up. The rate of bleed is slowing. Her mother and brother are staying with her today. Is there anything I should know about here?"

"I've left some notes on your desk."

"Thanks, Fred."

He went into his surgery and read through the notes before forcing Isobel and the miscarriage from his mind until he saw his final patient to the door at a quarter to one. He sat on a corner of his desk for a few moments dreading having to tell his parents. He knew his father especially would always see Isobel as a scarlet woman and would view the miscarriage as being her fault. But it had to be done and he heaved himself off the desk, picked up his medical bag, and went down the stairs for his hat and overcoat.

His parents were in number 67's morning room and looked up expectantly as he was shown in.

"What a lovely surprise." His ageless brown-haired mother, seated on the huge sofa upholstered in green velvet, smiled as he bent and kissed her cheek.

"I'm afraid I have some bad news," he began immediately as he went to one of the matching armchairs and shook his father's hand. "Isobel is having a miscarriage."

His mother clapped a hand to her chest and his father pressed his lips together.

"How is she?" his mother asked.

"She was extremely upset," he replied. "But she is slowly coming to terms with it now. Mrs Henderson and Alfie Stevens are staying with her today."

"Poor Isobel. You'll stay to luncheon?" she asked, getting up and smoothing down her high-necked burgundy-coloured dress before ringing for one of the house-parlourmaids.

Will's eyebrows shot up as she returned to the sofa. Was that it? He glanced at his father, who still hadn't spoken, before nodding.

"Yes. Thank you, Mother."

"I want a word with you, Will, before we eat." His father rose from the armchair and did up the buttons of his frock coat. "Come with me."

Reluctantly, Will followed his grey-haired father outside and closed the back door.

"I'll come straight to the point," his father said as they went down the steps before turning to each other on the dug-out and swept garden path. "This is Isobel's third miscarriage. She doesn't seem to be able to carry a child to term. I think it is time for you to think about her undergoing a hysterectomy."

Will stared at his father in disgust. "I'll pretend I didn't hear that."

"Be realistic, Will. How many times do you want her to go through this?"

"A hysterectomy?"

"Or an ovariotomy. One or the other."

"Remove Isobel's ovaries?" The very thought made Will feel nauseous. "No. That is little more than butchery."

"Well, what do you suggest? Unless you'd prefer to abstain from sexual relations with your wife altogether?"

Will exhaled a shaky breath. "No."

"Well, in that case…"

Will didn't wait to listen. He ran up the steps, opened the back door and went inside. He strode through the house, only pausing in the hall for his medical bag, hat and overcoat before going out and slamming the front door behind him.

Ramming his hat onto his head, he pulled his overcoat on and walked out of Merrion Square, not caring where he was going.

Twenty minutes later, he found himself on Brown Street in the Liberties. He gazed up at the Dutch Billy-style gable-fronted house he had lived in for almost five years noting how it was reoccupied and relieved it wasn't standing empty. Turning away, he made his way to a tenement house on Pimlico, climbed the stairs and knocked at the door to his former housekeeper's rooms, hoping Mrs Bell was at home.

She opened the door, wearing a black dress and white apron as always and beamed at him in delight for a moment before frowning.

"Dr Fitzgerald. Come in."

"Thank you." Taking off his hat, he went into her kitchen.

"You look like you could do with a cup of tea."

"Yes, please."

She hung a kettle on a crane over the open fire then

pointed to a chair. "Sit yourself down and tell me what's wrong."

"Isobel is having a miscarriage," he told her as they sat at the table.

"I'm so sorry to hear that," Mrs Bell said, her face creasing in sympathy. "Really I am. How is she?"

"Putting a brave face on it."

"And how are you?"

He stared across the table at her. She was the first person to ask him that and he couldn't help himself as the tears came.

"I'm so sorry," he sobbed, pulling a handkerchief from his trouser pocket and wiping his eyes.

"Jaysus, Dr Fitzgerald, has no-one else asked you how you are?" she demanded and he shook his head.

"My father wants me to consider having Isobel's womb or ovaries removed – anything to prevent her conceiving again. But I can't. I can't allow her to be butchered like that."

"No, of course not. Listen to me, Dr Fitzgerald." Taking his hands, Mrs Bell gripped them tightly. "Don't give up."

"But I don't think I could bear for her to go through this again."

"My mother had four miscarriages," she told him. "I was her fifth baby and, by all accounts, it was a completely normal pregnancy. So, don't you give up, do you hear me?"

"Four miscarriages?"

She nodded. "And, after me came my three brothers. We were all perfectly healthy, there wasn't a thing wrong with any of us. You and Isobel will have a baby, I'm sure of it."

"Thank you," he whispered.

"Don't give up."

"No."

"Good. I'll make some tea." She patted his hands, got up, lifted a brown teapot down from the dresser and took off the lid. "You're needed here, Dr Fitzgerald," she said, scalding the teapot with boiling water from the kettle. "The people need you back."

"Even after all but deserting me only a couple of months ago?" he asked bitterly, returning his handkerchief to his trouser pocket.

"A lot of people are sorry about that now. Come back?"

"Mrs Bell, my new practice has only been in existence for a month. Fred and I are still building up our patient lists. A good number of my father's patients were very sorry to see him retire suddenly and have gone elsewhere. At the moment I simply can't start again here."

"But if you could, you'd try?" Mrs Bell added two spoonfuls of tea to the teapot before reaching for the kettle again and filling it.

"Yes, but it could never be full time like before."

"Even just one surgery a week would make such a difference."

Will rubbed his forehead. "Where?"

Mrs Bell gave him a little smile as she put the teapot on the table. "Here. Downstairs."

"On the ground floor?"

"Yes. There are two empty rooms at the moment."

"I'll have to discuss it with both Isobel and Fred. I don't want to be too far from Isobel at present."

"Yes, of course. But she could come along, too?" Mrs Bell suggested. "Get her to help and be involved? She doesn't seem to be squeamish. You told me once she'd helped you get a

marble out of Annie Dougherty's throat. Think about it."

Half an hour later, Will got up to leave. "Thank you for listening. And for the tea."

"I'm glad you came for a chat, Dr Fitzgerald. Bring Isobel with you, the next time you call."

On his way out of the tenement house, he tried the door of the rooms on the ground floor. It was unlocked and he went inside. The room was large and rather dark, but that was due to the glass in the window being filthy. The next room wasn't quite as big and was a little brighter. It would make an ideal surgery but he turned on his heel and walked out. It wasn't just him he had to think of now. This would be a surgery far more than ten minutes walk away from Isobel and number 30. Apart from that, Fred might not be at all happy with the prospect of his practice partner setting up a surgery elsewhere.

Out on the street, Will put on his hat and buttoned up his overcoat. That morning's gale had blown the snow clouds away and the sun was shining for the first time in… he couldn't remember. He'd never heard of a woman having that many miscarriages and then going on to have four children with no complications. Banishing his father's disgusting surgical suggestions from his mind, he smiled and walked away to begin house calls.

Isobel did a double-take when Will came into the morning room, kissed the top of her head, then nodded to her mother and Alfie. He seemed a little brighter but it was also clear from his tear-stained cheeks that he had been crying.

"Well, we'll go home now." Mrs Henderson got to her feet and Alfie did likewise.

"Thank you for staying with Isobel today."

"Not at all, Will. Alfie and I were happy to keep her company."

"I feel well enough to call on Mother tomorrow," she told him and he smiled.

He saw her mother and Alfie out himself and she heard Mary, their other house-parlourmaid, tell him dinner would be ready in ten minutes.

"How are you really feeling?" he asked, coming back into the morning room and closing the door.

"I honestly feel much better. The bleeding is definitely slowing down."

He nodded. "I'll examine you again later."

"What did your parents say?" she asked, following him to the fireplace and turning his face towards hers as he held out his hands to warm them. "They made you cry," she added, smoothing a forefinger down his cheek and he grimaced.

"I didn't realise it was so noticeable. I wiped my eyes with my handkerchief but I should have washed my face before I began house calls."

"Tell me what happened, Will?"

"My father made me extremely angry. It was Mrs Bell who made me cry."

"You went to see Mrs Bell? Come and sit down and tell me what happened." She led him to the sofa and they sat down. "What did your father say?"

Will pressed his lips together for a moment. "I'd rather not repeat it, other to say I will not be taking his advice."

"His advice?" she echoed. "His medical advice? Does he think I should have an operation? Would it increase my

chances of not miscarrying in future?"

"No. He is still under the impression that you have had three miscarriages and believes you will never carry a baby to full term. He wants you to have either a hysterectomy or to have your ovaries removed so you will never be able to conceive again."

Her jaw dropped and she stared at him, her heart pounding in a mixture of revulsion and terror. "No. Oh, Will, no. Promise me you'll never allow that," she begged, grabbing his cold hands.

"I promise – I swear – I will never allow that to happen to you," he said, lifting her hands to his lips and kissing them.

"Thank you," she whispered, fighting back tears of relief.

"I was so angry I walked out of the house. I walked and walked and found myself on Brown Street. I saw that the house has new tenants in it, then I called to see Mrs Bell."

"How is she?"

"Very sorry to hear about you."

"So why did she make you cry?"

"She asked me how I was and—" He sighed. "I couldn't stop myself."

"Oh, Will." She flushed with shame. Everyone had been fussing around her and utterly neglecting him. He rested his head on her shoulder and she stroked his hair. "I'm so sorry. I know how much you wanted to be a father."

"When you were miscarrying last year and disappeared, I put all my efforts into finding you. When I did find you, I was so happy I didn't want to dwell on the fact you'd lost our child. This time, I've been with you all the time and I wanted to be strong for you. So when she asked me, it just all came pouring out."

"I'm so sorry." She held him tightly as he wept again.

"I'm glad I can cry," he murmured. "Even though I make a terrible mess." Raising his head, he sniffed and spluttered a laugh.

Pulling his handkerchief from his trouser pocket, she dried his eyes before handing it to him so he could blow his nose.

"Mrs Bell told me something you need to hear," he went on, putting the handkerchief back in his pocket. "She said her own mother had four miscarriages but she was the result of the fifth pregnancy. She also has three brothers. All their pregnancies were completely normal."

"Four miscarriages?"

Will smiled. "That's what I said, and I have to admit I've never heard of a woman having so many miscarriages and then going on to have four healthy babies, but I have no reason not to believe her. That is why I will never ever allow you to be operated on."

She nodded. "Thank you."

"There's something I want to discuss with you but I'll do it over dinner." He got to his feet and held out a hand. "I had no luncheon in the end and I'm ravenous."

Taking his hand, she got up and he escorted her into the breakfast room.

"Mrs Bell told me the people there want me back," he began as they ate slices of a delicious steak and kidney pie with carrots, potatoes and gravy.

"They all but deserted you."

"Apparently, they regret it now."

"But you can't go back. What about the Merrion Street Upper practice?" she asked.

"Mrs Bell said even if I were to do only one surgery per week, it would be an enormous help."

"Where? You said the house in Brown Street is now occupied."

"It is, but I wouldn't need a house. There are two rooms on the ground floor of Mrs Bell's tenement house," he explained. "I had a quick look and they need a good clean but other than that they are ideal, and if I earn back the rent of the rooms I'll be happy."

"You need to discuss this with Fred."

"I will, but you're my wife and I wanted to discuss it with you first because if I do start a weekly surgery there, I'd like you to assist me."

"Me?" She was pleasantly surprised. "How?"

"Remember Annie Dougherty who had the marble stuck in her throat?" he said and she nodded. "Annie would have choked to death if you hadn't been there to help me."

"But I'm not a nurse…"

"No, but you did tell me once that you nursed a rabbit back to health after you found it caught in a trap. I'd like you to be on hand to assist me if needed."

She smiled. "Speak to Fred."

"I will."

"Now, eat."

When Will examined her before they went to bed, the bleeding had reduced to spotting. The physical side of her miscarriage was almost over. How long it would take for the two of them to recover from it mentally, she didn't know.

The next morning before their surgeries started, Fred sat quietly behind his desk and didn't interrupt as Will related what Mrs Bell had told him.

"Four miscarriages?" Fred pursed his lips when Will finished. "I've never heard of a woman having that many then going on to have four normal pregnancies."

"Neither have I but Mrs Bell wouldn't have lied in order to placate me."

"No. And she wants you to go back to the Liberties."

"Yes. One surgery per week."

"Would one surgery per week be enough?" Fred asked.

"I don't want to do anything to jeopardise our practice here, Fred. If I do go back, one would have to be enough. Do you have any objections?"

"Well, I have to admit it is very soon for you to be setting up shop elsewhere but, no, I have no objections. I hope you've discussed this with Isobel?"

"I have. Thanks, Fred."

"Can I be a fly on the wall when you tell your father?" Fred gave him a grin but Will tensed.

"It's none of his business."

"Why?" Fred's grin vanished. "What's happened?"

"Father wants Isobel to have a hysterectomy or an ovariotomy," Will said, unable to keep the disgust out of his voice.

"The answer to women's troubles – whip the ovaries out." Fred rolled his eyes. "No. Absolutely not. Especially if what Mrs Bell says is correct. When you think the time is right, try for another baby. If Isobel miscarries, then we will talk again. Agreed?"

Will nodded. "Agreed."

After house calls that afternoon, Will walked through a heavy fall of snow to Pimlico and updated Mrs Bell. She gave him the landlord's name and address, he went straight there

and negotiated a reasonable rent for the two rooms. That done, he returned to Mrs Bell.

"The rooms are mine on a month-to-month basis," he told her.

"Oh, I'm so glad. When do you think you can begin and on what day?"

"I don't know yet. The landlord has agreed that the two doors and two windows will be replaced as soon as possible. As medicines will be kept there, the two rooms must be secure. The rooms themselves need to be scrubbed from top to bottom and I have to bring the desk, chairs and examination couch I used in Brown Street here. I also need to find some chairs for the waiting room... it could be a fortnight."

Mrs Bell nodded. "I'll round up some chairs for you and put the word out that you're coming back."

"For one surgery per week," he clarified. "One. Please make that clear."

"I will. I'm so glad," she said again. "Now, go and tell Isobel."

Will nodded and kissed her cheek.

He found Isobel standing alone at the bottom of the steps in number 30's snowy garden and despite wearing her new black and white coat and a black scarf and gloves, she was hugging herself in an effort to keep out the cold.

"I've rented the two rooms," he announced and kissed her lips. "When the doors and windows are replaced, I can begin to clean."

"No, we will begin to clean," she said, giving him a wobbly smile.

"What is it?" he asked softly.

"The spotting has stopped."

The miscarriage was over. "And do you feel tired?" he asked, not quite knowing how to reconcile his sorrow at the loss of their second child with the consolation that he and Isobel could now look to the future and try for another child in due course.

"No, I'm not tired," she replied. "Just sad."

"I know," he whispered, lifting her hands and kissing them.

"I thought I might call on Margaret tomorrow instead of waiting for her to call here. I would hate for there to be any awkwardness between us."

"Yes, do. And, after dinner this evening, I think we should call to number 67."

"Oh," she said simply and he heard the reluctance in her voice.

"I want to tell Father I will not be taking his medical advice and that I'm returning part-time to the Liberties," he explained with a wry smile. "He won't take it well but I don't care."

An hour later, they were shown into his parents' morning room by Tess, one of the house-parlourmaids. Both his mother and father looked up from their books in surprise as the door was closed behind them.

"Will and Isobel." His mother put her book on a side table before getting up from the sofa. "Oh, Isobel, my dear," she said, kissing Isobel on both cheeks then making way for his father, who rose from an armchair and kissed Isobel's hand. "How are you?"

"I'm much better, thank you."

"Good," his mother replied. "Would you like some tea? Your poor cheeks are frozen."

"No, thank you, Sarah. We've not long finished dinner. I enjoyed the walk here, it was very invigorating, and we'll walk home as well."

"Father," Will began at once. "I have called to tell you that Isobel and I will not be taking your medical advice and—"

"For God's sake, Will," his father snapped, thumping a fist on the back of one of the armchairs. "Isobel's your wife. How many more times do you want her to miscarry?"

"I don't want her to miscarry at all." Will's voice rose.

"Then see sense. Isobel clearly cannot carry a baby to term. If her ovaries are removed—"

"Stop it," Isobel shouted and both Will and his father turned to her in astonishment. "I do not want my ovaries to be removed and I would much prefer it if the two of you didn't speak about me as if I weren't here."

"Isobel," his father began irritably. "Think about—"

"Dr Fitzgerald," she interrupted him again. "I will have a child one day, even if I have to stay in bed for the entire nine months."

"Whether or not you stay in bed most likely has nothing to do with it but—"

"I also came to tell you that soon I will be holding one surgery per week in Pimlico," Will interrupted his father this time, firmly changing the subject. "This afternoon, I rented two rooms downstairs from Mrs Bell's rooms. I have discussed it with Fred and he has no objections."

"I think we should all have a drink," his mother leapt in with a forced laugh. "Sherry for Isobel and I, Will, please."

Isobel and his mother sat down on the sofa and Will went to the drinks tray on a side table in a corner of the room. His

father's silence spoke volumes but he had been told and that was an end to it. Will poured the sherries and passed them over before turning to his father who had sat down in an armchair.

"Whiskey, Father? Or would you prefer a brandy?"

"No, whiskey, please."

Will reached for the whiskey decanter, feeling his father watch him. Lifting the stopper, he poured two helpings, went to his father and held out a glass. His father took it with a brief nod of thanks and lifted it up.

"I suppose we had better drink to the future, then."

"The future," they chorused, holding up their glasses.

Sitting down in the other armchair, Will glanced at the clock on the mantelpiece as Isobel and his mother wisely changed the subject again and began to discuss the extraordinary weather.

They left half an hour later and outside on the pavement, Isobel stood with her back to the wind as Will put on his hat.

"That was awful," he said, having to hold his hat firmly on his head as another icy gust blew along Merrion Square South. "I'm sorry."

"We all know where we stand now."

"Yes, and I'm sorry for making you feel excluded."

"It's just as well I can speak up for myself, isn't it?" she said, giving him a mischievous grin. "I think your father despairs of us."

"He now knows he can't walk all over us."

"Yes, but at the same time, Will, I don't want us both to fall out with him."

They turned as the front door of number 68 opened and Mrs Harvey came out, wearing her favourite evening dress of deep red silk satin with a matching cloak. Behind her came Mr Harvey in white tie and tails, and he was followed by Frank, their footman and Claire, one of their parlourmaids.

"Will. Isobel." Mrs Harvey smiled and nodded to them. "How lovely to see you both."

"Can't stop, I'm afraid," Mr Harvey ushered his wife towards a waiting carriage. "We're off to a dinner and we're rather late."

Frank opened the carriage door and the Harveys' got in. Frank closed the door, the carriage moved off, and he went back into the house. From the front door, Claire gave them both a long look and Isobel opened her mouth to speak before reluctantly closing it. There was no point in even attempting to exchange pleasantries. Claire would never forgive her for lying about Will. The maid went inside and the front door slammed shut.

"Mr Harvey doesn't know how to act towards me," she said. "And Claire will always hate me."

"It's awkward for Jim."

"I know. I was the second of their maids to fall pregnant and he insisted I be dismissed. Mrs Harvey was always kind to me, though, and I feel I should call on her but she was once my employer and it would be too awkward for me. Apart from that, Claire would bang the front door even harder and I'd rather not be responsible for it falling off its hinges."

Will laughed, took her arm, and they hurried out of Merrion Square and along snowy and deserted Fitzwilliam

Street Lower and Upper. Turning from Fitzwilliam Square East onto the south side of the square, she stopped.

"What is it?" he asked.

"Each time I turn this corner, walk along the pavement and see number 30, I still can't quite believe the house is ours. It's huge and I am determined we will raise our children in it."

Will raised her hands to his lips and kissed them.

They settled on the sofa in the morning room but within minutes Will fell asleep and gently, she extracted *The Irish Times* from his fingers. She leant back against him and smiled as he automatically put an arm around her. He was lovely and warm and soon she felt drowsy herself and dropped the newspaper onto the floor.

She woke with a jump hearing the clock on the mantelpiece strike the hour and counted the chimes. It was ten o'clock and the fire was low. She slowly got up off the sofa so as not to wake Will, went to the fireplace and added a shovel-full of coal from the scuttle. She was straightening up when the door opened and Gerald, their footman, came in.

"I'm sorry to disturb you, Dr Fitzgerald, but there's a footman at the areaway door asking for you. He's come from the Wilson residence on Merrion Square on behalf of Dr Frederick Simpson. He says it's urgent."

Will swung his legs off the sofa, stood up and rubbed his eyes. "Thank you, Gerald. I'll speak to him."

He left the room with Gerald, returning a few minutes later, his face pale.

"What is it?" she asked anxiously.

"It's Cecilia," he replied with a grimace. "She's had a fall

and gone into labour. Fred wants me to assist in a caesarean."

"A caesarean?" she repeated. "But isn't Cecilia only..?"

"About six months pregnant, yes. Her father dismissed Dr Smythe and Fred is her doctor of two hours ago, apparently. I'm going to have to go, Fred wouldn't have sent for me if it wasn't urgent. Don't wait up for me." He kissed her lips and left the room.

She returned to the fireplace, watching as the coal began to burn. She didn't envy Will assisting in the delivery of his former fiancée's premature baby, which in all probability wouldn't survive. She couldn't pace the floor, Will would be gone for hours. Sitting down on the sofa, she sighed. It was too early to go to bed. Retrieving the newspaper from the floor, she turned up the large oil lamp which stood on a side table and forced herself to read.

When Will was shown into Cecilia's bedroom, he was greeted by a scene which made his jaw drop. Fred, drenched in sweat, had clearly not wanted to wait any longer before performing the caesarean. He had the baby in the crook of his arm and was cutting the umbilical cord. A young red-haired maid was standing across the double bed from him, a hand clapped over her mouth, her blue eyes bulging with a mixture of revulsion and horror.

Shrugging off his frock coat, undoing his cufflinks and rolling up his sleeves, Will went to the washstand.

"Please fetch more warm water," he instructed the maid as he poured some water into the basin and scrubbed his hands. "Fred?" he asked as the maid gratefully ran from the bedroom.

His friend glanced up at him momentarily. "I couldn't

wait for you to arrive. Dr Wilson and Dr Smythe rowed over how long to allow the labour to progress before intervening. Dr Smythe was dismissed and long gone before I got here. Cecilia's exhausted and the baby is unresponsive. According to Dr Wilson, Dr Smythe should have performed a caesarean hours ago. He said that despite being retired and Cecilia being his daughter, he would have done it himself, but his hands were shaking so much he couldn't hold the scalpel. So he sent for me. Take the baby."

Will took the baby from him. It was a boy but was limp and lifeless and much larger than he would have expected. Lying the baby on a towel on a pale green padded bedroom chair beside the washstand, Will cleared his mouth but the baby still didn't breathe.

"Is it dead?" Fred demanded.

"No," he replied, getting down on his knees and blowing gently into the baby's mouth. It made no difference and he did it again, blowing a little harder. Again, it made no difference and Will got to his feet. Taking the baby by the ankles, Will held him upside down and slapped his bottom. Nothing. Will slapped the baby harder. Nothing. "Come on," he urged. "Breathe."

"Is the baby dead?" Fred demanded again.

"No, he's not dead." Will gripped the baby's ankles tightly and began to swing him in a low but wide arc.

"Will, for God's sake, don't do that."

"Fred, just see to Cecilia while I see to the baby." He swung the baby again and gave his bottom a sharp slap. "Breathe," he whispered. "Come on, breathe." Hearing a gasp, Will quickly laid the baby on the chair again as the boy began to wail. "At last." Will gave the baby a grin. "You've got

a good pair of lungs." He wrapped the baby in the towel and turned to look at Fred, who was removing the placenta, then at the door as it opened and the maid came in with an ewer.

"The water, Dr Fitzgerald."

"Thank you," Will replied. "You can put it on the washstand."

"Is it all right?" She nodded at the wailing baby.

"It's a boy and he's absolutely fine. Please hold him for a moment."

"And Mrs Ashlinn?" she added, taking the baby, and he went to his medical bag and threaded a length of silk thread through the eye of a suture needle.

"Too early to tell, I'm afraid," Fred replied, doing a double-take as Will held out the needle and silk to him. "Will..?"

"I sutured the uterine incision after delivering huge twin boys and there was no infection," he told Fred. "Do it now, or the blood loss will certainly kill her."

After few seconds indecision, Fred took the needle and silk from him and glanced at the maid.

"Where is Dr Wilson?" he asked her, while Will threaded another length of silk to stitch the skin together.

"In the morning room with Mrs Wilson, Dr Simpson."

Fred stitched the internal and then the external incisions before straightening his back and stretching.

"There. Thank you, Will. And well done for not fainting, Teresa. You can tell Doctor and Mrs Wilson that I will be down to speak to them shortly."

The maid smiled, passed the baby back to Will, and bobbed a quick curtsy before leaving the bedroom. When the door closed, Will went to the bed.

"This is not a six-month baby," he said while Fred cleaned Cecilia's abdomen then lowered her nightdress. "It's not even a seven or eight-month baby," he added as Fred went to the washstand and washed his bloodied hands and arms instead of replying. "Answer me, Fred," he finally snapped. "This baby is full term, isn't it?"

"Yes, it is," Fred replied, turning away from the washstand, and Will exhaled a humourless laugh. "Clive is the father."

"Did you know Cecilia was having sexual relations with Clive behind my back?" he asked.

"No, I did not," Fred replied emphatically, reaching for a clean towel and drying himself. "I knew the moment I saw Cecilia that the baby was full term, but I made Dr Wilson confirm it. I'm sorry, Will. If I could have kept it from you, I would have, but I needed your help here tonight. What the hell were you doing to the baby?"

"I'd seen it done with a piglet who wouldn't breathe."

"A piglet?"

"Yes. And it breathed, too."

Fred's eyebrows rose but he gave Will a tired grin. "Can you stay here while I speak to the Wilsons?"

"Of course."

"Thank you. I'll try not to be long." Fred wiped his face and neck with the towel, shrugged on his frock coat and left the bedroom.

"Let's clean you up," he said as the baby stopped wailing and he laid the boy down on the padded bedroom chair again. Reaching for a small towel, he dampened it. He wiped the baby down, dried him and wrapped him up in a clean towel, then brought him to the bed.

He stared at the deathly-pale blonde woman who almost became his wife, willing her to live. The pain, humiliation and anger he felt at her throwing him over and marrying another man were long gone and with that other man now dead, the baby needed a mother all the more.

"Will?"

He jumped, not having heard the bedroom door open. Cecilia's mother, her hair now more grey than blonde, was standing in the doorway wringing her hands.

"Mrs Wilson." He gave her a brief nod.

"Dr Simpson says it is touch and go. Do you agree?"

"I'm afraid I can't say," Will replied. "Dr Simpson attended to Mrs Ashlinn, not me."

"He also said you saved the baby's life. That it was something to do with a piglet…"

"I helped him to breathe, that's all."

"May I hold him?" she asked, sitting down on the other pale green padded chair beside the bed.

"Of course." Carefully, he placed the baby in her arms. "He needs to be fed."

"That is being arranged."

"Good. Well, I'll go now."

"Please tell me she'll live, Will?" Mrs Wilson asked, her voice shaking.

Will glanced at Cecilia again. "She's strong. She survived the cab accident."

Mrs Wilson nodded as he shrugged his frock coat on. "I know she hurt you deeply. Are you happy now?"

"Yes. I'm very happy. I love my wife very much."

"I'm glad. Thank you, Will, for all your help."

"You're very welcome." Picking up his medical bag, he

went out, leaving her sitting forlornly by the bed.

He met Fred and Cecilia's white-haired father downstairs in the hall and paused to shake Dr Wilson's hand.

"Thank you for coming, Will."

"Not at all."

Fred gave him a grateful nod and Will nodded in reply before he was shown out.

Despite it being bitterly cold, he decided to walk home, hoping he hadn't given Mrs Wilson false hope.

He let himself into number 30, put his medical bag on the hall table and hung his hat and overcoat on the stand. He extinguished the gas lamp which had been left lit then a further two on the first and second-floor landings before creeping into his and Isobel's bedroom.

"Will?" She turned up the oil lamp.

"Sorry," he said, closing the door. "I didn't mean to wake you."

"I wasn't asleep. What happened?" she asked, sitting up as he got undressed.

"Dr Smythe left Cecilia in labour too long before admitting defeat. The baby – a huge boy – was born not breathing but I revived him. Cecilia, on the other hand, was exhausted even before the caesarean."

"Will she live?"

"It really is touch and go. But, as I told her mother, she did survive the cab accident."

"How long do you think the baby will live?"

"He won't die," he replied and she gave him a sharp glance. "The baby was full term," he explained with a grim smile and her eyes widened. "According to Fred, who questioned Dr Wilson, Clive is the father. It certainly isn't me as I never had sexual intercourse with Cecilia. I'm long

past being angry with her," he added as Isobel opened her mouth, no doubt to ask why on earth he was being so calm about it. "But I do wish she'd had the decency to end our courtship sooner and not accept my proposal of marriage."

"Perhaps Cecilia discovered she was pregnant only after she accepted your proposal."

"Perhaps," he mused. "But she should have thrown me over sooner."

"Did Fred know she was having sexual intercourse with Clive behind your back?"

"He says he didn't and I believe him."

"I'm sorry you found out the way you did," she said and squeezed his cold hands as he got into bed. "Will, you're freezing."

"I walked home."

"Please tell me you're all right?" she asked softly.

"It was an odd feeling to be holding Cecilia's child," he admitted. "But, yes, I'm all right."

The breakfast room door opened as they were about to eat and Isobel looked up from her bowl of porridge as Florrie came in.

"Dr Simpson is here, Dr Fitzgerald."

"Please show him in, Florrie," Will replied.

She was shocked when Fred came into the room, still wearing his overcoat and scarf. Under the dark stubble, his face was grey with fatigue.

"Cecilia has regained consciousness," he announced. "She is extremely weak but will live. It really was touch and go for a while but she regained consciousness at four o'clock this morning."

"And the baby?" Will asked.

"The baby is fine."

"I'm glad," she said. "Have you eaten, Fred?"

He gave her a little smile. "No. I haven't been home yet. I wanted to let Will know first."

"Then, sit down and join us," she said.

"Thank you." Unwinding the grey scarf from around his neck, he shrugged off his overcoat and laid them over the back of a chair before pulling out the adjoining chair and sitting down at the table opposite her. "And thank you for coming so quickly last night, Will, but I couldn't wait for you to arrive before beginning the caesarean. Dr Smythe should have done it hours before."

"You did well."

"So did you with the baby," Fred replied before turning to her. "I expect Will didn't tell you that he swung the baby by the ankles to get him to breathe."

"Swung the baby?" she repeated.

"I'd seen it done before with a piglet," Will explained. "It clears the airway."

"How old is Dr Smythe?" she asked.

"Somewhere around eighty." Fred rolled his eyes. "Someone will die needlessly in his care before long."

"Can't he be persuaded – and if not persuaded – then be made to retire?"

"He may not be able to take up other employment or afford to retire," Will said. "Not all doctors are as lucky as my father and Cecilia's."

"Have a word with your father all the same, Will," Fred told him. "Dr Wilson said Dr Smythe is no longer capable of safely practising medicine."

"Very well," he replied.

Will served Fred some porridge from a dish on the sideboard then poured him a cup of coffee and they continued with their meal. When Will and Fred got up to leave, she followed them out to the hall.

"I was thinking of calling on Margaret today. Will she be at home, Fred?"

"Yes, she will. I need to go home to wash, shave and change my clothes and I'll let her know. She'll be delighted to see you."

"Are you going to call this morning?" Will asked her. "I thought that after house calls this afternoon, I could show you the rooms on Pimlico and then call to see Mrs Bell."

"I'll call this morning." Reaching up, she kissed his lips and saw them out herself.

An hour later, Isobel was admitted to the Simpson residence on Ely Place Upper and shown into the morning room where a fire was blazing in the hearth. The sudden extreme change in temperature made her cheeks tingle and she began to regret not passing her coat and scarf to the butler. Margaret, dressed in a chocolate brown high-necked day dress, rose from a sofa upholstered in pale yellow silk satin and clasped her hands.

"Isobel, I'm so glad you have called. How are you?"

"I'm very much recovered, thank you," she said with a brave smile. "You are blooming."

Margaret smiled self-consciously and laid a hand on her small belly. "Baby is moving regularly now."

"Have you thought about names?" she asked as they sat down beside each other on the sofa.

"Well," Margaret replied slowly. "If it is a boy, I did

mention Duncan after Fred's father, but Fred wouldn't hear of it, even as a middle name."

"Perhaps one of Duncan's middle names, if he had any?" she suggested, fighting an urge to unbutton her coat, pull her handkerchief from the sleeve of her new sapphire blue dress and fan herself with it.

"Yes. Except, I honestly don't know if he had any." Margaret gave a little shrug. "But there is plenty of time for Fred and I to come to a decision. I must thank you for feeding him this morning."

"He was in dire need of coffee and porridge."

"Between them, Fred and Will saved both Mrs Ashlinn and her baby."

"Yes, they did," she replied simply and Margaret shuffled awkwardly.

"I'm sorry, Isobel. It must have been very difficult for both you and Will."

"He did admit it was odd to be holding Cecilia's child, but I've never met her and I have to admit I am curious to see the woman silly enough to give Will up."

Margaret reached out and squeezed her hands. "He loves you very much."

"I love him very much. And he will hold our child one day."

That afternoon, Isobel and Will walked to Pimlico to inspect the two rooms. The doors and windows had been replaced and Will went upstairs to Mrs Bell's rooms, returning with a key to the new front door.

"Mrs Bell is making a pot of tea," he said, unlocking and opening the door for her.

The first room was large with a fireplace and Will walked

past her to the door to the second room. He opened the new door then took the key from the lock. This room was smaller, also with a fireplace, and had probably been a bedroom. It would be ideal as a surgery.

"We can begin to clean now," she said, noting the grime and a mixture of dust and very fine ash from the fires which lay on every surface.

"You approve, then?" he asked and she nodded.

"These two rooms are just right – no stairs to climb, no having to sit and wait in the hall – yes, I approve of them very much."

"Good." He held her in his arms and kissed her, pulling gently at her lips. "I love you, Mrs Fitzgerald."

"Then, lock the doors," she whispered, sliding one hand around the back of his neck and reaching for his trouser buttons with the other.

"Isobel, no," he said, standing back from her. "It's far too soon."

"Please don't be afraid to make love to me, Will," she begged and he grimaced.

"I'm not afraid."

"I think you are afraid. If you don't want to risk getting me pregnant again—"

"Isobel, of course, I want us to try for another child," he interrupted irritably. "But not yet – and I don't want Mrs Bell to hear our raised voices," he added in a whisper when she opened her mouth to demand why not yet. "We'll discuss this later at home," he said, holding out a hand. "Let's go upstairs for a cup of tea."

Tea? She didn't want tea, she wanted him. Biting back a retort, she reached out and took his hand.

Mrs Bell kissed her cheek as they went into the kitchen. "How are you, Isobel?"

"I'm very much recovered, thank you," she replied automatically, forcing a smile. "And thank you for speaking so frankly to Will about your mother," she went on sincerely.

"Every word of it is true. In time, yourself and Dr Fitzgerald will have lots of beautiful babbies."

"Yes, I hope so," she said quietly, glancing at the kitchen table. Mrs Bell had lifted her best floral patterned china cups and saucers down from the dresser. "You've gone to a lot of trouble for us."

"This tea set was a wedding present and it only gets used on very special occasions like this – your first visit here as a married couple."

"Thank you, Mrs Bell."

"Sit yourselves down while I pour the tea."

An hour later, they walked back to number 30 in silence but when Will closed the front door and hung his hat on the stand he caught her arm as she unbuttoned her coat.

"Don't go upstairs yet, Isobel, I want to talk to you as a doctor." He led her into the morning room, pushed the door closed with his behind and leant back against it. "What I was trying – badly – to say is that I think it's too soon for you to fall pregnant again. You became pregnant very soon after the first miscarriage and your body needs to have a rest," he explained. "So – and this is your husband who adores you speaking – I will obtain some condoms because," he bent forward and whispered in her ear, "I love making love to you."

She smiled, feeling his lips on her neck. "And it's been too long," she said as he straightened up.

"Yes, it has. A few months, Isobel, and then we'll try again for the first of our lots of beautiful babbies."

That finally made her laugh and she cupped his cheeks in her hands. "I love you, Dr Fitzgerald, and I'm sorry for being selfish. I should have realised by now how difficult it is for you as both my husband and my doctor."

"A few months," he repeated softly. "And in the meantime, we can enjoy ourselves."

Chapter Two

The following Monday, a gradual thaw had begun and a smoke-fog hung over Dublin. Will walked to the practice house half an hour early in order to write to two suppliers of fish bladder condoms, preferring to correspond from and have them sent to him there to avoid any embarrassment at number 30.

Hanging up his hat and overcoat in the office, he froze hearing a thud and then a moan from upstairs. He ran up the stairs two at a time and tried the door to his surgery but the room was still locked. He went along the landing, opened the door to Fred's surgery and couldn't help but stand and watch for a few moments. Fred was on his knees behind the desk, his head between the thighs of a young blonde woman seated in his chair, her head thrown back as she moaned and implored him never to stop.

"Fred."

Fred jumped, straightened up and stared at him in consternation. "Will—"

"I think you should leave now." He addressed the young woman remarkably calmly and she stood up allowing the skirt of her black cotton dress to fall. Grabbing her straw hat

and black woollen shawl from the desk, she pushed past him and left the room. He heard her run down the stairs and a moment or two later, the front door slammed.

Fred got to his feet, pulled up his drawers and trousers and did up the buttons. "Will—" he began again but Will held up a hand.

"I could have been Eva coming to unlock all the doors."

"I know. I'm sorry. Margaret won't let me near her and—"

"That was the first and last time here, Fred. Do I make myself clear?"

Fred exhaled a humourless laugh. "You sounded exactly like your father, then."

"Had my father caught you here with a prostitute?" he asked, Fred looked away and Will took it for a yes. "Well, I mean it, Fred."

"Do you?" Fred demanded, turning back to him. "Christ, you can be so fucking holier than thou sometimes, Will. You wouldn't be a tiny bit frustrated, would you? I take it you haven't fucked Isobel since she lost the baby? Here." Fred opened a desk drawer, lifted out a small red box and threw it at him. The box hit Will on the chest and fell to the floor. "Condoms. Take them and fuck your wife tonight."

Will strode across the room, seized Fred by the throat and held him up against the wall. "First – my marriage is none of your concern. Second – your marriage is none of my concern. And third – if I find you here with a prostitute again, you will be out. You're an excellent doctor but it was little wonder my father never made you his practice partner – you're far too bloody immature."

"Your father always wanted you to become his practice partner," Fred croaked. "But you preferred to work in a fucking slum. You have all this and you still want to go back to the Liberties."

"How many times do I have to tell you that Brown Street is not a slum and neither is Pimlico. I'm going back because I'm needed there." Hearing the front door close, he let Fred go and stepped back from him. "You will not bring prostitutes here again," he repeated quietly, then turned and left the room, stepping over the box of condoms.

Sitting down at the desk in his surgery, he closed his eyes for a few moments to suppress his temper before opening a desk drawer and lifting out some headed notepaper. He wrote the two letters then went straight out to post them so they would be amongst the first postal collections of the day.

After surgery three and a half hours later, he walked home without speaking to Fred again. He went into the morning room and found Isobel seated on the sofa reading a newspaper.

"Can we go to Pimlico this afternoon and clean the two rooms?" he asked her by way of a greeting.

"Yes, of course, we can," she replied, closing and folding the newspaper before putting it on the arm of the sofa. "What is it? You sound angry."

"I caught Fred in his surgery with a prostitute," he said and her eyebrows rose but other than that, she didn't seem at all surprised. "Needless to say, we argued. Oh, Christ." Resting his hands on his hips, he stared up at the ceiling. "Have I made a terrible mistake going into partnership with Fred? Marriage hasn't matured him, the death of his father hasn't matured him, impending fatherhood hasn't matured him…"

"Could you run the practice on your own?" she asked and he lowered his head.

"Yes, provided the number of patients stays as it is now but, ideally, the practice needs twice the number of patients we have now, and how would it look if I were to dissolve the partnership after such a short period of time?" Isobel's frown gave him his answer. "I've given Fred one more chance," he went on. "And if he throws it back in my face, then he's out. Do you think Margaret suspects anything?"

"She seemed quite happy when I called but we aren't really close enough friends for her to divulge anything too personal."

"No, I suppose not. I'm sorry." He bent and kissed her lips. "But sometimes Fred infuriates me."

"Fred's your oldest friend and you care about him. Which is why I think you should either postpone starting the surgery in Pimlico for a while. Or involve him, too."

"Fred has the same attitude to the Liberties as my father and I don't want a repeat of what that led to."

"Well, it was just a suggestion," she said with a little shrug.

"No, it's a wonderful suggestion and if I broke Fred in gently—" He halted, seeing her smile. "Thank you," he continued. "I'll discuss it with Fred. The last thing I want is to fall out with him like I have with my father."

"Shall we clean the rooms in Pimlico this afternoon, then?"

"No," he decided. "Not until I've spoken to Fred. I have only three house calls to make this afternoon. Afterwards, I'll take you out for tea or coffee – whatever you'd prefer. When the condoms arrive, I will make love to you for an entire afternoon."

"When the condoms arrive?"

"I've ordered condoms from two manufacturers," he explained. "And I'll make my choice from them, although I know which Fred prefers."

"Oh?"

"He threw a box of them at me."

"Will, did you and Fred fight?" she asked slowly.

"Almost," he admitted, staring down at his shoes like a naughty schoolboy. "I grabbed him by the throat."

"For God's sake, Will," she snapped, getting to her feet. "What if Eva or your patients heard or saw you?"

"I know, I know. It won't happen again." She gave him a long look and he grimaced. "It won't happen again, Isobel," he repeated in a firm tone and this time she gave him a satisfied nod.

"You can take me out for coffee this afternoon. And perhaps a stroll around St Stephen's Green? Then, on our way home, we'll call to Ely Place Upper and invite Fred and Margaret to dinner in the next few days so you and he can discuss the future. Agreed?"

"Agreed," he replied quietly then went to the fire to warm his hands.

At half past three, they were seated at a corner table in a café on Grafton Street and Isobel smiled as she stirred milk and sugar into her cup of coffee.

"What is it?" he asked.

"I wrote the character reference I used for the position of parlourmaid at the Harveys' over there." She pointed to a table at the window. "And I wrote quite a few other letters to you here as well."

"I loved receiving your letters," he said, reaching out and squeezing her hand.

"I refused to admit it to myself that I loved receiving yours. I was falling in love with you even though I knew I shouldn't, but I couldn't help it. Can we do this again? Come here for coffee, I mean, because when I sat here writing to you I never dreamt that one day I'd be sitting here with you as your wife."

"Of course we can," he replied softly. "I still have to pinch myself, too. I love you, Mrs Fitzgerald."

They strolled around the frozen lake in St Stephen's Green, before walking the short distance to number 1 Ely Place Upper. They were shown into the morning room, which thankfully wasn't as oppressively hot as on her previous visit. Seated in an armchair, Fred uncrossed his legs, got up and threw his cigarette into the fire. He tensed on seeing Will but smiled and nodded politely to her.

"Margaret is lying down. I'll just—" He went to ring for a servant but she caught his arm.

"Let Margaret rest, Fred," she told him and he nodded again. "Will and I called to invite Margaret and yourself to dinner. You and Will have important matters to discuss."

Fred stared at her, realisation dawning on his face that she knew of the incident at the practice house. "Yes, we do."

"Tomorrow evening or the evening after that?" Will suggested.

"Tomorrow?" Fred asked. "We have no other invitations. Margaret is beginning to feel very self-conscious of her size. A small private dinner will be very nice, thank you."

"Tomorrow it is. Seven o'clock. It's good to see you, Fred." Will held out a hand and, after a moment's hesitation,

Fred shook it. "Please give our regards to Margaret."

"I will, and thank you for calling," Fred replied and saw them out himself.

She decided on onion consommé, poached salmon with steamed vegetables and a fruit salad with cream to follow and spoke with Mrs Dillon as soon as they got home. The housekeeper began compiling a list and Isobel left her to it.

"It's nothing too elaborate and I'm not fond of meals with umpteen courses," she explained to Will as she joined him in the morning room. "But it's a solid enough meal."

"It sounds delicious."

"Yes." She sat down on the sofa and wrung her hands. "I also instructed Mrs Dillon to prepare the dining room and drawing room as it would look very odd if we didn't eat in the dining room but…" Tailing off, she shuddered.

Will moved up the sofa and put an arm around her. "Don't think of that meal," he whispered. "This house is ours now and the dining room looks completely different."

It was true. Since her short-lived meal with Hugh Lombard, who had been intent on making her his mistress and, as with the rest of the house, the dining room had been decorated and all the furniture replaced.

"You're right. I'm sorry, I'm just being silly."

"No." She felt him kiss her hair. "Just always remember that this house is ours now."

A copy of *The Irish Times* was lying on the desk as Will went into his surgery the next morning. He put his medical bag down on the floor and glanced at the advertisements on the front page. What was he supposed to be looking at?

"Page four," Fred informed him from the doorway.

Will went to the page and his heart sank. *Doctor Saves Infant's Life Through New 'Piglet Procedure'.* The article described how he had saved the life of the premature newborn son of the late Clive Ashlinn Q.C. Will was named but Fred, and how he had saved Cecilia's life, was not.

"This is nothing to do with me, Fred."

"No?"

"No," he replied firmly. "The detail in this article could only have come from a doctor and I haven't spoken to Cecilia's father since that night."

"Well, Dr Wilson certainly told someone after I'd spoken to him."

"I'm sorry, Fred. This article should be about you. You saved Cecilia's life."

"Yes, but not with the 'Piglet Procedure'," Fred muttered. "I'll see you this evening."

Will sighed and closed the newspaper.

"Will?" About to run up the steps to number 30 and escape the cold just before one o'clock, Will turned hearing his father's voice. "Have you seen *The Irish Times*?"

"I have," he replied shortly as his father stopped beside him. "Come inside, it's freezing." Will hurried up the steps, opened the front door and they went into the hall. "Who was responsible for that sensationalist article?" he demanded, quickly closing the door and putting his medical bag on the hall table.

"I met Ken Wilson and he told me—"

"He clearly didn't tell you the baby was full term," Will interrupted and his father's jaw dropped.

"Full term?"

"Yes," he replied, taking off his hat and hanging it on the

stand. "And, thanks to you, all those who can count and know Cecilia was the one who ended our engagement and married Clive Ashlinn with undue haste, now know why – she was pregnant with his child after having sexual relations with him behind my back. For God's sake, Father, did you not stop for a moment to think – to count back the months? If the baby had been conceived after Cecilia married Clive, it wouldn't have survived five minutes – if even that – no matter what was done to try and revive it. Fred saved Cecilia's life. He performed a difficult caesarean – that old fool Smythe should have done it hours beforehand – and I get all the credit for clearing the baby's airway. It's completely ridiculous. Please don't do it again."

His father's eyebrows rose in clear offence. "The practice needs more patients and it was an ideal opportunity to obtain some publicity for you. As well as that, I was going to ask you to submit a paper to the *Journal of Irish Medicine*."

"On how to swing a baby by its ankles? Thank you, Father but, no. Ask Fred for one on the caesarean."

"We receive papers on caesareans all the time."

"Well write an editorial on elderly doctors and how they put their patients' lives at risk."

His father nodded. "I have heard complaints about Smythe before but he cannot be compelled to retire until…"

"He does actually kill someone." Will rolled his eyes. "While you're here, could you come into the breakfast room, I need to speak to you about Fred."

They went inside and Will closed the door to the hall. The table was laid for luncheon and his stomach began to rumble.

"Is Fred in trouble, Will?" his father asked.

"Yesterday morning, I caught him in his surgery with a young woman."

"A young woman? You mean a whore?"

Will winced. He hated the term. "I mean a prostitute. And it doesn't seem to be the first time he's brought one to the practice house."

"I caught him twice with one." His father sighed. "I thought that now he is going to be a father…"

"It would seem that has only made matters worse. Needless to say, we had 'words' about it. I told him if I caught him with a prostitute there again, he'd be out and—"

"You can't dissolve the partnership so soon, Will," his father interjected firmly. "How would it look?"

"Father, Fred's sexual excursions are none of my business, but he will not indulge his urges at the practice house. He and Margaret are coming here to dinner this evening and I want to try and build bridges with him but I also think he misses his father greatly."

"We all miss his father greatly."

"Could you speak with him, please?" Will asked. "Perhaps bring him to your club for a drink occasionally?"

"Be a father figure to him, you mean?"

"Yes. I'm finding it very difficult to be a friend to him at the moment and the newspaper article certainly hasn't helped matters."

His father nodded. "It was well intended."

"I know it was," Will conceded. "But don't expect Cecilia or her parents to be too pleased about it either."

"No," his father replied quietly. "How is Isobel?"

"A little nervous about the dinner as it's our first but other than that she is very well."

"Good. Well, I'll let you begin luncheon."

"Please don't tell Fred I've spoken to you about him?" Will asked.

"I won't."

"Thank you for calling, Father, and my love to Mother." He saw his father out and turned as he shrugged off his overcoat, hearing the morning room door open. "My father," he told Isobel, hanging the overcoat on the stand.

"Yes, I heard his voice," she said and closed the door. "Will, have you seen today's *Irish Times*?"

"Fred showed the article to me." Taking her hand, they went into the breakfast room. "He isn't happy about it. My father has just told me he is responsible."

"Oh."

"I've asked him not to do it again."

"You didn't row, did you?" she asked.

"No. I didn't row with Fred either."

"Good." She gave him a little smile. "For a moment, I thought you were going to tell me Fred has refused to come this evening."

"Fred and Margaret are definitely coming to dinner this evening," he assured her. "I have some house calls to make this afternoon, but I should be home before six o'clock."

Isobel was in the drawing room by the time Will arrived home and his brown eyes widened as they took in her evening dress. It was new, short-sleeved, and deep red in colour. His eyes rested on her cleavage and she exhaled an exasperated sigh.

"It is cut too low, I knew it."

"No. It's stunning. You are stunning. Oh," he added

softly. "The condoms can't arrive quickly enough."

"Don't mention the condoms," she whispered. "I'm trying not to think about them. Go and get changed," she said, giving him a gentle push.

The servants had worked hard and both the drawing room and dining room looked magnificent lit for the first time by the new gas lamps. Fires had been lit early in the morning and, despite it freezing sharply all day, both rooms were pleasantly warm as she made a circuit of them waiting for Will.

"Mrs Fitzgerald?" Will was standing in the drawing room doorway dressed in white tie and tails and she couldn't help but stare. Would she ever get used to the fact that this handsome man was her husband? She hoped not. She never ever wanted to take him for granted. "Shall we do, do you think?" he asked with a grin.

She went to him and kissed his lips. "I think we shall do very well, Dr Fitzgerald. Ah." She smiled, hearing voices on the stairs. "They're here."

Mary showed Margaret and Fred into the drawing room and Isobel kissed their cheeks.

"Thank you for coming. Come and sit by the fire, you must be frozen. Dinner will be served shortly."

The three-course meal was delicious and, silently thanking Mrs Dillon for being such an excellent cook, Isobel got up from the table.

"It's time to allow the doctors to have a chat," she announced lightly and she and Margaret went into the drawing room. "Some more lemonade?" she asked Margaret as she walked to the drinks tray.

"Yes, please."

"I think I'll have some, too," she added, reaching for the jug. "I don't particularly like sherry and my mother always looks horrified when I ask for whiskey or brandy."

"Don't let me stop you."

"Thank you, but I'd prefer lemonade." She poured two glasses and passed one to Margaret. "Please, sit down."

"Thank you." Margaret chose the sofa and smoothed a hand down the bodice of her sky blue evening dress before resting it on her small belly. "This is a beautiful room."

"Yes, it is," Isobel replied as she sat down at the other end while glancing at the pale gold wallpaper and the sofa and two armchairs upholstered in burgundy silk satin. "Will and I really must use it more. Perhaps in the summer."

"Isobel, while it is just the two of us, there is something I think you ought to know."

"Oh?" she replied a little apprehensively.

"I know Will caught Fred with a prostitute in his surgery. In fact, I know Fred uses prostitutes regularly."

Isobel had to consciously close her mouth. How on earth had Margaret found out? Surely Fred wouldn't have been foolish enough to disclose to his wife of less than a year that he uses prostitutes? She took a sip of lemonade and put her glass down on a side table, not quite knowing how, or if she should respond.

"I have discussed the matter with Fred and he assures me he will be more discreet in future," Margaret went on.

"In future?"

"I've known all along that Fred will not be faithful to me," Margaret told her matter-of-factly. "My only stipulation during our discussion was that he use condoms with the prostitutes."

"I see."

"Oh, dear, I think I've shocked you, Isobel."

It will take much more than that to shock me, she smiled wryly to herself. "No, not at all," she said. "I'm glad you feel you can confide in me."

"Thank you. I could never speak like this to my other friends but with you…"

"Being a fallen woman..?"

"I wasn't going to put it quite like that." Margaret put her glass beside Isobel's. "But I have discovered I do enjoy sexual relations as well. However, I know I will never fully satisfy Fred. And I would rather we did not engage in sexual relations while I am pregnant," she said, laying a hand on her belly again. "So he finds release elsewhere. With my blessing."

"I must admit I could never give Will my blessing to—"

"You and Will are very lucky. You both love and satisfy each other."

"Yes, we do."

"But you cannot give him a child."

Isobel tensed. "I will give him a child, Margaret."

"I hope for your sake you are right, Isobel. Will is a very handsome man and I know for a fact that there are many ladies in Dublin who would welcome him into their bed and—" Margaret broke off and screamed as Isobel struck her hard on the cheek.

Will closed the double doors to the drawing room after Isobel and Margaret. He filled Fred's glass and then his own with port before re-taking his seat at the head of the table as Fred lit a cigarette.

"My father was responsible for *The Irish Times* article," Will began and Fred's eyebrows rose and fell but he didn't reply. "I've asked him not to do it again."

Fred drew on the cigarette and exhaled the smoke slowly. "The meal was delicious."

"Yes, it was. Fred, I want to ask you something."

"I'm not going to bring prostitutes back to the practice house anymore, Will."

"It's not about that. It's about Pimlico. I want to ask you if you would consider doing one surgery per week there, too?"

This time, Fred's eyebrows shot up and stayed up. "Me?"

"You've proved you can carry out procedures in difficult circumstances but you must never refer to the area as a slum again and you must never do what my father did and leave a patient too soon because where that patient lives disgusts you. Three children are without a mother because of his snobbery."

"What's brought this on?" Fred asked. "You were fully prepared to do one surgery there yourself and not involve me at all."

"I'd like to involve you as well because the last couple of days has made me realise I really don't want to lose your friendship. Will you consider it?"

"Yes."

"Thank you." Relieved, Will raised his glass. "Good health, Fred."

"Good health." Fred touched Will's glass with his own. They drank and Fred glanced around the room, clearly admiring the gold and cream striped wallpaper and the new walnut sideboard, dining table and chairs. "You've done a great job with the house."

"Yes, it did turn out well. Isobel and I—" he broke off, hearing a scream from the drawing room.

When they reached Isobel and Margaret, Isobel was standing in the middle of the floor with her hands on her hips and a stunned Margaret – seated on the sofa – was holding a hand to her cheek.

"What happened, Isobel?" he demanded, while Fred went to his wife, who burst into tears.

"I will not be told in my own home that I'd better give you a child because you are a very handsome man and many Dublin ladies would welcome you into their bed," Isobel shrieked.

His jaw dropped. "What?"

"Margaret isn't the lady she appears to be. And she keeps resting a hand on her blasted belly just to rub in what a wonderful wife she is. In fact, she is such a wonderful wife, she has given her husband her blessing to find sexual satisfaction with prostitutes."

Fred gasped. "Christ, Margaret, you told her that?"

"I thought she would understand," Margaret cried. "Isobel admitted it to me herself that she's a fallen woman."

"Because of a seduction," Fred clarified. "I really do apologise, Isobel."

"I have never been struck on the face before," Margaret croaked, tears trickling down her cheeks, and Fred pulled a handkerchief from his trouser pocket. Kneeling down, he tilted her chin up and awkwardly dabbed at her eyes before passing the handkerchief to her.

"Well, Will." Fred stood up. "So much for our marriages being none of each other's business."

"Isobel and I will have a child one day, Fred, whether we

make it ourselves or not. And that is all I am going to say on the subject."

Fred nodded and glanced at Margaret. "And my wife would like to apologise."

Will doubted very much if Margaret liked the prospect of apologising one bit but he and Isobel waited.

"I am sorry," Margaret said quietly. "I've never been able to discuss such matters with a friend before and I'm afraid I got rather carried away. I do apologise, Isobel."

"And to Will," Fred added and Will cringed.

"You have my apologies, Will. It's clear to see how much you and Isobel love each other." Margaret gave him a weak smile before wiping more tears away. "May we start again, Isobel?" she asked her hesitantly. "I really would like to have you as a friend."

"I think we should have some tea." Isobel went to go to the rope and ring for a maid but Margaret got up and caught her hand.

"I think Fred and I should go. But I would like it very much if you and Will could come to us for tea one afternoon very soon. Please?"

Isobel glanced at him and he gave her a brief nod. "Yes," she said in a flat tone. "Very soon. I'll ask our footman to find you a cab."

"There's no need," Fred said. "I asked your maid to bring our cabman into the servants' hall to wait for us."

"I'll see you out." Will rang for a maid, opened the door and followed Fred and Margaret downstairs. In the hall, he passed Margaret her cloak and Fred his overcoat and hat as Mary came up the steps from the servants' hall. "Doctor and Mrs Simpson are leaving," he informed her.

"I'll tell the cabman, Dr Fitzgerald," she replied and returned to the servants' hall.

"Isobel and I will see you both very soon," he said, opening the front door.

"Yes, Will," Fred said simply and went down the steps after Margaret.

Will closed the door, ran back up the stairs to the drawing room and Isobel halted in her pacing up and down in front of the fireplace.

"I will not be spoken to like that and about such matters in my own home, Will. Not by Margaret – not by anyone. You are my husband – mine – and I will give you a child one day."

He lifted her hands to his lips and kissed them, inwardly cursing Margaret for rubbing salt into the open wound left by the miscarriage. "Isobel, you are a wonderful wife to me and I love you and – yes – we will have a child one day."

"If you hadn't been in there," she gestured towards the dining room, "building bridges with Fred, not only would I have struck Margaret – I'd have dragged her down the stairs and thrown her out of the house as well."

"I'm so sorry."

"No, I'm glad I got to see what Margaret's really like. And if she thinks I believe her for one second when she said Fred had her blessing…"

"Margaret's jealous of us?"

"Despite me not being able to give you a child, yes, she is. If Fred wasn't your oldest friend, I'd never want to see or speak to her again," she said and heaved a sigh to calm herself. "But I must. What did Fred say about Pimlico?"

"He's going to consider it," he told her, wishing he had more positive news.

She gave him a humourless smile. "And after this disastrous evening, he'll turn you down."

"I'll speak to him again in the morning."

"And I suppose I had better call on Margaret and make amends."

He nodded then kissed her forehead. "Well, at least the meal was delicious," he said and was delighted when she spluttered a laugh, threw her arms around his neck and hugged him.

At ten o'clock in the morning, Isobel stood on the steps outside number 1 Ely Place Upper clapping her gloved hands together in an effort to warm them while waiting to be admitted. This was going to be an ordeal but it had to be done. The butler opened the door and she forced a smile.

"Mrs Isobel Fitzgerald to see Mrs Margaret Simpson."

"I'm afraid Mrs Simpson is not receiving callers this morning, Mrs Fitzgerald."

"Could you please give her my name?" she asked, determined not to have had a wasted walk through a shower of sleet.

"Yes, of course." The butler went back into the hall, returning a few moments later. "Mrs Simpson asks that you join her in the morning room."

"Thank you," she said, pulling off her black gloves as he showed her into the room.

"Isobel." Margaret, wearing a purple day dress she favoured, got up from the sofa.

"I'm sorry." They spoke at the same time and smiled uneasily.

"Come and sit down, Isobel." They sat down on the pale

yellow sofa and Margaret clasped her cold hands. "You've probably guessed that I'm jealous," she said and Isobel felt herself flush. "You and Will love each other so much and I know I will never have what the two of you have. I love Fred and Fred loves me in his own way and I thought I could change him but I've been married long enough to him now to know I never will."

"Soon the baby will take up a lot of your time."

"Yes, and Fred and I would like very much if you and Will would consider being godparents."

"Oh." After the previous evening's events, this was the last thing she had expected. "Well, I'll discuss it with Will."

"Thank you. You'll stay for some tea?"

"Only if you're having tea as well."

Margaret shook her head. "Isobel, I'm horrified at insulting you and saying those things about Will yesterday evening. I went far too far and I apologise again."

"You've clearly been told of my past and heard the gossip circulating about me," she said. "It's no secret that I am a fallen woman. I wasn't a virgin when I married Will. I'm extremely lucky to be in the position I'm in now – with a loving husband and a beautiful home. I just wish I could give him a child." Her gaze dropped to Margaret's small belly. "And I'm jealous of your pregnancy. Will says we'll adopt if need be but I so want to give him a child we created together."

"I hope you will." Margaret sounded sincere and Isobel nodded gratefully. "And so we have both confessed a jealous secret to each other."

"Yes, we have. Margaret, I'm sorry. I find it very difficult to allow myself to befriend people. The last friend I had was

Claire, the other parlourmaid in Mr and Mrs Harvey's house on Merrion Square, but I was deceiving her by secretly visiting Will and when she found out she never forgave me. I simply don't know if I can truly befriend someone again."

"Can you please try?" Margaret asked quietly. "I do have acquaintances, but not a proper friend – and certainly no-one to discuss marital matters with – and with Fred and Will being best friends…"

"I can only try," she said, squirming at not just her unenthusiastic response, but at the prospect of discussing marital matters with Margaret or, indeed, anyone except Will.

"Would you like some coffee?" Margaret added brightly. "I suddenly have a fancy for some coffee."

It was stifling in the room and Isobel smiled, glad for the opportunity to take off her coat. "Some coffee would be very nice, thank you."

She left an hour later and called to number 55 Fitzwilliam Square. Slowly but surely, her widowed mother was making friends and acquaintances and these days it was rare to find her at home. To Isobel's surprise, Alfie and not Gorman the butler opened the front door.

"Can't stop, I'm afraid," he said, winding a pale blue scarf around his neck. "I'm on my way to a lecture. Mother is in the morning room and Mr Ellison is here again."

"Again?" she asked sharply. "Why is he here? Is something wrong?"

"No, not at all. He called to tell Mother and I that tenants have been found for the house on Westland Row and the two houses on the Rathmines Road."

At last. Her mother, Alfie and herself had been left rental

properties in Mr Henderson's will, including two brothels in the red light district of Monto, north of the River Liffey. The brothels had been quickly sold and the proceeds used to purchase a second property on the Rathmines Road. With Christmas and New Year intervening and the properties having needed decorating, it had taken what seemed like an age to have the houses occupied with tenants.

"Good. Thank you, Alfie, see you soon." She went into the morning room and Mrs Henderson beamed at her in delight.

"Isobel. How lovely. How are you?"

"I'm very well, thank you, Mother," she said, bending and kissing her cheek. "Mr Ellison," she added as the grey-haired solicitor got up from an armchair and shook her hand. "Alfie tells me you have found tenants for the houses."

"Yes, I have, Mrs Fitzgerald. The Rathmines Road tenants move in next week. A retired gentleman in one house and a young couple with a newborn baby in the other."

"Oh." She forced a smile and sat next to her mother on the huge sofa upholstered in gold-coloured velvet. "How nice."

"And a bank manager and his wife for the Westland Row house," Mr Ellison added, re-taking his seat. "They move in tomorrow."

"Tea?" her mother offered.

"No, thank you. I've just called on Margaret Simpson and we drank a pot of coffee dry."

"Goodness." Mrs Henderson's eyebrows shot up. "Is so much coffee wise in her condition?"

"I don't know, but she enjoyed it all the same."

"How was the dinner? Isobel and Will had Frederick and

Margaret Simpson to dinner yesterday evening," her mother informed Mr Ellison.

"It was very pleasant," she managed to reply in a neutral tone. "The meal was delicious. We were very lucky to find Mrs Dillon, she's a very competent housekeeper and an excellent cook."

Good grief. She only just stopped herself rolling her eyes. How she hated making small talk. She'd never been good at it. Perhaps discussing marital matters with Margaret might not be such an awful prospect after all.

Will was about to open the door to his surgery when Fred's surgery door opened and he looked out.

"There you are. Come in for a moment."

Will followed Fred inside and closed the door. "How is Margaret this morning?"

"She's very well, but I have to say, it's not every week I almost get throttled by you and my wife gets struck by yours."

Will just managed to bite his tongue. "Can we please put those incidents behind us?"

"Yes, of course, and you'll be very relieved to hear that two packages are waiting for you on your desk. Out of the two, I'd suggest the package I've left on top. They're good quality and I'd better stop there as I'd rather you didn't attempt to throttle me again."

"Was it just the condoms you wanted to speak to me about?" he asked crisply.

"No, I wanted to let you know that I'd be happy to take one surgery per week in Pimlico."

Will couldn't hide his astonishment. "Are you sure?"

"I'm positive. It's always good to challenge one's self and the caesarean made me realise my work needs rather more than haemorrhoids and gout."

"I never thought you'd say yes."

Fred smiled. "Never say never. So, when do we begin?"

"Well, the windows and two doors have been replaced, but the rooms themselves are filthy and need cleaning. Isobel and I haven't got round to that yet."

"The four of us could view the rooms this afternoon?" Fred suggested. "You and I can make a list of what we're going to need and then you and Isobel can come home with Margaret and I for afternoon tea? Yes?"

"Yes."

"Good. We'll call for you both at three o'clock. Now, go and inspect your packages." Fred slapped his shoulder.

Will went into his surgery, closed the door and put his medical bag down behind the desk. Picking up the top package, he unwrapped it and put the plain brown paper to one side. He opened the small red box and lifted out one of the condoms. It was extremely flimsy and he hoped it would be strong enough.

Hearing a sharp knock at the door, Will went to swipe the condoms onto the floor behind the desk with his arm until he heard Fred's voice.

"It's me." The door opened and Fred laughed, irritating him. "Those condoms are the best." He nodded at the red box. "Take my word for it."

"Oh." He returned the condom to the box and put it, the brown wrapping paper, and the other package in a desk drawer. "Thank you."

"No, I should be thanking you for acquiring some

condoms. The sooner you and Isobel begin having sexual relations again, the safer Margaret and I will be."

"Fred—" he began but his friend gave him a wink and left the room. Will grimaced. Fred was right, he missed making love to Isobel and she had shown in Pimlico how she missed making love, too. Tonight. He gave himself a determined nod before smiling as his first patient came into the surgery.

When he arrived home just before one o'clock, Isobel was speaking with Mrs Dillon in the hall.

"Luncheon will be five minutes, Dr Fitzgerald," the housekeeper told him as he put his medical bag on the hall table before hanging his hat and overcoat on the stand.

"Thank you, Mrs Dillon." Taking Isobel's hand, he led her straight into the breakfast room and closed the door. "The condoms have arrived," he said and she exhaled a little gasp of joy. "This evening, I will make love to you."

"I will count down the hours, Dr Fitzgerald," she replied softly.

"And Fred has agreed to join me in Pimlico for one surgery per week."

"Oh, I'm so glad. When do you start?"

"We haven't set a date yet, but this afternoon the four of us are going to view the rooms. Fred and I will make a list of what we'll need, then Fred has invited us to Ely Place Upper for afternoon tea."

"Afternoon tea?" she echoed with a comical groan. "This morning, Margaret and I drank an entire pot of coffee."

"How was she?"

"Apologetic. She wants us to be friends and I said I would try, but I can never be a true friend to her. I can never be a true friend to anyone – except you."

"You can only try and be as true a friend to her as you are able," he said softly.

"But she wants us to be godparents to the baby."

"Oh."

"Has Fred never mentioned it?" she asked.

"When he first told me Margaret was pregnant I mentioned in passing if he would be looking for godparents, but all he said was, 'we might be'. Do you want to be a godparent?"

"I don't see that we have much choice. And I hate to say it, Will, but with him joining you in Pimlico—"

"I'll be keeping an eye on Fred, don't worry," he assured her. "He won't be using the rooms in Pimlico to entertain prostitutes."

"How can you keep an eye on him from here?"

"I can't," he admitted. "But Jimmy can. He and his mother live next door. I hate not being able to trust Fred but he's brought this on himself."

"Yes, he has," she said as the door opened and Florrie came in with the soup tureen.

Fred was admitted to number 30 just after three o'clock, they joined Margaret in a cab and travelled to Pimlico. By Margaret's shocked expression as she viewed the two rooms, Will realised she had never been inside a tenement house before.

"This is ideal." Fred walked around the first room then into what would be the surgery, nodding approvingly at the new windows and doors. "Needs a damn good clean, though."

While Isobel went with Margaret to wait in the cab, Will and Fred compiled a long list of requirements.

"The desk, chairs and examination couch I used in Brown Street are in one of the guest bedrooms at number 30." Will put the list in the inside pocket of his frock coat. "You and I can clean these rooms then bring them here at the weekend. We'll try some of the furniture warehouses for a lockable cupboard and more chairs at the weekend, too. Shall we try and aim to begin here in a fortnight?"

"A fortnight." Fred smiled and they shook hands.

The cabman was standing on the pavement outside the tenement house, his bowler hat pushed to the back of his head while he smoked a cigarette. By Margaret's expression of fascination, as she turned away from him and peered out of the other cab window at two small barefoot boys chasing a terrier-type dog along the opposite pavement, Isobel realised she had never been in the Liberties before.

"My mother would be horrified if she knew where I was," she told Isobel with a little smile as if having read her mind. "But my mother is horrified by many things."

"So is mine, but Pimlico is respectable. So is Brown Street, where Will used to live."

"It is just so different here. I would be quite content to sit here all afternoon and just watch the people."

"While I worked for the Harveys', I used to sit in St Stephen's Green and watch the people there."

"Did you enjoy working for them?" Margaret asked curiously. "As a servant?"

"Yes, I did," she replied. "Very much so. The work was hard when I was a parlourmaid, not quite so hard when I was Mrs Harvey's lady's maid, but I was continually at her beck and call and I often had to wait up until the small hours for her to return from dinner parties."

"You don't have a lady's maid, do you, Isobel? I don't know where I would be without mine."

"No, I don't feel I need one. If I need help with my clothes, I ask Will."

"Will?" Margaret echoed, shooting her a wide-eyed glance.

"He very much enjoys undressing me. He is quite competent at dressing me, too."

"Good gracious me. Fred has never touched my clothes in that way. I don't think he would know where to start."

"Then, educate him," Isobel told her simply and Margaret peered out of the window at the cabman again. Isobel could almost hear her brain whirring.

"I could not go to Fred's bedroom."

Why not? He is your husband, Isobel answered silently. "Then, invite him to yours. Leave a letter or note in his medical bag or in his frock coat's inside pocket."

"If I do, it will be well after Baby is born."

"Whenever you feel comfortable enough to do so. Ah, here are Will and Fred. All done?" she asked, as Will opened the cab door and they climbed inside.

"All done," he confirmed. "And all being well, we begin our surgeries in two weeks' time."

That evening, as soon as she finished eating and put her dessert spoon down, Will got up from the head of the table and held out a hand.

"Now?" She laughed, getting up and taking it.

"Now," he replied, leading her to the breakfast room door and opening it for her.

In the hall, Florrie passed them on her way to the front

door and they halted to see who the caller was. Florrie opened the door and Mr Ellison took off his hat and nodded to the maid before glancing at the two of them at the foot of the stairs in a little surprise at seeing them there.

"I do apologise for calling so late," the solicitor began immediately. "But as I was leaving my office for the day, I received a telegram from India."

Isobel's heart began to thump nervously. Will's elder brother, Edward, was a major in the army and stationed in India.

"India," Will repeated in a flat tone. "Please, come inside, Mr Ellison."

Florrie took the solicitor's hat and they went into the morning room.

"I must explain a little," Mr Ellison continued. "Ronald Henderson was your brother's solicitor and on Ronald's death, I inherited his clients. The telegram is from your brother's commanding officer, Lieutenant-General Beresford. Dr Fitzgerald, I'm afraid there is no easy way to break this news to you; Major Edward Fitzgerald died of cholera two days ago at the Station Hospital at Deolali. I'm very sorry."

Isobel clapped a hand to her mouth then threw a glance at Will. He stood frozen in shock in front of the fireplace.

"What about his wife and son?" she asked Mr Ellison as the solicitor opened a black leather briefcase, extracted an envelope and passed it to Will.

"Why was this telegram delivered to you? Why did it not go to his wife or to my parents?" Will demanded, pulling the Post Office Telegraphs form out of the envelope and they read the scrawling handwriting together.

Deeply regret to inform you that Major Edward Fitzgerald died of cholera at Deolali Station Hospital on January 24ᵗʰ. Letter follows.

Lieutenant-General G. M. Beresford
Commander-in-Chief
Bombay Army

"Your brother left strict instructions that the telegram should come to his solicitor and for his solicitor to break the news to you, Dr Fitzgerald. Your brother also instructed that this letter be put into your hands in the event of his death." Reaching into the briefcase, Mr Ellison took out a second envelope and handed it to Will.

"Have you read this letter?" he asked as she took the telegram and its envelope from him.

"Yes, I have. It was also part of your brother's instructions that his solicitor read the letter first so he could be on hand to offer advice."

"I see." Will opened the envelope and Isobel saw his hands shake as he held the letter so she could read it, too.

Dear Will,

I have never been a good correspondent, but this letter needs to be written.

I took Mr Henderson on as my solicitor as I needed my own legal man completely separate from Father's and because there are a number of facts that you, as my brother, need to be aware of.

John, whom you believe to be my son with Ruth is, in fact, my son with an Indian woman named

Purnima Sharma. Ruth knew nothing of Purnima and, as a result, Ruth and I are no longer living together as husband and wife. Ruth returned to London when she learned Purnima was expecting my child and I have not heard from her since.

Purnima died giving birth to John and her family passed him on to me. Naturally, I could not bring up a son alone and in India, so I brought John to London and he is being cared for in a children's home which was recommended to me.

Purnima was the love of my life but I could never have married her. I knew it and Purnima knew it. The six months I spent in London on administrative duties was my futile attempt to try and forget her. It did not work. When I returned newly-married to India with Ruth, within days I had sought out Purnima and it was as if I had never been away.

I am endeavouring to obtain a permanent posting in London so I can try and be a father to John but, having already called in all the favours owed to me in order to obtain the six-month London posting and the two months leave to bring John to London, it is proving difficult. If you are reading this letter, Will, and very much to my regret, it has not happened.

I am sorry, Will, that I have never been much of a brother to you. I am especially sorry that I have been such a coward about all this and that it is now up to you to inform Father, Mother and Ruth and to pick up the pieces.

Edward

There was a silence as Will folded the letter, put it back in the envelope and leant it against the clock on the mantelpiece. Isobel could sense his anger boiling up and it wasn't long before he exploded.

"Christ Almighty. All of Edward's letters have been complete and utter lies. How did the bloody fool ever think he could get away with this?"

"Do you have the name and address of the children's home?" she asked Mr Ellison as she returned the telegram to its envelope and placed it in front of Edward's letter.

"Yes, I do."

"And do you know anything of Ruth?" she continued. "She needs to know Edward is dead."

"Not a thing, I'm afraid."

"Ruth was brought up by an aunt," Will said. "My parents have the address."

"Good," she replied.

"Did Edward leave a will, Mr Ellison?" Will added.

"He did. John is the sole beneficiary of approximately five hundred pounds."

"And he is in a children's home." Will rolled his eyes. "I wish you had read this letter sooner, Mr Ellison."

"I'm sorry, Dr Fitzgerald, but it was Major Fitzgerald's instructions that the letter only be read by both his solicitor and yourself in the event of his death. The instructions contained no mention of a child. If they had, I may have been able to reason with your brother."

"Is there anything else?" he asked the solicitor.

"As Major Fitzgerald did not divorce his wife, and as John is his illegitimate son, there is the possibility that she may contest the will."

78

Will exhaled a long sigh. "What do we do first?"

"You must decide what to tell your parents," Mr Ellison replied and Will frowned.

"I don't understand?"

"Will your parents accept an illegitimate half-Indian grandson, Dr Fitzgerald? By placing the boy in a children's home in London, it would appear that Major Fitzgerald did not think they would."

Will stared at Mr Ellison. "I don't know," he replied quietly. "But my parents need to know about John, whether they like it or not."

"My deepest condolences, Dr Fitzgerald."

Will gave him a weak smile and they shook hands. "Thank you for coming to inform me. I will break the news to my parents in the morning. When I have discussed John with them, I will call to see you."

Mr Ellison nodded, clearly not envying Will's task one bit.

"I'll see you out, Mr Ellison," she said and they went out to the hall and she closed the morning room door.

"You never met Major Fitzgerald?" the solicitor asked.

"No, I didn't. And I haven't met his wife either. Mr Ellison, do you know what kind of children's home John is in? Is it respectable?"

"I'm afraid I don't know, Mrs Fitzgerald. I will find out."

"Thank you."

"Your mother and brother are well, I hope?"

"They are very well, thank you," she said, lifting his hat from the stand and passing it to him before opening the front door. "Good evening to you," she added and he went out. She closed the door and hurried back to the morning room. Will was standing in front of the fireplace staring into the fire. "Will." She turned him around and saw the mixture of fury and grief in his eyes. "I'm so sorry," she whispered, taking him in her arms.

"How do I tell them?" he asked and she felt him give a helpless little shrug. "How do I tell my parents Edward is dead and that he'd been lying to us all?"

"I'll be with you," she said, knowing it sounded feeble. "Will," she went on as he went to the drinks tray and poured them both a brandy. "Will your parents accept an illegitimate half-Indian grandson?"

He turned around with the two glasses in his hands. "I honestly don't know."

"How old is John, exactly?"

"Well, the John that Edward told us about was born on 26th January 1878, which makes him three years old today. Whether this John is the same age, I don't know."

"Edward didn't send any photographs of John to your parents?"

"No." Will passed her a glass and she took a sip. "And they never questioned it. I think they rather assumed there were no photographic studios in India. Isobel, my parents are going to be heart-broken about Edward, so we have to decide what to do about John."

"And Ruth," she said as he drained his glass and put it back on the drinks tray. "Her husband is dead and she needs to know. She also might be able to tell us something about John's mother. But in the meantime – John?"

"You're thinking what I'm thinking, aren't you?" he asked.

"Yes," she replied at once. "We should give John a home here."

"Are you absolutely sure, Isobel? I know what I said when—"

"I'm absolutely sure. We both want a child and John needs a home."

Will nodded. "We need to go to London as soon as possible. In the morning, I have to tell my parents their eldest son is dead. This evening," he continued, taking her glass and placing it beside his on the drinks tray. "I need to make love to you."

She was led upstairs, into their bedroom and he lit the oil lamp before kicking the door closed with a foot. Turning her around so her back was to him, he quickly pulled the pins from her hair and undressed her. He wasn't rough but he was too urgent and as he pulled his own clothes off, he lost a shirt button in the process.

Opening a drawer in his bedside table, he reached for the red box of condoms. He lifted the lid off, took one out and laid it on the bedside table. Flattening it, he took each end in his fingers and pulled at it as if to see how pliant it was. The condom wasn't very flexible and he grimaced.

"Will," she said softly. "Will, let me."

"You've used one before?"

"Only one man insisted on using a condom," she told him. "I didn't know what to do with it and I tore it. He was furious and demanded another girl. The next day, Maggie showed me how to use one with a cucumber. So, no, I haven't used one before with a man but if you don't stop pulling at it like that you're going to tear it." He nodded and passed it to her. "Now, get onto the bed and lie down."

He did as he was told, she put the condom back into the box and followed him onto the bed. She kissed his lips then kissed her way down his chest and down to his groin. Wrapping her fingers around him she slid them up and down the exquisite hardness making him grunt. She reached for the condom and he watched her slide it on.

"There," she said as she straddled him, walked forward on her knees and sank down.

She rode him slowly, rotating her hips, before placing her hands on his shoulders and allowing him to clasp her waist and lift her up and down. She could feel his heavy breathing against her breasts until he took a nipple into his mouth, rolling the tip around with his tongue.

Suddenly, he wrapped his arms around her and rolled them over so he was now on top. He thrust hard into her before withdrawing and instructing her to turn over onto her hands and knees. She gasped as he slipped into her from behind. He felt so much deeper inside her and she had to pull air into her lungs as he began to stroke in and out. Her hands reached up to grip the brass bedstead, her hair cascading down her back and he swept it to one side so he could kiss the length of her scar.

They moved slowly, her arms curling back around his neck and he cupped her breasts as he kissed and nibbled her shoulder. When he moaned into her ear, it tipped her over the edge and she pushed back onto him crying out as she came. Grunting her name, he began thrusting erratically as he climaxed before falling sideways onto the bed bringing her with him.

They were both gasping for air and it was a minute or so before either of them could speak. Leaning over her, he kissed her lips.

"Thank you," he whispered. "I needed you."

They walked to Merrion Square straight after breakfast, each step making Will's legs feel more and more like lead. Tess showed them into number 67's morning room, where his mother was seated on the sofa. His father was bending to kiss her cheek, clearly about to leave for the *Journal of Irish Medicine*, but straightened up as Tess closed the door.

"Is there something wrong?" his father asked him. "Your surgery begins in ten minutes."

"A message is on its way to Fred to tell him I won't be taking surgery this morning."

"What's happened?" His father began to look wary and Will breathed deeply in and out to calm himself.

"Please sit down, Father."

Silently, his father sat on the sofa.

"Yesterday evening, Mr Ellison called to number 30," Will began. "He had received a telegram from Edward's commanding officer, Lieutenant-General Beresford. Edward is dead. He died of cholera three days ago at the Station Hospital at Deolali."

His father exhaled a long breath while his mother bent her head, covering her face with her hands.

"The telegram went to Mr Ellison," his father said. "Why?"

"Edward had instructed that it go to his solicitor. Edward had also sent a letter to his solicitor at the time – Mr Henderson – which Mr Ellison passed on to me as I was only to read it in the event of Edward's death."

"You? Why?"

"So I would be the one breaking the news to you, Father."

"What was in the letter?"

"Some hard truths."

"Tell me."

Will took another deep breath. "John is not Edward's son with Ruth."

His mother's head jerked up from her hands. "What? Then, who is his mother?"

"An Indian woman named Purnima. She died when John was born and her family passed him on to Edward. But Ruth knew nothing about Purnima and she returned to London when she learned of Purnima and that Purnima was pregnant with Edward's child."

Both his parents stared at him open-mouthed.

"Did Ruth and Edward divorce?" His father spoke first.

"No."

"Where is John now?" his mother asked. "Where has he been all this time?"

"In London. In a children's home."

"Oh." His mother burst into tears. "All of Edward's letters—"

"Have been complete and utter fiction," Will finished as his father got up and went to one of the windows.

"Oh, Edward." His mother fumbled in her sleeve for a handkerchief and blew her nose.

"We need to come to a decision about John," Will continued.

"What is there to decide?" his father said harshly without turning around. "The boy is a half-caste."

Will winced. "The boy is Edward's son. And, according to Mr Ellison, he is the sole beneficiary in Edward's will."

"But what about Ruth?" His mother spoke up. "If she and Edward did not divorce, she may have a claim on Edward's estate."

"Mr Ellison did mention that possibility," Will told her and heard his father swear under his breath. "But we really need to come to a decision about John, Father. He's your grandson, he can't be left in a children's home."

"This house will not be inherited by a half-caste bastard and that is final. Tell the children's home to find a family who will take him in."

And with that, his father strode out of the room, banging the door closed behind him.

Will stared at the door for a few moments before squeezing his eyes shut to try and calm himself.

"Will?" Hearing his mother's voice, he opened them and turned to her. "Your father is upset, he loved Edward so much."

"That may be so, but there is still a little boy to think of who is now an orphan and needs a home."

"Your father won't accept him, Will. Not in his present state of mind."

"Then, Isobel and I will give John a home at number 30."

His mother twisted around to look at Isobel. "Are you sure? Especially after what you've just been through?"

"We're sure."

"Thank you. When will you go to London?"

"As soon as possible," Will replied. "Hopefully this evening."

"Will." His mother got up and clasped his hands. "Thank you for telling us. It must have been horrendous for you."

"It was," he admitted. "I knew you would be distressed but I never thought Father would disown his own grandson because of where the boy's mother is from. I always thought he was more broad-minded than that."

"Do you know anything about her?" his mother asked.

"No, not a thing. We're hoping Ruth might so I need her aunt's address from you. I'm going to speak to Fred and then I need to speak to Mr Ellison."

"Yes, of course."

"I'll stay here until you return," Isobel told him.

"Thank you," he said, kissing her cheek then his mother's and leaving the room.

In the hall, he glanced at the stairs before running up the steps two at a time. Dr Fitzgerald senior was in the drawing room seated at the writing desk with his back to the door.

"Is there anything I can do, Father?"

"No," his father replied without looking at him. "I'm writing a death notice for *The Irish Times*."

Will walked out of the room without replying and called to Isobel as she went to go up the stairs to the bedrooms after his mother.

"I'll be back as soon as I can," he whispered. "I'm sorry, I realise you didn't know Edward."

"I'll try and get your mother to talk about him. It will be good for her and I'll learn about both Edward and Ruth. I don't know what to do about your father, though. I daren't go near him."

"I'll speak to him again when I get back," he said, not relishing the prospect one bit.

He kissed her lips then went downstairs, put on his hat and overcoat and left the house.

At the practice house, Fred was coming down the stairs and glanced at him in surprise. Taking Fred's arm, Will led him past their patients and into the dispensary.

"What's happened?" Fred asked. "I was told a family emergency."

"Fred, Edward's dead."

Fred's eyes widened. "Dead?"

"He died of cholera three days ago at the Station Hospital at Deolali in India."

"Christ, Will, you shouldn't be here. You should be with your parents."

"Isobel is at number 67. Fred, Edward fathered John with an Indian woman called Purnima and when Ruth found out about Purnima and the pregnancy, she left him and returned to London."

For once Fred was lost for words for a few moments. "Is there anything I can do?"

"Find a locum for tomorrow or ask the non-urgent cases to return on Monday as I'll be back by then. Edward placed John in a children's home in London. Isobel and I are going there to fetch him and to try and find Ruth."

"You're bringing the boy back to Dublin?"

"John is my nephew, Fred. My father has already disowned him but I won't. He's three years old and both his parents are dead. I can't leave him in a children's home and Isobel agrees with me that we'll give him a home at number 30."

Fred's face crumpled with sympathy. "I'm so sorry, Will. If there's anything else I can do. Anything at all."

"Thanks, Fred."

"When are you leaving?"

"I'm not sure – hopefully this evening – I have to go and see Mr Ellison then go to the shipping office. What was the name of the hotel Margaret and you stayed at in London?"

"The Tower Hotel. We found it excellent."

"Thanks, Fred, I'll send them a telegram."

Three hours later, Will returned to number 67 and found Isobel alone in the morning room.

"We sail for Holyhead this evening."

"Good," she said, getting up from the sofa. "I'll send someone to number 30 to ask Mary and Florrie to pack for us. I persuaded your mother to lie down," she added. "Your father went out shortly after you left, he hasn't returned, and I'm starting to worry."

"He was to deliver a death notice to *The Irish Times*."

"Will, walking there and back doesn't take this long."

"I think I know where he might be. I'll go and see."

Will went out, across the street and into the garden in the centre of Merrion Square. His father was seated on a bench with his hat in his hands staring into space. For the first time, John Fitzgerald looked all of his sixty-six years. His hair was more white than grey and the lines on his forehead and at the corners of his eyes had never been more prominent than now. Will sat down beside him and racked his brains for something to say. Instead, his father spoke first.

"Edward should have been the doctor, not you. It was always the eldest Fitzgerald son who went into medicine but he wanted none of it and you wanted nothing else."

"It was the army or nothing with Edward."

"Yes." His father sighed. "But I never thought I'd lose him to disease."

"Isobel and I are going to London this evening to bring John home with us, find Ruth and—"

"No, Will, you will leave that boy where he is."

"He is my nephew and your grandson and I will bring him home—"

"He is neither one thing nor the other—"

Will turned to face him. "I never thought I would ever hear you say things like this. Do not blame John. Edward brought this mess upon himself and, if you so wish it, we will not bring John anywhere near number 67. But Isobel and I are bringing him home to number 30 with us and that is final."

Isobel did a double take when the morning room door opened and Will stood in the doorway white-faced. The front door slammed, his father walked along the hall and she heard him go upstairs.

"You've rowed," she said unnecessarily.

"My father was across the street in the garden and he looked like an old man for the first time. He doesn't row like an old man, though. He wants John to be left where he is. The upshot is that John will not be brought here."

Her heart sank. "But we don't know how your mother feels about John yet."

"I'll speak to her and tell her she will be welcome to visit John at number 30. But I don't want this to come between her and my father. They've lost their eldest son and they are going to need each other."

Will's parents came downstairs for luncheon but the delicious vegetable soup, roast chicken, and trifle was eaten in silence.

"Mother," he began before anyone got up from the table. "I don't know if Father has spoken to you, but Isobel and I are going to London this evening to collect John. And we are most definitely giving him a home with us in Fitzwilliam Square."

"No," his father snapped.

"Yes," Will replied firmly.

"Dr Fitzgerald." Isobel intervened before another row broke out. "If you do not wish to acknowledge John, or to visit him, then so be it."

"You will be most welcome to visit John in Fitzwilliam Square, Mother, if you so wish," Will added. "But Isobel and I will be raising him."

"And what about the children you claim you will have?" Dr Fitzgerald senior asked, putting great emphasis on the word 'claim' and Isobel fought to control a flush of indignation.

"Number 30 is big enough for more than one child, don't you think?" Will replied.

"Can you find a locum to cover for you while you're away?" his father asked instead of answering.

"Fred is seeing to it. He and I were to bring a desk, examination couch and chairs to Pimlico this weekend. I need to go and tell Mrs Bell that won't happen now." He got up from the table. "I won't be too long." He squeezed her shoulder and went out.

"I'll have to go shopping for things for John," she said.

"There are some of Edward and Will's toys you can have," her mother-in-law told her. "Edward broke most of his and Will would always try and repair them but some are still intact. We still have their cradle somewhere as well."

"John might be a little big for a cradle but the toys will be very welcome, thank you," she said, as Will's father got to his feet.

"I'm going to the *Journal* offices to explain my absence."

"Now?" his wife asked.

"They'll be wondering where I am. I won't be long."

He went out and Will's mother gave her a sad smile. "They both need to be doing something."

"I hope you aren't angry at Will and I?" Isobel asked her as they went into the morning room and sat down on the sofa. "We can't leave Edward's son in a children's home."

"No, of course not, and I hope John accepts his grandson eventually." Sarah Fitzgerald's voice shook and Isobel reached out and held her hand. "I simply cannot fathom any of this," she whispered. "Edward. My beautiful son."

"Tell me about him?"

"Edward was an enormous baby and he took a full day to be born. I swore never to have another baby but then Will came along. Someone bought Edward a set of toy soldiers for his sixth birthday and that was it – he was going to join the army. His father and I thought he'd grow out of it, especially his father, as he expected Edward to go into medicine. But, no, Edward was going to join the army and it was Will who wanted to become a doctor. Edward met Ruth while on an administerial posting in London. He was so happy when he returned to India and he told me how eager he was to show Ruth how beautiful the country was. At least we thought Edward was happy, more than ever when he wrote and told us how proud he was to have a son…" Will's mother tailed off.

"We won't let John forget his father," Isobel assured her. "And if you have a photograph of him which we could put it in his bedroom—" She stopped. Which bedroom should John have? The bedroom next to hers and Will's, probably.

"What are you thinking?" Will's mother asked with a little smile.

"John's bedroom. His will be next to Will's and mine, so we can hear him if he cries."

"And he probably will, poor child."

"Yes. We'll all be complete strangers to him. Will and I are also going to try and find out about his mother."

"Purnima," Will's mother mused. "I wonder what she was like. Beautiful, I suppose, to have turned Edward's head."

"We only know what Edward wrote about her in his letter."

"Ruth may know more but will probably be less than kind." Sarah grimaced and shook her head. "We honestly thought Edward and Ruth were happy together."

"Who knows what it's like to be an army wife in India. Did Ruth ever write to you?"

"No. John and I only received letters from Edward. We barely know Ruth. We only met her for the first time the day before the wedding. Are you in a fit state to travel to London?" she asked suddenly.

Isobel nodded. Her monthlies hadn't returned yet but it would probably take time for her body to fully recover from the miscarriage. "I am very well," she replied truthfully for the first time. "Thank you, Sarah."

Chapter Three

A cab brought Will and Isobel through snowy London streets to the Tower Hotel at just after eight o'clock the following morning. They had slept on the train from Holyhead in Wales so they left their luggage, hats and coats in their double room on the first floor, went to the hotel's dining room for breakfast, then took a cab to Mrs Thompson's Home for Children. It was respectable, Mr Ellison had told Will, but that was all the solicitor had been able to find out.

They alighted from the cab outside a large white Georgian detached house, Will paid the cabman and he rang the doorbell. It was answered by a young maid who looked them up and down.

"May I help you?"

"Doctor and Mrs Fitzgerald from Dublin," he said, taking off his hat. "Mrs Thompson is expecting us."

"Do come in."

"Thank you."

They went into a tiled hall devoid of furniture or ornaments of any kind and the maid knocked at a door to their right before opening it.

"Doctor and Mrs Fitzgerald, Mrs Thompson."

A dark-haired woman in late middle age and dressed in black rose from behind a large mahogany desk as they went into the office.

"I am Mary Thompson."

"William Fitzgerald," he said, reaching across the desk to shake her hand. "This is my wife, Isobel."

"Do sit down."

"Thank you." They sat on the two chairs in front of the desk.

"Your solicitor, a Mr Ellison, sent a telegram on your behalf informing me of the death of Major Fitzgerald, that you are his brother, and that you will be giving John a home in Dublin. Do you have supporting documentation?"

"I do," Will replied, pulling an envelope from his overcoat pocket. "Baptism certificates for myself and my brother, Edward."

He passed them over and Mrs Thompson read them before nodding and handing them back to him.

"Thank you."

"May I ask how long John has been here?" Will asked, returning the certificates to the envelope and his overcoat pocket.

"Since he was two months old."

"And how old is John now?" he added and Mrs Thompson shot him a sharp glance. "I'm afraid my late brother misled all of us," he explained. "My parents and I were under the impression that John was the son of my brother and his wife and was still living in India."

"I see. Well, John has just turned three years old."

"John has been here for almost three years?" Isobel exclaimed.

"That is correct. Major Fitzgerald brought John here himself."

"What do you know about John's mother?" Will asked. "We know little or nothing."

"Not a thing, but we do have a photograph."

Will nodded, relieved there was something. "Is John healthy?"

"Extremely healthy. He does not speak, however."

"At all?"

"Not one word. He is very observant, he just does not speak."

"Has he been examined by a doctor?" Will asked.

"Yes, of course." Mrs Thompson both looked and sounded offended. "There is nothing physically wrong with the boy. We do our best here, Dr Fitzgerald, but nothing can make up for the lack of a home and a family. Do you have children yourselves?"

"Not yet," Isobel replied. "We are not long married."

"So you have little experience of children?"

"We want very much to give John a home," Isobel went on. "We are his family, and we will have the support of both our mothers."

"Does John know his father is dead and that my wife and I are going to give him a home?" Will asked and Mrs Thompson shook her head.

"No, he does not. I thought it better not to tell him in case you did not come."

"I see," Will replied and exchanged a glance with Isobel, also clearly wondering how to break the news to John and what reaction it would bring.

"Before I bring you to John—" Mrs Thompson got up

from her chair and retrieved a cardboard file from the top of a tall mahogany filing cabinet. Returning to the desk, she sat down and extracted two forms from the file. "I need you to sign these forms, here and here." She pointed to the bottom of each form then picked up a pen and opened a bottle of ink. "It is to acknowledge that you will now be responsible for the boy."

Taking the pen from her, Will quickly read the forms then dipped the nib into the ink and signed them both.

"Thank you, Dr Fitzgerald." Mrs Thompson blotted his signatures, put one of the forms in a desk drawer then placed the second form in the file and passed it to him. "Let me bring you to John."

They followed her upstairs, along a corridor and into a long dormitory containing approximately twenty narrow single beds with small chests of drawers standing in between them. Boys ranging in ages between two and five were sitting on their beds or playing on the bare floorboards with colourful wooden building blocks. One little boy, however, was seated alone in a far corner with his back to them.

"John Fitzgerald," Mrs Thompson called and the boy turned and stared up at them with eyes so dark they were almost black. Other than that, Will had to fight back tears at how like Edward he was. John's straight brown hair, his long nose and his wide mouth were all Edward. "Up you get."

"No, stay sitting." Will took Isobel's hand and they went forward and sat down on the floor beside him. "Hello, John," he said, noting the boy's clothing as he didn't want John to catch a chill when they left the home. John, like all the boys in the dormitory, was wearing a white shirt, a brown waistcoat and brown morning coat, knee-length brown trousers and black boots – all of which had seen better days. "My name is Will. I'm your uncle, brother to your father, Edward. This," he indicated Isobel, and the boy looked at her, "is my wife, Isobel. We didn't know you were here otherwise we would have come a lot sooner, but we would very much like for you to come and live with us. Would you like that, John?"

John stared impassively at him and behind him, Will heard Mrs Thompson clear her throat.

"As I said, Dr Fitzgerald, the boy does not speak."

"Well, we will have to try and rectify that, Mrs Thompson," he said, twisting around to look up at her. "We would be obliged if you could arrange for his belongings to be packed."

"Yes, of course. Molly?" Mrs Thompson nodded to a red-haired nursemaid who hurried out of the dormitory.

Will got to his feet and walked with Mrs Thompson to a window. "Are there any outstanding fees I need to be aware of?"

"Major Fitzgerald always paid in advance so, no there are not, Dr Fitzgerald."

"Thank you," he replied, grateful for her honesty. "Is there anything else you can tell me about John? His favourite foods, for example?"

"John's file contains everything you need to know, Dr Fitzgerald," she said as Molly returned with a small trunk.

"This is the trunk Major Fitzgerald had with him with John's belongings," Molly explained, putting the trunk down on a bed about halfway along the dormitory. "I'll miss John," she added, opening a chest of drawers, lifting the clothes out and packing them in the trunk. "He's always so well behaved."

"Thank you for looking after John, Molly." Will picked the little boy up as Isobel got to her feet, took the trunk from the nursemaid and they followed Mrs Thompson downstairs to the hall. "Thank you for all you've done for John, Mrs Thompson."

"Not at all, Dr Fitzgerald. Goodbye, John."

Molly opened the front door for them, they went down the steps and onto the pavement where Will hailed a cab.

The hotel had provided a child's bed in their room and Will sat John on it as Isobel set the trunk down on the double bed.

"Are you hungry, John?" she asked and Will glanced at the boy, hoping for a response, but again he just stared impassively.

They sat on their bed and began to go through the file. It contained a form, signed by Edward, with the date John Edward Fitzgerald was admitted to the children's home. John's birth certificate showed that although he was born in Nashik, Maharashtra, India, Edward had registered the birth in London. It also confirmed John's mother was Purnima Sharma and that John's date of birth was 26th January 1878 – the date Edward had supplied in his letters. Will lifted up a photograph of Edward and Purnima taken in a photographic studio against a painted backdrop of trees. She was wearing a sari but was clearly pregnant.

"She was beautiful," Isobel murmured.

"Yes. And John has her eyes. Everything else he's inherited from Edward."

"Did Edward like eggs?" she asked.

"I don't think Edward had a favourite food. Not that I can remember, anyway, but," he flicked through the other forms in the file before pulling one out, "yes, eggs are John's favourite food."

"We could try John with some scrambled egg for luncheon?" she suggested, going to the boy, picking him up and kissing his cheek. "Would you like some scrambled egg, John?" she asked but he just stared at her.

"This afternoon, I need to call on Ruth's aunt and see if Ruth is living there. If not, and if the aunt refuses to tell me where she is, I will have to place an advertisement in *The Times*. I also want to call on Jerry. I want to hear his opinion on John."

"I'll go through John's belongings and see what we must buy for him immediately."

"And I think I should tell him about Edward now," he added. Otherwise, I will just keep putting it off, he finished silently.

Isobel nodded and sat down again on the double bed with John on her lap. "We have something to tell you, John," she said and Will took a deep breath.

"Isobel and I honestly didn't know you were here in London otherwise we would have come a lot sooner. Edward – your father – didn't tell us you were here. We didn't know until we heard some sad news. I'm very sorry to have to tell you this, John, but your father died in India a few days ago."

He waited for a reaction but John simply gazed at him without any emotion. He glanced at Isobel and she gave him a little shrug before he turned his attention back to the boy.

"You probably know this already, John, but your father was in the army in India and he told me in a letter that he was trying to be sent back to London so he could be with you. Sadly, he died before that could happen. But—" Will continued in a brighter tone. "You are going to come and live in Dublin with Isobel and me and we will look after you. You will have your own bedroom and toys and a garden to play in."

Again, he waited for a reaction but, again, there was nothing and he fought to hide a grimace.

"Well, I am very hungry." Isobel smiled down at him and the boy raised his dark eyes to her face. "And I think we should all eat something now."

Will nodded, they went downstairs to the hotel dining room and two cushions were placed on a chair so John could sit at the table. Ordering three portions of scrambled egg on toast, so as to not make John feel left out, Will was relieved to see that once Isobel cut the meal up and passed John a spoon, the boy ate it all without any further assistance.

"I have no idea how long I'll be," he said, as he shrugged his overcoat on an hour later and she passed him his hat. "But if I'm not back by six o'clock, you and John go ahead and have dinner."

She nodded and he kissed her lips then caught John staring curiously at them. He crouched down.

"I have to go out but Isobel will stay here with you. Be a good boy for her?" John just stared back and Will swallowed a sigh before ruffling his hair.

He took a cab to the address in Wimbledon his mother had given him and rang the doorbell of a semi-detached house. A maid opened the door and he smiled politely.

"My name is William Fitzgerald. Is Miss Jones at home?"

"I shall inquire, sir." The maid went back inside and a

couple of minutes later the door opened again and Ruth, not her aunt, stared up at him.

"Will."

"Would it be possible to speak privately to you, Ruth?"

Her blue eyes narrowed suspiciously but she held the door open for him and he stepped into the narrow hall. He passed his hat to the maid before following Ruth into a small and cluttered parlour.

"Edward has told you at long last, then," she said as he closed the door. "I couldn't stay with him, you do understand that?"

"Ruth, could you sit down, please?"

"Why? I'm not going back to India and that is final. You've had a wasted journey, Will."

"Please, Ruth," he added quietly and she went to an armchair upholstered in floral damask and sat down. "Two days ago, Edward's solicitor received a telegram from Edward's commanding officer, Lieutenant-General Beresford. Edward is dead. He died four days ago of cholera at the Station Hospital at Deolali."

Her mouth opened but no words came out. She got up from the armchair and stood in front of the fireplace with her hands on her hips and her blonde head bent.

"Ruth," he went on. "We knew nothing of what happened between you. All of Edward's letters to us were lies."

"Edward was good at lying." Lifting the skirt of her royal blue dress, she turned around suddenly. "So you know nothing about—"

"John? We didn't know the truth until Mr Ellison, the solicitor, presented me with a letter which was only to be opened in the event of Edward's death."

"The boy is here in London somewhere."

"Yes. My wife and I collected him from the children's home this morning."

"What will you do with him?" she asked.

"Give him a home with us in Dublin," Will said and she pursed her lips. "Ruth, what happened out there?"

"Purnima lived a few miles away in Nashik," she explained. "Nashik was where officers went for a change and to play golf. I knew Edward had a wandering eye but Purnima was the most beautiful woman I have ever seen so it was little wonder he became infatuated with her. He expected me to do what other army wives do and turn a blind eye but I couldn't, especially when I learnt she was pregnant. So, I returned to London."

"But you did hear from him after that?" Will asked and she nodded.

"Oh, yes. He sent a telegram informing me Purnima had died giving birth to a boy. He actually had the nerve to ask me to return to India and raise the child otherwise he would have to place the child in a children's home in London. That was the last I heard from him as I didn't reply."

"Why didn't you divorce him?"

"I couldn't afford to," she replied matter-of-factly. "My aunt owns this house and lives on a small private income. I have gone back to teaching, passing myself off as a widow, but I simply don't earn enough to have pursued a divorce case through the courts." She exhaled a short sigh. "Now I don't have to lie anymore."

"I'm sorry," he said and was astonished when she laughed.

"Oh, Will, it's not your fault. Edward deceived us all and has left it to you to pick up the pieces."

"Yes, he has."

"You are really going to raise the boy?" she asked, sounding incredulous.

"Yes. He has been in a children's home since he was eight weeks old. It is not John's fault that he exists."

"No," Ruth conceded quietly. "How have your parents taken all this?"

"They are distraught at Edward's death. Angry at his lies. And my father will not accept 'a half-caste bastard' as his grandson."

"May I see the boy?"

Will couldn't contain his bafflement. "You want to see John?"

"I want to see Edward's son," she said firmly. "Then, I will be able to put Edward behind me and carry on with my life."

"I really don't—"

"Please, Will," she begged. "Allow me to see the boy and then I will be content."

"Ruth, you need to know that John is the sole beneficiary of Edward's will."

"I expected nothing less," she replied with a little smile. "I relinquished all rights to anything of Edward's when I left him. Please, may I see the boy, Will?"

He sighed. "Very well. Join us for coffee tomorrow morning at the Tower Hotel at eight o'clock while we have breakfast. We leave for Holyhead straight after we've eaten."

"Thank you. I just need to see him otherwise I will always wonder. You mentioned a wife. You are happy, Will?"

"Yes, I am, thank you. Shall I ring for some tea for you?"

"No, not unless you would like some?"

"No, thank you. I truly am sorry, Ruth. Edward was my brother, I thought I knew him, but it seems none of us knew him at all."

Ruth saw him out and he put on his hat and walked to the end of the street where he hailed a cab, instructing the cabman to bring him to Harley Street.

He paid the cabman and went up the steps of a Georgian townhouse into Jerry Hawley's medical practice. He was about to go into the waiting room when a surgery door opened at the far end of the hall and his dark-haired friend and a young woman with auburn hair came out. Jerry glanced along the hall and gasped in amazement.

"Will? What on earth are you doing in London?" He ushered Will and the young woman into the surgery then shook Will's hand warmly. "Lillian." He turned to her. "This is Dr Will Fitzgerald. Will, this is Miss Lillian Parsons."

"At last." She grinned and they shook hands. "A face to put to all the stories Jerry has told me."

"I'm delighted to meet you, Miss Parsons."

"Oh, Lillian, please. Provided, I can call you Will?"

He nodded. "Of course."

"What are you doing here?" Jerry asked.

"Can we sit down?" he suggested. "It's rather a long story."

"I'll wait out there." Lillian pointed towards the hall.

"There's no need," Will told her quickly and she smiled.

"Speak to Jerry in private. I'll wait."

"Thank you."

Jerry closed the door after her and motioned for Will to sit down before sitting down behind the mahogany desk. Will told him all and when he finished, Jerry sat back in his chair shaking his head.

"I can't believe it. My condolences, Will."

"Thank you. I think I only really believed it myself when I saw John sitting on the dormitory floor with Edward's hair, nose and mouth but eyes as black as coal."

"And he doesn't speak at all?" Jerry asked and Will shook his head.

"Not a word so far. He clearly understands what we say to him but—"

"Will, all of this will be completely overwhelming for him."

"But we were told he has never spoken."

"Do you think he was bullied? I mean, does he—"

"No, he doesn't look particularly Indian. But—" Will grimaced. "It's a distinct possibility he was bullied, given the fact that he did come to the home directly from India."

"Children can be incredibly cruel to one who is even the slightest bit different to them."

"Yes. Poor little lad. Oh, and Ruth wants to see him."

Jerry pulled a hesitant expression. "Is that wise?"

"Probably not, but Isobel and I will be there."

"And me?" Jerry suggested. "If you'll allow?"

"Won't you have surgery?"

"Tomorrow is Saturday," Jerry reminded him and Will gave Jerry a tired smile.

"So it is. Well, yes, of course. Come to the Tower Hotel for coffee at eight o'clock tomorrow morning while we have breakfast. We leave for Holyhead straight afterwards. Are you free this evening?"

"I was to escort Lillian home and then go out for a meal."

Will took out his pocket watch. It was half past five. "Why don't you both come to the hotel for dinner and meet Isobel and John?"

Jerry nodded, got up and opened the door. "Lillian, could you come inside?"

Will gave Lillian an edited version of his reason for being in London and her eyes widened in first astonishment then sympathy.

"Oh, Will, you have my condolences. How awful for you and for the poor little boy. Yes, I would very much like to meet him and your wife. But—" She turned to Jerry. "We'll need call at home first so I can tell Mother and Father where I'll be."

"Yes, of course. Give me a few minutes to finish up here and we'll hail a cab."

Isobel went through John's belongings, laying the clothes out on the double bed. There were two of everything but, she took a quick look at the boy, the brown morning coat and short trousers he wore would very soon be too small for him. John was going to need all new clothes. At the bottom of the trunk was a small carved wooden elephant and she went to him with it.

"What's his name?" she asked, sitting beside him on the small single bed, but John just snatched the elephant from her and clutched it to his chest. "My brother, Alfie, could never pronounce elephant when he was little. He always called them effalumps." She laughed. "But you'll be able to say elephant, I'm sure of it."

There was no response so she ploughed on.

"Will is my husband and we've been married a few months. We live in Dublin, which is in Ireland, and Will is a doctor. My mother and Alfie live very close by and they are very eager to meet you. Will and I are lucky enough to have a large house. We live there with Mrs Dillon, our cook and housekeeper, Annie, our kitchenmaid, Florrie and Mary, our house-parlourmaids, and Gerald our footman. Like Will said, you will have your own bedroom and there is a long garden for you to play in. Would you like to play in the garden?" she asked but John was staring at the elephant.

Gently prising the elephant from him, she put it to one side and held his hands.

"Please don't be afraid to speak to us, John. Neither Will nor I will ever frighten you. We hope you'll be very happy living with us."

At a quarter to six, her stomach began to rumble. It was time for dinner.

"Are you hungry, John?" she asked, and he glanced up at her momentarily from the elephant. "I am. I think we should have something to eat."

In the hotel dining room, she chose a corner table and a waiter provided two cushions for John to sit on before handing her a menu.

"Now, let's see," she said softly, wondering what she could order for the little boy.

"Cecilia?" Hearing someone call out, Isobel glanced towards the door to the foyer. A blonde woman of about thirty wearing a black silk taffeta dress similar to her own and a black velvet cloak was glancing around the dining room before calling out again. "Cecilia? John? Is there a John

Fitzgerald here? If there is a John Fitzgerald here, could he please stand up."

Before Isobel could stop him, John slid off the cushions and the woman wound her way through the tables towards them with a wild expression in her blue eyes.

"So you are Edward's son."

"Who are you?" Isobel inquired, picking John up and sitting him back on the cushions.

"Ruth Fitzgerald and I'm delighted to make your acquaintance at last, Cecilia," she said and Isobel tensed. "I remember Will's last letter to Edward before I left India," Ruth continued before Isobel could correct her. "It was full of questions to Edward on how he had courted me and how he had proposed to me and whether I was happy living as an army wife in India." Ruth exhaled a hysterical laugh and Isobel squirmed as the other diners began to stare at them. "If only poor Will knew that Edward was the last person he should be writing to for advice on courtship and marriage. I sincerely hope you are happy in your marriage, Cecilia."

"You are mistaken, Ruth," she said quietly. "I am not Cecilia. My name is Isobel Fitzgerald, and I am Will's wife."

"Goodness me." Ruth's eyes bulged and she clapped a hand to her chest while looking Isobel up and down. "Second choice, and about to bring up your dead brother-in-law's bastard."

"You've said quite enough," Isobel snapped. "Please leave."

"Is this lady distressing you, Mrs Fitzgerald?" the waiter asked, approaching them hesitantly.

"Yes, she is," Isobel replied. "Could you please escort her from the hotel?"

"If you lay one finger on me," Ruth informed the young man, "I will call for a constable."

"Well, what do you want?" Isobel demanded.

"To look at Edward's child." In one swift movement, Ruth lifted John from the cushions and stood him on the table. "Edward's bastard," she said, stepping back and surveying him. "Edward's bastard with an Indian whore—"

"That's enough." Isobel heard Will's voice and saw him winding his way through the tables with Jerry and an auburn-haired woman of about her own age dressed in silver-grey following him. She quickly lifted John off the table and held the little boy tightly in her arms, feeling him trembling. "Ruth, come with me."

"Don't you dare touch me, Will," she warned.

"You either come with us now, Mrs Fitzgerald," Jerry told her. "Or we will be the ones calling for a constable."

Ruth relented and Jerry escorted her from the dining room.

"Are you both all right?" Will whispered.

"Yes. Just keep her away from John."

He nodded and went after Jerry and Ruth, leaving her with the young woman.

"Allow me to change the tablecloth and place settings, Mrs Fitzgerald." The waiter began to pick up the cutlery.

"No," she replied, eyeing the auburn-haired woman standing awkwardly across the table from her. Who on earth was she? "Thank you, but we will dine in our room later."

"Of course," the waiter replied and left them.

"Isobel?" The woman began hesitantly. "I am Lillian Parsons. I'm a friend of Jerry's," she added and flushed.

"Oh." Isobel gave her a relieved smile. "I'm very pleased

109

to meet you, Lillian. Shall we go upstairs?" she suggested and Lillian nodded.

She carried John out of the dining room, the eyes of all the diners on her. She couldn't see Will, Jerry or Ruth in the foyer as she passed through and went up the stairs with Lillian behind her. In their room, she kissed John's cheek, put him down on his bed and went to the window. Although it looked out over the street in front of the hotel, she couldn't see any of them and she turned back to John who was gazing up at her with huge black questioning eyes.

"We'll eat soon, I promise," she told him. "Will is dealing with the nasty lady," she continued, as Lillian closed the door.

"That poor woman seems quite unhinged."

"She is Will's newly-widowed sister-in-law."

"Oh, I see," Lillian replied slowly and Isobel frowned. "I met Will at Harley Street and he told me why you are in London," Lillian explained. "Had you met her before?"

"No, never, and I hope never to meet her again," she went on and Lillian nodded. "Shall we begin again?" she asked, and they both laughed. "I am Isobel and this—" Picking the little boy up, she kissed both his cheeks. "Is John."

"What a beautiful child," Lillian said softly. "I am Lillian," she told him, but he just stared at her.

"John is rather overwhelmed," Isobel said as the door opened and both Will and Jerry came in.

"Isobel," Will began. "Jerry has invited us to stay with him and—"

"But what about Ruth?" she demanded.

"We put her in a cab and told her that if she attempts to

come near John again we will contact the police." He clasped her face in his hands and kissed her lips. "I'm so sorry. She was calm when I left her. John—" Taking the boy from her, Will kissed his cheek. "This is Jerry, one of my best friends. Jerry, this is John."

"Hello, there young man." Jerry shook John's hand. "I'm very pleased to meet you. Would you like to come and visit?"

John simply stared at Jerry and Isobel gave Jerry a little smile. "Thank you for inviting us."

"Not at all. I was going to eat out this evening but John needs to eat soon and go to bed. So, unless you think it's terribly low brow, we could call at a fried fish restaurant and buy five portions of fish and chips."

"Fish and chips?"

"Don't tell me you've never had fish and chips?" he asked. "Deep-fried chipped potatoes?" She shook her head. "Well, you're in for a treat and, I don't know about the fish, but John will love the chips."

"Good. Well, give Will and I a few minutes to pack and pay the bill."

Fifteen minutes later, the five of them were in a cab on their way to the best fried fish restaurant in London, according to Jerry. He and Will went inside, returning with five portions of fish and chips wrapped in newspaper. They smelled delicious and her stomach rumbled loudly.

Jerry lived in a suite of rooms on the first floor of a Georgian house in Kensington. He lit the gas lamps while Will left the luggage in the guest bedroom. Jerry then retrieved plates and cutlery from the kitchen and brought them into a small dining room. Will transferred the food from the packages to the plates while Jerry went to set and light fires in the parlour and bedrooms.

Isobel sat down at the dining table with John on her lap and Will put two plates on the table in front of her. She passed John a chip before taking one herself. John watched her curiously as she put it in her mouth before doing the same. The chip was delicious and she smiled as he chewed and reached for another one.

She cut John's piece of fish into small pieces and handed him a fork then started on her own meal.

"Well?" Jerry returned and sat down at the head of the table.

"The fish and chips are delicious," she said. "But my mother would have a fit if she could see us now."

"As would mine," Lillian declared with a gleeful grin, sitting down opposite her. "Thank you, Will," she added, accepting a plate from him. "Mother must never hear of this, Jerry."

Well over three-quarters of John's portion had to be divided between Will and Jerry but the little boy had clearly enjoyed it. As Isobel finished her meal, John rested his head on her shoulder.

"Time for bed." Will smiled, got to his feet and lifted the boy up.

Jerry followed them into the guest bedroom and handed her some bed linen. He then returned to the dining room and she could hear him stacking the plates and clearing the table. While she and Lillian made the bed, Will opened John's trunk and lifted out his nightshirt before undressing him.

"Isobel."

"What is—" she began and clapped a hand to her mouth

as she took in the umpteen scars and scabs – some dirty and starting to bleed – and bruises of varying colours across John's buttocks.

"Fetch Jerry would you, please?" Will asked.

She hurried across the hall to the dining room, grabbed Jerry's hand and brought him back to the bedroom.

Jerry gasped and shook his head. "Some of those scars are years old by the look of them."

"The bruises aren't," Isobel whispered.

"No, poor little mite. It looks like he received regular canings."

"We need to go back to that horrible home tomorrow and—"

"No, Isobel," Jerry interrupted. "Don't go near the place. Leave it to me. I'll report the home to the authorities. I'll fetch my medical bag and we'll clean John up. The bruises will just have to heal themselves, I'm afraid."

Jerry went out and Will tilted John's chin up. The little boy looked ashamed and Isobel had to blink away tears.

"We're not going to hurt you, John," Will told him softly. "Jerry is a doctor, too. No-one will ever do that to you again, I promise. Jerry and I are going to clean your bottom and put a bit of ointment on it to help it get better."

Will and Jerry cleaned the open sores and applied the ointment as gently as they could. It must have been painful for the little boy but John didn't make a sound. Isobel dressed him in the blue and white striped nightshirt, telling him they weren't going away, that they would be in the very next room. He used the chamber pot then was placed in the centre of the double bed and he was asleep before any of them had kissed him goodnight.

"Have either of you heard of Mrs Thompson's Home for Children?" Will asked Lillian and Jerry as the four of them stood around the double bed watching John sleep.

"No," Jerry replied and Lillian shook her head. "There are hundreds of such places all over London, some little more than baby farms. I will do my level best to get it closed down, Will, I promise."

"Thank you."

"Mr Ellison told Will the place was respectable," she said.

"Evidently, outwardly only, Isobel," Jerry said. "Poor John. He's going to need a lot of love, care and attention from you both to build his trust."

"And he'll get it," she replied, bending and kissing John's forehead.

They followed Jerry to the parlour and he bade them sit down before picking up two crystal decanters from the drinks tray.

"Whiskey or brandy? I'm afraid I don't have sherry, Isobel."

"It doesn't matter," she said with a little smile, sitting down beside Lillian on a brown leather sofa. "Brandy for me, please."

"And for me, please, Jerry," Lillian said.

"And I'll have a whiskey, please," Will added as he sat down in one of the leather armchairs and Jerry turned back to the tray and poured the drinks.

"Thank you," Isobel said, taking a glass from him. "It's been quite a day for John – for all of us."

"I still can't believe it." Jerry passed glasses to Lillian and Will before sitting in the other armchair with his own glass.

"For Edward to lie to you all like that and keep his son a secret."

"He was always impulsive," Will replied. "Which was why we were surprised he persisted with his ambition of joining the army. Being the second son, I was the one expected to join up. It's strange how things turn out."

Lillian finished her brandy, got to her feet, and both men stood up. "It's nine o'clock," she said. "I'd better go home. It was lovely to meet you both."

"I'm sorry you witnessed what you did at the hotel," Isobel said, getting to her feet, and Lillian pulled a sympathetic expression.

"Ruth shouldn't have behaved as she did but, at the same time, I can understand why. Her husband was unfaithful, fathered a child with a local woman, and then asked that she raise the child. There is only so much a person can tolerate. But," Lillian added in a lighter tone. "Ruth has seen John and we can only hope she can now carry on with her life."

"I hope so, too," Isobel replied, giving Lillian a hug and a kiss on the cheek.

"I hope we meet again soon."

"We do, too." Will smiled and kissed her cheek.

"I'll hail you a cab, Lillian," Jerry said and escorted her from the room.

"I'm exhausted," Isobel told Will and placed her empty glass on the drinks tray. "If you don't mind, I'll go to bed."

"Not at all," he replied. "Goodnight." He kissed her lips, she left the parlour and walked along the hall to the guest bedroom.

She turned the gas lamps down a little before climbing onto the bed. Smoothing brown hair back from John's forehead, she kissed it and lay down watching him sleep. Within moments, she was fast asleep too.

Will sat down in the leather armchair, exhaled a long sigh and rested his head back.

"It's been a long day and I'm worn out," he announced when Jerry returned to the parlour and sat down opposite him in the other armchair.

"There's no need to be polite, Will. If you want to go to bed as well..?"

"Not just yet." Will lowered his head and sipped his whiskey. "There are a few things I want to discuss with you."

"Oh?"

"Have you ever heard of a woman having four miscarriages and then going on to have four perfectly normal pregnancies?" he asked.

"I've heard of a woman having three miscarriages and then carrying the fourth pregnancy to term," Jerry replied. "How is Isobel? I was so sorry to receive your letter."

"She wanted the baby – we both wanted the baby. We never thought the first child we'd raise together would be Edward's three-year-old son."

"You are going to try again for a child with Isobel?" Jerry asked.

"Yes, but not for a few months. We decided that even before we knew about John."

"Good. And how are you?"

Will gave Jerry a comical smile. "Hoping I'm up to the task of being 'father' to John, knowing my own father wants nothing to do with him. Hoping that in time John will be able to trust us both and speak. And, as well as that, I'm hoping I haven't made a huge mistake in deciding to go back to the Liberties and bringing Fred with me. We haven't been getting on of late."

"You mentioned in your last letter that you don't think he's come to terms with the death of his father."

"No, and I caught him with a prostitute in his surgery. We almost fought," he added and Jerry's eyes widened. "It wasn't the first time he's done it. Father caught him with prostitutes at the practice house in the past. I just don't know what to do with him. Isobel suggested offering him a surgery in Pimlico and I did, hoping to build bridges and that he'd turn me down. But he accepted."

Jerry sighed. "Fred can be a law unto himself."

"The way he's going, he's going to find himself in trouble with the law. With Edward in India and you over here, Fred is like a brother to me. But now I think we're just too different and it's probably selfishness on my part – I'm too used to running a practice on my own – and now I'll be continually be wondering what the hell Fred is up to."

"You were always the most determined out of the three of us," Jerry declared and Will smiled.

"I don't know about that – Dr Jeremiah Hawley of Harley Street."

"The most stubborn, then. How many chances have you given Fred?"

"One last chance."

"Would you prefer to run the practice alone?"

"It's always been a multi-doctor practice with partnerships—"

"I know that but would you?" Jerry persisted and Will grimaced. "I'll take that as a yes."

"I can't run the practice alone plus a second one in Pimlico. Last year, a patient died needlessly because I couldn't attend to her and I sent my father instead. No." He sighed. "For now – and I hate to say it about him – I'm just going to have to put up with Fred."

"No, Will." Jerry was firm. "Not if he thinks he can ride roughshod over you. You've given him one last chance, if he throws that back in your face, dissolve the partnership. What if it became public knowledge that Fred was entertaining prostitutes in his surgery or elsewhere?"

"The practice would be finished."

"Exactly. And I have to say this – the Pimlico surgery…"

"Is the ideal place for entertaining," Will finished. "I know, and someone will be keeping an eye on him but, oh, God, you must think I'm such a fool."

"No, not at all. I'd probably have done the same in your position. I'm sorry you're having to deal with Fred alone."

"Not anymore," Will admitted. "I've asked my father to bring Fred to the Trinity Club and to try and be a father-figure to him, seeing as I have failed utterly as a 'brother'."

"I hope it works."

"I hope so, too. Now, enough about Fred. Tell me how you are?"

"Very well. The practice is flourishing and I'm going to ask Lillian to marry me."

Will's face broke into a grin. "That's great news."

"I'm not counting my chickens."

"The best of luck, Jerry."

"Thanks, Will. And, if she does say yes, I'd like you to be my best man."

Will gave him another grin. "It would be a pleasure."

"At least you won't drag me around the majority of London's pubs before finishing up in a disgusting brothel."

"No," Will replied quietly. "I won't."

"More whiskey?" Jerry offered.

"No, thanks, it's time for bed. Tomorrow will be another long day."

"It's good to see you, Will."

"And you, Jerry. Thanks for accommodating us all and for listening."

"Not at all."

"When will you be in Dublin again?" Will asked.

"Next month, for a week. It's my mother's sixtieth birthday. You, Fred and I could meet one evening?"

"Call to number 30, and we'll arrange it."

Will crept into the guest bedroom and turned the gas lamps up. Both Isobel and John were fast asleep but Isobel was on the bed still fully-clothed. Gently, he laid a hand on her shoulder and she woke with a jump.

"What time is it?" she murmured.

"Just after ten. Has John stirred at all?"

"No, I don't think so."

"Perhaps we should get him to use the chamber pot again? Just in case." Pulling the pot out from under the bed, he reached for the little boy, who began to whimper and struggle. "It's all right," he assured him. "It's me, Will. Isobel's here, too. Come and use the chamber pot and then we can all go to bed." Standing John in front of the pot, he lifted the nightshirt and John relieved himself. "Good boy. If you need to use the chamber pot again, don't be afraid to wake one of us."

He lifted the boy into the bed and John curled up and went back to sleep.

Will and Isobel got undressed, pulled on a nightshirt and nightdress and after he turned down the gas lamps, they got into the bed on either side of John.

"I can only begin to imagine what he's been through," Will whispered. "But we will bring him out of himself."

"Yes," she replied and kissed John's forehead.

"Goodnight." Will leant over and kissed her lips and they settled.

Isobel wondered how John would cope with the long train journey from London to Holyhead in Wales but he seemed content to kneel on one of the seats in their compartment and stare intently out of the window at the snow.

He was utterly fascinated by the boat and they spent all of the chilly early evening crossing of the Irish Sea up on deck.

"Look, John." Will picked him up and pointed into the distance where the lights of Dublin were just visible. "That's Ireland. Not long now. We'll soon be home."

The little boy fell asleep with his head on Will's shoulder as they travelled from the North Wall Quay passenger terminus to Fitzwilliam Square by cab. It was just after ten o'clock when Isobel closed number 30's front door behind them. John and his trunk were carried straight upstairs where the bedroom beside theirs had been prepared and she lit the gas lamps. The boy was undressed then dressed in his striped nightshirt and Will cleaned and applied ointment to the sores on his buttocks. John was encouraged to use the chamber pot then lifted into bed, kissed goodnight, and the gas lamps turned down a little.

"Mrs Dillon." Isobel greeted the housekeeper downstairs

in the hall with a tired smile. "We'd like to speak to you about John. Please, come into the morning room."

They sat down and John's reluctance to speak, plus his injuries, were explained to the shocked housekeeper.

"The poor little lad—" she began just as the door opened and Mary came in.

"I can hear the boy screaming, Doctor, Mrs Fitzgerald."

They all ran up the stairs to the second floor and found John on the landing shaking with fright. Isobel picked the little boy up and held him tightly, kissing his cheeks and stroking his hair to calm him.

"It's all right, John, I'm here now," she whispered as he stared wide-eyed at Mary and Mrs Dillon. "This isn't going to work," she added to them. "John can't be left on his own two floors up from us. Do you or Florrie have any experience as nursery maids?" she asked Mary.

"No, I'm afraid not Mrs Fitzgerald," Mary replied and she nodded.

"That's all right, Mary."

Wrapping John up in a blanket, she passed him to Will who carried him downstairs to the morning room and a 'bed' was made up for him on the sofa.

"We're going to need an experienced nursery maid," she told Will as they watched John sleep.

"Yes, so we're going to have to open up the nursery."

"I didn't want that, I wanted him to be with us as much as possible, but he clearly needs to be somewhere he feels safe and at home in."

"I agree." Will rang for a servant and Mrs Dillon came in a few minutes later.

"Would you be able to find us an experienced nursery

maid, Mrs Dillon?" Isobel asked.

"Forgive me, Mrs Fitzgerald, but the boy needs a nanny, not a maid. The poor little lad is overwhelmed by what he's been through and his change in circumstances. He needs care from a trained nanny, the stability of a home in the nursery, and lots of love from yourself and Dr Fitzgerald."

Isobel sighed but Will squeezed her hand. "I know you didn't want a nanny," he said. "But Mrs Dillon is right. Mrs Henderson was raised by a nanny who was an absolute horror by all accounts," he explained to the housekeeper.

"She was cruel to my mother and I swore I would never employ one," Isobel added.

"I will look for suitable candidates, Mrs Fitzgerald, and you and Dr Fitzgerald will naturally have the final say in who is taken on."

"Very well," Isobel replied quietly.

"Thank you, Mrs Fitzgerald. We'll open up the nursery first thing in the morning and begin cleaning and make a list of what needs to be bought or replaced. Florrie tells me she is one of ten children so, if you'll agree, she will care for Master John in the nursery until a nanny is found."

"Yes. Thank you, Mrs Dillon." The housekeeper left the room and Isobel sat down on the sofa beside John. "I promised myself that no child of mine would ever have a nanny. Alfie and I only ever had a nursery maid."

"We must do what is best for John. And if that means a nanny…"

"I know. I'm just tired and hoping very much that I'm capable of being a mother-figure to him."

"I said more or less the same thing to Jerry – that I hope I'm up to the task of being 'father' to John. I'm not going to lie to you, Isobel, it's not going to be easy, but we have many people to call on for advice."

She nodded. "Shall we go to bed?"

"Yes. Let's get a good night's sleep and install John in the nursery tomorrow."

The nursery, with two small bedrooms off it, was located on the top floor of number 30 next to the servants' bedrooms. Isobel brought John there straight after breakfast to show him where he would be living and the boy glanced around the room and at the walls papered in a warm yellow colour. The dust sheets covering the furniture had been removed, the windows thrown open and Florrie and Mary were in the process of not just dusting, but wiping down every surface. Mrs Dillon was walking from room to room with a notebook compiling a list but stopped and smiled at them.

"Mrs Fitzgerald. And Master John."

"That looks like quite a long list, Mrs Dillon."

"I'm afraid it is. The furniture is perfectly serviceable and we will make do for today and tonight, but a new fire guard, rugs, towels, bed linen and such like specifically for the nursery need to be purchased and I will see to that tomorrow. What I found in the chest of drawers has been here for a long time by the look of it and no nanny will want to use any of it, I'm afraid."

"No. The nursery isn't too small and old-fashioned, though, is it?" she asked anxiously. "It was decorated, along with the rest of the house, but I don't know when it was last used."

"No, not at all. I'm pleasantly surprised at how bright and airy these rooms are."

"That's a relief. I would like these rooms to be as homely as possible."

"We'll do our best, Mrs Fitzgerald."

"Thank you."

"And how is Master John this morning?" The housekeeper asked, taking one of his hands but John pulled it back.

"John slept very well and woke my husband so he could use the chamber pot. Didn't you?" She smiled at John. "You were such a clever boy."

"Very clever." Mrs Dillon agreed.

"My husband has gone to see his mother to tell her about her grandson. He may bring her back here with him."

Mrs Dillon nodded. "There is chicken soup for luncheon and plenty for one more."

"Thank you, Mrs Dillon. I'll let you get on. I'm going to show John the garden."

They went downstairs, out the back door and down the steps. Standing John on the lawn, now clear of snow but rather sodden, she sat on the bench and waited to see what he would do or even say. John stood stock-still, looked around him at the snow still lying in the corners the sun didn't reach and then at her with a puzzled expression as if to ask, "What do I do now?"

"This is our garden," she explained. "When Will and I moved in, the garden was very overgrown with weeds but we engaged a gardener who pulled out all the weeds and cut the grass. Now it looks very neat and tidy, despite all the snow we had. Would you like to play out here, John?"

The little boy turned back to the garden then walked across the lawn to the flower bed. Crouching down in front of a group of snowdrops, he reached out and touched one and she joined him.

"Aren't they pretty?" she asked and he nodded. It was the

first time he had clearly responded to her and she bent and kissed the top of his head. "They were flattened by the snow but they're recovering well now. In a few weeks' time, the daffodils will be in bloom but snowdrops are the first flowers to bloom in this garden. Some flowers have a scent – a smell – but some, like snowdrops, don't. I don't know why. Maybe Will does, we'll ask him when he comes back."

"Ask me what?"

She jumped and glanced over her shoulder at the back door. Will and his mother were standing at the top of the steps and when John turned around Mrs Fitzgerald senior burst into tears.

Tess showed Will into his parents' morning room and he was relieved to find his mother seated alone on the sofa wearing a black taffeta dress.

"You're back." She got up and kissed his cheek. "How was it? How is the boy?"

"Shall we sit down?" he said instead and they sat side by side on the sofa where he told his mother all. When he finished, she rose from the sofa and went to one of the windows.

"Edward would not have put his son in such a place if he knew John would be treated in a cruel way. Will he be scarred for life?"

"Yes, I'm afraid so."

"And he really does not speak?"

"Not one word. But he is the most observant child I have ever seen so I would hope that in time, he will speak."

"And what on earth did Ruth want with the boy?"

"She said she wanted to see him," he explained. "I

suspect that when she did, it was all a little too much for her."

"She sounds utterly disturbed to me."

"Think of what she's been through."

His mother sighed and turned to face him. "Yes, you're right. I must write to her. How has Isobel taken all of this? She must have expected a lively three-year-old boy and instead…" Tailing off, his mother let her hands drop to her sides helplessly.

"Both of us want what is best for John, so we are going to engage a nanny. We put John to bed last night and a few minutes later one of the maids rushed into the morning room to tell us John was screaming. We hadn't heard a thing. He needs the run of a nursery but, unlike Edward and I, John needs a trained nanny, not a nursery maid. I hope that the nursery, the nanny, and Isobel and I can bring him out of himself."

"I'd like to help, too," his mother said quietly. "If you'll allow?"

"Of course." Getting up, he joined her at the window and kissed her cheek. "You're his grandmother."

"Does he look like Edward?"

"Yes. He has his mother's very dark eyes but everything else is Edward."

"I had better prepare myself, then."

Ten minutes later, they walked to number 30, where Mary informed him that Mrs Fitzgerald junior and Master John were in the garden. He opened the back door and followed his mother onto the steps. Isobel and John were crouching down at a group of snowdrops in a flower bed across the lawn from them.

"…Maybe Will does," she was telling the boy. "We'll ask him when he comes back."

"Ask me what?" he called and she looked over her shoulder and John turned around. His mother gave a little gasp, burst into tears and Will took her arm. "Come and sit down, Mother," he said softly, helping her down the steps and to the bench.

His mother sat down, pulled a handkerchief from her sleeve and dried her eyes as Isobel led John to them.

"Mother, this is John," he said, sitting the little boy on the bench beside her. "John, this is your grandmother. She is my mother and your father's mother."

"Oh, you are so like Edward," she said and John stared curiously at her. "Was Isobel showing you the pretty snowdrops?" she added but John just continued to stare at her.

"Your grandmother has lots of pretty snowdrops in her garden." Isobel sat on the arm of the bench and John peered up at her. "Would you like to see them, John?" she asked and Will's eyes widened as John nodded gravely in reply. Will met her eyes and she gave him a little smile. "And Mary, Florrie and Mrs Dillon are preparing the nursery. John will have his own lovely bedroom and somewhere to play when it's raining."

"Shall we all have a look at your father and Will's toys and see if there are any you would like to have to play with?" Will's mother suggested.

"Would you like that, John?" Will asked and John glanced up at him for a moment before nodding. "Good." He gave the boy a grin. "We'll do that very soon."

"Will you stay to luncheon, Sarah?" Isobel asked.

"I'd like that very much, thank you."

"Good. I'm relieved the snow is all but gone but it's still rather chilly. Let's go inside."

John was installed in the nursery that evening and shown his bedroom, which contained a small single bed, a bedside table and a chest of drawers.

"Florrie is going to be here with you," Isobel assured him. "If you need anything, she will be sleeping in the bedroom right next to this one. You won't be on your own, I promise. Will is going to clean your bottom and put more ointment on, we'll kiss you goodnight, and I will be here when you have breakfast in the morning. Then, I want to bring you to meet my mother while Florrie, Mary, and Mrs Dillon finish making the nursery nice for you. You're not going to be on your own, John," she promised him again and, to her relief, he nodded.

"The sores are getting better," Will told John as he finished applying the ointment. "Do they hurt as much now?" he asked and John shook his head. "I'm glad. Now, use the chamber pot, good boy."

After using the chamber pot, Will lifted John into the bed and they sat down on either side of him.

"Florrie will be next door," Isobel reminded him. "And Will and I shall be sleeping just downstairs. Sleep well," she added softly and kissed his cheek.

"Goodnight, John." Will kissed his forehead.

They went out to the nursery, where Florrie was seated in front of the fire with some sewing. Putting it to one side, she got up.

"I'll look in on him in a few minutes, Doctor, Mrs Fitzgerald."

"Thank you, Florrie, and if you need anything just ring down to the servants' hall."

"Yes, Mrs Fitzgerald."

They went downstairs to the morning room and settled on the sofa.

"I hope he sleeps," she murmured.

"You've re-assured him as much as you can. And he mustn't get used to sleeping in the same bed as us."

"No. Are his sores really getting better?"

"Yes, they are. And he's reacting to us." Will kissed her lips. "We're going to bring him out of himself, I know it."

Before Will left for the practice house in the morning, the two of them went upstairs to the nursery. To her delight, John, with Florrie's help, was seated at the square table tucking into a boiled egg with toast 'soldiers' and she kissed his cheek.

"Did you sleep well? she asked and he nodded. Sitting beside him, Florrie also nodded and smiled.

"Master John slept very well. He even used the chamber pot without my help. He's being a very good boy."

"Good." Will kissed the top of John's head. "I have to go and take a surgery – that's when my patients come to see me at the practice house – but I'll be back for luncheon. Be good for Isobel and Florrie, won't you?" John nodded and picked up another 'soldier' and Will gave him a grin.

Florrie followed the two of them out onto the landing and closed the nursery door.

"There wasn't a peep out of him last night. I looked in on him a few times during the evening and before I went to bed and he was fast asleep. And he did use the chamber pot himself. If only some of my little brothers were like him."

"No attempts to speak?" Will asked and Florrie shook her head.

"No, nothing, Dr Fitzgerald, but I talk to him all the time."

Will nodded. "Thank you, Florrie," he said and the maid returned to the nursery. "Isobel, I'd better go," he added, turning to her and kissing her lips. "See you at luncheon."

Isobel went back to John and smiled as Florrie helped him to scoop the last of the boiled egg out of the shell.

"I think you enjoyed that," she said and he nodded as he chewed the last mouthful. "This morning, I'm going to bring you to meet my mother. She lives across the square from here. My brother, Alfie, might be at home, too. Shall we fetch your coat?" He nodded again, slid off the chair and went to his bedroom. "We won't be too long," she told Florrie as she followed him.

"Yes, Mrs Fitzgerald."

She helped John into his morning coat, did up the buttons and carried him downstairs. In the hall, she donned her own coat and hat and they left the house. Standing on the steps, she let John gaze around the square.

"It's called Fitzwilliam Square," she said. "The gardens in the centre can only be used by the people who live here. They simply call it a garden, but I don't because there are many individual areas in which to walk and explore – the lawn in the middle, the paths, and under the trees. Gardens within the garden, if you like. On a nice day, I'll show them all to you."

They went slowly down the steps and walked around the railed-off gardens to number 55. Gorman, the butler, admitted them and she put a hand on John's shoulder.

"Good morning, Gorman. May I introduce my husband's nephew, John Fitzgerald? John, this is Gorman, who is my mother's butler."

"I'm very pleased to meet you, Master John." Gorman inclined his head but John just gazed back impassively. "Mrs Henderson and Mr Stevens are in the morning room, Mrs Fitzgerald."

"Thank you," she replied as Gorman opened the door for them.

"Mrs Fitzgerald and Master John Fitzgerald," he announced and they went inside.

Her mother got up from the sofa and Alfie from an armchair, both looking intently at the little boy.

"This is John," she said, leading him across the room and kissing their cheeks. "John, this is my mother and this is my brother, Alfie." John stared at them and she picked him up. "John is a little shy," she explained. "The past couple of days have been a lot to take in."

"Yes, of course," her mother replied. "Hello, John. Good gracious me." She clapped a hand to her chest. "What on earth should he call me? Sarah is his grandmother but I am no relation whatsoever."

Isobel turned to Alfie but he seemed as flummoxed as she was and she grimaced. She should have talked this over with Will.

"Well, I'm just Alfie." He gently lifted John's hand and shook it. "I'm very pleased to meet you, John. I've never had a nephew of sorts before."

"I'd have to discuss it with Will, but John could call you Grandmamma Martha?" she suggested. "Would you be happy with that, Mother?"

"Grandmamma Martha?"

"It seems John is going to call Sarah Grandmother, so this would avoid any confusion. Unless you would rather not be called Grandmamma?"

Her mother glanced at John. "Well, yes, then. If everyone else is agreeable, I would very much like to be called Grandmamma."

"Thank you."

"How was London?"

She met her mother's eyes directly, silently telling her they would speak about it at another time. "We stayed with Will's friend, Jerry, in his rooms in Kensington," she said instead. "We even ate deep-fried fish and chipped potatoes. Are they available in Dublin?" she asked Alfie.

"I'm afraid I have absolutely no idea but I'll try and find out."

"Thank you, Alfie. John enjoyed the train but he really enjoyed the boat, didn't you?" she asked and he nodded. "John loved looking at the snowdrops in number 30's garden. May he see the snowdrops here?"

"Of course he may." Her mother smiled and the four of them went outside.

"Look at them all, John." She pointed to the varying-sized groups of snowdrops in the flower beds as they went down the steps from the back door.

"Let me take him?" Alfie held out his hand to John, who immediately looked up at her for approval. She nodded, John clasped Alfie's fingers, and they set off to view the flowers.

"He hasn't spoken," her mother whispered.

"He doesn't."

"At all?"

"No. He's only just beginning to trust Will and I. I'm afraid we've been advised to find a nanny for him."

"Oh, Isobel, no."

"Will and I will choose the nanny carefully," she assured her. "John was treated very badly at the children's home. Outwardly it was respectable, but John was caned regularly and over a long period of time. His buttocks are scarred and there are sores which Will is treating."

Clearly appalled, her mother clapped a hand over her mouth.

"We thought John could live with us," Isobel went on. "But last night we found him at the top of the stairs looking for us and very upset. I didn't want to have to engage a nanny, but with what he's been through he needs the run of a nursery where he can be looked after properly."

"What is the nursery like?" her mother asked. "Everything was covered with dust sheets when Mr Ellison and I viewed the house."

"In good condition, according to Mrs Dillon. It's needed a good clean and some items are being replaced. John seems to have settled in very well."

"And what about you and Will? How are you both coping?"

"Will is confident that John will speak. We try to be with John as much as we can and talk to him as much as we can." She glanced at Alfie, who was laughing at something with John staring curiously up at him. "Let's join them."

"I think these are the best snowdrops in Dublin," Alfie declared as they approached. "But I'm not too sure if John agrees."

The groups of snowdrops were very impressive but she turned to the boy. "Do you like them, John?"

The little boy nodded and slipped his hand into hers. She gave it a reassuring squeeze and he squeezed it in reply. Looking down at him, he looked up at her at the same time and gave her a grin.

As Will closed the front door to the practice house, he heard raised voices and then a slap. Eva ran out of the office and Will had to drop his medical bag and grab her shoulders as she tripped over the skirt of her bottle green dress and almost fell.

"Eva?" he demanded as Fred appeared at the office door, a hand on his cheek. "What on earth is happening?"

"A slight misunderstanding, Dr Fitzgerald."

"Slight?" he repeated, steadying Eva then letting her go. "What I heard sounded rather more than slight."

"Very well." Eva smoothed her dress down. "I'm afraid I took great exception to being called 'an interfering old bat'."

Will's jaw dropped and he looked from Eva's indignant face to Fred's ashamed one. "Fred – explain."

"There's nothing to explain. I'm afraid I lost my temper. Please accept my sincere apologies, Eva."

"I accept your apology, Dr Simpson," she replied crisply and Fred stepped aside as she returned to the office.

"I'll speak to you after surgery," Will informed Fred as the front door opened and a lady in late middle age wearing a chocolate brown dress, cloak and hat came in. Realising he still had his own hat on, he quickly took it off. "Good morning," he said and opened the door to the waiting room for her before picking up his medical bag and going to the coat stand in the office.

Hanging up his hat and overcoat, he frowned. Eva had the patience of a saint. She had been practice secretary for the past twenty years and had always dealt professionally with both patients and doctors. For how long had there been ill-feeling between her and Fred? Turning, he walked to the door and closed it.

"The patients, Dr Fitzgerald," Eva began, sitting down at the desk.

"They can wait. What brought this incident on?"

"I'd rather not say, Dr Fitzgerald," she replied, picking up a pen before putting it down again.

"Well, I would rather you did, Eva, please. I want to get to the root of any animosity between yourself and Dr Simpson and try and resolve it."

Eva sighed. "I arrived early in order to update some of the patient files and there was a… girl seated on the steps."

"A girl?"

"A prostitute, Dr Fitzgerald. I asked her to move along and she said she would not and that she was waiting for her Freddie."

"Her Freddie," Will repeated flatly, closing his eyes for a moment in an effort to subdue his temper.

"I'm afraid it's not the first time I've found a prostitute here, Dr Fitzgerald, and—"

"You've caught Dr Simpson with prostitutes here in the past?"

"Many times, Dr Fitzgerald," she replied wearily. "But this morning was the first occasion I've found one seated on the steps as bold as you please, decked out in – well – almost a dress and more lip rouge and powder than I thought possible. This is a respectable medical practice, Dr

Fitzgerald, and I'm afraid I saw red – literally."

"You should have come to me, Eva," Will said as calmly as he could.

"Oh, Dr Fitzgerald, you've had enough to deal with recently."

"I meant, long before this."

"I thought Dr Simpson would see reason. Unfortunately, he refuses to, and I'm afraid it is time for me to consider my position here."

"Please don't do anything hasty, Eva. I will speak to Dr Simpson."

"I am sorry, Dr Fitzgerald, with you recently bereaved and just back—"

"You have absolutely nothing to be sorry for," he assured her. "I will speak to Dr Simpson."

Leaving the office, he went upstairs and into Fred's surgery without knocking and kicked the door closed.

"And still it goes on."

"I beg your pardon?" Fred asked, getting up from his chair behind the desk.

"Prostitutes, Fred," he whispered fiercely. "Prostitutes in here. Prostitutes sitting on the front steps—"

"Will—"

"What the hell is wrong with you, Fred?"

"I have syphilis," he replied, his voice little more than a whisper, and Will leant heavily on both hands on the desk, hoping he wouldn't throw up.

"How long have you known?" he asked.

"Months."

"And you've continued to treat patients?" Will roared before squeezing his eyes shut and breathing deeply in and out as there was a knock at the door and it opened.

"Surgery, Doctors," Eva told them.

"In a few minutes, Eva," Will managed to reply calmly without turning around and the door closed.

"I have no lesions on my hands." Fred held them out palms upwards then turned them over. "I would never—"

"You should never have continued to practise medicine once you knew. Right." Will straightened up, forcing himself to think clearly. "You will retire from medicine immediately and I will take on all your patients. Were you showing symptoms before Margaret became pregnant?"

Fred shook his head. "But that doesn't mean she and the baby don't have it."

"You performed a caesarean on Cecilia."

"Well, I wasn't going to ask you to do it," Fred snapped.

"You also examined Isobel," Will reminded him, hearing his voice shake.

"I didn't touch her, Will, I swear. I looked, that's all. It was clear she was miscarrying and I told her that when you and she were a little calmer, you would examine her. There is no possibility of my having infected Isobel or Cecilia. It's Margaret and the baby I'm worried about."

"Have you noticed any symptoms on her body?" Will asked and Fred shrugged.

"I haven't seen her body in months."

"Have you not been examining her?" Will added incredulously.

"Yes, but not her vaginal area."

Will breathed deeply in and out again and counted to ten. "Well, someone needs to."

"Would you do it?"

"Under what pretext?" he demanded. "Because I take it you haven't told her you're ill? You just prefer to block it all out and cavort with prostitutes."

"No, I haven't told her," Fred replied quietly. "Tell her… oh, God, I don't know what to tell her…"

"We'll think of something. Do you know when you may have become infected?"

Fred nodded. "The drunken night before my wedding – in Sally Maher's brothel."

Will's stomach constricted. "Are you sure?"

"I hadn't had sex with a prostitute without using a condom in months before that night and afterwards it was only Margaret until she fell pregnant and she wouldn't let me near her," Fred explained. "Since then, I've used a condom every time. It had to be that night in Monto." Fred sat down in his chair behind the desk and ran a hand across his jaw. "Her name was Maggie. What was yours called?"

"Rose," he replied. "She's dead."

Fred's eyes widened. "How do you know that?"

"There was a piece in one of the newspapers shortly afterwards about a woman who drowned herself in the Liffey. She was identified as Rose Green, a prostitute from Monto."

"Poor girl."

"We need to think of a reason for you retiring from medicine, Fred. Would you mind very much if I were to speak to my father?" he asked and Fred shook his head.

"No, but please don't tell anyone else apart from Isobel."

"I won't, I promise."

"Thank you. Hopefully, your father will have a plausible excuse."

"Yes. I'm so sorry, Fred."

His friend gave him a rueful smile. "The three of us each chose a girl based on the colour of her hair. I'd never been with a redhead before. Curiosity killed the cat, eh?"

Chapter Four

Isobel twisted around in her chair as the morning room door opened shortly before one o'clock. Will came in and closed the door then peered around the room before finding her seated at the writing desk near the window.

"Isobel, I need to ask you something."

"Anything," she replied, putting her pen down on a list of clothes and toys which needed to be purchased for John.

"When Fred examined you the evening you began to miscarry, did he touch you?"

"No, he said he wanted to see the amount of blood and that it would be more proper if you examined me later when both you and I were a little calmer. Why?" she asked before her heart began to pound with terror. "Oh, God – Fred's ill – he has syphilis – doesn't he?"

"Yes, and you must not tell anyone, Isobel."

"Has he infected me, Will?" she added, hearing her voice shaking.

"No," he replied and she burst into tears of relief. "No, he hasn't. But he may have infected Margaret and the baby."

She exhaled a shocked breath and wiped the tears away with her fingers. "Are you going to examine Margaret?"

"Yes," he replied and she heard the reluctance in his voice as he sank down onto the sofa with his head in his hands. "And that's not all," he murmured.

"Tell me," she said and he slowly raised his head.

"Fred became infected at Sally Maher's brothel the night before his wedding," he told her and she clapped both hands to her cheeks. "From the redhead called Maggie."

"But we were all examined the day you visited," she whispered.

"Maggie's symptoms may not have been evident yet or the examination wasn't thorough enough."

"Oh, God." Getting up from the chair, she clutched her head. "The bloody brothel. For the first time, I had managed to go for days without thinking of it. Now, I'll never be able to forget. Oh, God, poor Maggie – poor Fred – but how many others have they both infected?"

"Fred says that since Margaret became pregnant and wouldn't allow him near her, he has used a condom with all the prostitutes he's been with. But Maggie... who knows," Will replied in a weary tone.

"What happens now?" she asked, fighting to pull herself together. "And what can I do to help?"

"Fred has retired from medicine and I have taken on all his patients. After luncheon, I'm going to see my father."

"You're not going to ask him to return to medicine, are you?"

"No, that's out of the question, but I need his help to come up with a plausible reason for Fred retiring and we need to discuss what Fred can do now to earn a living while he still can."

"You also need to replace Fred at the practice. You can't

cope with all the patients alone. Nor with the surgery in Pimlico," she went on sadly.

"No," he replied. "I'll go and see Mrs Bell as soon as possible."

"What have you told Eva?"

"I told her I sent Fred home to reflect on whether he wanted to continue working at the practice," he said and she gave him a puzzled frown. "This morning, Eva found a prostitute sitting on the steps outside the practice house waiting for 'her Freddie'," he explained. "When Eva confronted Fred about it, they rowed and Eva slapped his face."

"Did anyone see or hear the row?" she asked, sitting down beside him and he shook his head.

"I heard Eva slap Fred. Luckily, there were no patients present." Covering his face with his hands, he groaned then dragged his fingers down his cheeks. "I should have noticed Fred was ill."

"Your mind has been full of other things," she said softly. "But you know now and you and I will help Fred and Margaret as best we can."

"Yes," he replied and kissed her temple.

"Come and eat." Getting up, she held out a hand and he got up and took it.

"How is John?" he asked as they went into the breakfast room.

"Very well. He grinned at me."

"Progress." Will lifted her hand and kissed it.

After Will left to go and see his father, Isobel hurried around the gardens to her mother's home. Gorman showed her into the morning room where Alfie was seated in an armchair reading a newspaper. On seeing her, he closed it and got to his feet.

"You look flustered, Isobel. What is it? What's wrong?"

"Can I ask you about David?" she asked.

"David? Why?" he replied cautiously, dropping the newspaper onto the seat of the armchair.

"Has he found a practice?"

"No, not yet. To get more experience of dealing with patients he's been doing locum work here, there, and everywhere. Why?"

"I was just curious," she said and grimaced when Alfie gave her a long sceptical look. "I'm afraid I can't say, Alfie, I'm sorry."

"I see. Well, can you tell me about John?"

"Yes, I can." They sat down side by side on the sofa and she told him all. "And Will treats the sores every evening," she finished and Alfie shook his head.

"The poor little lad. No wonder he doesn't speak."

"He needs to build up a lot of trust first."

"He trusts you – the way he grinned at you."

"That was the very first time," she admitted and Alfie's eyebrows shot up. "The first of many grins, I hope. Where's Mother?"

"She's taking your mother-in-law out to luncheon."

"Good. I'm glad they've become friends," she said and, to her surprise, Alfie roared with laughter. "What is it?"

"Mrs Fitzgerald senior isn't the only new friend Mother has."

"I'm glad to hear it. I was hoping Sarah would introduce Mother to her friends and acquaintances and I'm delighted Mother now has many female friends."

"And one male admirer."

Isobel frowned. "Who?"

"Mr Ellison. I've lost count the number of times he has called here on one flimsy pretext or another."

"Has Mother said anything?"

"No, nothing, and whenever I mention him, Mother changes the subject. How would you feel if he were to court her?"

She shrugged. "I don't know – I've never even considered the possibility – is he after her money and this house?" she asked suddenly.

"He's quite well-off himself so, no."

"Is he a bachelor?"

"A widower. His wife died of cancer five years ago."

"How do you know all this?"

"It's amazing what snippets of information you can acquire in Trinity's law faculty," Alfie replied. "How would you feel if he were to court her?" he asked again.

"I've always found him pleasant and direct to deal with. Alfie, I just want Mother to be happy, but it's only a couple of months since Mr Henderson died. How did you feel when she met him?"

"After Father and all he put her through, I hoped she had found happiness at last. And she thought she had, too, so I can't help but be concerned."

"The next time Mr Ellison calls, send for me and I'll call if I can."

Will called to number 67 but Tess informed him that his mother was out to luncheon with Mrs Henderson and his father was lunching at his club before returning to the

Journal of Irish Medicine. Will walked to Hume Street and was shown into his father's office. It was the first time he had been there and his father got up from a chair behind a large leather-topped desk in surprise.

"Will?"

"Can we be overheard here, Father?" he said by way of a greeting.

"No, why?"

"Because no-one must hear what I'm about to tell you."

"I see. Well, sit down," his father said, pointing to a chair in front of the desk.

"I'd prefer to stand if you don't mind," he said, placing his medical bag on the chair. "Father, there is no easy way to tell you this but Fred has syphilis."

His father closed his eyes for a moment. "Does he know how long he has been infected?"

"Yes. Since just before his wedding," Will replied and his father sighed. "He doesn't know whether Margaret and the baby have been infected but I would be very surprised if they are not."

"And he has been practising medicine all along."

"Yes, but he has now retired. And I don't know what to do," Will confessed. "What excuse can I give for Fred retiring at his age? He also needs to make a living for as long as he possibly can. So, I was hoping…"

"That I could find him a position here," his father finished.

"Yes."

"First things first. Someone must examine Margaret."

"I will," he said reluctantly. "I'll call to Ely Place Upper this evening. Oh, God," he went on, raising his eyes to the ceiling. "After Isobel's mother, I swore I would never again attend to anyone I knew socially."

"It has to be done."

"Yes. Is there anything Fred can do here?"

"Leave it with me, Will. I haven't been editor long and I cannot start shoe-horning friends into positions but I will do my best to find Fred employment somewhere."

"Thank you."

"And what will you do now?" his father continued. "The practice needs a new doctor."

"I haven't thought that far forward yet," he said, the very thought of having to replace Fred filling him with dread.

"Well, you need to now. Fred told me the newspaper article brought in a good number of new patients. You must not risk losing them, Will. You cannot run the practice alone."

"No," Will replied, silently berating Fred for discussing the practice with his father. "I'll start looking discreetly for a new doctor tomorrow."

"Will you treat Fred?"

"Yes, if he's agreeable. Thank you for listening, Father."

"Your mother has told me about the boy," his father added as Will picked up his medical bag and went to turn and leave the office.

"The boy's name is John."

"Is he mentally retarded?"

"No, he is not," Will replied adamantly. "John is the most observant child I have ever seen. He needs to make sure he can fully trust us before speaking. He was treated atrociously in the children's home."

"So your mother said."

"And there is no doubt he is Edward's son."

"Your mother said that, too."

"And Isobel and I are going to do our absolute best for him."

His father nodded and Will left the office to begin house calls.

Four hours later, he closed number 30's front door behind him and saw Isobel coming down the stairs as he put his medical bag on the hall table and hung his hat on the stand.

"How is John?" he asked.

She smiled and helped him off with his overcoat. "He's exploring every inch of the nursery with Florrie," she said. "I've been to see Alfie," she continued, hanging the overcoat on the stand beside his hat.

"I've been to see Father," he replied as they went into the morning room. He closed the door and sighed. "I'm going to examine Margaret this evening and Father is going to try and obtain a position for Fred at the *Journal of Irish Medicine*."

"Would you like me to come with you this evening?" she asked, sounding a little hesitant. "Say no if you think I'll be in the way."

"I would like you to come and sit with Fred. If it is bad news, it would be best with the two of us there."

"How did your father take the news?"

Will shrugged. "You know my father. He's advised me to find a replacement for Fred as soon as possible but..." He tailed off and made a helpless gesture with his hands. "How do I replace Fred?"

"You can't run the practice alone," she said softly. "So that is why I went to see Alfie."

"Oh?"

"I asked him about David Powell."

"David is less than a year qualified."

"But Alfie tells me he's been doing a lot of locum work to build up his experience. Would you consider him, Will? Even as a locum until you do find someone permanent?"

"Where is he working as locum now?"

"I don't know. Naturally, I couldn't say why I was asking, but it shouldn't be too hard for you to find out, should it?"

"No, it won't," he conceded.

After kissing John goodnight at seven o'clock, they walked to number 1 Ely Place Upper. After passing their hats and coats to the butler, they were shown into the morning room. Fred had clearly told Margaret why they were calling as her face was white and tear-stained. She got up from the sofa and took a deep but unsteady breath.

"Shall we get this over with, Will?" she said, ringing the bell for a servant.

"Yes." He opened the door for her and they went out to the hall.

"Bring warm water, soap and a towel to my bedroom immediately," she instructed a maid, who was hurrying up the steps from the servants' hall. "And knock, Dorothy, do not come straight in."

"Yes, Mrs Simpson," the maid replied and Margaret walked on with Will following her up the stairs to the second floor and into her very feminine pale pink bedroom.

"Before we start," she said while he closed the door. "Did you know Fred was infected?"

"Not until he told me this morning, no."

"You, Fred and Jerry went to a brothel the night before my wedding. Does Isobel know you frequent brothels?"

"She knows about that night," he replied, hearing a knock at the door. "I have not been to one since." Opening the door, he took an ewer of water, a bar of soap and a towel from the maid. "Could you bring up another ewer of warm water, please?" he asked her. "I shall need to wash my hands again thoroughly."

"Yes, Dr Fitzgerald," she replied and he closed the door.

Shrugging off his frock coat, he laid it on a bedroom chair. He undid his cufflinks and rolled up his shirt sleeves before washing and drying his hands. Turning to the bed, he forced from his mind the fact that Margaret was his oldest friend's wife and proceeded to question and examine her. He sighed as he straightened up, hearing another knock at the door and Margaret grabbed his arm before he could ask the maid to come in.

"What is it, Will? Tell me?"

"I'm afraid my examination has proved to be inconclusive," he told her and she held her hands out helplessly.

"What does that mean?"

"Did Fred explain to you what the symptoms of syphilis are?"

Margaret flushed. "Yes, he did."

"I can't see any visible symptoms but that doesn't mean you aren't infected. It is called being asymptomatic."

"So what happens now?" she asked.

"If you are infected, this stage may continue for years – even decades – before the tertiary stage—"

"But what about my baby?" she interrupted.

"Margaret, I'm sorry, but there is no way of knowing

whether the baby is infected, as well." This information was too much for her and she burst into tears. "Margaret, please calm yourself."

"Calm myself?" she screeched. "I'm going to die and my baby's going to die and it's all because the three of you fucked whores the night before my wedding."

Will stepped back from the bed. "Would you like me to send Fred up to you?"

"No. I never want to see him again. I'm moving out. I'm going home to Dame Street."

"Margaret," he snapped. "This is your home, and do you really want to explain to your mother why you've left your husband of less than a year?" She stared at him open-mouthed. "If you'll agree," he continued calmly. "I will provide you and your baby with the best care."

"And what about Fred?"

"I will provide you, your baby, and Fred with the best and most discreet care. Do you agree?"

"I agree," she replied and he squeezed her arm.

"Good. After I've washed my hands, I'll listen to the baby's heartbeat." Going to the door, he opened it and took the ewer of water from the maid. "I may need your help, so please wait there on the landing," he whispered, she nodded and he closed the door.

He washed and dried his hands then lifted his stethoscope out of his medical bag. Returning to the bed, he placed it over Margaret's abdomen. He couldn't hear a thing apart from Margaret's agitated breathing so he moved the stethoscope a little. Then moved it again. And once more before straightening up.

"When did you last feel the baby move?" he asked in as

neutral a tone as he could manage while putting the stethoscope back in his medical bag.

"I—" She gave him a blank stare.

"Or kick?"

"I'm not sure," she replied. "A few days. Perhaps a week. Why do you ask? Oh, God, Will, what's wrong with my baby?" Margaret demanded as he went to the door and opened it.

"Could you ask Dr Simpson and my wife to come up here at once, please?" he asked the maid, who bobbed a little curtsey before running down the stairs.

"Will?"

Closing the door, he returned to Margaret, sat on the edge of the bed and clasped her hands. "I can't hear a heartbeat," he told her gently.

"What do you mean?"

"Margaret, your baby is dead."

"No." She gave him a dismissive little smile. "No, I don't believe you."

"I'm afraid it's true."

"No," she whimpered. "Not my baby."

"I'm so sorry," he whispered, hoping he wasn't going to start crying as well.

"Will?" He jumped, not having heard the door open, and he twisted around as Fred came in with Isobel right behind him. "We met Dorothy on the stairs and—"

"I need to speak with you, Fred," he said, getting up off the bed.

"The baby's dead," Margaret wailed before he could usher Fred from the bedroom and Fred's jaw dropped in horror.

"I'll sit with her." Isobel pushed past Fred and went to Margaret as she covered her face with her hands and began to weep.

"Come onto the landing." Taking Fred's arm, Will led him out of the bedroom and closed the door. "There's no heartbeat and Margaret hasn't felt movement or kicking for up to a week," he explained. "As well as that, my examination for syphilis was inconclusive," he added and Fred's face contorted.

"What have I done, Will?" he sobbed. "What have I done?"

"You didn't know."

"Well, I should have known," Fred roared. "I should have known how fucking irresponsible it was to bring you and Jerry to a brothel the night before my wedding when you didn't want to go."

"Fred." He gripped his friend's shoulders. "Listen to me, Fred – we need to deliver the baby."

"A caesarean."

"Yes."

"I'll do it."

"What?" Will was horrified. "No, absolutely not."

"Yes, Will," Fred insisted. "Margaret's my wife and it's highly likely she has syphilis. I don't want you to risk becoming infected. You may administer the chloroform and monitor Margaret's heart rate, but I will carry out the procedure."

"Very well," Will conceded. "Let's prepare."

Isobel tried to calm Margaret but it was impossible. Had syphilis killed the baby she wondered as Margaret wept, rocking back and forth on the double bed, completely oblivious to her presence.

The door opened and Will and a tearful Fred came inside.

"Isobel," Will said softly. "Fred needs to speak to Margaret."

She squeezed Margaret's hands before sliding off the bed and following Will onto the landing.

"Fred's going to perform a caesarean and deliver the baby—" he began.

"Fred is?" she exclaimed.

"It has to be Fred. Even though my examination was inconclusive, it's highly likely Margaret has syphilis, too."

"Because it has to be syphilis which has killed the baby?" she asked and he nodded. "Is there anything I can do?"

"No, not really," he said with a sad little smile. "But thank you for asking."

"I'll wait in the morning room."

"Isobel, it could take hours…"

"I'd still like to wait," she said, reached up to kiss his lips, then went downstairs.

In the morning room, she sat down on the sofa with a newspaper but after glancing at the front page she knew she wouldn't be able to concentrate on it. Putting the paper to one side, she got up and went to look at the photographs on top of the piano which stood in a corner of the room.

There were studio portraits taken at the time of Fred and Margaret's wedding, including the bride and groom, the bride with her attendants, and the groom with his two best friends. Others were of Fred's parents and another older couple – possibly Margaret's mother and her late father –

and a photograph she had seen before of Will, Fred and Jerry when they graduated from Trinity College.

She turned, hearing the door open and Will's father stared at her in surprise as he was shown into the room.

"Isobel?"

"Dr Fitzgerald."

"Is Fred at home?"

"Yes, he is," she replied and waited for the butler to close the door. "I'm afraid I have terrible news. Margaret's baby is dead and Fred is performing a caesarean—"

"Fred is?"

"Will told me it has to be Fred," she explained. "Because it's highly likely Margaret has syphilis, too, and it has killed the baby."

"Oh, good God Almighty." Dr Fitzgerald senior sighed. "How long has it been?"

"Not long – only a few minutes."

"I see." He grimaced and shook his head. "I called to tell Fred I have found a position for him at the *Journal*. Would you like me to stay?" he offered and she nodded gratefully.

"Yes, please. Will told me it could take hours."

"I'll send the footman to tell Sarah I will be late home – if at all. Excuse me, Isobel."

He left the room and she went to the fireplace. She added a shovel of coal to the fire then looked for the decanters. They were on a tray on a round mahogany table across the room from her and she was pouring herself a brandy when Will's father returned.

"I thought I would help myself," she said. "Whiskey or brandy?"

"Whiskey, please," he replied as he joined her and she

poured him a generous helping. "Margaret and Fred." He held up his glass.

"Margaret and Fred." She touched his glass with hers.

"Brandy?" he queried.

"I don't like sherry," she told him. "I've never liked sherry. I can tolerate whiskey but I much prefer brandy."

"I see."

"My mother doesn't approve either."

"I don't disapprove, I just…" He tailed off and shrugged.

"You don't know what to make of me?" she suggested. "It doesn't matter. It has reached the point where I no longer care what people think of me."

"And I admire you for it."

"You do?" she asked in surprise.

"You are a strong woman, Isobel. I admire strong women. Cecilia would have been utterly wrong for Will, I see that now. Unfortunately, it seems Edward did pick the wrong woman."

"I'm afraid I only saw Ruth at her worst, so I can't really comment. But Purnima was beautiful so it's not surprising she turned Edward's head."

"You've seen a photograph of her?" Dr Fitzgerald senior asked.

"There was a photograph of Edward and her amongst John's belongings."

"Edward wanted his son to see his parents."

"Yes, he did. Except John hasn't seen it yet. The photograph was kept in his file at the children's home, and I meant to have it framed once we returned to Dublin, only I haven't done it yet. But I will."

"You seem quite prepared to be a mother to the boy."

"John never knew his real mother and he hasn't had a mother-figure in his life so he doesn't know what a mother is, but I will try my best. He's never dared to trust anyone before either, but Will and I are making progress. And I hope," she continued boldly, "that one day you will want to meet John."

"Perhaps."

Perhaps is better than no, she concluded and sipped her brandy.

"Had you ever dealt with a case like Margaret's?" she asked.

"No, I hadn't dealt with syphilis in a pregnant woman but I have read case studies and it is truly horrific."

"Can anything be done for Margaret and Fred?"

"There are those who think mercury treatments—"

"But mercury is poisonous, isn't it?"

"Yes, it is. And no, Isobel, there is no cure."

Two hours passed before the door opened and Will came in. If he was surprised to see his father sitting in one of the armchairs, it didn't show on his face. He looked wretched and her heart went out to him.

"It's done," he said.

"How is Margaret?" she asked.

"Recovering. The baby was a boy. Fred wants him buried with Duncan in Mount Jerome Cemetery. In the morning, I'll arrange the funeral and burial."

"What about a name?" she added.

"Fred says they may name him Nicholas after Margaret's late father."

"How is Fred?"

"Exhausted."

"And so are you," Will's father spoke up and got to his feet. "Isobel, take him home."

"But Fred—" Will protested.

"I'll stay with Fred, Will. Go home."

"Does Mother know where you are?"

"She knows I'll be late home – if at all. Now go home."

Taking their hats and coats and Will's medical bag from the butler in the hall, Isobel ushered Will out of the house and he stood on the pavement with his hands on his hips.

"That was awful." He sighed. "Truly awful."

"Let's find a cab."

"Can we walk?" he asked as she helped him with his overcoat before passing him his medical bag and hat. "I need some air."

"Yes, of course," she replied, giving him an appreciative smile as he helped her with her coat and she put on her hat.

"Why did my father call?" he added as they crossed Ely Place Upper before turning onto Hume Street.

"He's found Fred a position somewhere at the *Journal*. He didn't say what and I didn't like to ask."

"Good, I'm glad."

"Are you hungry? Shall I ask Mrs Dillon to cook you something?"

"No, I'm not hungry, I just need to sleep."

In the hall of number 30, she put his medical bag on the table then hung his hat and overcoat on the stand. Hanging her own coat and hat beside them, she led him upstairs and into their bedroom. He was almost out on his feet and she could only speculate on the condition poor Fred must be in. Sitting Will down on the bed, she took off his clothes and dressed him in his nightshirt.

"Thank you," he murmured, getting up as she lowered the bedcovers.

Climbing into bed, he curled up and closed his eyes. He was fast asleep before she had pulled the covers over him.

She woke as Will opened the bedroom door and went onto the landing. When he returned with two ewers and placed them on the washstand she sat up.

"I want to call on Margaret and Fred before I start surgery," he explained as he began to shave. "Fred will oversee Margaret's recovery from the caesarean but I want to keep an eye on them both. And I need to tell Eva that Fred has left the practice. Oh, and as I'm dealing with all the patients now, I'll probably miss luncheon. Actually, I will miss luncheon as I have to call to the clergyman at St Peter's and then to Daltons."

"Well, make sure you eat a good breakfast, then," she said and he smiled at her in the washstand mirror.

He ate a bowl of porridge, four triangular slices of toast and marmalade and a cup of coffee before she accompanied him to the front door.

"Give Margaret and Fred my condolences," she said, helping him on with his overcoat then passing him his hat and medical bag.

"I will." He kissed her lips and opened the door. "See you this evening."

Closing the door after him, she went upstairs to the nursery and found John dipping a toast 'soldier' into a soft boiled egg. So far, it appeared to be his favourite meal and her heart leapt as he smiled at her as she pulled out a chair and sat at the table beside him.

"I must go out this morning but after luncheon, Florrie

and I will bring you clothes shopping. Afterwards, we'll go to St Stephen's Green and feed the ducks. Would you like that?" she asked and John nodded even though he clearly didn't know what ducks were. "Good boy. Finish that egg and I'll see you soon."

Ten minutes later, she was admitted to number 55, only for Gorman to tell her Mr Stevens had just left to attend a lecture. Hoping she could catch up with Alfie, she hurried out of Fitzwilliam Square and saw him ahead of her on Pembroke Street Lower.

"Alfie?" she called and he stopped and peered over his shoulder.

"Isobel." He smiled. "What is it?"

"I won't delay you, but can you tell me where David is doing locum work at the moment? Will needs a locum as soon as possible."

"Why? What's wrong with Dr Simpson?"

"His wife's unborn baby died and had to be delivered by caesarean yesterday evening," she explained and Alfie's face contorted in sympathy. "Please don't tell anyone yet, will you?"

"I won't, I promise. David is at Dr Ferguson's practice on York Street."

"Thank you, Alfie. I'll go straight there."

David Powell was speaking to a red-haired gentleman in the hallway but glanced at her as she closed the front door and did a double-take.

"Mrs Fitzgerald?"

"Isobel, please. May I speak with you for a moment?"

"Of course." Turning back to the red-haired gentleman and excusing himself, David went with her outside onto the steps.

"Alfie told me where to find you," she said in a low voice. "Will needs a locum as quickly as possible, so I immediately thought of you."

"That's very kind, but I'm locum here until the end of the week."

"Do you have time to meet Will today or tomorrow? Either at the practice house on Merrion Street Upper or at number 30?"

"I could call to number 30 this evening?" he suggested and she nodded.

"We'll see you this evening. Thank you, David."

He went back inside and, with nothing more she could do, she went home.

After luncheon, with a bag of bread crusts from Mrs Dillon in her handbag, Isobel, Florrie and John slowly made their way to the Switzers department store on Grafton Street. John was measured and Isobel bought him two vests and two pairs of socks and drawers, followed by two shirts, two brown waistcoats, two pairs of short brown trousers and two brown morning coats. They continued on to a boot and shoe seller, where John's feet were measured and Isobel bought the little boy his first ever pair of new boots.

In Hodges Figgis, two picture books and a child's first book of letters and numbers were purchased and in a toy warehouse, John was bought a set of wooden farm animals. That would do for now she decided, as she had yet to see which of Edward and Will's toys would be suitable for him.

They carried the packages to St Stephen's Green but the grass at her spot near the lake was too damp to sit on so the three of them stood under the trees instead. Isobel exchanged a smile with Florrie as they watched John's enthralled face while he observed the ladies, gentlemen and children walking past, listened to the chatter and occasional laughs and shouts, and smelt the odour of damp vegetation. His dark eyes widened all of a sudden as a drake jumped out of the water and waddled towards them.

"Shall we give him some bread?" she asked and John nodded. Delving into the paper bag, she brought out a piece of crust and passed it to the boy. "Throw it down for him," she instructed and John dropped it. The drake edged forward, snatched the crust and ran away with it.

"Try another piece," Florrie suggested and Isobel held out the bag. John reached inside for a crust and threw it towards the lake this time. "Look." Florrie pointed at a group of ducks swimming towards them. "The others want some, too."

John reached into the bag again, threw another crust at them and four ducks began to fight for possession.

"We'll have all of them here, soon." Isobel threw a handful of crusts as far as she could in the direction of the lake. "That one with the green head and neck is a male duck called a drake. The others must be his wives. Throw them the last few pieces of crust."

John did as he was told and they watched the ducks either gobble down the crusts or swim away with their prize.

"We'll have to come back soon with more crusts and bring Will with us when he isn't so busy," she added, returning the now empty paper bag to her handbag, and John nodded. "We need to see how much he knows about ducks." John nodded again and she smiled. "I like it here. I like the trees, I like the lake and I like watching people. Before I married Will, I used to sit here and watch people –

see what they were wearing and wonder where they were coming from or going to. Now, I'm here with you and Florrie."

She bent and kissed his cheek then smiled at John's disappointed face as the last of the ducks swam away. Suddenly, she jerked upright and John gave her a puzzled glance. What was that? She felt the fluttering in her belly again and, in case Florrie noticed something was wrong, she fought to control her breathing. No. It couldn't be. John frowned at her and she managed to give him a reassuring nod before putting her half of the packages under her left arm and taking his hand. It was time to go home.

Three-quarters of an hour later, she was seated at the dressing table in hers and Will's bedroom flicking through the small diary she had bought to record her monthlies and other pertinent information. She miscarried on Monday, January 17th. She and Will made love for the first time afterwards on Wednesday, January 26th – the evening they learnt of Edward's death – and Will had worn a condom. It was now Wednesday, February 2nd – only a week later. Could the condom have torn or burst? Even if it had, she couldn't possibly be feeling movement just one week into a pregnancy.

Closing the diary, she stared at her puzzled reflection in the mirror for a few moments before her eyes bulged. Her mother was a twin. Her mother's twin brother had died at a year old but the fact remained that there were twins in her family. Surely the only explanation was that she had been carrying twins but miscarried one of them.

Getting up from the dressing table, she stood in front of the wardrobe mirror and undid the jet buttons on the front of her mourning dress. Shrugging it off her shoulders, she let the dress billow to the floor then opened the waistband of her small bustle frame and threw it, her corset, petticoat and chemise onto the bed. Lowering her drawers a little, she ran her hands over her stomach. It was flat, but not as flat as it had once been and she clapped a hand over her mouth, not knowing whether to laugh or cry.

She was pregnant – still pregnant! She should be jumping for joy and telling Will. But she couldn't. Not after the dreadful events of the previous evening and especially with the baby's funeral yet to come. Her news would simply have to wait until a more appropriate time.

Will arrived home just after six o'clock. He looked worn out and she hugged and kissed him before they went into the breakfast room for dinner.

"The baby has been named Nicholas Frederick Simpson," he told her. "The funeral is tomorrow morning at eleven o'clock at St Peter's Church and Nicholas will then be buried beside Duncan in Mount Jerome Cemetery," he added, holding her chair as she sat down then taking his seat at the head of the table. "I've cancelled surgery and arranged for a cab to be here at ten o'clock. Will you come?"

"Of course I'll come. Did you tell your father?"

"Yes. He and Mother will attend, too."

"How are Margaret and Fred?"

"Numb," he replied quietly. "They know Nicholas was the only child they will ever have. I also made an appointment with Mr Ellison to dissolve the partnership."

"Isn't it very soon to dissolve—"

"Fred insisted. He's accepted my father's offer of the position of deputy editor of the *Journal of Irish Medicine*."

"I'm glad."

"So am I. My father can keep an eye on Fred and the *Journal* offices are only a couple of minutes walk from number 1."

"Now, Will, don't be angry," she said, reaching out and squeezing his hand.

"Why would I be angry?" he asked with a tired smile.

"I discovered where David Powell is doing locum work. I went to see him and he's coming here this evening."

"What did you tell him?"

"I told Alfie that Fred and Margaret's baby had died and you were looking for a locum. David only knows you are looking for a locum as quickly as possible. Nothing else."

Will nodded. "Thank you. I just didn't have time to see to it today. What else did you do today?"

"This afternoon, Florrie and I brought John shopping for clothes, boots, books and toys. Afterwards, we went to St Stephen's Green and fed the ducks. You must come with us next time."

"I'll try. Did he enjoy it?"

"Very much so," she replied, reaching for the jug of water and filling their glasses. "He loved the ducks and he loved being out and about with Florrie and I. Will, I'm deciding against engaging a nanny," she announced, putting the jug down and his eyebrows rose and fell. "I'd rather John didn't have to begin again with a stranger, especially a nanny. What do you think?"

"Not all nannies are cruel sergeant majors like your mother's," he declared. "But, you're right. Florrie is as competent a nursery maid as she is a house-parlourmaid. It will be better for John to continue building trust in you and myself – and Florrie," he concluded with a nod and she leant over and kissed his lips.

"I'll ask her later if she'll continue as nursery maid and—" She stopped as the door opened and Mrs Dillon came in with two dinner plates.

"Mary has just answered the front door to a Dr David Powell, Doctor, Mrs Fitzgerald," the housekeeper said, placing one plate of succulent sliced roast beef down in front of her and the other plate in front of Will.

"Could you ask Mary to show Dr Powell into the morning room, please, Mrs Dillon?" she replied. "And tell Dr Powell that Dr Fitzgerald missed luncheon but he will be with him when he finishes his dinner."

"Yes, Mrs Fitzgerald."

The door closed and Isobel lifted the lids off the serving dishes, spooned some sliced carrot and parsnip onto Will's plate before adding two potatoes and a little gravy. "Eat."

He smiled and picked up his knife and fork. "Yes, Mrs Fitzgerald."

While Will spoke with David, she went upstairs and helped to put John to bed, applying the ointment herself to the almost healed sores on his buttocks. She kissed him goodnight and Florrie followed her from John's bedroom into the nursery.

"I've never looked after a child so well-behaved, Mrs Fitzgerald," the maid said, closing the bedroom door.

"Sadly, we know what was done to make him so. Has he made any attempt to speak to you, Florrie?"

"No, Mrs Fitzgerald."

"I thought to see and to feed the ducks for the first time might have prompted him to say something."

"I'm sorry, Mrs Fitzgerald."

"Oh, Florrie, it's not your fault," she assured her. "I do want to ask you something, though," she added, pulling a chair out from the table. "Please, sit down."

They sat at the table and she glanced approvingly around the nursery. The room was as clean as a new pin, the warm yellow wallpaper gave it a cosy atmosphere, and the new red rugs on the floor added a splash of colour. But it was very bare. Pictures needed to be bought for the walls and, although John loved his wooden elephant and the new farm animals, he needed more toys to play with – and some educational toys, too.

"Florrie," she began. "Mrs Dillon advised me to engage a nanny for John but I want to ask you if you would be prepared to continue as John's nursery maid permanently instead?"

"Me, Mrs Fitzgerald?" Florrie looked and sounded astonished.

"John likes and trusts you as much as my husband and I," she continued. "And I would rather he didn't have to begin again with a stranger. You don't have to answer straight away, Florrie. I know it must be rather isolating for you to be up here alone with John but I will try to be here as much as I can and I doubt very much if a nanny would appreciate what could be seen as interference from me."

"Would you employ another house-parlourmaid to replace me?" Florrie asked.

"Yes, I would. Mary can't be expected to do all the work on her own."

"The house does need two house-parlourmaids." Florrie nodded and Isobel began to cross her fingers under the table.

"Mrs Fitzgerald, I don't need time to think about it. I would very much like to continue as John's nursery maid."

Isobel's face broke into a wide smile. "Oh, I'm delighted. Thank you, Florrie. We'll tell John the good news tomorrow."

Downstairs in the morning room, she found Will and David at the drinks tray.

"Meet the new locum." Will gave her a clearly relieved grin. "Brandy?"

"A very small one, please," she said and he turned back to the decanters. "I'm so glad. When do you start, David?"

"Next Monday. Will has also been telling me about his time in Brown Street and the Pimlico surgery."

"Oh?" She accepted a glass of brandy from Will. "Thank you."

"To Isobel." Will raised his glass. "Thank you for seeking David out."

"To Isobel." David smiled and they all touched glasses. "I'd very much like to see the rooms you rented, Will."

"I'm afraid I can't bring you to see them until next week. I've had to cancel surgery tomorrow because of the funeral and I'll be catching up on Friday."

"Of course," David replied. "Please give Dr Simpson and his wife my sympathies."

Will stood in front of the wardrobe mirror buttoning up his frock coat. He'd hardly slept and he looked terrible, the only colour in his face was the dark circles under his eyes. He hated funerals and this one was going to be heart-breaking. Feeling a hand on his shoulder, he jumped. Isobel was standing behind him wearing her black silk taffeta mourning dress and a small black tricorn hat her mother had given her.

"The cab is here," she said softly and he nodded.

The cab brought them to Ely Place Upper and McDonnell, the butler, admitted them to number 1, Will noting the two carriages which stood outside. The first thing he saw when he followed Isobel into the house was the tiny oak coffin on the hall table and it was all he could do not to grab her hand, turn on his heel and order the cabman to bring them straight home.

"Will. Isobel." A grey-faced Fred greeted them from the morning room door.

"Fred."

"Margaret is insisting on attending both the funeral and the burial." Fred glanced briefly up the stairs. "There's nothing I, my mother, nor her mother can say to stop her. I expected her sister to be here but Elizabeth is unwell. Elizabeth's husband, Gordon Higginson, is here, though. Would you mind going upstairs to them please, Isobel, and hurrying them up?"

"Of course."

Will watched her go up the stairs before taking Fred's arm and bringing him into the morning room.

"Would Margaret listen to me if I told her as a doctor and not as a friend that she shouldn't attend?" he asked. "Especially so soon after the caesarean?"

"No," Fred replied. "Nicholas will be her only child and she insists on seeing him buried. I've borrowed a bath chair for her and Gordon and Mrs Dawson will travel with it in the second carriage. Have you found my replacement yet?"

"I've found a locum. A Dr David Powell. He starts on Monday. He's just under a year qualified so we'll see how he copes."

"You will, you mean. Have you made an appointment with Mr Ellison to dissolve the partnership?"

"Yes, it's on Monday," Will replied. "When have you decided to start at the *Journal of Irish Medicine*?"

"Your father left it open – whenever I feel I can begin – but it will probably be Monday. Margaret and I must attempt to start living what passes for a normal life as soon as possible."

Will nodded and, hearing footsteps on the stairs, they both walked out to the hall.

Margaret, dressed from head to toe in black, was being carried slowly down the stairs by Gordon Higginson, a tall gentleman in his forties Will remembered from Fred and Margaret's wedding. Following them were Margaret's mother, Fred's mother, and Isobel.

"Margaret." Will lifted the thick black lace veil covering her face and kissed her white cheek. "My deepest sympathies."

"Thank you, Will," she replied while Gordon Higginson quickly stood back as Fred strode past without acknowledging any of them and picked up the coffin before walking out of the house to the first of the waiting carriages.

Will and Isobel followed Margaret and Gordon, Mrs Dawson and Maria Simpson out of the house. He helped Isobel into their cab and it followed the two carriages to St Peter's Church on Aungier Street for the funeral service.

At the graveside in an icy cold but thankfully dry Mount Jerome Cemetery, Will couldn't take his eyes off the tiny coffin in Fred's arms. Feeling Isobel slip her gloved hand into his, he fought an urge to kiss her and hold her in his arms and gave her fingers a squeeze instead. Tonight, he would hold her and kiss her until they both fell asleep.

With clear reluctance, Fred passed the coffin to John Dalton, the undertaker. It was slowly lowered into the grave and Will raised his head. His parents were standing opposite him and he gave them the briefest of nods before turning his attention to Margaret, seated stock-still in the bath chair with a blanket over her knees. Her weeping mother and mother-in-law were standing on either side of her, each with a hand on her shoulder, and he noted how Fred made no attempt to move closer or to give comfort to any of them.

The short burial service over, they all returned to Ely Place Upper. Gordon Higginson carried Margaret straight back upstairs, her mother, mother-in-law, Isobel and a maid all following to help to return her to bed.

Tea and sandwiches were served in the drawing room on the first floor and Will went to one of the side tables, took three of the tiny triangular sandwiches and put them on a plate. He brought the plate to Fred who was standing alone at a window with his hands in his pockets staring down at the street.

"Eat," he said, gently nudging Fred with the plate.

"I can't."

"You must."

"Bring them upstairs to Margaret."

"Margaret is being served luncheon on a tray as we speak. So, eat."

Sighing, Fred selected a ham sandwich and bit into it. "Thank you for coming today," he said with his mouth full. "I was dreading it – especially the burial."

"So was I," Will admitted and Fred nodded as he chewed, swallowed and ate the remainder of the sandwich.

"Whenever Margaret is well enough, and you both feel up to it, call to number 30."

"We will. Thank you."

"And I'd like you to consent to me attending to you both."

Fred shot him a sharp glance. "Would you really want that, Will?"

"It's not a question of what I want, but one of what you both need. And that is a doctor who is also a friend and who will do his absolute best for you both."

"Will, I don't know if I could put you through what is to come. Especially after what happened with my father…"

"Think about it, Fred. Talk it over with Margaret and we'll speak again."

"Very well."

"Good." Will held up the plate and Fred selected another sandwich. "And if you want to talk privately about anything or everything, you know where to find me."

"Thanks, Will."

"And I'm sure Isobel is saying the same to Margaret. The two of you can talk to the two of us – together – or separately."

Fred nodded again and glanced towards the door. Will followed his glance and saw Isobel coming towards them.

"Margaret is having some soup and her mother and your mother will sit with her," she told Fred.

"Thank you, Isobel."

"We're going home now," Will said. "Remember what I told you."

"Yes, Will." Fred gave them a tired smile. "Thank you."

"Mother. Father." Will greeted them as they walked to the door. "We'll call soon."

"Do," his mother replied. "Has Fred had some tea?"

"Two tiny sandwiches, no tea," he replied and his mother went to the tea tray. "Thank you for taking Fred on at the *Journal*," he added to his father in a low voice.

"Have you found a locum?"

"Yes. He starts on Monday."

"Good. You look exhausted."

"He is exhausted," Isobel spoke up. "And we're going home."

After a late luncheon, Isobel went in search of Mrs Dillon. The housekeeper was in the kitchen, closing the door of the range's firebox and they stepped outside into the garden.

"Was it a big funeral, Mrs Fitzgerald?"

"No, very small. They didn't want any fuss."

"That's understandable."

"Mrs Dillon," she went on. "I've decided against employing a nanny. John is content with Florrie and I don't want him to have to start again with a stranger. I've asked her if she will continue to be his nursery maid and she has agreed."

"Well, as you take such an active role with the boy, Mrs Fitzgerald, it's probably wise not to get a nanny in. Many of them don't like…"

"Interference," Isobel finished. "No. My mother's nanny certainly didn't and she was extremely cruel to poor Mother. This does mean we will need to find a replacement house-parlourmaid. Can you see to that, please?"

"Of course, Mrs Fitzgerald," Mrs Dillon replied. "Master John is a lot brighter now, isn't he?"

"Yes, he is. I had hoped he would have spoken by now, though."

"He will," Mrs Dillon replied in a confident tone. "He's come a long way in a very short time, and that's down to you, Mrs Fitzgerald."

"Thank you," she replied gratefully. "On Saturday, both my husband and I are going to take him to St Stephen's Green to feed the ducks."

Mrs Dillon smiled. "I'll put aside some crusts for him."

"Thank you."

She returned to the morning room, found Will fast asleep on the sofa and gently extracted the *Freeman's Journal* from his fingers. He needed to rest but he also had house calls to make so she decided to wake him in half an hour.

She went upstairs to the nursery where John was sitting on one of the new red rugs playing with the wooden elephant. Florrie was seated beside the fire knitting what looked like a scarf in brown wool. John smiled at her and Isobel got down on her knees on the rug beside him.

"Have you given Mr Elephant a name?" she asked and he shook his head.

"How about Alphonsus?"

She twisted around and Will gave them a grin from the doorway.

"Alphonsus the elephant is a bit of a mouthful," she said. "It might just have to be Effalump."

Will nodded, sat down on the rug and crossed his legs. "Mr Effalump Elephant is even more of a mouthful but let's ask John. So," he turned to the boy, "Effalump or Alphonsus?" John peered down at the elephant and shrugged his shoulders. "Effalump?" Will suggested and John nodded. "Effalump it is."

"I'm glad," Florrie spoke up from her chair beside the

fire. "I have an Uncle Alphonsus."

Isobel snorted a laugh and clapped a hand to her cheek. "Sorry, Florrie."

"No, don't be, Mrs Fitzgerald. It's an awful name and he hates it, too. Effalump is much better."

"As long as he is referred to by his full name." Will lifted John onto his lap. "Mr Effalump Elephant. Yes?" he asked and John looked up at him and nodded.

"We have some good news for you, John," she said and the boy turned to her. "Florrie has agreed to stay on as your nursery maid. Are you happy Florrie will be staying here in the nursery with you?" she asked and John nodded and smiled at Florrie then at her and lastly up at Will.

"Good." Will ruffled his hair. "Now, I must make some house calls, but I'll be back later to kiss you goodnight." She took John from him and he kissed them both before getting to his feet. "I'll see you later."

They retired early to bed that evening, and she exhaled a long relieved sigh that the day was over as she pulled back the bedcovers and reached under the pillows for her nightdress and Will's nightshirt.

"Can I kiss you?" he asked, taking the nightshirt from her. "I'm too tired to make love to you, I just want to kiss you."

"Anywhere in particular?"

"Your breasts," he replied, throwing his nightshirt onto one of the pale yellow bedroom chairs then reaching out and smoothing a thumb over one of her nipples. "Looking at Fred and Margaret at the cemetery, they may as well have been a hundred miles apart and will probably never share a bed again, while all I wanted to do was take you to bed, kiss you and try and forget all about today."

"Take me to bed, then," she said, throwing her nightdress on top of his nightshirt and he lifted her up and laid her down on the bed.

"I love you, Mrs Fitzgerald," he whispered, climbing onto the bed beside her and bending his head.

She stroked his hair as he licked and pulled at her nipples, thankful she could help him alleviate the horror and sadness of the past few days. Her hands slid down the back of his neck and she began to explore the muscles in his shoulders. They felt tense but she didn't want him to stop kissing her so she went back to stroking his hair as he rhythmically circled each nipple with his tongue before pulling gently at it with his lips. Her nipples were hard and sensitive and it wasn't long before she arched her back and moaned.

"Sorry," she said, running a thumb across his lips as he raised his head.

"Don't ever be sorry. I'm glad you're enjoying it, too." He yawned as he spoke and grimaced. "I'm worn out, but at the weekend I'll catch up on some sleep and we'll spend time with each other – and with John."

"The weekend," she agreed and pulled the bedcovers over them. "Sleep now. I hate seeing you look so tired."

They turned onto their sides and he eased her back against him, put an arm around her and cupped a breast. She felt him kiss her neck just below her ear and they settled.

Chapter Five

Will couldn't remember when he had last been this exhausted. It was a quarter to one on Friday afternoon, and he was seeing his final patient out of the practice house.

"My finals," he said aloud as he closed and locked the front door.

"What's that, Dr Fitzgerald?" Eva asked, hurrying out of the office.

"The last time I was this exhausted, I had just finished my finals," he told her and she gave him a sympathetic smile. "Thank you for all your hard work this week."

"Not at all, but I haven't been doing the work of two doctors."

"Dr Powell starts on Monday."

"I'll be here early to meet him and show him what's what. Now, go home to your wife."

"Thank you, Eva, but I have a few things to do here and then house calls to make before I can go home."

Five hours later, he found Isobel sitting on the garden bench in the dusk wrapped in a huge black shawl. She got up as he approached and kissed him.

"You look shattered."

"I am shattered," he admitted. "But this week is over, thank goodness, and on Monday I will gladly pass on some of Fred's patients to David."

"Only some?" she queried with a frown.

"I don't want to underestimate David but at the same time I want to break him in gently, so I went through the files of all Fred's patients and I allocated certain patients to David. I'll keep an eye on him and next Friday, we'll discuss how he's getting on. Father interrogated me every evening when I first started at the practice and I hated it, so I'll start with once a week and take it from there. Are you all right?" he asked suddenly and she nodded.

"Mother called this afternoon and we brought John out here for a while. After she left, I came back outside for a little time to myself, that's all. Dinner won't be long and when we've kissed John goodnight, you can fall asleep beside me on the sofa."

He gave her a thankful smile, she took his hand and they went inside. An hour later, they curled up on the sofa in the morning room. Accepting a cushion from her, he put it behind his head and she leant back against him with a book. He was so tired he didn't even see her open it.

He was woken by lips on his forehead and Isobel smiled down at him.

"It's eleven o'clock," she said softly. "We should go to bed."

He plodded up the stairs after her and she helped him to undress and to put on his nightshirt.

"Thank you," he murmured.

"You've had four hours sleep," she said as he got into bed. "I want you to get at least another eight."

"I will." He watched as she quickly let down her hair and plaited it before getting undressed and pulling her nightdress over her head. "This has been a horrible week. I'm so glad it's over."

"So am I." She got into the bed beside him. "I love you," she whispered and kissed his lips. "Now, sleep," she added, reaching across him and turning down the oil lamp.

Waking up and knowing he could simply go back to sleep was wonderful and he exhaled a contented sigh before kissing Isobel's shoulder and closing his eyes.

"Two more hours," she mumbled and he smiled.

"Yes, Mrs Fitzgerald."

When he opened his eyes again, Isobel leant over and kissed his lips.

"Feel better?" she asked.

"Much better. And I'm looking forward to spending more time with you and John. He is happy here, isn't he?"

"Yes. And he trusts you, me, and Florrie. That he still doesn't speak worries me a little but we just have to be patient."

After luncheon, they walked to St Stephen's Green and sat on a rug on the grass near the lake with John between them. Isobel opened the paper bag of crusts Mrs Dillon had supplied and John reached in and threw some towards the water. Three ducks swam towards them and Will watched John's enthralled expression as the ducks jumped out of the water and wolfed down the bread.

"Drop a piece there, John." He pointed to the grass just beyond their feet. "And we'll see if they'll come for it."

John reached into the bag and dropped the crust. One brave drake edged forward, snatched it and quickly waddled back to the lake. John grinned and clapped his hands and for a moment Will thought he was going to speak at last, but John merely pulled another crust from the bag and flung it at the other ducks. He met Isobel's eyes and she gave a little shrug.

"I really thought John was going to say something," he said when they returned to number 30.

"Patience." She smiled then turned as the morning room door opened and Alfie was shown in.

"I was in the gardens, making myself scarce, and I saw the three of you walk home so I thought I'd follow you."

"Is Mr Ellison is calling on Mother again?" Isobel asked. "Should I call, too?"

"What do you mean, again?" Will inquired before Alfie could reply.

"With all that's happened, I forgot to tell you that Mr Ellison appears to be courting Mother," Isobel told him.

"There's no 'appears' about it," Alfie added. "He calls to the house every few days."

"Has he spoken to you?"

"Mr Ellison doesn't need my permission to court Mother, Will."

"No, but has he?"

"No, he hasn't," Alfie replied. "But he knows that I know why he's calling. I also called to thank you for taking David on as locum, Will. He's looking forward to Monday."

"I'm looking forward to him starting, too. I dealt with all the patients myself last week. I don't want to have to do that again."

"When do you think Dr Simpson will return?"

Will didn't answer the question and Alfie flushed. "It's

none of my business. I'm sorry, Will."

"You and David must come to dinner soon," Isobel interjected brightly.

"That's very kind, but how, exactly?"

"We'll invite David and you will call at an agreed time and be 'persuaded' to stay to dinner," she said and Alfie mulled it over for a few moments before nodding.

When he had shown Alfie out, Will returned to the morning room and Isobel sat on the sofa making a helpless gesture with her hands.

"Someone needs to speak to Mr Ellison about him courting Mother so soon after Mr Henderson's death. If Alfie is reluctant to do it, then I will. On Monday."

James Ellison was showing a client out of his office as Isobel closed the law practice's front door behind her.

"Mrs Fitzgerald, good morning."

"Mr Ellison. Do you have a few minutes to spare?"

"I do. Come in."

They went into his wood panelled office, he shut the door and held a chair for her as she sat down.

"I'll come straight to the point, Mr Ellison," she said as he took his seat behind the large and plain mahogany desk. "What are your intentions towards my mother?"

He peered down at his hands for a moment and colour flooded his cheeks. "I admire your mother a great deal and I would very much like to court her."

"From what I have gathered, you already are. Mr Ellison, do I really have to remind you that it is only a couple of months since Mr Henderson died?"

Slowly, he raised his head. "No, you do not, Mrs

Fitzgerald, your mother said almost exactly the same thing to me. I am well aware we must be extremely circumspect and I will ensure that we are."

"Thank you," she replied gratefully.

"May I ask you something, Mrs Fitzgerald?" he asked.

"Yes, of course."

"How would you feel if I were to become your step-father?"

She stared at him for a moment. She barely knew anything about the solicitor and wondered how she should answer. "Mr Ellison," she began, deciding she needed to be cautious yet direct with him. "I knew Mr Henderson very little and, for reasons we now know all too well, he married my mother solely for companionship. I do not want to see my mother deceived and hurt again, so 'admiring' her is simply not good enough, I'm afraid."

Mr Ellison got up and went to the window. "I would not be marrying your mother simply for companionship," he said with his back to her. "I am not of the same persuasion Ronald was. I love your mother very deeply and she loves me equally deeply. Ours would be a marriage in the fullest sense of the word. Is that good enough for you, Mrs Fitzgerald?" he asked, turning back to her.

"Yes, it is," she replied. "Thank you for speaking so frankly."

"Your mother has told me of what she, you, and Alfie went through with your father. Let me assure you that I am not a violent man. Nor am I in pursuit of her money or property. I own the house I reside in and I believe myself to be well-off. I am fifty-five years old. My wife died of cancer almost six years ago and our son – our only child – died of consumption when he was fourteen years old." His voice shook as he spoke and she felt a sharp stab of pity for him.

"I'm very sorry to hear that."

"Thank you. When my wife died, I threw myself into my work and I expected to be alone for the rest of my life. Then, Ronald introduced me to your mother shortly before their marriage." He gave a little shrug. "I fell in love with her instantly. When Ronald died, I had to put my feelings aside and assist his widow and try and leave it at that but I found I just couldn't keep away."

"Alfie noticed how often you were calling to the house," she said as he sat down again. "And I had to come and speak with you as my mother has been through so much and you would be her third husband." Reaching across the desk she squeezed his hand. "Mr Ellison, I would be delighted to have you as a step-father."

"I am very relieved to hear that, Mrs Fitzgerald," he said and they exchanged a smile.

"Please call me Isobel."

"And I am James," he said and she nodded. "When a year has passed since Ronald's death, I will marry your mother."

When Will saw his final patient out of the practice house and went back upstairs, Fred's surgery door opened. Will stared for a moment as David's bearded face peered out at him. How long would it take for him not to expect his friend to be standing there?

"So?" He mustered up a smile. "How was it?"

"Very positive," David replied. "No-one commented on my age or possible lack of experience."

"I'm glad. Well—" Returning to his surgery, he retrieved

his medical bag from the floor behind his desk. "I must go. I'm glad to have you here, David."

"Thank you, Will."

Isobel was coming down the stairs when he arrived back at number 30 for luncheon.

"Did you go and see Mr Ellison?" he asked as he put his medical bag on the hall table then hung up his hat and overcoat.

"Yes, I did," she replied, taking his hand and leading him into the breakfast room. "I'll tell you while we eat."

He put his soup spoon down in the bowl with a clang when she finished speaking. "Mr Ellison's been in love with your mother all along?" he asked incredulously.

"Yes. And when Mr Henderson has been dead a year James will marry Mother."

"He asked you to call him James?" he asked and she nodded.

"After I asked him to call me Isobel."

"So it was quite a frank discussion?"

"Yes, and it had to be, Will. Luckily, he's well aware he will be Mother's third husband and there is a need to be cautious. What time is your appointment with him?"

"Two o'clock, so I need to finish this soup and leave, I'm afraid."

Three-quarters of an hour later, Will was sitting down in Mr Ellison's office, dreading what he was about to do but knowing it had to be done.

"Isobel has just told me of your discussion," he said and the solicitor smiled.

"It's been a long time since I've had to explain myself in such detail but it's natural Isobel is concerned for her mother and I was glad to do it."

"Well, as I will be your step-son-in-law in the not too distant future, please call me Will?"

"James." They shook hands and Will watched as the solicitor extracted some papers from a cardboard file. "You need to sign here and here." James pointed to the bottom of two documents then passed over a pot of ink and a pen.

Will signed the documents thus ending his brief partnership with Fred and sat back sadly in his chair.

"How are Dr Simpson and his wife?" James asked, blotting the signatures before returning the documents to the file and placing the file in a desk drawer.

"Bearing up as best they can," Will replied. "Fred is taking up a position at the *Journal of Irish Medicine* today."

"And have you found a replacement for him?"

"A locum. Dr David Powell."

"I wish you both well."

"Thank you."

James nodded and Will knew the solicitor understood perfectly well that the death of baby Nicholas wasn't the real reason for Fred to leave the practice. Babies died all the time and Will silently thanked James for not pursuing the subject.

"How is young John?" James asked.

"He is settling into number 30 very well. He's still not speaking, though. We must be patient."

On his way home after completing house calls, Will called to number 67 and found his mother in the hall pulling on a pair of black gloves and preparing to go out.

"Oh, Will, I was just about to call to number 30 to see John."

He smiled and kissed her cheek. "John and Isobel will be delighted to see you. I went to see James Ellison this afternoon," he told her. "My partnership with Fred is over," he added, hearing his voice shake.

"I'm so sorry," she said. "Your father called at Ely Place Upper and accompanied Fred to the *Journal* this morning."

"That was good of him. I'll call to the *Journal* and walk Fred home this evening."

"How is Margaret?"

"She is recovering physically from the caesarean but whether she will ever fully recover mentally from the loss of baby Nicholas…" He tailed off and his mother nodded.

"I will call on Margaret in the next few days."

"Thank you, Mother," he replied. "Isobel says she will call on her, too, and Father and I will keep an eye on Fred."

"Not many husbands would give up a partnership in a prospering medical practice to spend more time with their wife," she added. "Even for a wife whose unborn baby died and who will never carry another."

"You're right," Will replied simply, both answering his mother and confirming her suspicions that there was much more to the story behind Fred's departure from the practice than what was being put about.

"How was the locum's first surgery?" his mother asked, changing the subject brightly as they left the house. "Do forgive me, I don't know his name."

"David Powell," Will told her, taking her arm. "He says very well. We'll discuss his first week on Friday—"

"Unlike your father, who cross-examined you each evening when you first started at the practice," she said and he grimaced.

"Yes. I certainly don't want to put David through that ordeal."

At number 30, Mary was sent upstairs to the nursery to ask Mrs Fitzgerald and Master John to come downstairs to the morning room. His mother's face beamed with delight when Isobel came in with John holding her hand.

"Your grandmother is here to see you," Isobel told the little boy and he grinned at her. "How are you, Sarah?"

"I'm very well, thank you, and how is this young man?"

Will picked John up, sat him on his grandmother's lap, and she kissed both his cheeks. "John has two new sets of clothes and a pair of new boots and he is enjoying playing with Mr Effalump Elephant."

"Good gracious me, such a name."

"Alfie couldn't pronounce elephant when he was little," Isobel explained. "John loves Mr Effalump Elephant. Don't you, John?"

John replied with a slow nod and his grandmother stroked his cheek with a forefinger. "Your father's favourite toys were his soldiers. You must come to number 67 and we'll get them out and see if you like them, too."

John looked up at Isobel for approval. She smiled and he did the same.

An hour later, Will escorted his mother back to Merrion Square before continuing on to the offices of the *Journal of Irish Medicine* on Hume Street. His father was in the hall, replacing a book on a shelf and nodded to him as he closed the front door and hung his hat on the stand.

"How's Fred?" Will asked in a low voice. "I thought I'd accompany him home."

"He's looking through some past editions to get a feel of the *Journal*. We lunched at the Trinity Club and he was quiet, but leaving practising medicine behind is a huge step."

"Yes, it is. Which office is he in?"

"It's just along here."

Will followed his father along the hall and waited as he knocked briefly at a door to their right before opening it. His father's sharp intake of breath made Will peer over his shoulder.

"No." Pushing his father to one side, Will ran into the office where Fred was slumped in his chair, a syringe and an empty vial of morphine on the desk in front of him. Will pulled open Fred's black cravat and took it and his collar off. "He's not breathing."

Hauling Fred from the chair and lying him down on the floor on the faded floral rug, Will began to try and resuscitate him, pumping his chest and blowing air into his lungs until he felt hands on his shoulders.

"Will, stop." His father felt Fred's neck for a pulse. "He's gone."

"No—" Will attempted to pump Fred's chest again before his father dragged him away and he found himself sitting on his behind in the middle of the floor gasping for breath.

"He's dead," his father told him and closed the office door.

"Did you do this?" Will demanded and his father bent and grabbed Will's cravat with one hand while clenching his other hand into a fist. Will braced himself but, instead of punching him, his father let him go and he fell onto the floor on his back.

"No, I did not do this," his father replied tightly. "What happened with Duncan was exceptional. Fred could have had years of being asymptomatic ahead of him."

"I know that. Christ," he whispered, clutching his head.

"Will, listen to me," his father commanded. "Were you Fred's doctor?"

Will lowered his hands and peered up at him, struggling to think clearly. "I had suggested to Fred that I attend to him and Margaret but he hadn't given me a reply. I was going to ask him again today."

"So, how do you want to deal with this?"

"Deal..?" Will glanced from his father to Fred then up to his father again. "I don't—"

"Do you want to get the coroner involved? Have to testify at a public inquest? Have everyone know Fred was a syphilitic? Have him buried at night with no religious ceremony like all other suicides?"

Will shuddered at the prospect. "No, of course not, but—"

"Then, Fred's cause of death will be a heart attack and Fred will be remembered with dignity," his father concluded quietly. "Agreed?"

"But Fred's... He was only thirty-one..."

"Are we agreed, Will?"

Will stared up at his father. "We'll never get away with it."

"We will. I'll go and speak to John Dalton immediately."

"Father?" Will called after him as he went to the door. "No-one is going to believe Fred died of a heart attack."

"What do you know of Fred's grandfather?" his father asked.

"Little or nothing," Will admitted. "He died long before Fred or I were born."

"That's right. Of a heart attack aged thirty-six. He

dropped dead on the pavement right outside the College of Surgeons and the incident was reported on in most of the newspapers. I'm sure the staff in the National Library will be happy to assist you if you wish to do some research."

Will didn't reply to that but struggled to his feet instead. "Is there anyone else here?" he asked as he swayed, feeling light-headed, and had to grab the desk to steady himself.

"No. I was about to suggest to Fred that we leave when you arrived. I'll try and be as quick as I can at Daltons," he said, peering past Will, before going to the desk and picking up the syringe and the vial of morphine then leaving the office.

Will took a few deep breaths then crouched down beside Fred and searched his pockets. Apart from Fred's wallet in the frock coat's inside pocket and a handkerchief in a trouser pocket, they were empty. Will went back to the desk and opened the drawers but all they contained were sheets of headed notepaper, envelopes, a pen and a bottle of ink and some old copies of the *Journal*.

Closing the drawers, he sat down but got up a moment later and returned to Fred. Crouching down again, Will pushed up the left arm of Fred's frock coat, undid the cufflink then slid the shirt sleeve up. There was a faint mark at the crook of Fred's elbow but it was only noticeable if someone was actually looking for it. Will pulled down the shirt sleeve and fastened the cufflink before pulling down the arm of the frock coat.

"I would have done my absolute best for you, you bloody fool," he said, his voice hoarse with emotion. "Why the fuck didn't you let me help you?"

Exhaling a shaking breath, he fought to contain himself.

There would be time to cry later. He was going to have to lie to everyone first. Except for Isobel. He couldn't lie to her. But what about Margaret? Would she believe Fred died of a heart attack? How would she react? Would she be hysterical? Or would she be furious at being left alone to her fate? Either way, he needed a woman to be present when he would break the news.

Leaving the office, he straightened his black cravat and walked unsteadily along the hall before opening the front door and going out onto the steps. A small boy wearing neither coat nor boots was sitting on the kerb about fifty yards along the street in the direction of St Stephen's Green. Will waved at him but the boy was looking the other way. Raising his fingers to his lips and hoping he still could, Will whistled loudly, the boy turned and Will beckoned the boy to come to him.

"Want to earn yourself a shilling?" he asked as the boy approached.

"I do."

"I want you to go to number 30 Fitzwilliam Square. Go to the front door and ask for Isobel Fitzgerald and bring her here to the offices of the *Journal of Irish Medicine* at once. Tell her Will has sent for her. Have you got that?"

"Yes, sir."

"Good lad."

The boy ran off and Will glanced up and down the street but there was no sign of his father. This was awful. How long was his father going to be?

Isobel looked at the clock on the morning room mantelpiece. It was a quarter past six, she was starving and the steak and kidney pie Mrs Dillon had made for dinner was drying out in the oven. Where on earth was Will? It couldn't take this long to walk his mother and then Fred home.

She got up from the sofa as the door opened, expecting it to be Will but, instead, Mary came in.

"There's a boy at the front door asking for you, Mrs Fitzgerald."

"Thank you, Mary." She went to the front door and found a barefoot boy of about eight or nine years old on the steps. "I'm Mrs Fitzgerald."

"Isobel Fitzgerald?"

"Yes."

"You're to come with me to the offices of the *Journal of Irish Medicine.* Will's sent for you."

Has his father been taken ill, she wondered, but nodded. "Let me put on my coat and hat."

Ten minutes later, she was knocking at the front door to the *Journal* offices. It opened, and an agitated Will stared first at her and then down at the boy. Even in the unforgiving light from a nearby gas lamp Will looked terrible. His face was devoid of all colour and sweat was glistening on his upper lip. Her heart began to thump anxiously. What had happened here?

"Thank you for being so quick." He passed the boy a coin then pulled her inside and closed the door.

"Is it your father?" she asked and he shook his head.

"It's Fred. He's killed himself." She staggered back a couple of steps, suddenly feeling faint with shock and Will quickly reached for her shoulders to steady her. "Isobel?"

"I'm fine," she lied. "How?"

"An overdose of morphine. My father says he had no hand in it," he added before she wondered if she should ask. "Isobel, Father and I have agreed to make it look as though Fred suffered a heart attack."

"But how? Fred's the same age as you."

"There's a history of heart disease in the Simpson family. Fred's grandfather died of a heart attack aged only thirty-six. This is the only way – you know how suicides are treated – we can't allow Fred's syphilis to become common knowledge at an inquest."

"No, but what are you going to tell Margaret?" she asked and grabbed his hands as he grimaced. "You're going to lie to her as well, aren't you? Oh, God, Will, no – you can't lie to Margaret—"

"Do you want to tell Margaret that her husband has killed himself and has left her alone, childless and infected with syphilis?" he demanded.

Isobel raised a shaking hand to her forehead. "No," she had to admit. "Would you like me to be present when you tell her?"

"Yes, I would, please," he replied and she nodded, peering past him down the hall lined with floor to ceiling bookcases and lit by four gas lamps.

"Where is Fred?"

"In his office. My father has gone to speak to and fetch John Dalton. I hope they aren't much longer, Fred's just lying on the floor…"

She squeezed his hands, feeling him trembling. "Let's go and sit with Fred."

"Would you not rather wait in Father's office?" he asked as they walked along the hall and she shook her head.

"Let's sit with Fred," she said, hearing a key being inserted into a lock and she continued on while Will went back to the front door.

She halted at the doorway of a small office at the far end of the hall. Fred lay on the floor on a faded floral rug. Hugh Lombard, lying on his back on the drawing room floor at number 30, flashed in front of her eyes and she had to force herself to blink and tear her eyes away from Fred, spotting his collar and black cravat on the desk.

"Father, Mr Dalton." Will greeted Dr Fitzgerald senior and the undertaker with unmistakable relief in his voice and she glanced at the front door as the two men came inside. "I sent for Isobel," Will added and she stepped away from the office doorway. "To be on hand when I break the news to Margaret."

"Isobel." Will's father nodded to her and Mr Dalton did likewise as they passed her.

"Dr Fitzgerald. Mr Dalton."

The three men went into the office and a couple of minutes later Will and Mr Dalton went outside to a hearse. Isobel stood back as they returned, carrying an oak coffin into the office, and the door was closed.

She went to the stairs and sat on the steps to wait, tears of sorrow at the loss of Fred coupled with tears of rage at Fred for thinking only of himself stinging her eyes. This was the second time Will had been taken for granted and expected to pick up the pieces. As well as that, to conceal the true cause of Fred's death was a huge risk to take. If it was discovered Fred had committed suicide, an illegal act in the eyes of the law, Will could be struck off the medical register and face criminal charges. You must not cry, she ordered herself, blinking the tears away. This isn't the time or the place. For now, you must be strong for Will – and lie to everyone about how Fred died.

When the office door opened again, she reached for the banister rail and hauled herself to her feet as Will and Mr Dalton carried the coffin outside to the hearse.

"Fred will be taken to Daltons' mortuary chapel," Will's father told her. "Now, Margaret must be told."

It took less than two minutes for the three of them to walk from Hume Street to number 1 Ely Place Upper. They were shown into the stifling morning room where Margaret slowly and carefully got to her feet.

"Is Fred not with you?" she asked, walking towards the door before halting abruptly and turning to them in alarm as it was closed. "Why isn't Fred with you?"

Isobel went to her and clasped her hands. "Shall we sit down?" she suggested softly. "Will has something to tell you."

Margaret allowed herself to be guided back to the sofa and they sat side by side as Will came forward and got down on one knee in front of them. His movements were stiff and unnatural, as he held the heartbreak inside, not allowing himself to relax for fear it would bring forth a flood of emotion. Fighting back more tears, it was all Isobel could do not to grab his hand and run from the room with him.

"I went to the *Journal* offices this evening to see how Fred had spent his first day and to walk him home. I met Father in the hall and we went to Fred's office. Margaret." Will laid a hand on top of hers. "When we went inside, Fred was dead."

"Dead?" Margaret whispered, giving him a blank stare.

"It was his heart," Will added softly.

"But – but – he was too young for his heart…"

"Fred's grandfather died young of a heart attack."

"Oh." Margaret frowned. "Yes. Someone told me that."

"Margaret," Will's father spoke for the first time. "May we fetch your mother?"

She shook her head. "Mother is at Aunt Abigail's home in Co Wicklow."

"Your sister and brother-in-law, then?"

"Yes. Please."

"I'll have Elizabeth and Gordon sent for." Will's father went out to the hall.

"It was Fred's heart?" Margaret looked back at Will. "Not the—?"

"No, it wasn't that," Will replied. "I tried to revive him but he was gone. I'm so sorry."

"You've been so good to us, Will."

For a moment, Isobel thought Will's barely-contained composure was going to crack but he gave Margaret a weak smile.

"Fred was my oldest friend. I had suggested to him that I attend to you both. That offer still stands with you."

"Thank you, Will. Where is Fred now?"

"My father is friends with John Dalton of Dalton and Sons the undertakers and he went to see him," Will explained. "Fred has been taken to Daltons' mortuary chapel."

"Daltons buried my father. I remember there was snow the day of the funeral and it took an age to get to the cemetery—" Margaret peered over Will's shoulder as his father came back into the morning room. "Fred's mother must be informed."

"I'll go to Rutland Square and tell Maria," he said and Will twisted around.

"Are you sure?"

"Yes." Dr Fitzgerald senior made an almost imperceptible jerk of his head towards the hall and Will got up and followed him from the room.

"Would you like some sherry?" Isobel asked Margaret. "Or, perhaps, something stronger?"

"I don't know," Margaret murmured, closing her brown eyes for a moment. "I can't believe it. I keep expecting Fred to come in at any moment. Do you think he suffered?"

"From what I gather, it would have been very quick," Isobel replied.

"I'm glad. What am I going to do now, Isobel?"

"You need to take one day at a time," she told her. "And remember what Will told you – that he will attend to you – if you so wish."

"Yes. You really don't have to stay—"

"I will stay with you until your sister and brother-in-law arrive," she assured her as the door opened and Will returned.

Half an hour passed until she heard voices in the hall and she and Will got to their feet as a blonde woman a few years older than Margaret was shown in.

"Oh, Margaret," she began, tears spilling down her cheeks while her husband followed her into the room and the door was closed behind him.

"Elizabeth." Margaret held out her hands. "Thank you for coming so quickly. This is Dr Will Fitzgerald and his wife, Isobel," she added, nodding to them.

Elizabeth glanced briefly at them both before brushing

past Isobel without a word, sitting down on the sofa in the space Isobel had just vacated and clasping her sister's hands.

"Of course, I came quickly, you silly thing."

"Margaret," Will called softly. "Isobel and I are leaving now."

"Thank you, Will. And you, too, Isobel." Margaret gave him and then her wobbly smiles.

Will exchanged nods with Gordon Higginson, they went out to the hall and Will closed the door.

"There was no need for Elizabeth to be so rude to you," he said, lifting her hand and kissing it.

"It doesn't matter, Will. Let's go home."

"We can't – not just yet. I promised Father I'd go to number 67 and break the news to Mother and explain where he is."

"Oh." Her stomach rumbled. "Yes, of course."

They walked hand-in-hand to Merrion Square and Tess showed them into the morning room. Will's mother laid a book beside her on the sofa then got to her feet.

"Is your father not with you, Will?"

"No, and he may not be home for some time."

"Why? What's wrong? Did you not call to the *Journal* offices?"

"Mother." Will clasped her shoulders and inhaled and exhaled a deep breath. "It's Fred. He's dead."

Sarah stared up at him in disbelief. "Dead? Fred? What happened?"

"A heart attack."

"Oh, Will—"

"Isobel and I stayed with Margaret until her sister and brother-in-law arrived. Father has gone to break the news to

Maria Simpson. I don't know how long he'll be."

"Oh, Will," his mother began again. "Fred was so young…"

"Yes, he was."

"How is Margaret?"

"It hasn't sunk in yet."

"Oh, this is awful." Sarah shook her head. "Where did it happen?"

"In his office at the *Journal*. Father and I found him. I tried to resuscitate him but…" He tailed off and his mother reached up and kissed his cheek.

"Fred's grandfather died of a heart attack, too. He was no age at all."

"Thirty-six."

"I'm so sorry, Will."

He nodded and turned away from her, his stomach rumbling loudly. "Excuse me," he murmured.

"You haven't eaten." His mother went to the rope and rang for a maid. "I went ahead with dinner alone and—"

"No dinner for me," Will told her. "Thank you."

"Could we have some tea, please?" Isobel spoke up. "And perhaps some sandwiches, too?" she added, meeting Sarah's brown eyes directly before looking at Will, telling her silently that Will needed to eat something whether he liked it or not. "Will's father will be hungry when he comes home."

"Yes, he will. Where is Fred now?"

"Daltons," Will replied and his mother nodded as the door opened and Tess came in.

"Some tea and sandwiches please, Tess."

"Yes, Mrs Fitzgerald," she said and went out.

When the tea and sandwiches arrived, Isobel put two tiny

triangular ham sandwiches on a plate and passed it to Will. He nibbled at one sandwich before dropping the plate onto the floral rug, racing across the room to the writing desk and vomiting into the wastepaper basket.

"Oh, God," he gasped as Isobel and his mother reached him. "I'm so sorry. I didn't know what else to use."

"It doesn't matter," Sarah soothed, ringing for a maid.

"Could you manage a little tea?" she asked softly, running a hand up and down his back and feeling him tremble.

"I don't know. I'd better not."

"Maybe we should go home?" she suggested but he shook his head.

"No, I want to wait until Father returns."

"Come and sit down, then," she said, leading him back to the sofa. He sat beside her still trembling and she caressed his hands.

When Tess came in, Sarah passed her the waste paper basket and asked for some boiled water.

"You need to drink something," his mother told Will as Tess went out. "And it will be easy on your stomach."

"Yes. Thank you. You haven't eaten, Isobel." He reached down to the rug for his plate and passed it to her. "Finish these sandwiches."

He looked up and Isobel followed his gaze as his father came into the room and closed the door behind him. Dr Fitzgerald senior looked as awful as Will and his wife went to him and kissed his cheek.

"Come and have some tea," Sarah said softly and he sat in his armchair.

"I escorted Maria to Ely Place Upper and she's now with

Margaret, Elizabeth and Gordon. Margaret's mother is being sent for." He sighed and ran a hand across his jaw. "To say Maria is devastated would be an understatement. I'll call on them first thing in the morning."

"How did Margaret seem?" Will asked.

"I think it will take a little time for Fred's death to sink in."

"If she needs me, I will be at the practice house in the morning. Isobel, the practice can't be run by two locums," he added as she opened her mouth to protest. "As well as that, I want to break the news to Eva myself."

"Certify Fred's death and I'll call to the practice house for the certificate so his death can be registered and the funeral arranged," Will's father told him and Will nodded.

"Ah, good." Sarah cleared a space on the side table as Tess returned with a teapot and another cup and saucer. "Thank you, Tess." She poured Will a cup of boiled water and passed it to him before re-taking her seat in the other armchair.

"Boiled water?" his father inquired.

"I vomited," Will explained. "I'm afraid I made rather a mess of the waste paper basket."

His father waved a hand dismissively. "Drink that and go home to bed, it's late. We'll talk again tomorrow."

"Father, I'll send Jerry a telegram in the morning but if he can't attend the funeral, I would like to be one of the pallbearers."

"I would, too. I will mention it to Margaret. What about the eulogy?" his father added and she felt Will tense. "Shall I do it?"

"No," he replied resolutely and she stared at him in dismay. "I will do it."

"I'll read a lesson, then," his father said and he nodded. "Good."

"Drink some water." She nudged him gently and he raised the cup to his lips while she ate one of the ham sandwiches. She was relieved to see him finish the water and put the cup and saucer on the table. "Let's go home."

At the front door, his mother took his face in her hands. "I am so sorry, Will. I know how much you loved Fred."

All he could do was nod, kiss her cheek and shake his father's hand.

They walked home in silence with an arm around each other's waists. The gas lamps in the hall and on the upstairs landings had been left lit but the rest of the house was in darkness. They hung their hats and coats on the stand then went into the morning room and she lit the oil lamp while Will sat on the sofa with his head in his hands. She dropped to her knees and held him tightly as the tears finally came and he wept great big gasping sobs into her chest. Stroking his hair, she let him cry until he sniffed and raised his head. His eyes were red and swollen and she gently kissed each of them.

"I'm going to miss Fred so much," he croaked.

"I know. We all will."

"I never thought he would do something like this — I should have—"

"No," she interrupted firmly, clasping his wet cheeks in her hands. "You did everything you possibly could for Fred. You couldn't mind him like a child. He was a grown man and a doctor. You have absolutely nothing to berate yourself for."

"At least he didn't do it at home. Imagine if Margaret

had found him. We had to lie about the cause of death – we had to."

"I know. And, perhaps, that is why Fred didn't do it at home."

Will stared at her for a moment before nodding. "Perhaps, but who knows what was going through his mind."

"Try not to think about that," she said, pulling his handkerchief from his trouser pocket and passing it to him. "Let me help you as much as I can."

"I have to send Jerry a telegram. I wouldn't want to hear it in a telegram, but he must be told Fred has died." He exhaled a long breath then wiped his eyes. "And I must call to Jerry's mother and tell her. That will have to be tomorrow afternoon."

"In the morning," she continued. "Would you like me to come to the practice house with you for when you tell Eva?"

"There's no need, but thank you for offering. I'll go early and break the news to her and if she wishes to go home, David and I will manage. But if you could call on my mother, please? She was very fond of Fred. And I will call there for you on my way home for luncheon."

"I will."

"Thank you for being there this evening. It was horrendous."

"Are you absolutely sure you want to deliver the eulogy?" she asked. "It will be awful for you."

"I know, but if I don't do it, I'll always regret it. I'll write it all down and if you could keep the copy in your handbag..? Just in case..? I'd rather not have to unbutton my frock coat and pull it out of the inside pocket in front of everyone."

"Of course I will," she replied softly. "And you will tell

me if there is anything else I can do?" she asked and he nodded. "Good. Let's go to bed."

She got to her feet a little too quickly and multi-coloured dots danced in front of her eyes, the room spun around and Will just managed to catch her before she fell. He sat her down on the sofa and knelt where she had just been.

"Isobel?" He held her face in his hands. "What is it?"

"It's nothing—"

"It is not nothing. You almost fainted."

"Oh, Will, I didn't want to tell you yet."

"Tell me what?"

"I'm pregnant," she whispered and his eyes widened in shock.

"You've missed a monthly?"

"No, I haven't missed one." She grimaced and fought to express herself clearly. "What I mean is, I haven't had a monthly since the miscarriage. Will, I've been pregnant all along. My mother was a twin but her brother died at a year old. It's my belief that I was carrying twins but one died, I miscarried it and this baby is the surviving twin."

"I need to examine you," he said as her stomach rumbled loudly. "But you must eat first. I'll make you a sandwich – a proper sandwich." He kissed her forehead and helped her to lie down on the sofa. "I won't be long."

Cursing the bout of dizziness, she stared at the shadows cast by the oil lamp onto the ceiling while he left the room and her stomach rumbled again.

He returned with two plates of sandwiches and she sat up slowly as he passed one plate to her before sitting beside her with the other.

"Thank you." She wolfed down the first half of the ham

sandwich but ate the second in a more ladylike manner before wiping her mouth and putting the plate on a side table. "It was delicious."

"I enjoyed mine, too. My stomach had started to rumble as well. I can make you another?" he offered, putting his empty plate on top of hers.

"No, one sandwich was enough, thank you."

"Good." He opened the door then turned down the oil lamp. "Let's go upstairs."

He extinguished the gas lamps in the hall and on the first and second-floor landings, and they went to their bedroom. He lit the oil lamp on his bedside table, helped her to undress and his jaw dropped when he saw her stomach.

"What is it, Will?" she demanded, her heart racing. "Is there something wrong?"

"You are still pregnant," he said, his voice shaking. "I should have noticed."

"You've been exhausted—"

"You're my wife, Isobel, I should have noticed you are pregnant," he added, his voice rising, and he blew out his cheeks in an effort to calm himself. "Have you felt any movement?" he asked and she nodded.

"Yes. A fluttering every now and again. Is there something wrong?" she demanded again. "Should I be bigger than this?" she added, laying a hand on her stomach. There was no pregnancy belly yet, merely a roundness, and she fought back tears.

"No, not at just over three months. This." He laid a hand over hers. "This is completely normal."

"Are you pleased?" she asked tentatively. "With what happened to Fred and Margaret's baby and now Fred's death… I wanted to wait and tell you at a more appropriate time."

"I want to cry again," he told her, clasping her face in his hands, his voice thick with emotion. "But because you've made me so very happy and because Fred will now never know I'm going to be a father. It's…" He tailed off struggling to find a suitable word and kissed her lips instead. "Thank you."

Chapter Six

Will opened his eyes, reached out and stroked Isobel's hair. Bittersweet was the word he'd been unable to think of. What was it Fred had said last year following Duncan's death about Margaret's pregnancy? Something along the lines of he had just lost a parent but he was gaining a child. Will sighed. In the space of a few hours yesterday, he had lost his oldest friend but he had learnt of the new life growing inside Isobel.

Sliding a hand down her body, he stopped when he reached her stomach and laid it over the roundness. This was the child they feared they would never have and he kissed Isobel's temple as she stirred and raised herself onto an elbow.

"Hungry?" she murmured.

"Yes, I am. Are you?"

"Some porridge would be nice," she said.

"Good. And, Isobel, if I'm late for any meal – eat – don't wait for me. You need nourishment – now more than ever."

Making sure Isobel, like him, ate a bowl of porridge, two triangles of toast and marmalade and drank a cup of coffee, he followed her into the hall. She helped him on with his overcoat, passed him his hat and medical bag and he kissed her goodbye before kissing his hand and placing it over her stomach.

After deliberating at the telegraph office and reluctantly concluding that it was impossible to break the news gently to Jerry in a telegram, he supplied only the barest details of Fred's death.

He arrived at the practice house just before Eva and held the front door open for her. She unlocked the office door, they went into the shelf-lined room and hung up their hats and coats.

"Could you come and sit down please, Eva?" he asked.

"Yes, of course."

He held the chair behind the desk for her as she sat down before carrying a second chair from a corner of the room and sitting beside her.

"Eva, I'm afraid I have some terrible news about Dr Simpson," he began. "Fred died yesterday evening," he went on softly and Eva clapped a hand to her mouth. "He had a heart attack in his office at the *Journal*."

"Oh, Dr Fitzgerald…"

"I can hardly believe it," he said truthfully and her face crumpled in sympathy.

"You shouldn't have come in today, Dr Fitzgerald."

"I couldn't allow Dr Powell to deal with all the patients. It nearly killed me last week." He winced at his bad choice of words and she reached out and patted his hands. "I don't know when the funeral is yet but we will cancel surgery on that day."

"Yes. Oh, Dr Fitzgerald, I'm so shocked."

"There is a history of heart disease in the Simpson family."

"Yes." She frowned. "Yes, there is. Dr Simpson's grandfather died young. Oh, it's so cruel, his poor wife…"

"Would you like to go home?" he asked gently and she shook her head.

"You're very kind to ask, but I would prefer to stay. We did have our ups and downs but I would like to attend Dr Simpson's funeral."

"Of course. My father is calling to Ely Place Upper this morning and should learn when it will take place."

"How is your father?" she asked.

"Stunned. He broke the news to Fred's mother. He's known her a long time but to have to tell a mother her only child has died…"

"Poor Mrs Simpson. Oh, it's so awful."

"Yes, it is. If anyone asks, please tell them I will only be able to do the most urgent house calls today."

"I will. Oh." She half-turned as they heard the front door open and close. "There's Dr Powell."

"I must tell him," he said and they got up. "I also need to certify Fred's death and my father is to call for the certificate. Eva," he added. "If at any time you would prefer to go home, just tell either myself or Dr Powell."

"Thank you, Dr Fitzgerald."

He went upstairs, knocked and went into – he mustn't call it Fred's surgery anymore – and found David opening the window to a gap of about an inch. He sighed. How many people had he broken the news to now? David turned to him with a smile which quickly faded.

"What's wrong?"

"Fred Simpson died of a heart attack yesterday evening."

David's dark eyes widened. "Will, you shouldn't be here."

"You can't deal with all the patients yourself and we will cancel surgery the day of the funeral."

"I can't believe it. A heart attack? He was only a few years older than I am."

"Fred was the same age as me – thirty-one since December. I've told Eva and asked her if she would rather go home but she says she would prefer to stay. We'll both keep an eye on her, yes?"

"Yes, of course. Gosh, Will." David shook his hand. "I'm sorry."

"Thank you. We'll muddle through as best we can this morning and I'm only doing urgent house calls this afternoon. I've sent a telegram to Jerry Hawley - he, Fred and I were best friends – but I need to go to Kingstown and break the news to his mother. She was very fond of Fred – everyone was very fond of Fred." He grimaced. "Well, we'd better get on."

Sitting down at the desk in his surgery with a medical certificate, he stared at it for a few moments before blinking away tears and opening a bottle of ink. Picking up his pen and dipping the nib into the ink, he filled in the details but put the pen down without signing the certificate. He had never falsified the cause of death on a medical certificate before but this was for Fred. Picking up the pen again, he added his signature and blotted it before placing the certificate in an envelope.

He brought the envelope downstairs to the office and left it with Eva then forced Fred's death from his mind and escorted his first patient upstairs to his surgery.

Three hours later, he closed and locked the front door and followed Eva and David into the office.

"Thank you for being such a wonderful practice secretary." He lifted Eva's hand and kissed it. "It was a terrible shock and you coped admirably. Did my father call for the medical certificate?"

"Yes, he did."

"Good. Did anyone mention Fred, David?"

"No, nobody did."

"His death notice will probably be in one or more of the evening newspapers and in tomorrow's *Irish Times*. We may have some callers."

He walked to number 67 and was shown into the morning room. His mother was seated on the sofa as usual and Isobel got up from one of the armchairs and kissed his cheek.

"Are you hungry?" she asked.

"A little. Is Father home?"

"Not yet," his mother replied.

"The best time to find me at home will be this evening. I am doing only the most urgent house calls this afternoon and then I must break the news to Mrs Hawley."

"Please tell her I will call on her in the next few days."

"I'll tell her. Well." He bent and kissed his mother's cheek. "Isobel and I must go home for luncheon. We both need to eat."

To Isobel's relief, Will ate a hearty luncheon before leaving the house. She left the house herself a few minutes later, walked around the gardens to number 55, and was shown into the morning room.

"Alfie." Her brother was alone in the room, seated at the writing desk, and he twisted around to look at her. "Where's Mother?"

"Out to luncheon with a new acquaintance." He put his pen down and got to his feet. "You look flustered."

"Fred Simpson died yesterday evening," she told him and Alfie's eyes bulged. "A heart attack."

"A heart attack? At his age? Good God, I don't know what to say."

"When you see David, could you ask him to please keep an eye on Will? To say he's distraught doesn't even begin to describe..." She tailed off and sighed.

"Yes, of course," he replied. "I'm meeting David this evening. When is Fred's funeral?"

"We don't know yet, but I hope Will's friend, Jerry, can come over from London. Will needs to talk about Fred with someone who knew him longer than I did."

"Please give Will my condolences?"

"I will. And, Alfie, while we're alone – and please don't be angry – I need to tell you I went to see James Ellison and I asked him about Mother."

Alfie's eyebrows rose. "Oh?"

"We had quite a frank conversation and the upshot is that James loves her and he's loved her ever since Mr Henderson introduced her to him. And when the first anniversary of Mr Henderson's death has passed, James will marry Mother."

"James?" Alfie echoed. "You're on first name terms with him? It must have been a very frank conversation."

"I had to question him, Alfie. He will be her third husband."

"I know, and I'm not angry. I just wasn't sure if I should interfere. Have you spoken to Mother about it?"

She shook her head. "I haven't had a chance. But I will."

"How's John?"

"Very well. But still not talking."

"Do you think he will?"

"I don't know," she replied simply.

"I'll come to number 30 when I get a chance."

"How's the studying going?" she asked, looking past him at the textbooks stacked on the writing desk and at the open notebook beside them.

"Very well. It's hard work, but I love it."

"I'm glad," she said and he nodded, turning back to the desk.

"Poor Fred," he murmured, picking up a textbook then putting it down again. "I hope it was quick."

"What is it?" she asked gently.

"I found Father after he had his heart attack."

"Oh, Alfie." Grabbing his hands, she squeezed them. "I'm so sorry. I didn't know."

"I was in the garden and I heard a crash from inside the house," he explained. "I knew Father was in his study so I went there and he was on the floor beside his desk. I think he was dead before he even fell."

"I'm so sorry, it must have been terrible for you."

"Telling Mother was worse. I didn't know how she would react, but she was remarkably calm. And, talking of frank conversations, we decided there and then that we should leave Ballybeg – start our lives again in Dublin – and I'm so glad we did because within months I was a medical student at Trinity and Mother and I had found you again."

She laughed and hugged him tightly. "I couldn't believe it when Will told me his very first patient was Mother and that she and you were living nearby. Can the studying wait?"

she asked, gesturing to the textbooks on the desk.

"Yes, it can."

"I didn't mean to upset you."

Alfie gave her a dismissive smile. "Life is short. We need to make the most of it."

"Yes, we do. Come back to number 30 with me and we'll wrap John up warm and bring him out to the garden."

Alfie carried John and Mr Effalump Elephant downstairs from the nursery, down the steps from the back door and stood the little boy on the lawn.

"Has Mrs Dillon been cooking rocks for you to eat?" he asked and John shook his head. "No? Well, goodness me, what have you been eating?"

John looked at her and she smiled. "The same as Will and I, but John loves a soft boiled egg with 'soldiers' for breakfast, don't you?" He nodded and she pointed to the elephant. "Let's see how Mr Effalump Elephant likes the garden."

They were 'walking' the elephant on the lawn when Isobel turned, hearing the back door close. Mary was coming down the steps and Isobel went to her.

"Dr John Fitzgerald is here, Mrs Fitzgerald. I've shown him into the morning room."

"Oh." She threw a glance at his grandson. "Thank you, Mary. I'll be with him shortly."

"Yes, Mrs Fitzgerald," Mary replied and Isobel returned to Alfie and John.

"Will's father is here."

"Go to him," Alfie replied. "I'll look after John."

"Thank you." She went inside, hung up her hat and coat, and found Will's father warming his hands at the fireplace in the morning room.

"Isobel."

"Dr Fitzgerald. I'm afraid Will's not home yet. I don't know how long he'll be."

"That's quite all right, I've come straight from Ely Place Upper to tell you that Fred's funeral will be the day after tomorrow at eleven o'clock at St Peter's with burial afterwards in Mount Jerome Cemetery."

"How is Margaret?" she asked.

"Alternating between sorrow and anger."

"Poor Margaret. Have you eaten?" she added.

"No, I haven't. I came straight here so I wouldn't have to go out again this evening."

"I can ask Mrs Dillon for some onion soup?"

His face brightened. "Thank you, that would be very welcome, then I must return to the *Journal* offices."

She rang for Mary then sat down on the sofa while Will's father sat in one of the armchairs. "I still can't believe it."

"Neither can I. I delivered Fred and he screamed the house down. I thought one day he'd be carrying my coffin, not me carrying his. We need to make the most of life, it can be so tragically short."

"Alfie said something similar when I told him."

"How is he?" Dr Fitzgerald senior asked. "Forgive me, he's in his first year at Trinity, isn't he?"

"Yes, he is, and he says he loves it. Father wanted him to become a clergyman but Alfie had his heart set on becoming a doctor."

"Please give him my best wishes?"

"Thank you, I will. Oh, Mary," she said as the door opened. "Could you ask Mrs Dillon for some of the onion soup from luncheon, please?"

"I think Master John prefers oxtail, Mrs Fitzgerald."

"Yes, he does, but the soup isn't for him."

"Oh." Mary flushed. "I'm sorry, Mrs Fitzgerald."

The maid went out and Isobel gave Will's father an awkward smile.

"How is the boy?" he asked.

"Very well. He has a hearty appetite."

"Is he speaking yet?"

"No, not yet. I—" she began but the door opened again and Mary came in.

"It's Master John, Mrs Fitzgerald, he's fallen over and cut his knee."

She quickly followed Mary to the back door. Alfie was carrying John up the steps and into the house.

"I'm sorry, Isobel."

"These things happen." She turned hearing Will's father's voice and saw him stare intently at the boy. "May we invade your servants' hall, Mrs Dillon?"

"Yes, of course, Dr Fitzgerald," the housekeeper replied. "I'll fetch some warm water."

"Thank you. Sit the boy on the table," he instructed Alfie, who sat John down on the long dining table. The little boy's right knee was bleeding and covered in grass stains. "What were you up to?"

"Trying to do a cartwheel," Alfie explained. "It didn't quite go according to plan."

"Your father and uncle were just the same. Thank you." Will's father accepted a bowl of water and a cloth from Mrs Dillon. "Let's clean this knee then I'll have a look at you."

The knee was cleaned, the blood wiped away and soon a clot formed.

"Oh, dear, that will be a scab in next to no time." Alfie sighed. "I used to pick at mine."

"Don't pick at yours, will you?" Will's father instructed the boy, who shook his head. "It's there to protect the cut and it will fall off when the cut is healed." Lifting the boy up, he stood him on the table. "Well, you're Edward's son all right. Do you know who I am?" he asked, John shook his head again and Dr Fitzgerald senior smiled. "I'm Will's father and your father's father – I'm your grandfather. I'm very pleased to meet you." He held out a hand and John stared at it before looking at her. She gave him an encouraging smile and John shook it. "Do you like living here?" The boy nodded and Will's father ruffled his hair. "I'm glad."

"The soup is heated, Mrs Fitzgerald," Mrs Dillon whispered to her. "And I've sliced some soda bread and made a pot of tea as well. Mary and I will bring it all up to the breakfast room."

"Thank you. Sorry about all this."

"Boys will be boys, Mrs Fitzgerald."

"They certainly will." Dr Fitzgerald senior laughed. "Shall we go upstairs?"

They went into the breakfast room, and John was seated on a cushion at the table while Mrs Dillon brought in the soup, soda bread and butter dish and Mary carried in the tea tray.

Isobel poured the tea then buttered a slice of soda bread and added some marmalade from a dish on the sideboard as Will's father ate his soup. Dr Fitzgerald senior, she noticed, couldn't keep his eyes off John as she passed the boy the soda bread and he grinned his thanks to her.

When John finished his bread and marmalade, she reached for a napkin and wiped his mouth and hands before picking him up. "It's time for this young man's lie-down. Say goodbye to your grandfather, John."

John held out a hand and Will's father stared at it for a moment before shaking it warmly.

She carried John upstairs to the nursery and Florrie took him from her.

"John cut his knee and he'll have a scab soon," she told the maid then kissed the little boy's cheek. "But he met his grandfather for the first time. Will and I will kiss you goodnight later," she said and John nodded.

Downstairs in the hall, Alfie was closing the breakfast room door.

"I must get back to my books, Isobel. I'm so sorry about John, I only took my eyes off him for a split-second."

"Some good did come of it. I'll call to see Mother soon." She gave him a hug and a kiss before seeing him out.

She returned to the breakfast room and Will's father got to his feet.

"Thank you for the soup, Isobel."

"You're very welcome, Dr Fitzgerald, and thank you for attending to John."

"He's a fine little boy."

"He is, and I'm confident he will speak. I'll see you out."

Will arrived home just before six o'clock and his face registered at first surprise and then astonishment when she related the events of the afternoon to him.

"I thought it would never happen – Father meeting John."

"Never say never," she said and kissed his lips. "How was Mrs Hawley?"

"She was very upset when I told her. We chatted for about half an hour, remembering the occasions when Fred and I were invited to stay. It was silly really, Kingstown is only a short train ride away, but it always felt like we were miles away from Dublin and on holiday. Fred and I used to share the guest bedroom at the front of the house next to Jerry's and, no matter the time of year, we always used to keep the window open so we could hear the sea. Fred loved the sea but he never learnt how to swim, of course. Typical Fred."

A telegram was delivered for Will just as they were about to go into the breakfast room for dinner. He tore open the envelope and pulled it out.

"It's from Jerry," he told her. "He's on his way."

"I'm glad."

"Yes." Will re-read the telegram with clear relief before putting it back in the envelope. "He was planning on coming to Dublin for his mother's birthday. Maybe he has brought that forward. I'll let Father know first thing in the morning. Jerry will probably want to be a pallbearer as well. This evening, I must write Fred's eulogy."

John was climbing into bed when they went upstairs to the nursery bedroom to kiss him goodnight.

"How's your knee?" Will lifted John's nightshirt and examined the scab. "It will get itchy but try not to scratch it." John shook his head and Will smiled. "Good boy."

John lay down and they leant over and kissed him.

It took Will less than an hour to write the eulogy. As she read it, tears stung her eyes before rolling down her cheeks. All she could do was nod as she passed the sheets of notepaper back to him. She was dreading the funeral just as much as he was. How Will was going to stand up in front of what was sure to be a huge congregation of mourners and deliver these beautiful words about his oldest friend without breaking down, she really didn't know.

In the morning, she made sure Will ate a good breakfast before seeing him out. She spent an hour with John before leaving the house and walking to number 1 Ely Place Upper. The butler opened the door and over his shoulder, she saw Margaret's sister coming down the stairs dressed in black. Their eyes met for a brief moment before Elizabeth turned to the butler.

"No callers, McDonnell," she said loudly and clearly, going into the morning room and closing the door behind her.

"I'm sorry, Mrs Fitzgerald," the butler told her apologetically.

"It's quite all right. I'll call again after the funeral."

McDonnell closed the front door and Isobel walked away. Deciding to call on her mother, she began a circuitous route back to Fitzwilliam Square so as not to call while her mother was still at her usual late breakfast. Turning onto Hume Street, she saw Will's father leaving the *Journal* offices and hurrying along the pavement ahead of her putting his pocket watch away. Quickening her pace and about to call out a greeting, a cab stopped at the junction with St Stephen's Green, he went to it and opened the door. Inside, a woman leant forward, raising the black veil covering her face and he kissed her cheek. Isobel's eyebrows rose. The woman was Maria Simpson, Fred's mother.

Will's father glanced around him and Isobel ran up the steps of the nearest house, hoping he hadn't seen her. She made a pretence of ringing the doorbell but watched out of the corner of an eye as he got into the cab, the door closed and the cab set off in the direction of Earlsfort Terrace.

Turning away from the house, she frowned to herself. Where were they going? More to the point, what were they doing together? Surely all of Fred's funeral arrangements were complete by now? Will's father had seemed extremely ill at ease being there – and so he should. St Stephen's Green was hardly a suitable location for a clandestine rendezvous – if that's what it was. Puzzled, Isobel continued on back to Fitzwilliam Square.

Her mother was seated on the enormous sofa in the morning room reading a periodical but put it on a side table and got up.

"Oh, Isobel, Alfie told me about Dr Simpson – it's awful. When is the funeral?"

"Tomorrow morning. Will's friend, Jerry, is coming from London."

"How is Will?"

She sighed. "This has hit him hard. And I'm dreading the funeral because Will is giving the eulogy but I'm relieved at the same time that Jerry will also be there. I just hope Will can get through the eulogy without breaking down. He wrote it yesterday evening and it made me cry."

"And how is poor Mrs Simpson?"

"I haven't seen Margaret since Will broke the news to her. I've just come from number 1 but I wasn't allowed inside."

"Why not?" her mother asked sharply.

"My past appears to have reached the ears of Margaret's sister and she has taken a dislike to me. I'm not offended, it's been quite a while since I cared what others think of me, but I would have liked to have spoken to Margaret. I'll try and speak to her at the funeral, I'm sure Elizabeth will not wish to cause a scene in public."

"No. Well, I am delighted you have called." Her mother kissed her cheek and they sat down side by side on the sofa. "As there is something I would like to tell you."

"About James Ellison?" she asked and smiled when her mother blushed.

"Is it so obvious?"

"Alfie couldn't help but notice the number of times Mr Ellison was calling here."

"You and Alfie have spoken about Mr Ellison? Do you like him?"

"Do you?" she teased and her mother blushed an even deeper red.

"I love him, Isobel. And he loves me. And we are to be married."

"But there is something worrying you, isn't there?"

"He will be my third husband."

"It's not your fault you were widowed twice," Isobel told her gently.

"No, but all the same…"

"I like Mr Ellison, and so does Alfie. We both want you to be happy. Yes, there will be gossip, but there is always gossip."

"That is true."

"So." She clasped her mother's hands. "Have you made any plans yet?"

"Well, James and I are unofficially engaged-to-be-married but our engagement will not be announced in *The*

Irish Times until after the first anniversary of Ronald's death. I insisted on waiting as, I suppose, I did marry Ronald with undue haste after your father died. We haven't set a date for the wedding but we must."

"I am delighted for you, Mother, really I am."

"Oh, Isobel, I'm so relieved."

"Why?" she asked in surprise.

"Well, I couldn't help but notice that you didn't like Ronald, and I was very much afraid you might not like James either."

"Mother, I barely knew Mr Henderson, but I have spoken with Mr Ellison on a number of occasions and I believe he is a very fine man."

"Thank you. Would you like some coffee instead of tea?"

Isobel smiled. "Coffee would be lovely."

Will returned to number 30 for luncheon, put his medical bag on the hall table and hung up his hat and overcoat. Mary came out of the breakfast room and told him that Mrs Fitzgerald was out, so he went into the morning room and had just sat down in an armchair with *The Irish Times* when the door opened and Mary came in.

"There is a Dr Jeremiah Hawley to see you, Dr Fitzgerald."

Quickly folding the newspaper, Will dropped it on the floor beside the chair and got to his feet. "Show him in, Mary, thank you."

Jerry came into the room, Mary closed the door, and the first thing Will saw was the exhaustion in his friend's face.

"Jerry." Hugging him for the first time in years, Will fought back tears. "I'm so glad you've come and I'm so sorry about the telegram, there just wasn't time for a letter. Officially, Fred had a heart attack like his grandfather but—" He sighed. "The truth is that Fred killed himself. An overdose of morphine."

Jerry's jaw dropped. "Jesus Christ."

"Only five people know the truth, Jerry – Isobel, my father, John Dalton, myself – and now you – we couldn't allow the truth to get out."

"No, of course not." Jerry looked around for the sofa and sank down onto it. "Jesus Christ," he whispered again. "Why?"

"Because he had syphilis," Will told him and Jerry closed his eyes for a moment. "Most likely contracted the night in Monto before his wedding."

"What about Margaret?" Jerry asked and Will grimaced.

"Although Margaret is showing no outward symptoms, I believe she also has syphilis. Her baby died in the womb and Fred delivered him by caesarean last week."

"Fred did?"

"He insisted and I assisted. The baby was a boy. He was named Nicholas after Margaret's late father and he was buried in the same grave as Duncan Simpson. Fred will now be buried alongside them."

"Christ." Jerry shook his head.

"How long can you stay?" Will asked.

"A month. Luckily, the locum could start immediately, so I can stay on for Mother's birthday. When is the funeral?"

"Tomorrow at eleven o'clock at St Peter's. I've asked to be a pallbearer and I will also deliver the eulogy. Father has been helping with the funeral arrangements and I can send a message to him if you'd like to be a pallbearer, too?"

"Yes, I would, thank you. Oh, Fred…" Jerry exhaled a shaky sigh and Will gripped his shoulder.

"When did you last eat?"

"I took the overnight sailing from Holyhead and I had breakfast at six o'clock this morning."

"Then, you'll stay for luncheon, unless your mother is expecting you?"

Jerry shook his head. "I've just come from Kingstown. I went straight home so I could tell Mother but she said you had called yesterday afternoon. Thank you, Will, I was dreading telling her."

"I thought she should be told before she'd read the death notice in *The Irish Times* and we chatted for a while about the 'holidays' Fred and I had there at the seaside."

Jerry gave him a weak smile. "Fred never did learn how to swim, did he?"

"No. Nor ride a bicycle."

Jerry spluttered a laugh then shook his head again. "I just can't believe it. Who found him?"

"Father and I found him in his office at the *Journal of Irish Medicine*. It was his first day. Father had accompanied him there and I called to walk him home."

The door opened and Jerry got to his feet as Isobel came in.

"Jerry." She reached up and kissed his cheek. "I'm so sorry we're meeting again in such dreadful circumstances. When did you last eat?"

"At six o'clock this morning."

"Then, you'll stay for luncheon. I'll let Mrs Dillon know."

She left the room and Jerry smiled. "You have a wonderful wife."

"Yes, I do. When will you have one?"

"Lillian accepted my proposal and when we set a wedding date I'll let you know."

"Congratulations, Jerry."

"Thank you, Will. Oh, I wish Lillian could have met Fred. All she's seen of him is the atrocious photograph of us when we left Trinity."

"I think we were still drunk."

"Well, Fred certainly was – I'm sorry," he said in a shaking voice. "I just can't believe he's gone."

Will put an arm around Jerry as he sobbed. "We must see more of each other," he insisted and Jerry nodded. "Isobel and I will come to London and yourself and Lillian must come here."

"Yes." Jerry pulled a handkerchief from his trouser pocket and dried his eyes. "We must never lose touch."

"No." He gave Jerry another hug as Isobel returned. "Jerry and Lillian are getting married," he told her and her face brightened. "And we are invited."

"That's wonderful." She kissed his cheek again. "Congratulations. I'm looking forward to meeting her again."

"How is Margaret?" Will asked and she shrugged. "Isobel?"

"Elizabeth saw me at the front door and I wasn't admitted to the house."

"Elizabeth?" Jerry queried.

"Elizabeth Higginson, Margaret's sister," Isobel explained. "She seems to have heard of my past and disapproves of me."

"She's a bloody rude and arrogant woman," Will declared.

"I will speak to Margaret tomorrow, whether Elizabeth likes it or not."

"Good." He kissed her forehead. "Is luncheon ready?"

"It is."

When they had eaten, Will saw Jerry onto a train at Westland Row Station before walking to the *Journal* offices on Hume Street to speak to his father.

"Jerry has come and would like to be a pallbearer as well," he began, sitting down on the chair in front of his father's desk. "I also told him the truth."

"Are you planning on telling anyone else?" his father asked and Will tensed.

"No, I'm not, but Jerry deserved to know how Fred really died. I also need to know if you mean to acknowledge John as your grandson?"

His father sat back in his chair. "The boy still doesn't speak."

"He will speak, given time."

"How can you be so sure?" His father gave him a long look. "It is clear he adores Isobel, yet he doesn't speak to her."

"He will."

"I want Bertram Harrison to see the boy."

"A psychiatrist? No."

"Then, tell me why the boy remains silent?" his father demanded.

"John will speak," Will replied quietly before changing the subject. "How is Margaret?"

"Bearing up. Has Isobel not called on her?"

"She did, this morning, but Elizabeth Higginson would not have her admitted to the house."

His father's eyebrows rose. "Well, Elizabeth cannot deny access to the funeral to those she does not approve of."

"No, she can't."

"I have arranged for a carriage for tomorrow morning. Your mother and I will call for you and Isobel at half past ten."

"Thank you, Father."

He caught up on house calls before returning to number 30. Isobel was in the nursery sitting on one of the new red rugs reading to John and both of them gave him a bright smile. He bent and picked John up and kissed his cheek.

"What was Isobel reading to you?" he asked and waited for an answer. John pointed to the book on Isobel's lap but Will shook his head. "What is it called?"

"Will—" Isobel began, getting to her feet, but he held a finger to her lips.

"Tell me the name of the book, John," he said but the boy shook his head. "Why not?" he asked as gently as he could but John just looked away. "Will you read a book to Isobel and I one day?" To his relief, John turned back to him and nodded. "Good boy."

"Will?" Isobel turned on him as soon as they left the nursery.

"John needs to know that we want him to speak."

"But he does know."

"I don't think he does. I think we – and John – are getting too used to the fact that he doesn't speak."

"What has Jerry been saying?" she demanded.

"It wasn't Jerry. My father wants John to see a psychiatrist."

She stared at him for a moment before shaking her head. "No, absolutely not."

227

"I agree. But we must try harder to get John to speak."

"Yes, but not like that. You were making John nervous."

"We must make it seem like a game we're all playing, then. Mother mentioned Edward's toy soldiers, we could use those?" he suggested and she nodded.

"Your father won't visit John until he speaks, will he?"

"He didn't say it in so many words but, no."

She rolled her eyes and he followed her downstairs.

At half past ten in the morning, he was waiting at the front door with Isobel beside him as the carriage carrying his parents come to a halt. His stomach felt as if it were full of lead but Isobel gave his hand a little squeeze, he closed the door and they went down the steps. She was carrying a copy of the eulogy in her handbag as a precaution he hoped he wouldn't need. Each word was etched in his mind but who knows how he would react getting up in front of all the mourners to pay tribute to Fred.

At St Peter's Church on Aungier Street, he escorted Isobel and his mother inside to a pew occupied by Mrs Hawley then went back outside to wait for the hearse with his father and Jerry. When the funeral cortège arrived, he glanced at Jerry as they went to the hearse. His friend's face was grey. Here was the ultimate proof Fred really was gone.

The oak coffin was carried inside and they went to the pew and sat down. Isobel held his hand and further along the pew, he was relieved to see Mrs Hawley lay a comforting hand on Jerry's knee. The funeral service passed in a haze until Isobel patted his hands and he got up and made his way to the lectern on wobbly legs. Gripping the sides tightly, he stared out over the congregation breathing deeply in and out in an effort to calm his racing heart. The church was full and there were even a few men standing near the door.

"Fred and I were born within a week of each other in December 1849," he began. "As our fathers were best friends, Fred and I spent an enormous amount of time together in each other's homes – playing – and later studying. We met Jerry Hawley at what is now Wesley College and from then on the three of us were the best of friends."

Inhaling and exhaling another deep breath, he continued. "The three of us had one thing in common – our fathers were medical men – and we wanted to be medical men, too. Everyone expected Fred to become a surgeon like his father but Fred insisted on accompanying Jerry and I to Trinity College and studying medicine there instead.

"Fred could have been a fine surgeon, he could perform complex procedures in difficult circumstances, but surgery's loss was general practice's gain. Fred's vast medical – and surgical – knowledge, his compassion and his ability to listen to patients without interruption was a combination which ensured Fred was an exceptional doctor.

"Margaret and Maria—" He peered down at them seated in the front pew between Mrs Dawson and Diana Wingfield, Maria's sister, their faces hidden by black lace veils. "Fred loved you both so very much. I can't even begin to imagine how immense your suffering is but please never forget that as well as your families, you have many, many friends ready to cry with you and talk and listen.

"As for Fred himself..." Will tailed off and sighed. "He was complex. At times I found him both infuriating and frustrating and he had a sense of humour which can only be described as unique, yet I never wanted to lose him as a friend. Tragically, he has left us all far too soon and far too young but we must be grateful that he was here with us at all. Thank you, Fred, for brightening, not just my life, but the lives of everyone who knew you and loved you."

He returned to the pew and sat down. Isobel lifted his left hand to her lips and kissed it then held out one of his handkerchiefs. Raising his right hand to his face, he found his cheeks wet with tears and he took the handkerchief from her and wiped them away.

All too soon, the coffin was borne outside to the hearse for Fred's final journey to Mount Jerome Cemetery.

At the graveside, Will and Isobel, his parents, and Jerry and his mother found themselves opposite Margaret, her mother and mother-in-law, Diana Wingfield, and Elizabeth and Gordon Higginson. As the coffin was lowered into the grave, Isobel held his hand tightly as he leant forward to read the brass coffin plate.

Frederick Simpson M.D.
1849-1881
At Rest

At rest. Straightening up and exhaling a shaky breath, Will could only hope that was true.

Before Elizabeth and Mrs Dawson had a chance to lead Margaret away, he ushered Isobel and Jerry towards her.

"My deepest condolences, Margaret."

"Thank you for your lovely words, Will," she said. "Please call soon – both of you."

"Thank you, Margaret," Isobel replied. "We shall."

"Margaret." Jerry lifted her gloved hand and kissed it.

"My deepest sympathies."

"Jerry?" She peered up at him through her thick black lace veil. "Oh, Jerry, you came all the way from London."

"I couldn't not be here."

"Thank you, Jerry," she managed to add before she was led away.

Glancing around the cemetery before returning to the carriage, Will exchanged a nod with Eva Bannister as he and the practice secretary noted with approval the large number of mourners who had braved the damp and dreary weather to bid farewell to Fred.

Mary was opening the front door as he and Isobel went downstairs that evening after kissing John goodnight. Jerry was on the steps with his hat in one hand and a bottle in the other.

"The finest single malt I could find," he said, holding the bottle up. "We need to give Fred a good send off."

"We do. Come in. Thank you, Mary."

They went into the morning room and Jerry put the bottle on the drinks tray.

"I escorted Mother home, wandered around the house for a bit, then went out and hailed a cab," he told them. "Would you like some whiskey, too, Isobel?"

"Thank you, no, I won't have a drink." Isobel sat on the sofa and glanced at Will with a raised eyebrow while Jerry poured two helpings of whiskey, silently asking him if they should tell Jerry she was pregnant. He nodded and she replied with a little smile.

"Will?" Jerry passed him one of the glasses and they sat down in the armchairs.

"Thank you."

"To Fred." Jerry held his glass up and they clinked glasses.

"Fred. And to Isobel," he added and Jerry frowned. "Isobel is pregnant," he explained and Jerry gave him a grin.

"That is wonderful. When is the baby due?"

"In just under six months time."

"Six?" Jerry repeated.

"It's our belief that Isobel miscarried a twin."

"Good God."

"No-one else knows yet," she said. "Will and I were waiting until the funeral was over before telling anyone."

"Of course. My congratulations. I'm delighted for you both. And how is John?"

"Very well," he replied. "But he still doesn't speak. And my father wants a psychiatrist to assess him."

Jerry pursed his lips. "That might just make things worse."

"I agree. We will have to make a more concerted effort to encourage John to speak."

"If there is anything I can do to help while I'm here, please tell me," Jerry said and he nodded. "I have reported the children's home to the authorities," he went on and Isobel reached out and gave his hand a squeeze. "I'll let you know the outcome."

"Thank you, Jerry. Tell me about the three of you at the Wesleyan Connexional School," she added and he and Jerry exchanged a smile.

"Well, Will was so nervous on our first day he was sick on the schoolroom floor," Jerry told her.

"Thanks for reminding me," he replied in a dry tone and Jerry raised his glass with a grin. "Fred and I both thought

Jerry was very exotic – coming all the way from Kingstown."

"You and Fred hadn't known Jerry at all before that?" she asked and he shook his head.

"No, we didn't. We took pity on him when we saw that he was absolutely hopeless at rugby football."

"I hated rugby football," Jerry declared. "Not so much the running but the muck. I always seemed to end up face-down in the mud. Will and Fred would always haul me to my feet and Fred would pass me a handkerchief so I could clean my face."

"Fred carried a handkerchief while playing rugby football?" she asked incredulously.

"Fred always carried a clean handkerchief," he told her. "And then Jerry would ruin it." He smiled and rested his head back. "We were three small boys when we started at Wesley. Three small boys who wanted to be medical men like our fathers. You wouldn't have thought it, but Fred was the cleverest of the three of us. At Trinity, I lost count of the number of lectures he'd slip out of. He'd lean over and whisper—"

"'This is very dull, I'm off,'" Jerry finished with a grin. "And yet he never fell behind nor failed any exams."

"We really should have hated him," he continued. "But we couldn't. Fred was Fred."

After an hour, Isobel stood up. It was time to leave the two friends to their whiskey and memories of Fred.

"I think I'll go to bed and read for a while."

"Please don't feel as though—" Will began as he and Jerry got to their feet.

"I don't. You both need to chat about Fred without

having to explain for my sake. Call again soon, Jerry."

"I will." He reached for her hand and kissed it. "Goodnight, Isobel."

In the hall, she met Mrs Dillon coming down the stairs with an empty mug.

"I had brought Florrie some cocoa," the housekeeper explained.

"She isn't too isolated up there, is she?" Isobel asked.

"No, not at all. Master John keeps her busy and both Mary and myself are up to the nursery regularly and I allow Annie to keep Florrie company when I don't need her in the kitchen. I do want to speak to you about Florrie's replacement, though, Mrs Fitzgerald. I let it be known that the household is looking for another house-parlourmaid and I was contacted by Mrs Anderson's Agency."

"An agency?"

"Yes. Mrs Anderson has a suitable candidate with excellent references but is having difficulty placing her with a household. There is one rather large problem."

"Which is?" Isobel prompted and Mrs Dillon shuffled uncomfortably.

"The girl is dark-skinned, Mrs Fitzgerald. I went to meet her at the agency today and she is very pleasant but is quite… dark."

"Would that be a problem for you, Mrs Dillon?" Isobel asked cautiously.

"Not for me, no," the housekeeper replied firmly. "In a previous household, I worked with a footman from the Congo, but I can't speak for Gerald, Mary, Annie or Florrie. It is most likely that they have never seen – never mind met – a dark-skinned person."

"Would you speak to them tomorrow, please, and I will speak to my husband."

"Yes, I will. Thank you, Mrs Fitzgerald. Goodnight."

Lying in bed, Isobel laid the palm of her hand on her stomach, feeling another stronger flutter.

"Hello," she said softly. "You're really letting me know you're there, aren't you?"

Two hours later, and about to turn down the oil lamp, the door opened and Will came in.

"I walked with Jerry to Baggot Street and waited until he hailed a cab," he said, closing the door behind him.

"Is he all right?" she asked and Will nodded as he got undressed.

"We'll try and meet up again before he goes back to London." He got into bed and put an arm around her. "You're not angry that he is the first to know about the baby?"

"No. Oh." Grabbing his hand, she placed it over her stomach. "That's the strongest flutter yet."

He smiled and kissed her forehead. "Who will we tell next?"

"I'd like to tell my mother," she said. "She was one of twins and this baby was one of twins, so I would like to tell her tomorrow."

"Yes. And we will call to my parents tomorrow evening when they're both at home. And one evening this week, I must show David the two rooms in Pimlico and hope he isn't too horrified."

"He seems quite open-minded."

"Yes, he does. I need to sit him down and discuss how he's getting on but tomorrow I must call to number 1. Fred never did give me an answer on whether he would like me to attend to himself and Margaret, so I have to speak to Margaret as a doctor and not as a friend. I'm not looking forward to it but it has to be done."

"And you." She turned his face towards hers. "How are you?"

"A bit up and down," he replied quietly. "I'll keep myself busy."

"Not too busy to take your wife out for coffee once a week and to feed the ducks in St Stephen's Green with John and I at the weekend? Soon I'll be waddling like the ducks but I'd like to continue with both for as long as possible."

"I'll never be too busy for that. And you'll never waddle."

"Hmm." She smiled. "We'll see in few months."

"You'll still be beautiful," he said and kissed her lips.

"Mrs Dillon has found a suitable replacement for Florrie."

"Oh? You sound a little hesitant."

"Mrs Dillon told me the girl is dark-skinned. Would that be a problem for you?"

"Not for me, no. But what about Mary, Florrie, Annie and Gerald?" he asked.

"I've asked Mrs Dillon to speak to them."

"Good. Well, we'll just have to wait and see what they say," he said and turned the oil lamp down.

Her mother was in the hall, having only just finished breakfast when Isobel was admitted to number 55.

"Isobel, how lovely to see you. Come into the morning room."

They sat on the sofa and Isobel held her mother's hands. "I've called because I have some good news – I'm pregnant."

Her mother's eyes filled with tears. "Oh, Isobel. Oh, I'm so happy for you."

"But that's not all," Isobel went on. "It turns out I've been pregnant all along."

"All along? I don't understand."

"Will and I believe I was expecting twins and one died and I miscarried it. I told Will that you were a twin."

Her mother nodded. "Miles died when he was a year old. Whooping cough. Oh, so you are—" She looked down at Isobel's waist. "Three months pregnant."

"Just over three," she clarified. "I am starting to show and I can feel the baby move."

"I am so happy for you. How is Will?"

"Shocked but delighted. My timing could have been better. I had a dizzy spell and I had to tell him the evening Fred died."

"How was the funeral?" her mother asked.

"Awful. But Will delivered the eulogy wonderfully and he and his father, and Will and Fred's friend, Jerry, were amongst the pallbearers and I think that helped. Jerry also called to the house last night and I left him and Will to reminisce."

"You should have come over here."

"Thank you, Mother, but I was tired and I read for a while."

"Look after yourself and the little one, won't you?"

She smiled. "I look after Will and Will looks after me. Is Alfie at home?"

"He was up and out an hour ago."

"Good grief, he used to be such a slugabed. I'm so glad he's enjoying being at Trinity."

"Would you like to tell him yourself?" her mother asked. "He's very fond of John and he'll be so delighted to be an uncle twice over soon. And me a grandmother."

"I would like to tell him, thank you, Mother."

When she returned to number 30, she went upstairs to the nursery and sent Florrie to the servants' hall for a cup of tea. Dressing John in one of his new morning coats, she brought him out to the garden and they were exploring the flowerbeds when Alfie called shortly before luncheon. The door to the servants' hall had been closed as she and John walked past and she guessed that Mrs Dillon was speaking to the servants about the possible replacement house-parlourmaid. John, she was delighted to see, remembered Alfie and gave him a grin.

"Mother said you have some news for me," he said, ruffling John's hair.

"I do, but let me bring this young man upstairs. It's almost time for luncheon, isn't it, John?" she asked and he nodded.

Alfie carried John to the nursery and they went to the window where the little boy gazed out over the square then down at the gardens where, through the bare branches of the trees, she could see a gentleman on the lawn in the centre walking a small dog.

"What a wonderful view," Alfie declared. "I never tire of looking out across the square from my bedroom. When the trees come into leaf, you and I must go on an expedition and I'll teach you what all the different trees are."

When Florrie returned, Isobel promised John she would be back later. She and Alfie then went downstairs and into the morning room.

"I'm pregnant, Alfie, and I've been pregnant all along," she announced and expressions of joy then astonishment followed by bewilderment crossed his face.

"How? No, wait a moment – twins," he said. "You must have originally been carrying twins. Good God. Oh, dear, that sounded awful." He gave her a tight hug. "Many congratulations, Isobel."

"Thank you. I can hardly believe it."

"And Will?"

"He's absolutely delighted." They turned and Will grinned at them as he closed the door. "It was a shock – I can't deny that – but I'm over the moon." He kissed her forehead. "We're going to tell my parents this evening and then we must think of a way of telling John."

"Tell him he'll soon have a cousin who will share the nursery with him."

"I think Will meant how to explain to John where the baby has come from without going into too much detail," she said.

"Well, I will gladly leave that up to you." Alfie laughed. "And now I must go. I have a lecture at two o'clock. Congratulations, and I will see you soon."

He left the room and she smiled at Will.

"Mother was very happy when I told her, too."

"I'm glad. My parents next." He pulled a comical face and escorted her into the breakfast room for luncheon.

At just after four o'clock that afternoon, Will went up the steps to number 1 Ely Place Upper, rang the doorbell and waited. And waited. Frowning, he rang the doorbell again and the door was flung open by an exasperated McDonnell.

"Dr William Fitzgerald to see Mrs Margaret Simpson," he said, noting how the older man was less than his usually perfectly-attired self.

"I'm afraid Mrs Simpson is no longer in residence, Dr Fitzgerald," the butler replied, straightening his black cravat before doing up his frock coat buttons.

"I see," Will replied, even though he didn't. "Would you have a forwarding address for her, McDonnell?"

"Mrs Simpson and Mrs Dawson have gone to stay with relatives in Co Wicklow," the butler told him abruptly. "Mrs Simpson left instructions to prepare the house so it may be put up for rent."

"I wish you well with the tenants."

The butler stiffened. "All the servants have been put on a week's notice, Dr Fitzgerald."

Will put his medical bag down. "I'm sorry to hear that. You've been butler here a long time, McDonnell."

"Almost thirty years. I must admit this morning's events were a great shock to us all."

"Mrs Simpson left only this morning?"

"Yes, Dr Fitzgerald, and I do not expect to see her again."

"I am sorry." Will put out a hand and the butler shook it. "If you – or any of the other servants – are in need of a character reference, call to number 30 Fitzwilliam Square and my wife and I will be happy to oblige."

"Thank you, Dr Fitzgerald, that is very kind. Good afternoon to you."

The front door closed, Will picked up his medical bag and went down the steps to the pavement. There, he paused and looked up at the house. He had been a regular caller here all his life and now the door was firmly shut. He turned away and, with nothing more he could do, went home.

After bringing Isobel up to date, they walked to number 67 as dusk fell. His father had just arrived home was passing his hat and overcoat to Maura in the hall and the maid showed the three of them into the morning room.

"We've called because we have some good news – Isobel is pregnant," he announced and held up a hand before his parents had a chance to respond. "She has been pregnant all along," he clarified. "It is our belief she was expecting twins but miscarried one of them."

"My mother was a twin," Isobel explained.

"Oh, Isobel." His mother got up from the sofa and hugged and kissed her. "I am delighted for you. And for you, Will." She reached up and kissed his cheek.

"Congratulations, Will." His father held out a hand and Will shook it.

"Thank you."

"Congratulations, Isobel." His father kissed her cheek. "Are you well?"

"I'm very well, thank you. Rather shocked but very happy, too."

"We would also like to borrow Edward's toy soldiers," he added. "We hope the fact they were his father's will encourage John to speak."

"Of course," his mother replied. "And you don't need to borrow them, Will. John can have the soldiers."

"Thank you. May I speak to you in private, Father?" Will asked.

"Of course," he replied and turned to the ladies. "Please excuse us."

They went upstairs, and in the chilly drawing room Will

lit two of the gas lamps and told his father of Margaret's sudden departure from Ely Place Upper.

"Do you think Margaret has told Maria that number 1 is going to be put up for rent?" Will asked.

"I don't know. But the house was Fred's and when he died, it passed to Margaret. The house is hers to do with as she pleases."

"But it's been the Simpson home for decades," Will protested.

"There is no-one else left to inherit it now," his father reminded him gently and Will raised his eyes to the ceiling hoping he wasn't going to cry. "And Margaret needs an income."

"Margaret needs a bloody-good talking-to," he snapped. "Because I doubt very much if she has told any of her family she has syphilis."

"You're not her doctor, Will. She's not your responsibility."

"No, but—"

"She's gone," his father interrupted firmly. "There's nothing more you can do for her. You need to look after your own wife now."

"Yes."

"I'm happy for you, Will. Truly, I am."

"Thank you, Father. I can still hardly believe it."

"Have you told the boy?"

"Not yet. We have to decide how to go about it in a way which won't make John feel as though he will be second best. He and the baby are cousins but they will be raised as siblings."

"I see."

"Do you?" Will demanded. "Do you or do you not want

to be grandfather to John? Because if you don't, tending to his knee and telling him who you are was a terribly cruel thing to do."

"You simply don't understand how hard losing Edward is for me. And for me to see how Fred's death has affected you more—"

"I'm furious at both of them for being selfish and cowardly," he interrupted. "Edward lied about his marriage and John, and Isobel and I are doing our best for the boy. Fred left a childless wife with syphilis behind and – yes, you're right – there's nothing more I can do to help Margaret. But Fred was more of a brother to me than Edward ever was. I'm sorry if that upsets you, Father, but it's the truth. Fred, Jerry and I went through more together than Edward and I ever did. Maybe when John begins to speak and I'm not quite so angry at Edward, then I might be able to mourn him, too."

"You cannot help everyone, Will."

"No, I can't," he conceded. "But I will continue to do my damndest to help as many people as I can. And I mean what I say – John and the baby are cousins but they will be raised at number 30 as siblings."

"Good," his father replied simply and Will stared at him in astonishment as he walked to the fireplace and stared into the empty hearth with his hands in his pockets. "You're right. Edward was selfish and a coward and that was because of me. I had expected him to follow me into medicine and when he insisted on joining the army I told him he had better make me proud. And he did. He was promoted to major at such a young age – but at the expense of his marriage – and he didn't have the courage to tell me it had failed, nor that he had fathered a son with another woman. Edward's son exists and is the way he is because of me."

That was quite a confession. "But John improves every day, Father. And you could help him to—"

"Will, the boy looks so much like Edward I don't know if I can bear to look at him again," his father admitted, turning to him with a helpless shrug. "Fred has a grave we can all visit but Edward is buried thousands of miles away in a country I have never visited nor know very much about. I still cannot quite believe he is dead. I keep expecting to receive a letter from him to say he will be home soon on leave. I simply need time to try and come to terms with the fact that Edward will never come home."

Will nodded. "Of course."

"I will look for the toy soldiers in Edward's bedroom myself. If they can help John in some way, however small, then I will be happy."

"Thank you."

"No, thank you."

"For what?" Will asked, genuinely puzzled.

His father smiled. "For being stubborn. For speaking your mind. For many things."

"Let's go and look for the soldiers together. Two pairs of eyes are better than one."

His father nodded, Will lit an oil lamp and they went upstairs to the second floor.

Isobel glanced at the clock on the mantelpiece. Will and his father had been gone for almost twenty minutes and she hoped they weren't going to be too much longer. She saw Sarah catch her glance and they exchanged a smile.

"Tea?" Sarah asked. "Or coffee? I've developed quite a taste for coffee."

"No, thank you, we will be having dinner as soon as we go home." Getting up from the armchair, she went to the windows and closed the curtains feeling her mother-in-law's eyes on her. "I have only just begun to show."

"Oh, dear, I'm sorry, Isobel. I didn't mean to stare. It's just that Edward was a huge baby and I showed from quite early on. But Will," she mused. "No, Will wasn't a big baby, he was just over six pounds."

"I'll be big soon." Isobel ran her hands over her stomach. "And I must admit I can't wait for the baby to show him or herself more. After the miscarriage, I thought I would never become pregnant again, never mind find myself still pregnant."

"I am so happy for you both." Sarah got up and squeezed her hand then held onto it. "Let's go upstairs and look for Edward's toy soldiers."

They climbed the stairs to the bedrooms and found Will and his father in a bedroom at the back of the house standing at a mahogany wardrobe with both the doors open.

"Here it is," Will was saying as he lifted a large wooden box off a shelf and placed it on the single bed.

Taking the lid off, his father picked up a red-coated toy soldier. "I hope these won't be too small for the boy – that he won't try and eat them, I mean. Edward was six when he was given this set."

"Will and I shall sit John down and tell him they are not for eating," she said, and they both turned and nodded. "What else is in the box?" she asked and went to the bed.

"Books," Will replied, picking two up. "A ball, alphabet bricks, marbles, a train set…"

"Take whatever you think John will like," his mother said.

"Thank you, Mother. Even though Isobel bought him a set of wooden farm animals, the only toy John has played with so far has been Mr Effalump Elephant. I think it was the only toy he had or was allowed in the children's home, so it's time he was introduced to more toys, including some educational ones. We'll take the toy soldiers, the ball, the alphabet bricks and the train set. And we'll be back for the rest when he's a little older."

Will's father found a smaller wooden box, they placed the toys in it and Will carried the box downstairs.

"Which of Edward's toys shall we give John first?" Isobel asked as she and Will returned to number 30. "The train set?"

"Yes," he replied simply, leaving the box on the hall table and opening the morning room door for her.

She gave him a sharp glance before going into the room. "What's the matter?" she asked as he followed her.

"My father believes John exists and is the way he is because of him," he said, closing the door.

She sat on the sofa as Will stood in front of the fireplace and recounted his conversation with his father. "That is a huge confession to make," she said and he nodded.

"It is. Father is never one for showing or divulging his feelings. We both said some harsh words but he's right about one thing. Fred's death has affected me more than Edward's, even though I'm furious at both of them for being selfish and cowardly. I can't mourn Edward because I'm furious at him for lying about his marriage and John, and Father can't accept John because Father thinks it's his own fault Edward

246

was a liar and a coward." He let his arms drop to his sides helplessly.

"Will, I'm glad you're angry because I am, too," she stated firmly, relieved to finally be able to reveal how she really felt on the matter. "I'm angry at both Edward and Fred for taking you for granted and expecting you to pick up the pieces after their deaths. But I'm especially angry at Fred because you had no choice but to lie about the cause of his death – not just to his wife and almost everyone who knew him – but on the medical certificate, too. If it's discovered you falsified an official document, I dread the consequences for you as a doctor and for the medical practice, and I don't think I'll ever be able to forgive Fred for putting you in such a position."

"I hesitated before signing the certificate," he admitted with a grimace. "But I signed it for Fred – to protect his reputation and Margaret's – and all I can do now is hope the certificate is filed away somewhere and forgotten about."

"I hope it is, too," she said, sounding far more confident than she felt. "I'm sorry, Will," she went on, reaching out a hand, which he took and sat down beside her. "I know Fred was your oldest friend and you loved him, but I had to say it."

"Don't be sorry." Raising her hand to his lips, he kissed it. "You speak your mind and I'm thankful that you do."

"Well, you may not want to hear this, but you need to spend more time with your father. From what you've said, you both know how the other feels now so go and see him more often. Tell him about John and which of Edward's toys he likes best. You have to remember that your father has lost his best friend, too, plus his son and his godson. You're his only son now and he needs you."

Will nodded. "And you'll continue to visit Mother?"

"Of course I will," she said softly. "I like your mother very much and she is so happy about the baby. We will use Edward's toys to help John. With the alphabet bricks, we can explain how each letter should be pronounced and try and get him to repeat them?"

"Yes," he replied quietly.

"And we must think of a way of telling John about the baby," she went on and he nodded again.

"I think we'll wait until you're a bit bigger, it might be easier for him to understand there is a baby inside you when there is more to see."

"Should we show him the photograph of his parents in the meantime, then?" she asked. "I finally had it framed this afternoon. Or is it still too soon?"

"No, I don't think so. We'll bring the photograph and the toys upstairs to him after we've eaten and before he goes to bed."

John was sitting on one of the red rugs playing with Mr Effalump Elephant when they went into the nursery. Will placed the box of toys on the table and Isobel joined Florrie in John's bedroom where the maid was turning down the bedcovers.

"We've decided to show John his mother and father," she explained and showed Florrie the photograph. "We also have some toys for him which belonged to his father. But we'll deal with the photograph first."

"Yes, Mrs Fitzgerald. Would you like me to stay?"

"You don't have to. This could take a little while."

"I'll go downstairs, then."

"Thank you, Florrie."

She sat down on the rug beside Will, who lifted John onto his lap.

"Isobel and I have something to show you," he began and she held out the framed photograph. "This is your mother and this is your father." John stared intently as Will pointed to the couple. "Your mother was called Purnima and she was from Nashik in India. Your father was called Edward and he was born here in Dublin. He was three years older than me. I'm afraid I don't know how old your mother was, but about Isobel's age, I would think. She was from a city close to where your father was stationed with the army and I'm afraid that is all we know about her. It's very sad, but they both died in India. Your mother died when you were born and your father died a few weeks ago of a disease called cholera."

"Would you like us to put the photograph in your bedroom so you can look at your mother and father?" Isobel asked and John glanced at her then turned his attention back to the photograph, grabbing it from her hands and flinging it across the room.

"No," he shouted, startling her, as the photo frame hit the wall, the glass shattering. "No. No. No."

"John." Will held him tightly as the little boy continued to shout. "John, it's all right. We'll put the photograph away. John, listen," he commanded, holding the boy's face in his hands. "We will put the photograph away until you want to see it."

"Don't want to see it ever," John mumbled. "Major Fisgered didn't want a bastard."

"Who told you that?" Will demanded. "Was it someone in the children's home? It was, wasn't it?"

"I'm a bastard. No-one wants a bastard."

"That is not true," she insisted. "It was very wrong to call you that."

"Your father did want you," Will added firmly. "I know he did because he told me in a letter that he was trying to get the army to send him back to London so he could be with you."

"Didn't want me," John mumbled again, one tear and then another trickling down his cheeks. "Sent me away because I'm a bastard."

"Well, we want you," she told him. "Will and I love you, John," she continued softly, pulling a handkerchief from Will's trouser pocket and drying John's eyes. "And you will always have a home with us here, we promise."

"Once we were told about you, Isobel and I went to London as quickly as we could because we wanted you and we wanted you to come and live here with us," Will said. "We only wish we had been told about you sooner. Never think no-one wants you. You are our little boy and we love you. Your grandparents love you and your Grandmamma Martha and Alfie love you and Florrie loves you, too – we all do."

John nodded and Isobel kissed his cheek. "Good boy."

"Your grandparents have given us some toys to give to you," Will told him and she got up, went to the table and quickly lifted the toy soldiers out of the wooden box so the boy wouldn't see them. She set the box down on the rug in front of them and Will reached for one of the alphabet bricks. "I was taught my letters with these." He placed the brick on the rug before reaching for some of the other bricks and arranging them until they spelt JOHN. "This is your name – J – O – H – N – John. Do you think you can say

John?" he asked and the little boy stared up at him. "John?"

"Everyone will think you are such a clever boy if you can say John," she said with a smile, desperately hoping he wasn't going to fall silent again. "John."

"John." Will nodded encouragement at him. "John Fitzgerald."

"John Fitzgerald," the boy whispered and Isobel's heart leapt.

"That's wonderful." Will grinned and ruffled his hair while she leant over and gave him another kiss.

"Clever boy."

"Yes," he said.

"You mustn't be afraid to speak to us," Will told him. "Promise Isobel and I that you are not afraid to speak to us."

"Promise," he replied and she clapped a hand to her mouth, hoping she wouldn't cry.

"Good boy." Will smiled. "Shall we surprise Florrie by you saying her name when she comes back? Yes?"

"Yes."

"What would you like to say to her?" she asked.

"Hello, Florrie."

"She'll like that very much. Shall we see what else is in the box while we wait for her to come back?"

"Yes."

"Now, let's see." Will reached in and lifted a wooden steam locomotive painted scarlet and black out of the box. "Ah, my train set. There are also some matching carriages – similar to the carriage the three of us were in when we travelled home from London – and a track. Shall we see if we can put it all together?"

"Yes."

"Come on, then." Will sat John down on the rug and between the three of them, they laid out the circular track and set the locomotive and carriages on it. "Let's give them a little push." He gently took John's hand and they pushed them around the track. "Can you remember the noise the locomotive made?"

"Toot-toot?" John suggested and they all laughed as the door opened and Florrie looked in at them.

"What would you like to say to Florrie?" Isobel whispered in his ear.

"Hello, Florrie."

The maid's grey eyes bulged and she clapped both hands to her cheeks. "Oh, hello, there, Master John. Oh, I'm so glad you've said hello."

"We're very proud of John for being such a clever boy." Isobel got to her feet. "Can I speak with you please, Florrie?"

"Yes, of course," the maid replied and Isobel kissed the top of John's head before going into John's bedroom. Florrie followed and closed the door. "Oh, Mrs Fitzgerald, however did you manage it?"

"It was the photograph," she replied. "Will told John about his parents and John went hysterical and threw the photograph against the wall. I'm afraid the glass went everywhere." She exhaled a shaky sigh. "It seems he was told in the children's home that his father didn't want him because he was a bastard."

Florrie's face crumpled in pity. "Was he afraid to say anything in case he was sent away from here?"

"Yes, it's possible, but I'm afraid we mustn't mention his father at all. The toys we brought him belonged to my husband and John's father but John must think they only belonged to my husband. John seems very taken with the locomotive. There are also some toy soldiers, which were his father's, and we'll have to take them away."

"Yes, Mrs Fitzgerald. Oh, I knew he would speak eventually, but not like this."

Isobel nodded. "We must all encourage him to continue to speak and we must all continue to assure him that we all want him and love him and that this is his home."

"Oh, the poor little boy."

"That children's home." Isobel fought to control her temper. "My husband's friend, Dr Hawley, has reported it and I hope it gets closed down for physical and mental cruelty. John may cry tonight, Florrie, and if he wants my husband and I then send for us, no matter what the time is."

"Yes, Mrs Fitzgerald."

"Thank you, Florrie. Let's get him ready for bed."

Fifteen minutes later, John was sitting up in bed with the locomotive standing on the bedside table beside Mr Effalump Elephant.

"We're so happy you are talking now." Will gave him a grin and John returned one. "Good boy. Sleep well and we'll play with the locomotive again tomorrow."

"Yes."

"Goodnight, John." She hugged and kissed him and he snuggled down under the covers.

In the nursery, Will extracted the photograph from amongst the remains of the frame on the floor.

"Is it damaged?" she asked and he shook his head.

"No, but I'm afraid the glass has gone everywhere."

"I'll sweep it up, Dr Fitzgerald," Florrie assured him.

"Thank you," he replied, picking the toy soldiers up off

the table. "We mustn't mention John's father, Florrie."

"Mrs Fitzgerald has explained, Dr Fitzgerald. The poor little boy, to tell him something like that…"

"We must encourage him to keep speaking."

"I will, Dr Fitzgerald."

"Thank you, Florrie, and if you need us – call us."

"Mrs Fitzgerald?" Mrs Dillon called as they were about to go into the morning room. "I have spoken with Annie, Florrie, Mary, and Gerald and they have no objections to the girl."

"The girl?" Will queried.

"The possible replacement for Florrie as house-parlourmaid," Isobel reminded him. "That is good news," she said, turning back to the housekeeper. "I would very much like to meet her."

"Of course, Mrs Fitzgerald. I will go to Mrs Anderson's Agency and arrange it."

In the morning room, Will put the toy soldiers and the photograph on the writing desk before sitting down on the sofa and running a hand across his jaw.

"I was confident John would speak eventually, but not in circumstances like that. And now I have to tell my parents that, yes, John is speaking at last, but they must not mention Edward in front of him. It's like we're taking two steps forward and then one step back."

"At least we are moving forward," she said and sat beside him. "I got such a shock when John started shouting."

"The photograph frame only just missed your head." He kissed her temple. "Who knows what else was said to him or in front of him in that place. Oh, God, I'm tired," he added with a groan. "Thank goodness it's Friday, it's been a terrible week. I'm meeting David at the practice house in the morning at eleven o'clock and we're taking a cab to Pimlico so I can show him the rooms, even though I'm beginning to have second thoughts."

"About starting a surgery there?" she asked and he nodded.

"I want to spend as much time as I can with you and John – and the baby when the time comes – and I can't if I'm on the other side of the city."

"Well, you've said all along there will be only one surgery per week and John and I could meet you on whatever day it is and we could all come home together."

"John can't walk all the way to Pimlico."

"No, we would go to St Stephen's Green first and then on to Pimlico. And on wet days, John and I will go and see your mother or mine. I want to keep as active as possible while I still can and it will be good for John to see more of Dublin. I don't want you to later regret not doing it," she added.

"Thank you," he replied gratefully.

"One thing, though; you'll need someone who will be able to come here to fetch you if you are needed urgently."

"Remember Jimmy?" he asked and she nodded. "He's a reliable lad. I'm going to leave enough money with him that he can come here by cab if need be. Plus, he lives next door, so he's right on the spot."

"You've got it all worked out."

"I hope so."

In the morning, he and Isobel went upstairs to the nursery where John was starting his breakfast.

"How are you this morning?" he asked. "Hungry?"

John smiled. "Yes."

"Good."

While Isobel sat down at the table and helped John with his boiled egg, Will followed Florrie into John's bedroom.

"There wasn't a peep out of Master John all night, Dr Fitzgerald," she told him. "And I looked in on him a couple of times."

"Thank you. I was worried he would stop speaking."

"He doesn't say much but he does speak and I'm so happy that he does."

"We're very relieved. Keep chatting to him."

"I will, Dr Fitzgerald," she replied.

"Thank you, Florrie."

They returned to the nursery and he kissed the top of John's head then Isobel's cheek before leaving to meet David at the practice house.

On Baggot Street, he took out his pocket watch. He had just enough time to walk to Ely Place Upper then call into the Shelbourne Hotel and reserve a dinner table for Isobel and himself for that evening.

Halting opposite number 1, he noted sadly how all the shutters were now closed before he walked back along Ely Place and went left onto Merrion Row, spotting his father ahead of him.

Will crossed over to the opposite pavement, followed him onto St Stephen's Green North and was about to call out a greeting when his father suddenly hurried across the street. On the steps of the hotel, Will turned as a cab stopped outside one of the entrances to the park, his father walked to it, opened the door and got in. Puzzled, Will watched as the cab set off in the direction of Earlsfort Terrace before taking off his hat and continuing on into the foyer to make the reservation.

Half an hour later, Will and David were standing in the smaller of the two rooms on Pimlico.

"This is ideal." David was nodding with clear approval. "And I'd very much like to help in any way I can."

"Are you sure?" Will asked. "It will be quite a commitment."

"I'm sure. I need the experience."

"Experience, David. Not experimentation."

"Of course."

"Well, two surgeries per week between us here will be wonderful. I was thinking about Fridays for myself. How about Tuesdays for you?"

"Tuesdays are fine."

"Good." Will gave him a grin and held out his hand. "Welcome to Pimlico."

"Thank you, Will." David shook it. "Let's clean these rooms. Where's the nearest shop so we can buy some bits and pieces?"

"It's not far. Come, and I'll show you some of the sights of the Liberties."

At just before half past twelve, Will was rolling down his shirtsleeves and fastening his cufflinks while David was closing the windows. The ceilings, walls and floors had been swept and every surface scrubbed clean. The rooms were now ready for furniture but that would have to wait until another day.

"Come to luncheon, David," he said, reaching for his frock coat, overcoat, and hat. "We'll find a cab on Cork Street."

"Thank you, Will, but I can't. I've arranged to meet Alfie. But I'll share your cab as far as College Green if that's all right?"

"Yes, of course. We'd better hurry, otherwise, I'll be in Mrs Dillon's bad books again for missing another meal."

He was closing the front door of number 30 as Isobel left the morning room.

"I have good news and good news and good news," he told her, hanging his hat on the stand and shrugging off his overcoat. "David will also be taking a surgery and we've just cleaned the two rooms, that's why I'm a little late."

"I'm so glad, about both," she said as he hung up his overcoat and kissed his lips. "Those rooms were filthy. What is the other good news?"

"I'm taking you out to dinner at the Shelbourne Hotel this evening. A cab will call for us at half past six."

"What's the occasion?" she asked as they went into the breakfast room.

"The last few weeks have been hell but we've come through and we need an evening out together."

"We do. I'll tell Mrs Dillon not to cook for us. Thank you."

Before changing their clothes that evening, they went upstairs to the nursery where John was in his bedroom on his way to bed.

"This evening, I'm taking Isobel to a hotel for dinner but we'll come and see you before we go," he told John. "You'd like to see us all dressed up?" he added and the little boy nodded. "Lift up your arms." John did as he was told and Will helped him into his nightshirt. "May I have a look at the sores on your bottom?"

"Yes."

Will raised the nightshirt. The sores were healed but scars remained.

"The sores are gone," he told the boy.

"They hurt."

"I know, but no-one will ever hurt you like that again," he said, lifting the little boy into the bed and Isobel tucked the bedcovers around him. "I have another surgery, that's where people who are sick come and see me, and David – he's another doctor who works with me – well, he and I spent an hour this morning cleaning the two rooms and we'll bring you to see them very soon. Florrie is going to read to you now and Isobel and I will be back when we've changed our clothes," he explained and John nodded.

"Master John asks me what I'm doing now, and why," Florrie told them in the nursery. "I still get a bit of a start, I'm not used to him speaking yet, but it's such a relief."

"It is, and we must all question him, too, and get him to build up his vocabulary."

"Yes, Dr Fitzgerald."

"We're making enormous progress, so we mustn't slip up now."

Chapter Seven

Isobel turned away from the dressing table mirror and caught Will staring at her. Standing up, she ran her hands down her front. Thanks to the tightly-fitting deep red evening dress and no corset, her pregnancy was clearly showing and very soon she wouldn't be able to wear the dress.

"I am going to have to go to the dressmaker," she told him, reaching for a shawl. "Soon, I'm going to burst through the seams of all my dresses."

"You're beautiful," he said softly and laid a hand on the roundness.

"That may be so, but I'm still going to need some new dresses."

"Order what you need."

"Thank you. You look very handsome."

He pulled a comical face. "I don't know why, but I never feel comfortable dressed in white tie and tails. I'm so used to wearing what my father refers to as 'workmen's clothes' in the evenings."

"There's nothing wrong with your black morning coat. Take no notice, you always look smart."

"Thank you. Let's go and see John before we go."

"Will?" she called as he went to the door and he turned back. "We're going to have to tell John about the baby because he's going to notice me getting bigger if he hasn't already."

"Yes."

He didn't sound very enthusiastic and she grimaced. "How did your parents explain human reproduction to you?"

"They didn't," he replied simply and her jaw dropped.

"What? Not even your father?"

"No. Fred's father told him and Fred told me in a typically Fred-like way."

"Fred?" she exclaimed and he nodded.

"Yes, and the following day I borrowed one of Father's medical textbooks and I read it from cover to cover on the floor under my bed with a candle. It's a wonder I didn't set the house on fire and ruin my eyesight at the same time."

"And did it satisfy your curiosity?"

He smiled. "No, because there were no diagrams and the book was written in such a dry style, I found it hard to follow and I didn't know where in the male and female body the author was referring to. It wasn't until I started at Wesley that the mystery of human reproduction was explained to me in a way I could understand."

"I can't believe your father didn't sit both you and Edward down and tell you."

"Sex was never mentioned in front of The Boys," he said and she rolled her eyes.

"I thought Ballybeg Glebe House was the only house in Ireland where sex was never mentioned in front of The Children."

261

"Well, John must not go through what we did," he said firmly. "We'll sit him down and tell him in the most simplistic of terms that you are expecting a baby and when he is older, we will explain it all to him."

"Yes. Now, let's go and see him."

John was sitting up in bed and Florrie was seated beside him with a book open on her lap. His dark eyes widened as he took in their clothes.

"Oh, don't Doctor and Mrs Fitzgerald look lovely, John?" Florrie asked and the little boy nodded.

"These are our going-out-to-dinner clothes," Will explained. "White tie and tails for me and an evening dress for Isobel. It's a beautiful colour, isn't it?"

"Yes," John replied. "Beautiful."

"We won't be back before you go to sleep so we'll say goodnight now." Isobel bent and kissed John's cheek. "Sleep tight."

"Yes," he replied and hugged her.

"Don't snore and keep Florrie awake," Will added and John gave him a sharp glance before he saw Will wink at him and squealed with laughter. "Goodnight. We'll see you in the morning."

"Your cab is here, Dr Fitzgerald," Mary told him as they went down the stairs to the hall and she helped them with their hats and coats before opening the front door.

"Thank you, Mary, goodnight," he said, following Isobel outside and down the steps. "It's George Millar, Isobel."

"Who?"

"The cabman who brought me to number 67 when I had typhilitis. George almost killed me but he helped to save my life at the same time so whenever I need a cab, I try and use him. He drives like a lunatic, but I've asked him for a more sedate pace this evening."

Clearly, George Millar's understanding of sedate was the opposite of Will's. She had to hold onto Will with one hand and the door handle with the other as the cab hurtled around corners with Will banging a fist on the ceiling ordering the cabman to slow down. When the cab was forced to stop on Merrion Row before proceeding on to St Stephen's Green, she couldn't help but turn to Will and laugh. He was looking out of the window and she followed his gaze.

"What's the delay?" she asked.

"I don't know, I can't see. George?" he called suddenly, opening the door and jumping out. "George, we'll walk from here."

"Right you are, Dr Fitzgerald. A gentleman is getting out of his cab in the middle of the street instead of allowing the cab to move out of the traffic. He's in no hurry at all. He's blowing kisses to the wife – Jaysis – it looks like he's giving the wife a proper old kiss goodbye now."

Will held her hand while she alighted from the cab and she went onto the pavement, walking to the nearest gas lamp while he paid their fare. The gentleman was leaning into a cab two ahead of theirs and when he drew back her eyes widened as gaslight fell on John Fitzgerald and Maria Simpson's faces. Reaching out, Maria clasped Will's father's cheeks in her gloved hands and kissed his lips. He then kissed Maria on the lips before lowering Maria's black lace veil and putting on his hat. When Will joined her on the pavement and took her hand, Isobel felt him tense when he saw who the gentleman was.

"What is my father doing?" Will muttered and they

watched his father close the cab door and cross the street without looking around before turning down Merrion Street Upper. "Strange," Will added as the cab moved off and the traffic began to flow again. "Let's go to the Shelbourne."

They were seated at a corner table in the hotel dining room, handed menus and she observed Will over the top of hers. His brown eyes skimmed through the offerings before he put his menu down on the table.

"What was my father doing abandoning Mother in a cab like that?" he whispered, clearly as much to himself as to her.

"Will, the woman in the cab wasn't your mother," she replied, putting her menu on the table between the cutlery and his eyes narrowed.

"So who was the woman in the cab?" he asked.

"The day before Fred's funeral, after I wasn't admitted to number 1, I decided to call on my mother," she explained. "Mother doesn't breakfast early these days so I took a longer route back to Fitzwilliam Square. I saw your father leave the *Journal* offices, hurry along Hume Street and open the door of a cab which had stopped at the junction with St Stephen's Green. A woman in the cab leant forward and he kissed her cheek. Your father looked around before he got in and the cab moved off in the direction of Earlsfort Terrace." She pulled a face but continued. "Will, the woman in the cab I saw your father kiss on the cheek that day – and on the lips today – is Maria Simpson."

"Why didn't you tell me you had seen Father and Maria together?" he demanded and Isobel threw a glance at a lady with a laugh like a braying donkey sitting at a table near the entrance to the dining room, grateful it was she and not them who was attracting the attention of all the diners.

"It was the day before Fred's funeral and your father simply kissed Maria on the cheek. I did think it was rather odd that your father met her in a cab on St Stephen's Green, but it was the uneasy way he looked around before getting into the cab which made me speculate if it was a secret assignation. I also wondered if they might be making last-minute funeral arrangements and going to Mount Jerome Cemetery. Will." She shrugged helplessly. "I was puzzled. I didn't know what conclusions to draw from what I saw."

"Well, what would you think if I told you that I also saw my father getting into a cab on Stephen's Green?" he asked, sitting back in his chair.

"When?"

"This morning, when I came here to reserve a dinner table for us. He was walking ahead of me on Merrion Row, crossed over to St Stephen's Green and got into a cab. The cab also moved off in the direction of Earlsfort Terrace."

"Why didn't you mention it?" she asked.

"Because Father was simply getting into a cab and I didn't see anyone else in it. Christ," he hissed under his breath. "What the hell is Father doing? I need to go and speak—"

"No." Grabbing his wrist as he went to get up, she held onto it tightly. "We saw your father turn down Merrion Street Upper so he's more than likely gone home. Do not confront him until you have more proof."

"You witnessed him kissing Maria Simpson's lips," he whispered in disgust. "What more proof is needed that he's carrying on an affair with her?"

"You need to be absolutely certain about this, Will."

They stared at each other then up at an approaching waiter and she quickly let go of Will's wrist.

"Are you ready to order, sir?"

"May we have another few minutes, please?" she asked and the waiter turned to her.

"Of course, madam."

"We'd better choose something." Will picked up his menu. "My father is not going to ruin this evening."

"No, and I won't allow the lady with the terrible laugh to ruin it either." They exchanged determined nods and she read through the menu. "The fantail of melon then the pan-fried trout for me, please. I'll decide on a dessert later. No wine, just a jug of water."

"I'll have the melon, too. And then the duck and—"

"Will, you can't have the duck," she interrupted. "What will John think when we tell him what we ate?"

Will sighed and read the menu again. "I'll have the trout as well, then." He gave the waiter their orders and they sat in silence for a few moments before he reached across the table and squeezed her hand. "We will enjoy this evening," he said softly but firmly as the lady brayed loudly again and they both swore under their breaths.

When their water arrived, Will filled their glasses then raised his.

"A toast," he announced. "To Fred. The four of us never did manage to come back here for a meal, but I know that wherever he is, Fred's in stitches at us toasting him with water and having to listen to—" He jerked his head in the direction of the lady with the braying laugh.

She smiled and touched Will's glass with hers. "To Fred," she said and they drank and put their glasses down.

"Can we walk home when we've eaten?" he asked. "Or do you think you'll be cold?"

"No, it's a mild evening and I'll enjoy a walk with you," she said and he nodded.

Their meals were delicious but the evening had been ruined and Will was quiet as they strolled home arm-in-arm, his mind clearly on his father. As they approached number 30, she could hear raised voices and they stopped. Tess, Will's parents' house-parlourmaid who doubled as his mother's lady's maid, was hurrying down the steps to a waiting cab while Mrs Dillon pleaded with someone from the front door.

"Doctor and Mrs Fitzgerald will be home soon. Please come inside and calm yourself."

"But I have no money to pay the cabman." Will's mother emerged from behind the cab smoothing down the skirt of her black dress and, to Isobel's horror, sank down onto the kerb bursting into tears.

"Christ," Will whispered and they ran to her. "Mother?"

"Oh, Will…"

"I'll pay the cabman, Mother. Isobel will escort you inside."

"Sarah." Clasping her mother-in-law's cold hands, Isobel raised her to her feet. "Come into the house, you're freezing."

"Tess, too?" Sarah asked and Isobel glanced at the girl. Usually, a capable maid, Tess' face was ashen. What on earth had she heard or witnessed?

"Yes, Tess, too. Come inside." Slowly they climbed the steps and went into the hall. "Mrs Dillon, this is Tess. Tess, this is Mrs Dillon. I think we could do with some tea – all of us," she added with a nod towards the maid, and the housekeeper took Tess' arm.

"Yes, Mrs Fitzgerald."

"Come into the morning room, Sarah." Isobel led her inside and sat her down on the sofa, hearing the front door close then silence as Will most likely hung up his hat and overcoat before his footsteps could be heard approaching the door.

"What's happened, Mother?" he asked, coming in and closing the door behind him.

"Oh, Will," she said in a shaky voice. "I don't know where to begin."

"Take your time."

"I have separated from your father."

Sarah knew about Maria Simpson. Isobel met Will's eyes and he agreed with the briefest of nods before crouching down in front of his mother.

"Why?" he asked softly.

"Your father was never one for openly expressing his feelings, but lately he's been extremely distant – even more distant than usual – and I put it down to him adjusting to not practising medicine anymore and the deaths of Duncan, Edward and Fred. But—" Sarah inhaled and exhaled deeply in an effort to compose herself. "Today, I discovered he has betrayed me with another woman. And has been doing so for quite some time."

"Do you know who the woman is?"

Sarah nodded. "Yes. And, oh, Will, it's so awful because I considered her a friend. It's Maria Simpson."

"How did you find out?"

"We saw them together."

"We?"

"I was out to luncheon with your mother, Isobel." Sarah

glanced at her for a moment. "We thought we would be adventurous and take the train to Kingstown for some sea air, luncheon and so I could call on Mrs Hawley. After we had eaten, we saw John and Maria strolling along the seafront as bold as brass. And then he kissed her – in public. He's never once, in all the years we've been married, kissed me in public. And I hate to admit it, but I fainted."

"Did you hurt yourself?" Will asked sharply and she shook her head.

"A bruised elbow, that's all. Poor Martha half-caught me as I fell and as soon as I was able, she brought me home. She's been so good and she didn't want to leave me but I insisted that I needed to confront your father alone."

"What did he say?"

"Well, he could hardly deny it. Oh, Will, they've been having an affair for years. We had the most terrible argument – the worst of our marriage – and I walked out."

"I'd better go and speak to him." Will went to get to his feet.

"No." Isobel and his mother spoke at once.

"No, Will," Sarah continued. "He's angry and I don't want you to row with him, too. Besides, this is between your father and I. Please, Will," she added as the door opened and Mary came in with a tea tray.

"How is Tess?" Sarah asked.

"She's having a cup of tea, Mrs Fitzgerald," Mary replied, putting the tray down on a side table.

"Poor Tess." Sarah sighed as Mary left the room. "She must have heard John and I shouting and was in the hall not knowing what to do. I simply grabbed her hand as I left the house."

"Mrs Dillon will look after Tess," Isobel assured her. "And Will and I will look after you. Could you pour the tea please, Will, while I have a quick word with her?"

In the hall, she unbuttoned and shrugged off her coat and hung it on the stand then went down the steps to the servants' hall.

"May I have a word, Mrs Dillon?" she asked as all the servants got to their feet.

"Of course, Mrs Fitzgerald." The housekeeper followed her into the kitchen and closed the door.

"Mrs Fitzgerald senior and Tess will be staying the night. Whether they stay any longer than that remains to be seen."

"Yes, Mrs Fitzgerald. I will have a guest room prepared and Tess can share with Mary."

"I'm afraid neither of them brought any nightdresses with them."

"Tess can borrow from Mary."

"And my mother-in-law can borrow from me."

"Yes, Mrs Fitzgerald. I didn't like to mention it in front of Mrs Fitzgerald senior, but Mrs Henderson called while you and Dr Fitzgerald were out. She wishes to speak to you urgently regarding Mrs Fitzgerald senior."

"I see. Thank you. How is Tess?" she asked.

"Quiet. We'll keep an eye on her. I went to the agency this afternoon and I spoke with Mrs Anderson about the girl," the housekeeper continued slowly, clearly not quite sure that this was the right time to bring up the subject. "And, if it is convenient to you, the girl can be here tomorrow at two o'clock."

"Tomorrow is Sunday, Mrs Dillon."

"Mrs Anderson is anxious to place the girl with a

household as soon as possible."

"I suspect Mrs Anderson wants the girl off her books as soon as possible."

"Yes, she does, Mrs Fitzgerald."

"It's just that I don't know if I will be free tomorrow. May I speak to you about this in the morning?"

"Of course."

"Thank you, Mrs Dillon."

She returned to the morning room and saw at once that Sarah had been crying.

"A room is being prepared for you," she said gently. "And Tess is staying here, too."

"I'm being so much trouble…"

"No—"

"But I've spoilt your evening," Sarah protested. "You look so lovely – both of you."

"Thank you," Will replied, getting up and sitting beside his mother on the sofa. "We had dinner at the Shelbourne Hotel. Isobel and I had the trout. I wasn't allowed to have the duck."

"Why ever not?" his mother asked.

"John loves the ducks in St Stephen's Green," she explained. "I didn't particularly want to have to explain to him why Will had eaten one of their cousins."

"How is he?"

Isobel met Will's eyes with a smile and he turned to his mother.

"John has started to speak," he said and Sarah clapped her hands to her face.

"Oh, Will. Oh, how wonderful."

"He doesn't say a lot, but it's a start."

"So he is happy here?"

"Yes, he is."

"And soon he will have a cousin in the nursery."

"Yes, he will." Isobel laid a hand on her stomach just as the door opened and Mary came in.

"I've just admitted Dr John Fitzgerald to the hall, Doctor Fitzgerald. Was that the right thing to do?"

Sarah's eyes widened in alarm but Will squeezed her hands and got to his feet.

"Yes, it was, Mary. Thank you. I'll speak to him."

"Don't row with him, Will, please?" his mother begged.

"I'll try not to," he replied and followed Mary from the room.

His father was standing at the front door and took in Will's white tie and tails with clear surprise.

"You've been out?"

"Isobel and I dined at the Shelbourne," Will explained as Mary scurried down the steps to the servants' hall. "Come upstairs."

"I want to speak to your mother," his father stated firmly and went to walk towards the morning room door.

"No." Will quickly blocked his father's way. "Mother doesn't want to speak to you. Come upstairs."

They went up the stairs to the drawing room where Will lit the gas lamps and waited for his father to speak.

A few moments of silence passed before his father spoke irritably. "Say something, then."

"I was waiting for an explanation from you," he replied, surprised at how composed he sounded. He certainly didn't feel in the least bit calm.

His father walked to one of the huge sash windows and gazed out over the lamp-lit square. "Duncan and I both pursued Maria but she threw me over for Duncan." He turned away from the window and gave Will a bitter smile. "So you weren't the only Fitzgerald to have his heart broken."

"I have no lingering feelings for Cecilia," Will told him. "None whatsoever."

"You say that now. What about in twenty – thirty – years from now?"

"I adore Isobel—"

"I thought I adored your mother," his father interrupted. "But Maria was always there at the back of my mind. Perhaps if I had never seen her again after she threw me over, matters may have been different. But she married my best friend, I had to socialise with her regularly, and I simply couldn't forget her."

"When did your affair begin?" Will asked.

"About a year before Fred was born," his father told him matter-of-factly.

Will's jaw dropped. "Fred was your son?"

"Yes."

"Did Duncan know?"

"Of course," his father replied. "That he had a 'son' left Duncan free to be with Ronald Henderson and forge a successful career."

"Are you telling me Duncan and Maria never had sexual intercourse?"

"Yes, I am. Duncan informed Maria he wasn't interested in her sexually – and why – on their wedding night."

Will's head began to pound. He went to the sofa and sat

down, pulling open his bow tie and collar. "So what you told me last year about you questioning Duncan after his outburst at Ronald Henderson's funeral was all lies. When did you find out about Duncan and Ronald?"

"Maria sought me out and told me about them the day she and Duncan returned from their honeymoon. Duncan was always quite secretive but I had absolutely no idea he preferred men to women until Maria told me. If I had known, Maria would have married me. The only reason Duncan pursued Maria was that he needed to marry and Maria would be a fitting wife for him. Will, your mother doesn't know I am Fred's father and she must never know."

"So you do care a little for Mother, then?" Will sneered. "The woman you married simply because she would be a suitable wife for you."

"Of course I care for her," his father snapped. "I've been married to her for thirty-six years."

"And fucking Duncan's wife all along."

"Don't be crude."

"But you knew Duncan had syphilis all along, too, didn't you?" Will realised with disgust, getting to his feet and rubbing his forehead.

"I recognised the signs early on, yes."

"And yet you allowed Duncan to continue to practise as a surgeon—"

"There were no lesions on his hands but I told Maria that Duncan had syphilis and, more recently, I knew Fred had discovered Duncan was ill and was monitoring him—"

"So you simply left it up to good old Fred." Will couldn't keep the scorn from his voice as he remembered how an exhausted Fred had broken down in tears and confessed how

274

he had been hiding Duncan's mistakes and behaviour from people for the best part of a year. "He never knew you were his father, though, did he?"

"No. Because I knew he wouldn't be able to keep it from you and ultimately from your mother."

"So what now? Are you going to give Maria Simpson up?"

"I can't."

"In that case, Father, it will soon become common knowledge that Mother has separated from you – and why."

"Will, I came here because I need to appeal to your mother to come home and to tell her that very soon Maria will no longer be a part of my life."

"Maria is dying, isn't she?" Will asked and his father nodded.

"Cancer. She has a tumour in her left breast. She can no longer walk far, hence all the cab journeys. Soon, she will be confined to bed and I doubt very much if she will live to see the summer."

"You can't expect Mother to return home and—"

"Your mother's a practical woman."

"She's just discovered her entire married life has been a complete charade." Will's voice rose and his head pounded even more. "She won't do it."

"She will," his father replied firmly. "She is my wife and once she calms down she will realise she doesn't want all of Dublin to know of her marital difficulties."

"You're making it sound as if it is all her fault," Will roared.

"Go and fetch her, Will."

"No, I will not. If you think you can shame her into returning home—"

"Will." Isobel was standing in the doorway. "We can hear you downstairs. Your mother is upset again."

"I'll go to her," he said. "Father is leaving."

"I am not leaving this house without your mother," his father announced stubbornly and Will glared at him before walking out of the room.

Isobel watched Will run down the stairs before turning to his father. John Fitzgerald's eyes took in her stomach's roundness and she felt him watch her as she walked across the large room to the drinks tray.

"Would you like some whiskey?" she asked.

"Yes, I would, thank you."

She poured the drink and passed the glass to him. "I know what it's like to have parents with an unhappy marriage. Will does not."

"Would your mother have separated from your father if he had not died?"

"No," she replied immediately. "My mother's family didn't want her to marry my father – he was a mere curate in the village near their home at the time – but she thought she loved him and she ran away from home to marry him. Then she discovered he was a selfish, cruel and violent man and that divorce was out of the question. She was trapped in a marriage to a man admired by his parishioners but violent towards – not only herself – but her children, too. Have you ever been violent towards your wife, John?" she asked, addressing him by his Christian name for the first time and his eyebrows rose at her bluntness.

"No. Never. Nor towards Edward or Will. I just—" He sighed. "I simply could not love Sarah the way I love Maria.

No doubt Will shall tell you all but..." He tailed off and sighed again.

"You want Sarah to come home with you and to put up and shut up like all wives are expected to do?"

"All wives?" he echoed. "I doubt very much if you would."

"No, I wouldn't. I don't need to remind you what Will and I went through – what I put Will through – before we got married? I had to know he was finished with Cecilia and that he truly loved me. I love him, John. I am a good wife to him and he will never feel the need to stray as long as he is married to me."

"In that case, you and Will are very fortunate."

They both turned to see Sarah at the door with a clearly disapproving Will standing right behind her.

"I would like to speak to my husband alone now, Isobel," Sarah continued in a brisk tone.

"Yes, of course. Will and I shall be downstairs."

Taking Will's hand, Isobel led him down the stairs to the morning room. He slammed the door and she waited for him to explode.

"The bloody arrogance of the man. Mother shouldn't be giving in to him like this."

"Let's just see what happens. At least your parents are discussing their marriage. Mine never did."

"Your parents' marriage wasn't a complete sham."

"A sham?" she repeated with a puzzled little shake of her head. "I don't understand."

Will paced the room while he explained and she gasped and grabbed his arm as he passed her for what seemed like the umpteenth time.

"Wait, Will. Stop for a moment. Fred was your half-brother?"

"Yes. He was my brother and I never knew." He finished in a whisper and she put her arms around him as he cried. "And Father wants Mother never to know," he sobbed. "How can we keep something like that from her?"

"Will," she said, hoping she could reason with him. "Think of your poor mother. It's bad enough her knowing of the affair. Imagine if she knew there'd been a child and that child was Fred."

Will raised his head and grimaced as she gently wiped his tears away with her fingers. "It would kill her. But my father deserves—"

"Will, Fred is dead, and soon Maria will be, too. When she is dead, your parents may be able to start again. Let's just wait and see if they can come to an agreement."

"Yes," he replied with clear reluctance in his voice.

"At least your father has never struck her," she added and Will's eyes widened.

"You asked my father if he has been violent?"

"I was brought up in a violent home, Will, I had to ask."

He nodded and kissed her lips. "We'd better make ourselves comfortable, they could be some time."

They sat on the sofa and he put an arm around her just as the door opened and his parents walked in.

"May we sit down?" Sarah asked, both appearing and sounding remarkably calm.

"Yes, of course," she replied and Sarah and John sat in the armchairs.

"We've had a frank discussion and I will be returning home tonight with John," Sarah announced.

Isobel felt Will tense. "Mother—"

"No, Will." Sarah held up a hand to stop him. "Please allow me to continue. I feel hurt, angry and betrayed but I will allow John to remain with Maria until she dies because John and I had two wonderful sons together. Edward is dead but his son is not. Will, your father has agreed to write young John into his will. The boy is a Fitzgerald and he will inherit number 67 when the time comes. As well as that, your father will sign an agreement entitling me to reside at number 67 for my lifetime. My grandson has his rightful inheritance, I am guaranteed a home until my death, and I am content."

"Very well." Will reached out and squeezed her hand.

"Could you please ring for Tess, Isobel?" Sarah asked. "I would very much like to go home and go to bed."

"I'll fetch her myself," she said, getting to her feet. "I need to have a quick word with Mrs Dillon."

Before going to the servants' hall, Isobel hurried upstairs to the drawing room and sat down at the writing desk. Pulling a sheet of notepaper towards her, she scribbled Sarah a note.

Dear Sarah,

I do not wish to alarm you but please consider appointing your own solicitor who can look over the will and the residency agreement for you. I can highly recommend Mr James Ellison. Will shall pay the legal fees.

Isobel

She blotted and folded the note and placed it in an

envelope. She then wrote a second note to reassure her mother.

> *Dear Mother,*
>
> *Thank you for calling to number 30 this evening. Please do not worry about Sarah. She is here at present but is returning to number 67 with John. I will call first thing in the morning and explain.*
>
> *Isobel*

Blotting and folding the note, she put it in an envelope and wrote *MOTHER* on the front so she wouldn't mix up the two envelopes. She got up from the desk and extinguished the gas lamps, went downstairs to the servants' hall and met Mrs Dillon coming out of the kitchen.

"I'm terribly sorry, Mrs Dillon, but my mother-in-law and Tess are returning to Merrion Square tonight. And tomorrow," she added. "I will be free to meet the girl at two o'clock. In the meantime, could Gerald deliver this note to number 55, please?"

"Yes, of course, Mrs Fitzgerald." Mrs Dillon took the envelope from her. "I'll instruct Gerald and call Tess for you."

The housekeeper went into the servants' hall and a few moments later Tess came out.

"Can we step outside for a moment, please, Tess?" It was dark, but she brought the maid down the garden towards the mews, well away from any prying eyes and ears. "I'm sure you know why my mother-in-law left Merrion Square this evening?"

"Yes, I do, Mrs Fitzgerald."

"Tess, my parents-in-law claim to have reached an agreement and are returning home together. I'm not asking you to spy on your mistress, and she is bound to be distressed by what has happened today, I would simply like for you to keep a close eye on her. If, at any time, you feel an argument is getting out of hand or feel afraid for her safety, please send someone for either myself, my husband or my mother or brother who live at number 55 Fitzwilliam Square."

"Yes, I will, Mrs Fitzgerald."

"Thank you. Could you also pass this note to her?" The maid nodded, took the envelope, and placed it in her apron pocket. "Thank you, Tess. We'd better go inside before someone comes to look for us."

They returned to the house and found Will and his parents waiting for them in a stony silence at the open front door.

"May Will and I call on you tomorrow, Sarah?" she asked and her mother-in-law's face brightened.

"Of course you may. In the afternoon? Despite it being Sunday, John and I shall be calling to the solicitor first thing in the morning."

"The afternoon it is," she said and turned to Will's father. "Goodnight, John."

"Goodnight, Isobel. Will." John nodded to him, but Will didn't reply, and John followed his wife and Tess out of the house.

Will closed the door and leant back against it, his face devoid of all colour. "Mother shouldn't have gone home with him."

"If she had felt in any way uncertain she would have stayed here. We'll call to number 67 tomorrow and I will ask

Mother to call the next day. I've asked Tess to keep an eye on your mother and she will also pass your mother a note from me recommending she consult James Ellison and ask him to inspect the will and the residency agreement and that you would pay the legal fees."

"Thank you."

"Can we go to bed now, Will?" she asked, suddenly feeling drained. "There's nothing more we can do tonight and I'm very tired."

"Of course, we can." Taking her face in his hands, he kissed her lips. "Thank you for everything you've done today."

Some hours later, Isobel woke with a jump feeling the baby move.

"Isobel, what is it?" Will asked, sounding wide awake and she blinked and squinted as he turned the oil lamp up.

"The baby's moving," she said, reaching for his hand and placing it on her belly. "How long have you been awake?"

"I haven't been to sleep," he replied with a shrug. "Everything has been going round and round in my head – Father and Mother – Father and Maria – Father and Fred – I just can't believe Fred was my brother."

"Do you think he knew?"

"Who knows. But I doubt it."

"Say no if you'd rather not," she began, hoping it wasn't too soon to suggest it. "But one day, we could visit Fred's grave..?"

"Yes, I'd like that very much," he said in a voice thick with emotion. "I'd like to go tomorrow afternoon. I have two house calls to make then I'll come to number 67 for you and see how Mother is."

"Tomorrow it is. Try and sleep now," she said softly.

"Does the baby often wake you up?"

"That was the first time. It will probably happen most nights from now on. I'll try not to wake you."

"It doesn't matter," he said. "I love you and I love feeling our baby move." Easing her back against him, he turned the oil lamp down and they slept.

After breakfast, and helping young John with his, Isobel walked around the gardens to number 55. Her mother was alone and still at her own meal but put her triangular slice of toast and marmalade down as Isobel was shown into the breakfast room.

"How is Sarah?" Mrs Henderson asked at once.

Isobel went to the sideboard and helped herself to a cup of coffee before pulling a chair out from the table and sitting beside her mother.

"There was quite a commotion last night. On our return from the Shelbourne Hotel, Will and I found Sarah and her maid outside number 30. Sarah was in a very distressed state, saying she had separated from John. We managed to calm her and she explained what she had seen in Kingstown, but then John arrived at the house insisting that he speak to her."

"Oh, dear."

"Will didn't want Sarah to speak with John but Sarah insisted and I'm glad she did but I'm not overly happy with the outcome."

"Why not?" her mother asked with a frown. "Your note said Sarah was returning to number 67 with John."

"Sarah agreed to return home with John on the condition that he write young John into his will," she explained. "Young John will inherit number 67 – and it is what he is entitled to – but as his grandfather was forced into it, I'm worried it will cause him to resent young John. In addition to that, an agreement will be drawn up enabling Sarah to reside at number 67 for her lifetime."

"What has Will said about it all?"

Isobel grimaced. "He and his father had 'words' last night and he thinks his mother shouldn't have returned home with his father. Mother, I hope you don't mind, but I wrote Sarah a note advising her to have the will and the residency agreement looked over and I recommended James Ellison."

Her mother flushed. "Why should I mind?"

"Well, I wasn't sure if I should involve James, but it is up to him whether or not to accept Sarah as a client."

"Yes, it is. Are you going to call on Sarah today?"

"This afternoon," she said. "Sarah and John are calling to John's solicitor this morning."

"Then, I will call on her tomorrow."

"Thank you. Yesterday must have been awful."

"It was," her mother said with a sigh. "There they were – John Fitzgerald and Maria Simpson – as bold as brass strolling along the seafront arm-in-arm. And then he kissed her. And Sarah fainted. I half-caught her but she still fell to the ground. It was almost an hour before she was calm enough to go home. We took a cab. She was in no fit state for the train."

"Did John and Maria see either of you?" Isobel asked and her mother shook her head.

"No. And I am extremely relieved they didn't. Can you imagine the scene if John and Sarah had been violent towards each other in public?" her mother said in a hushed tone and Isobel shrugged.

"I can't speak for Sarah, but John has never been violent towards her – and I doubt if he ever would be – but I have asked Sarah's maid to keep an eye on Sarah all the same."

Her mother stared at her open-mouthed. "You asked John Fitzgerald if he had ever been violent?"

"Yes, I did."

"Then, you are braver than I am, Isobel. I didn't dare ask Sarah."

"Mother, I needed to know whether their discussion – in my home – with young John sleeping upstairs – was likely to turn violent. Thankfully, it didn't, and Sarah believes she has struck a good bargain and she has allowed the affair to continue until Maria dies."

"Until Maria dies..?" her mother repeated in a puzzled tone as Isobel took a sip of coffee. "I don't understand?"

"Maria Simpson has cancer," Isobel explained. "She will not live to see the summer. I think Sarah was very much afraid John would force her out of number 67 and move Maria in until she dies, which is why Sarah insisted on a legal entitlement to reside in the house for her lifetime."

"Oh." Her mother's eyes bulged. "Good gracious – Sarah really did strike a hard bargain."

"Yes, she did. I just wish young John hadn't been used as a bargaining tool."

At just after two o'clock, Isobel stood up as the door opened and Mrs Dillon showed the prospective house-parlourmaid into the morning room.

"Susan, Mrs Fitzgerald," the housekeeper announced and left the room.

Susan had always been referred to as 'the girl' but she was, in fact, a young woman in her early twenties and she eyed

Isobel nervously. Isobel smiled to reassure her and pointed to the sofa.

"Please, sit down."

"Thank you," she said, sitting down at one end and Isobel sat at the other.

Susan's black hair was pulled into a bun at the nape of her neck and she wore a prim navy blue dress, not all that dissimilar to one Isobel had owned.

"I am Isobel Fitzgerald. Is Susan your real name?" she asked gently.

"No, Mrs Fitzgerald. My previous employer called me Susan as it was easier for him to remember. My real name is Zaineb Gamal. Here is my reference."

"Thank you." Isobel took the envelope and pulled out a sheet of notepaper. The character reference from an address on Mountjoy Square was glowing. She returned it to the envelope and passed it back, both angry and saddened that Zaineb was all but unemployable simply because of the colour of her skin. "Where were you born, Zaineb?"

"In London, Mrs Fitzgerald," she replied. "But my mother was born in southern Egypt. My father was also born in London. He served in the army but he was killed in India."

"I'm sorry," Isobel said and Zaineb gave a little shrug.

"I barely knew him. He and my mother... they were not married. He brought my mother to London when she discovered she was with child."

"Is your mother still in London?" Isobel asked.

"No, my mother and I moved to Dublin last year and Mother is the cook in a solicitor's residence on Mountjoy Square. It is the same address which is on my reference. I was employed there on trial as a parlourmaid but—" She peered down at her hands. "Clients and callers stopped calling as they did not wish for someone who looks like me to open the door to them. I could have worked in the kitchen, where no-one would have seen me but, unlike my mother, I am a terrible cook."

"I can't cook either," Isobel told her and gave Zaineb a little smile as she raised her head. "But Mrs Dillon is a wonderful cook. Have the wages, days off and the household been explained to you?" she asked.

"Mrs Dillon informed me of the wages and days off and a little of the household."

"Well, I will elaborate on the household. My husband is a doctor but his practice house is on Merrion Street Upper, so patients – or patients' servants – will only call here in an emergency. If they call here late in the evening, or during the night, only our footman will open the front door or areaway door to them. My husband's elder brother was in the army but died some weeks ago in India. My husband and I are raising his three-year-old son, John, as our own. John's mother was an Indian woman—"

"And you are raising him as your own?" Zaineb exclaimed before clapping a hand to her mouth for a moment. "I'm sorry."

"Did your father's family disown you?" Isobel asked and she nodded.

"My father was from a good family. They did not approve of my mother and I."

"I'm sorry to hear that."

"Thank you."

"John lives upstairs in the nursery and Florrie is now his

nursery maid, which is why we need to replace her. We have a small household but the work is still too much for one house-parlourmaid to undertake. The vast majority of our callers are family. My mother and brother live across the square and my husband's parents live on Merrion Square. And that is all," Isobel concluded with a smile. "And I would like to offer you the position of house-parlourmaid, Zaineb. Would you be able to start tomorrow?"

Zaineb's jaw dropped. "I can start today, Mrs Fitzgerald. Oh, thank you."

"You may move in today and begin tomorrow. Do you do have your own uniforms?"

"Yes, I have uniforms. Oh, thank you, Mrs Fitzgerald."

"And we won't be calling you Susan, here," Isobel told her as she got up and rang the bell for Mrs Dillon. "Zaineb is your name and you will be called by your name."

"Thank you, Mrs Fitzgerald. I'm very grateful."

"And if there are any problems – and I hope there won't be any – please speak to either Mrs Dillon or myself."

"I will," Zaineb replied and got up as the housekeeper came in.

"The new house-parlourmaid, Mrs Dillon," Isobel told her before adding, "Zaineb, not Susan. Zaineb will be moving in today and starting tomorrow."

"Yes, Mrs Fitzgerald." Mrs Dillon smiled in reply before ushering Zaineb from the room.

Isobel exhaled a contented little sigh as the door closed.

At three o'clock, Isobel was admitted to number 67 and Sarah got up from the chair at the writing desk as she was shown into the morning room.

"Isobel, thank you for your note. I shall bring a draft copy of the will and the residency agreement to Mr Ellison for his appraisal tomorrow morning."

"I'm glad. I hoped you wouldn't think I was interfering."

"No, not at all."

"How are you?"

Her mother-in-law's eyebrows rose and fell. "Very well, considering. I'm terribly sorry for turning up at number 30 and causing such a to-do last night."

"Sarah, I'm relieved you felt you could come to number 30 and our door will always be open to you if need be."

"Thank you, but that will not be necessary. I am content with the outcome of my discussion with John."

"Where is he?"

"John went out straight after luncheon to the *Journal* offices. He said he had some matters there he needed to attend to. Whether that is actually true, I cannot say."

"I see," she replied as the door opened and Tess came in.

"Are you at home to Mrs Maria Simpson, Mrs Fitzgerald?" she asked and Isobel's heart pounded apprehensively while Sarah gave the maid a brief nod.

"You may show her in, please, Tess."

"Yes, Mrs Fitzgerald."

"I'll go, Sarah."

"Thank you, Isobel. I would prefer to speak to Maria alone."

Maria Simpson was waiting in the hall wearing a black velvet cloak over a black taffeta dress and a ridiculously large black feathered hat. To Isobel's further unease, Maria gave Isobel a grim smile and inclined her head when Isobel passed her. Tess showed Maria into the morning room, closed the door then walked to the front door as Isobel heard raised voices.

"Could you wait a moment, please, Tess?" Isobel asked when the maid went to open the door.

Hearing a slap, a shriek and then a thud, she ran back along the hall and into the morning room with Tess right behind her. Sarah was standing in the middle of the floor with her hands clapped to her cheeks in horror while Maria lay flat on her back on the rug beside the brass fender which surrounded the hearth. Hugh Lombard and then Fred Simpson flashed in front of Isobel's eyes and she blinked furiously to rid the images from her mind before turning to Tess.

"Go and find a doctor – any doctor," she ordered. "Go, Tess – now." The maid ran from the room and Isobel got down on her hands and knees beside Maria.

"Is she dead?" Sarah demanded, her voice shaking. "I struck her and she staggered backwards, tripped over the rug and hit her head on the fender."

Isobel felt Maria's neck for a pulse, there was one, and she exhaled a relieved breath. "No, she's alive."

"Should we try and move her, Isobel?"

"No. Not if she's hit her head."

The front door slammed, footsteps ran along the hall and Isobel looked up as Will came into the room.

"Isobel – Mother – are either of you injured?"

"No," Isobel replied.

"Good. Tess." He turned to the maid, standing behind him in the doorway, and quickly moved aside. "Please escort my mother to the drawing room and pour her a brandy."

"Yes, Dr Fitzgerald." Taking Sarah's arm, Tess led her from the room.

"Isobel." Will closed the door after them, before crossing

the room and dropping to his knees beside her. "Tell me what happened," he said as he put his medical bag to one side then felt Maria's neck for a pulse.

"Your mother struck Maria and Maria tripped over the rug and hit her head on the fender."

"Were you present?"

"No. Your mother said she would prefer to speak to Maria alone. I was at the front door with Tess when I heard raised voices then a slap, a shriek and a thud. Your mother wanted to move Maria but I said no."

"Good," he replied and carefully removed a pin from Maria's hat, followed by another and another. Isobel frowned incredulously as no less than six hat pins were pulled out and placed beside the medical bag, followed by the hat itself. Will lifted Maria's eyelids and grimaced then used the tips of his fingers of both hands to gently examine her head, slowly feeling his way from the top of Maria's skull to the base. "Here," he murmured to himself. "Christ," he added in a whisper as he bent to inspect Maria's ears and the surrounding skin before lifting his hands away, his fingers covered in blood.

"Why is Maria bleeding from both ears?" she asked, suddenly fighting back nausea.

"Maria has a depressed fracture of the base of her skull which has caused bruising and bleeding to the soft tissue in her brain," he told her and Hugh Lombard flashed in front of her eyes for a second time. He had died of more or less the same injury on number 30's drawing room floor. "There is also bruising becoming evident behind Maria's ears which suggests the fracture extends from the base to both sides of the skull," Will went on as she squeezed her eyes so tightly shut that she was thankful when all she could see for a few moments were multi-coloured stars. "It is highly unlikely Maria will regain consciousness."

"How long does she have left?"

"Not long. Is my father here?"

"No, he went to the *Journal* offices after luncheon."

"Isobel, please send someone there to fetch him."

"I'll go," she said. "What shall I tell him?"

"That there has been an accident and Maria has been injured. Nothing more – I'll explain what has happened before he sees her."

"Should Maria be moved now?" she asked, glancing down at her face.

"Yes. I'll ask for help to move her to a bedroom."

"I'll ask the housekeeper that one be prepared."

"Thank you. Please ask for the pillows to be covered with some towels – and ask for a large towel to be brought here as well - I need to wrap it around Maria's head."

"Will, your mother…"

"I'll speak to her. Go and bring Father here." She nodded and he grabbed her hand before she could get up. "Are you all right?" he asked and she nodded again, despite her queasy stomach wanting to heave. "Isobel, I don't know how my father is going to react, so bring Maura with you."

"There's really—" she began.

"There is," he insisted. "Bring Maura with you."

"Very well."

"Good. And walk, Isobel, don't run."

"Yes."

He kissed then released her hand and she tried to ignore Maria's blood on it as she got to her feet and left the room.

Will pulled a handkerchief out of his trouser pocket and wiped his fingers before straightening Maria's arms and legs. As carefully as they could, he and Terence, the footman, carried Maria upstairs to the second floor, into a guest bedroom and she was placed in the freshly-made bed.

"Is there anything I can do, Dr Fitzgerald?" the housekeeper asked.

"Could you sit with Mrs Simpson, please, Mrs Rogers? I must speak to my mother."

"Yes, of course."

"Thank you. Please shout for me if you notice any change in her condition."

"I will."

His mother was seated on the sofa in the drawing room with a glass of brandy in her hands. On seeing him, she put the glass on a side table, her hand trembling.

"Could you wait outside, please, Tess?" he asked and closed the door after the maid. "Mother." Sitting down beside her on the sofa, he held her hands. "Maria has been brought upstairs."

"How is she?"

"Maria has a depressed fracture of the base of her skull," he told her gently. "She is unconscious and she is not going to wake up."

"I've killed her?"

"It was an accident."

"But she's going to die?" his mother persisted.

"Yes."

"She's going to die – here – in this house?"

"Yes."

"No."

His jaw dropped. "What?"

"I will not allow that woman to die in this house."

"But, Mother—"

"No, Will." She held up a hand to stop him continuing. "She came here to provoke me. Please remove her from this house."

"Provoke you?"

"She came here to inform me that your father is also father to Fred Simpson and if you do not remove her from this house, I will go upstairs and drag her down the stairs and out onto the street myself."

"Mother, she is going to die very soon."

"Not in this house," his mother replied stubbornly.

"You really would have her die in the street?" he demanded.

"As long as it is not in this house, I do not care where she dies."

Will fought to control his temper. "Mother, please—"

"Very well." His mother got to her feet and walked to the door. "I will remove her from this house myself."

"Mother." Following her to the door, he reached out and held it shut, deciding to be blunt. "When Maria hit her head on the fender, the base of her skull was crushed inwards and it has caused bruising and bleeding to her brain. Maria is now bleeding from the ears. She can't be carted through the streets in such a condition."

"Take her to number 68, then."

"Mother, please think," he begged. "Do you really want to explain why to the Harveys'?"

"Jim Harvey is a fool," she replied crisply. "But Harriett is a sensible woman and will understand. Step aside, Will, please."

Reluctantly, Will complied and his mother opened the door and went out.

Isobel took a deep breath and knocked at the front door to the offices of the *Journal of Irish Medicine* on Hume Street, hoping Will's father was there and not at his club as it didn't allow women inside. To her relief, the door opened and John stared first at her and then at Maura in surprise before a wary expression crossed his face.

"Isobel?"

"May I speak to you in your office, John?"

"Please, follow me." Leaving Maura to shut the front door, he brought Isobel along the hall, opened a door to the right for her and she went into a large wood-panelled office. "Please, sit down," he added as he closed the door.

"Thank you, but I would prefer to stand."

"What is it, Isobel? Is it Will? Sarah?"

"John, I was visiting Sarah when Maria Simpson called to the house—"

"Maria?" he interrupted sharply.

"Yes. I'm afraid there has been an accident and Maria has been injured. Please come—"

"Injured?"

"Will shall explain and—"

"What happened?" he demanded and she sighed.

"Sarah said she would like to speak to Maria alone, so I prepared to leave. I was in the hall when I heard raised voices, a slap, a shriek and then a thud. I returned to the morning room and found Maria unconscious on the floor. It seems Sarah hit her and Maria tripped over the hearth rug and struck her head on the fender."

"Is Maria dead?" he asked slowly.

"Will arrived almost immediately and examined her. Maria has a depressed fracture of the base of her skull which has caused bruising and bleeding to the soft tissue in her brain. Will does not expect her to regain consciousness."

"So, Sarah has killed her," he stated in a flat tone.

"No."

"No?" His eyebrows rose. "How else would you explain it?"

"My explanation can wait—"

"No, Isobel, I would like to hear it now."

She sighed again. "Very well. It is my belief that Maria came to number 67 to provoke Sarah into striking her and—"

"Provoke her?"

"Yes. John." She gestured to the door. "We really need to return to—"

"Maria would not provoke Sarah."

"Well, why did Maria call to number 67 today?" she asked. "When Maria passed me in the hall, she smiled at me. It was not the smile of a woman calling on a friend for a cup of afternoon tea. Did you and Maria see Sarah and my mother in Kingstown yesterday?"

"No, but—" His shoulders slumped. "Maria did know Sarah knew about us. Last evening, when Sarah walked out, I took a cab to the Wingfield house on Rutland Square to warn Maria and to instruct the servants not to answer the door in case Sarah went there."

"Well, Maria went to Sarah instead. Please, come with me, John, there isn't much time."

To her despair, he stood his ground. "I don't want to see Maria… broken."

"John." Reaching out, she held his hands. "Please come. Will was to bring Maria to a bedroom and make her as comfortable as possible. Please come."

"But Sarah—"

"I will look after Sarah," she said softly but firmly. "Come." Gently, she led him to the door and opened it. Maura was waiting in the hall and Isobel felt John tense. "Maura came with me on Will's orders to ensure I walked here and didn't run." Giving her stomach a little pat, she went to the coat stand, handed John his hat and overcoat and the three of them left the building.

They walked to Merrion Square in silence but inside number 67 there was anything but quiet. Upstairs, a door slammed and Will begged his mother not to go next door but she came running down the stairs with Will close behind her.

"That woman will not die in this house," Sarah informed John. "I'm going to speak to Harriett Harvey."

"No, you are not," he snapped. "Calm yourself, Sarah, you're hysterical."

"John, I am anything but hysterical. I am perfectly calm. I will not have my husband's mistress die in this house."

"Maria is not to be moved."

"She is – unless you would prefer that I announce to all of Dublin that Fred Simpson was your son – and why?"

"You wouldn't dare."

"No?"

They faced each other and for a horrible moment which went on for what seemed like an age, Isobel expected either one to strike the other, but John stepped to one side and Sarah went to the front door.

"Sarah, wait." Isobel caught her arm. "I think it would be best if I speak to Mrs Harvey."

"I have just said, Isobel, that I am perfectly calm," Sarah informed her in an icy tone.

"Yes, you are, Mother," Will spoke up and Isobel exchanged a quick glance with him. "But a little detachment is called for. Please allow Isobel to go."

His mother exhaled an exasperated sigh. "But—"

"Please, wait in the morning room, Mother."

"Oh, very well." Sarah walked away from the front door and John ran upstairs.

"Isobel." Will lifted her hand and kissed it. "If Harriett Harvey refuses, we will bring Maria back to number 30. If she lasts that long."

He opened the front door for her and Isobel went out and down the steps to the pavement. Reaching for the railings which divided the steps of the two houses, she breathed deeply in and out to calm herself before continuing on up the steps to the Harveys' front door and ringing the bell. The butler opened the door and nodded to her.

"Is Mrs Harvey at home, Mr Johnston?" she asked. "I need to speak with her urgently."

"Come in, Mrs Fitzgerald," he replied in his harsh Ulster accent. "And I will ask."

"Thank you," she replied, stepping into the hall, and the butler shut the door before going into the morning room.

She waited impatiently for him to return and a minute or two later, the morning room door opened and Harriett Harvey came out with the butler behind her.

"Isobel? Johnston said it was urgent."

"I'm afraid it is, Mrs Harvey."

"Then, please come in and sit down."

Isobel followed her into the room and the door was closed. Sitting on one of the reddish-brown leather sofas, she carefully made her request to the older woman, who sat on the opposite sofa wearing an exquisite burgundy-coloured dress she favoured. When Isobel finished, Mrs Harvey blew out her cheeks in a most unladylike way.

"I know it's a huge request to make," Isobel added. "And if—"

"No ifs." Mrs Harvey got up and rang for a servant. "Mrs Simpson may be brought here."

Isobel closed her eyes for a moment, feeling light-headed with relief. "Thank you. I'll go and let Will know."

"You'll do no such thing, Isobel, you're as white as a sheet. One of the maids will go. Ah, Claire," she said as the door opened. "Please instruct Mrs Black to have a bedroom prepared at once – it is an emergency – then go next door and tell Will Fitzgerald that his mother's request has been granted and a bedroom will be ready very shortly."

Isobel was seated with her back to the door but she could feel Claire's eyes boring into the back of her head before replying.

"Yes, Mrs Harvey."

The door closed and Harriett Harvey sat down beside Isobel and patted her hands.

"They shouldn't have sent you in your condition," she chided gently.

"I offered to speak to you. Sarah was going to come here, insisting she was calm, but she isn't at all calm."

"No. How absolutely horrendous this must be for her. Jim is no angel, I must admit, but thankfully he isn't clever enough to keep a mistress a secret from me. Hence his rather large photographic collection." Isobel fought to control a flush and Harriett laughed kindly. "I'm sorry, I'm embarrassing you."

"No, not at all. I just didn't know you knew about Mr Harvey's photographs."

"Some of them are quite beautiful in their own way."

"Mrs Harvey—"

"Please call me Harriett, Isobel, we are equals now."

"Harriett, then. I know this is your home, but if you would prefer not to be here, I am prepared to stay and be on hand if Will and his father need anything."

To her surprise, Harriett kissed her cheek. "I am so glad you suggested that. I am happy to make the house available, but I would much rather not be here when the time comes. I will go next door and keep poor Sarah company."

"What about Mr Harvey?"

Harriett glanced at a clock on the mantelpiece. "Jim is at his club and won't be home for at least two hours. Ring for tea or coffee."

"I will."

"Good. We must meet again under happier circumstances."

Harriett got up from the sofa and went out while Isobel stood up and wandered slowly around the room. At the windows, she saw Will and his father carrying Maria on a makeshift stretcher down the steps of number 67 then up the steps to number 68. She hurried out to the hall and opened the front door for them.

"Is the bedroom ready?" Will asked her as they came inside.

"Yes, it is, Dr Fitzgerald," Mr Johnston replied, walking

up the steps from the servants' hall. "May I be of assistance?"

"Yes, thank you, Johnston. If you could please take my father's place?"

Mr Johnston did as he was asked and John returned to the front door as Will and the butler began a careful progress up the stairs.

"Maria's sister, Diana Wingfield, has been sent for but she doesn't know to come to this address," John told her before closing the door.

"I'll look out for her," she said and he nodded and went upstairs.

She waited in the hall and looked up, hearing feet coming down the stairs. Mr Johnston gave her a kind smile.

"Mrs Fitzgerald, would you not rather wait in the morning room?"

"Thank you, Mr Johnston, but I would like to be here to greet Mrs Simpson's sister. Once she is here, I will wait in the morning room."

"Would you like some tea or coffee?"

"Coffee would be very nice, thank you. Oh." She turned back to the front door, hearing horses' hooves outside. "This must be her."

Mr Johnston opened the front door and Isobel went out onto the steps as the small grey-haired woman dressed in black she remembered from Fred's funeral got out of a cab and paid the cabman.

"Miss Wingfield?" she called before the woman walked up the steps to number 67.

"Yes?"

"I am Isobel Fitzgerald, John's daughter-in-law. Please come inside."

"Why is my sister not at number 67?" Miss Wingfield asked, struggling to maintain her composure.

"Please allow me to escort you upstairs." She extended a hand into the house. "And John will explain."

They followed Mr Johnston up the stairs to the second floor. The butler knocked at one of the guest bedroom doors and Will opened it.

"Miss Wingfield." He held the door open for her. "Please, come in."

"Thank you." Miss Wingfield went into the bedroom but Will came out onto the landing and closed the door.

"Father is to send for me when…" He tailed off and Isobel nodded. "We'll wait downstairs," he added, taking her hand.

"Harriett is with your mother," she said as they went into the morning room.

"I'm glad. How are you?"

"Starting to feel tired," she admitted, sitting down on one of the sofas. "But someone is bringing coffee."

"Good," he replied. "I'm relieved Miss Wingfield arrived in time."

"It will be soon, then?"

"Very soon. Moving Maria didn't help matters."

"Who is her doctor, Will? Should he be called?"

"I am her doctor," he replied. "She was one of my father's patients and when he retired, her care passed to me. But she never attended any of my surgeries and I didn't know she had cancer."

"Your father must have continued as her doctor."

"Perhaps. Or, perhaps, she refused all help. I simply don't know."

"Will, what is going to happen? Your father can't go home to your mother."

"I really don't know," he said. "Especially now Mother knows about Fred. Let's just deal with one thing at a time. And, for now, it's coffee," he added as the door opened and Claire came in with a tray and set it down on a side table.

"Thank you, Claire," she said.

"You are quite welcome, Mrs Fitzgerald," Claire responded crisply and left the room.

Reaching for the coffee pot, she poured them both a cup then added milk and sugar.

"Thank you." He took a cup and saucer from her, stirred and drank the contents in two gulps.

"More?"

"Yes, but drink yours, I'll help myself." He poured himself another cup and sat on the opposite sofa, only to get up again as the door opened and Mr Johnston came in. "Dr Fitzgerald senior is asking for you, Dr Fitzgerald."

"Thank you." Putting his cup and saucer on the tray, he squeezed her shoulder as he passed her and left the room.

Quickly drinking the contents of her own cup, she put the cup and saucer beside Will's and went out to the hall. Even from two floors down, she could hear Miss Wingfield crying and she hurried up the stairs. Diana Wingfield was on the landing outside the bedroom, her hands covering her face, but jumped and dropped her hands when she sensed Isobel's presence.

"Maria is dead," she whispered. "My sister is dead."

"I am so very sorry, Miss Wingfield. May I be of any assistance?"

"I don't know. John and your husband are doing…

whatever it is they need to do, and someone has been sent to Daltons, the undertakers. Maria is to be brought home to Rutland Square."

"Then, come downstairs to the morning room and have some coffee while the doctors are working."

Without waiting for a reply, Isobel took her arm, they went slowly downstairs and in the hall, she asked Claire for another cup and saucer.

"I have no-one left now," Miss Wingfield told her with a wobbly smile as she sat down on one of the sofas with her back to the door. "Maria was my only sister and my best friend and now she's dead."

Had she any inkling Maria intended to hasten her own death, Isobel wondered. "Have you heard from Margaret – Fred's widow?" she asked instead, sitting down beside Miss Wingfield on the sofa.

"Not a word since she upped and left for Co Wicklow without even as much as a goodbye to Maria or myself."

"I'm sorry to hear that," she said, forcing her weary brain to work out that Miss Wingfield was Will's half-brother's aunt. "You are most welcome to call upon me if you would like?"

"I would like that very much but—" Miss Wingfield hesitated. "Your mother-in-law?"

"Sarah is devastated by all this and I do need to be careful, but I don't need to ask her permission as to who may call on me."

"I knew the truth would get out eventually," Miss Wingfield said with a little shrug. "In fact, I am astonished all of it was not uncovered years ago. Dublin is far too small a city for any secret to be kept for long," she added and Isobel felt a sharp pang in the pit of her stomach. "Is Mrs Harvey with Sarah?"

"Yes, she is."

"Good. Poor Sarah. I begged Maria not to go anywhere near her but Maria would no longer listen to reason. Maria loved the sea, and when I heard her ask John to take her to Kingstown for the last time, I half expected him to return to Rutland Square and tell me she had drowned herself."

"So you knew Maria wished to hasten her own death?" Isobel asked, trying desperately to keep her voice neutral and not sound accusing.

"I suspected it," Miss Wingfield admitted. "But I never expected her to do it in such a dreadful way as this. Oh, how you must despise me…"

"No, not at all." Reaching out, Isobel held her hand.

"Yes," Miss Wingfield insisted. "Maria detested Sarah, you see. Maria was trapped in a sham of a marriage to Duncan while Sarah had a happy marriage to John. Sarah loved John so much – I say loved because Sarah must surely hate him now."

"Miss Wingfield—"

"Please call me Diana?" she asked, sounding a little hesitant. "Frederick always called me Aunt. Not Aunt Diana, just Aunt. Maria was the only person to call me by my name and now they are both dead and I feel so very alone."

"I am Isobel and never think you have no-one left because you do. Thank you, Claire," she added as the maid came into the room with the cup and saucer. "Do you take milk and sugar, Diana?" she asked, pouring the coffee.

"Just milk. Thank you, Isobel."

A few minutes later, Will put his head around the door to tell her he was going to the practice house. He didn't say why in front of Diana but Isobel knew he was going there to certify Maria's death. Half an hour passed before Will and John Dalton were admitted to the house together and a coffin was brought upstairs. Another fifteen minutes elapsed before the coffin was carried out of the house to the hearse and Diana went to a waiting cab with John to follow the hearse to her home. Mr Johnston closed the front door after them and Will shook his hand.

"Thank you, Johnston."

"Yes, thank you, Mr Johnston," she added. "And thank you to everyone who helped today. My husband and I are now going to thank Mrs Harvey and tell her that her house is her own again."

Chapter Eight

Tess showed them into number 67's morning room. His mother and Mrs Harvey were seated side-by-side on the sofa and Will bent and kissed his mother's cheek.

"Is Maria dead?" she asked him.

"Yes, Mother. John Dalton has been and Maria is being taken home to Rutland Square."

"Good."

"Harriett." Isobel turned to Mrs Harvey. "Thank you."

"Sarah has thanked me a thousand times, Isobel. I am glad I was able to help. Jim isn't home yet, is he?"

"No, he isn't."

"That is a relief." Mrs Harvey patted his mother's hands. "I'll go home now, Sarah. And remember, if you need to call for me – or come next door – then do. It doesn't matter what time it is – day or night."

"Thank you, Harriett."

He saw Mrs Harvey out, returned to the morning room and sat down in an armchair.

"Thank you," his mother said. "Today must have been horrendous for you both."

"What are you going to do now?" he asked and she gave

him a blank stare.

"Do? The woman is dead – and good riddance to her. This is my home and I will continue to live here."

"With Father?"

She shrugged. "That is entirely up to him."

"Mother, I will be attending Maria's funeral. Despite everything, she was Fred's mother, and she was always very good to me."

"Did you know Fred was your half-brother?"

He sighed and shook his head. "Father told me yesterday evening."

"You really didn't know?" His mother was incredulous.

"No."

"It must have been a terrible shock for you."

"For me?" His eyebrows shot up. "What about you?" he asked and she gave him a sad little smile.

"Take Isobel home, Will. She looks exhausted."

Sitting in the other armchair, Isobel did look pale but at the same time, he didn't want to leave his mother.

"Please come home with us, Mother?"

"No, I will not leave my home. Now, please take Isobel home."

"I'll call here first thing in the morning on my way to surgery." His mother nodded and he got up and kissed her cheek again. "We'll see ourselves out."

At number 30, he sank down onto the sofa in the morning room and held out his arms for Isobel. Instead, she crossed the room and stood in front of the fireplace.

"What's the matter?" he asked.

"Will, I told your father this, and I need to tell you as well. It is my belief Maria Simpson came to number 67 with the aim of provoking your mother into striking her and hastening her death. Diana Wingfield also suspected Maria wished to hasten her own death but she never expected Maria to do it the way she did. You extracted six pins from Maria's hat – six – on a day when there was little or no wind. One way or another, Maria was going to fall and she wanted one or more of the hat pins to pierce her skull and kill her, but her head struck the fender instead."

"Provocation." Sitting up straight, he ran a hand over his jaw. "That is Mother's belief, too. How did Father react?"

"He denied it at first but, deep down, I think he knew Maria didn't want a lingering death."

Will sighed and nodded. "Come and sit down." She sat beside him, he put an around her and kissed her temple. "I've spoken to John Dalton and I will be a pallbearer at the funeral. Jerry will want to be a pallbearer, too. I'll send him a telegram when I know when the funeral is."

"Your mother won't like you carrying Maria's coffin," she said, resting her head on his shoulder. "And I don't think you should do it either. For Maria to want to hasten her own death was one thing, but for her to use your mother to achieve it was just…" She tailed off and Will hugged her to him.

"Maria was Fred's mother. He adored her. I will carry Maria's coffin for Fred – and only Fred."

"Very well," she conceded. "What did you certify as the cause of death on the medical certificate?"

"A depressed fracture of the base of the skull caused by general debility brought on by advanced cancer of the breast."

"But that's the truth – more or less," she exclaimed, straightening up and turning to face him.

"Yes, it is. Maria had cancer. She was weak. She fell. We will keep the circumstances very much to ourselves."

In the morning, they walked to number 67 where Tess told them Mrs Fitzgerald senior was at breakfast and that Dr Fitzgerald senior hadn't come home the previous night.

They went into the breakfast room, where his mother was seated at the table buttering a triangle of toast.

"Mother," he said, bending and kissing her cheek. "How are you?"

"I'm as well as can be expected," she replied, motioning for Isobel to sit down. "This morning, I will bring the draft copy of the will and the residency agreement to Mr Ellison for his appraisal. Your father stayed away last night," she added, reaching for the dish of marmalade.

"I'll call to the *Journal* offices," he said, pulling out a chair for Isobel and holding it as she sat down.

"Don't row with him, Will," his mother warned. "Any grievance he has is with me."

"I won't. I'll go now and I'll return here after surgery." He kissed Isobel's temple and went out.

His father wasn't at the *Journal* offices on Hume Street and Will took out his pocket watch. Surgery began in ten minutes. Putting his watch back in his waistcoat pocket, he walked away.

Three and a half hours later, Will was back in Hume Street, only to discover his father hadn't come to the *Journal* offices that morning. Not sure whether to be angry or concerned, he returned to number 67 and updated his mother in the morning room.

"I'll find him," he assured her. "He may be at the Trinity Club."

"Don't you have any house calls to make this afternoon?" she asked. "If your father wishes to stay away that is his affair," she added, rolling her eyes at her unfortunate choice of words.

"I do have some house calls to make this afternoon," he said as he and Isobel returned to number 30 for luncheon.

"Then, I will call on Diana Wingfield when we've eaten. Your father might be with her arranging Maria's funeral."

"Thank you. I'll meet you there after my house calls."

At a quarter to four, a parlourmaid admitted him to the Wingfield residence on Rutland Square. He was brought upstairs to a large and very feminine drawing room on the first floor with cream wallpaper, pale pink curtains and a sofa and two armchairs upholstered in the same pale pink silk satin. Miss Wingfield and Isobel were standing at a large sash window where the older woman was pointing at something. There was no sign of his father.

"Dr William Fitzgerald," the parlourmaid announced, they both turned and Miss Wingfield nodded to him.

"Dr Fitzgerald. I'm afraid I can only repeat what I said to Isobel. I haven't seen your father since he left here yesterday evening at about seven o'clock. I assumed he was returning to Merrion Square. Would you like some tea?"

"Thank you, but no. I need to find my father."

"Of course."

"When is Maria's funeral?" he asked.

"Tomorrow morning at eleven o'clock at St Peter's Church. After moving here, Maria continued to attend Sunday service there, so it has been arranged that her funeral will take place there, too."

Yet another funeral at St Peter's, he noted wearily. "We will be attending."

"Thank you, Dr Fitzgerald."

"I'm worried about Father now," he said as he and Isobel left the house. "It's been almost twenty-four hours since anyone has seen him. I'll go to the Trinity Club and ask if he's there, or if he's been there."

"Before you do, have tenants been found for the Simpson house?" she inquired.

"I don't know. I walked there one day and all the shutters were closed and I haven't been back since."

"Does your father have a key to the house?"

"No, I don't think so." He stopped and stared at her. "You think he may be there?"

"I'm hoping he's there."

They walked on, hailed a cab, and within fifteen minutes were standing opposite number 1 Ely Place Upper. The shutters were still closed and the house appeared unoccupied but they crossed the street, he rang the doorbell and they waited. When no-one answered, he grimaced but she took his hand.

"Let's go around the back," she said, led him along the laneway which ran parallel to the house and into the garden.

They climbed the steps to the back door and he tried the handle. The door opened, revealing a broken lock, and they went inside.

Peering into the servants' hall, he saw it was empty and they continued on up the steps to the hall. Opening the door to the morning room, he stared through the gloom in surprise. The room was still fully furnished, complete with ornaments and photographs. McDonnell had told him Mrs Simpson left the servants instructions to prepare the house so it could be put up for rent but it looked as though they had simply walked out. Photographs of Fred and Margaret's wedding stood on the piano and he exhaled a long breath, hating to see the contents abandoned like this.

"I thought the house would have been packed up, not just left to gather dust." Isobel picked up the photograph of himself, Fred and Jerry at Fred and Margaret's wedding. "This is awful." Replacing the photograph, she went to the drinks tray. "Will. Look."

One of the three crystal decanters was missing.

"I want you to stay here while I go upstairs," he told her. "No."

"Yes," he insisted. "Please, Isobel. I don't know what condition Father may be in. Stay here."

"Very well. It's my guess he is in what was Maria's bedroom."

He nodded, kissed her lips and left the room. Running up the stairs to the bedrooms, he stood on the second-floor landing for a moment to get his bearings before walking to a bedroom at the back of the house.

Opening the door, the first thing he noticed when his eyes adjusted to the dim light in the room was the rumpled bedcovers. Walking around the double bed, he frowned when he found no-one lying on the rug. Turning, he jumped violently when he saw his father sitting on the floor in a corner watching him, the decanter empty between his legs.

"Father. Thank God."

"Get out."

"Let me help you up." Reaching for his father's arm, his father slapped his hand away.

"I said, get out."

"You're drunk and I'm not leaving you here. None of us should be here."

"None of us?" His father peered up at him bleary-eyed.

"Isobel is downstairs," he explained. "She guessed you might be here."

"You married a clever woman, Will. Maria was clever, too. I should have married her. I should have insisted that she marry me. Being a gentleman about it – allowing her to throw me over for Duncan – cost me my happiness."

"You were happy with Mother."

"At times," his father said with a little shrug. "When Edward was born. When you were born. But I should have married Maria."

Will stood back from him. "Well, you didn't marry her, but it still didn't stop you from being with her."

"In secret," his father roared. "Have you any idea what it was like trying to keep it a secret? Trying to keep the fact that Fred was my son a secret? You have never had to keep anything important a secret in your life."

Oh, but I have, Will contradicted him silently. "Let me help you up," he said instead, offering him a hand.

"No. I'm staying here."

"Father, the funeral is tomorrow morning."

"I know it is. I helped to arrange it, but I'm not going."

Will closed his eyes for a moment, fighting to keep his temper. "As far as everyone is concerned, Maria was your best friend's wife. You will go to the funeral because I will not make any excuses for you. Now, go home and go to bed."

"I'm never going back there. I'm staying here."

"Father, for God's sake—"

"Will," Isobel called sharply from the door and he turned to her. "Wait downstairs. Now."

314

Sighing, he walked past her and went down the stairs to the first-floor landing. Sitting on the bottom step, he lowered his head into his hands.

Leaving the bedroom door wide open to allow more light inside, Isobel crossed the room and carefully sat down on the floor in front of John. The baby fluttered hard and she gasped.

"Your grandchild is all but kicking now," she explained and he peered at her stomach.

"You shouldn't be sitting on the floor in your condition."

"Neither should you. Come home with Will and I. Sleep the alcohol off and we'll send someone to number 67 for clothes for the funeral."

"I'm not—" he began and shook his head before continuing, "I can't go to the funeral. I can't go and pretend. I've done it too many times – Nicholas' funeral – Fred's funeral – I just can't do it anymore."

"John." Inching a little closer to him, she held his hands. "Once more – just once more for Maria – because if you don't go, you will always regret not going."

"But I don't think I can bear seeing her being put into a hole in the ground," he whispered. "I helped to lift her into the coffin, I helped to carry the coffin to and from the hearse and I had to pretend I was indifferent, but I just can't do it anymore."

"You won't have to carry the coffin at the funeral," she assured him. "Will is one of the pallbearers. I will be with you. I will hold your arm."

"Sarah will be expected to be with me."

"Sarah will be ill," she said softly. "So I will be with

you and Will shall help to carry Maria. Yes?" He stared at her undecided so she tried again in simpler terms. "We will take one matter at a time. First – you can't stay here – this house belongs to Margaret. Second – you shall come home with Will and I and we will send someone to number 67 to tell Sarah where you are and to collect some clothes for you. Third – you will sleep the alcohol off. And fourth – in the morning you, Will, and I shall attend the funeral. You will only have to pretend once more."

"I only have to pretend once more?" he whispered and she nodded.

"Then—" They both looked up as Will came to them and crouched down. "Then, you will come home with us again and you can have all the time you need to decide what to do next."

"But you must hate me?" John said and Will shook his head.

"You're my father and I love you. Let us take care of you. Please?"

Slowly, John nodded and she squeezed his hands.

"You're going to have to help me up, Will," she said.

Taking her hands, he raised her to her feet then, between them, they managed to stand John up. With an arm around his father's shoulders, Will guided him from the bedroom. She quickly straightened the bedcovers and picked up the empty decanter before closing the door and following them down the stairs.

She returned the decanter to the drinks tray in the morning room then went to the back door and jammed a dining chair from the servants' hall under the handle.

"I'll hail a cab," she said as she passed them in the hall and opened the front door.

She had to walk a little way along the pavement before a cab approached along Ely Place and stopped for her. She hurried back to the house and pulled the front door closed as Will first helped his father into the cab, then her, before getting in himself.

At number 30, Will asked the cabman to wait and brought John into the hall. Mrs Dillon and Zaineb were coming up the steps from the servants' hall and the new maid's dark brown eyes widened in shock as she noted John's inebriated condition. Will continued on with him up the stairs to the bedroom which had been prepared for Sarah and Mrs Dillon quickly followed them.

"Zaineb," Isobel said softly and the maid tore her eyes away from the stairs. "How are you settling in?"

"Very well, thank you, Mrs Fitzgerald. May I be of assistance?" she asked, turning back to the stairs.

"Thank you, Zaineb, but no. Mrs Dillon will help my husband."

"Yes, Mrs Fitzgerald."

Isobel went into the morning room and sat down on the sofa, suddenly feeling exhausted. Resting her head back, she dozed, but jumped and went to get up when Will put his head around the door.

"You're sitting down, good – no – stay sitting." He came into the room, bent and kissed her lips. "Father is in bed and asleep. I'm going to Westland Row to speak to David about tomorrow's surgery. After that, I'll send Jerry a telegram and call to number 67. I must tell Mother where Father is, that she needs to be 'ill' tomorrow and collect some clothes for him. I don't know how long I'll be, so go ahead with dinner and give John a kiss from me."

When Maura admitted Will to number 67, he asked for some of his father's clothes to be packed, including mourning attire. The maid then showed him into the morning room and his mother got to her feet, closing and placing a periodical on a side table.

"Did you find your father?"

"Yes, he was in number 1. Isobel and I have brought him back to number 30 and he is in bed."

"In bed?" His mother stared at him, an eyebrow rising. "He was drunk?"

"Yes. Mother, you will be expected to accompany Father to Maria's funeral tomorrow but, under the circumstances, it would be better all round if you were to be 'ill'."

"Did your father ask you to dissuade me from attending?" she demanded.

"No, he didn't," Will replied firmly. "In fact, he didn't want to attend at all. It was Isobel who told him that if he didn't, he would regret it."

"Did she. Well, what shall it be, my illness?"

"A bad cold should suffice. I will be one of the pallbearers and I will make your excuses."

"And will your father return home after the funeral?"

"That I don't know. He told me he was never coming back here but I hope that was the alcohol speaking. Isobel has persuaded him to take matters one at a time and I think all of us should do that as well. I have asked for some of Father's clothes to be packed and I am going home now, tomorrow is going to be a difficult day."

"One thing before you go," she said as he went to kiss her cheek. "Fred's death. As he couldn't possibly have inherited Duncan's father's heart condition, what did Fred really die of?"

Will hesitated before answering. Could she be trusted to keep the truth to herself?

"Fred killed himself, didn't he?" his mother asked quietly and Will nodded. "Why?"

"He had syphilis," Will replied and his mother clapped a hand to her cheek. "It's highly likely he passed it on to Margaret and that it caused the death of baby Nicholas."

"Oh, God." His mother sat down on the sofa. "Oh, God, how awful."

"Mother." Sitting beside her, he clasped her hands and held onto them tightly. "You weren't told because Fred didn't want anyone to know he had syphilis. Only Isobel and myself, Father and John Dalton, and Jerry – and now you know. And, Mother, no-one must ever know Fred committed suicide. You know how suicides are treated, and can you imagine how Margaret would have reacted?"

"Are you telling me Margaret doesn't know Fred killed himself?" she asked incredulously and Will shook his head. "Do her family know she has syphilis?"

"No, they don't."

"But she's upped sticks and gone to her aunt's home in Co Wicklow. According to Frances Belcher, the house on Ely Place Upper is just standing empty."

"Please, don't tell anyone any of it Mother," he begged.

"I won't. My only grievance is with your father. Have you cancelled tomorrow's surgery?"

"There wasn't time. I've just been to see David Powell

319

and in the morning he will ask Eva to request that only the most urgent cases remain and he will see those patients. I'll call here tomorrow, but it will probably be the evening."

"There is really no need, Will."

"There is," he replied, kissing her cheek. "Goodnight, Mother."

At number 30, he climbed the stairs carrying a small trunk and opened the door to the guest bedroom as quietly as he could. His father was snoring, so Will went inside and turned the gas lamps up a little. Opening the trunk, he hung the clothes in the wardrobe before tuning the gas lamps down and leaving the room.

Isobel was sitting up in bed with a book on her lap as he closed the door to their bedroom.

"Mother will have a bad cold tomorrow," he told her while he got undressed. "Father has fresh clothes and mourning attire. And we need to get a good night's sleep."

At a quarter past eight in the morning, he left their bedroom and met the new house-parlourmaid on the landing.

"I'm Will Fitzgerald," he said. "You must be Zaineb."

"Yes, Dr Fitzgerald. I'm very pleased to meet you." She held up a floral patterned ewer and basin then glanced at the guest bedroom door. "Mrs Dillon sent me upstairs with some warm water and a basin for Dr Fitzgerald senior."

"I'll take them," he said and she passed the ewer and basin to him. "I hope you'll be happy here, Zaineb."

"Thank you, I'm sure I will be, Dr Fitzgerald."

Will went into the guest bedroom and found his father standing at the window looking out over the square still wearing one of Will's nightshirts.

"Would you like me to help you dress?" he offered,

putting the ewer and basin on the washstand before opening the wardrobe door.

"You went to number 67," his father said, turning and peering past him into the wardrobe at the clothes hanging up inside.

"I needed to see Mother and you needed fresh clothes and mourning attire. Let me help you get dressed?"

"I can manage."

"Very well. Breakfast is served in fifteen minutes and a cab will come for us at half past ten."

His father came into the breakfast room at half past eight, immaculately dressed in his best frock coat. He silently poured himself a cup of coffee at the sideboard before sitting down at the table and helping himself to a triangle of toast and marmalade.

"Would you not prefer something a little more substantial?" Isobel asked. "Some porridge perhaps?" she added, pointing to a serving dish beside the coffee pot.

"Thank you," he replied. "But, no, this will be sufficient for now. I may be a little more inclined to eat at luncheon," he added.

"Of course."

They arrived at St Peter's Church on Aungier Street at a quarter to eleven. Will escorted Isobel – wearing a large black silk satin shawl over her mourning dress to disguise her pregnancy – and his father to a pew before going back outside to wait for the hearse. He gave Jerry an edited account of Maria's death before exchanging sympathies with the other pallbearers and mentioning his mother's cold as the hearse and a carriage approached. Diana Wingfield alighted from the carriage dressed from head to toe in black, a lace veil obscuring most of her face.

"Miss Wingfield," he said simply, shaking her hand.

"Dr Fitzgerald," she replied and glanced at the church. "Your father?" she added quietly.

"He is inside with Isobel," he replied just as softly. "Unfortunately, Mother has a bad cold and is unable to attend," he continued in a normal tone. "She sends her sympathies."

"Thank you, Dr Fitzgerald."

He accompanied her inside before rejoining the other pallbearers. The coffin was borne into the church, placed on the bier, and he sat down beside Isobel. His father sat on her other side as if turned to stone. Miss Wingfield was seated alone in the front pew, her back ramrod straight but every so often she would tremble and he hoped she wouldn't collapse.

When the coffin was placed in the hearse, he joined Isobel and his father in the cab for the short journey to Mount Jerome Cemetery.

"Did you speak to Miss Wingfield?" he asked her.

"Yes, and she is disappointed Margaret hasn't attended," Isobel replied and he glanced at his father, who was staring intently out of the window, then back at Isobel. She gave him a little nod, telling him that the worst – the burial – was yet to come and the two of them would need to take care of him. Will nodded in reply. "Other than that," she continued. "There is a large attendance and she is very touched by it."

At the cemetery, they made sure his father stood in between them with Miss Wingfield on Isobel's other side. Will felt his father brace himself as the coffin was lowered into the grave and glanced anxiously at him every couple of minutes. When the burial service ended, his father stood utterly still with his head bent, while Miss Wingfield received condolences from the mourners.

"Father," he said when just the four of them remained at the graveside. "I'm going to accompany Miss Wingfield to her carriage. I won't be long."

His father didn't reply so he took Miss Wingfield's arm and they walked away.

Isobel turned to John. His brown eyes were fixed on the coffin and she gently laid a hand on his arm.

"I'm going to make a circuit of this group of plots. When I return we will have to leave."

She received no response so she left him, meeting Will on the path halfway around the circuit.

"Isobel?"

"Your father needed a little time alone," she said as Will took her hand and they made their way slowly to a corner where they could see John standing at the graveside hugging himself and clearly in great distress. Discreetly looking away, she saw how pale Will was. He had never witnessed his father in such anguish before and she lifted his hands to her lips and kissed them. "We need to bring him home now, Will, the gravediggers are waiting to fill the grave."

Returning to John, he raised his head and smiled at her through his tears.

"Thank you," he whispered, pulling a handkerchief from one of his trouser pockets and wiping his eyes. "I needed to say goodbye."

"Let's go back to number 30, John. It is vegetable soup for luncheon today."

As she was about to turn away, he caught her hand. "Thank you for speaking to me so frankly, Isobel. I would have regretted not attending."

She nodded and they walked to the corner where Will was waiting. "Let's go home."

She was relieved to see John eat a hearty luncheon and when they went into the morning room and sat down, he asked them to hear him out.

"I cannot expect Sarah to forgive me for thirty-six years of deceit and divorce is out of the question, so I am going to look for rooms for myself. I hope it won't take more than a few days—"

"Rooms?" Will interrupted. "And how do you propose to keep the fact you and mother are living separately a secret? You may as well get divorced and—"

"Will." She nudged him to make him stop. "John, I really think Sarah should be part of any discussion regarding your future living arrangements. When Will visits his mother this evening, I suggest he asks her to call here – perhaps tomorrow evening – and a calm discussion be held then. Yes?"

"Yes," John and Will conceded quietly.

"Good." She got to her feet and the two men also stood up. "As it's a dry day, I think we should bring young John out into the garden. Would you like to join us, John?"

"I—" Will's father hesitated for a moment before nodding. "Yes, very much so."

Will smiled. "I'll go upstairs and fetch him."

Isobel and John put on their coats and went outside. They sat on the bench and he glanced around the long and narrow garden.

"You've done wonders here."

"Thank you. It's the result of a lot of weeding and tidying and having the grass cut. All the flowers and shrubs in the beds along the walls were just hidden by the weeds."

"You don't think I should look for rooms either, do you?" he asked suddenly and she twisted around a little so she could face him.

"No, I don't. Once it becomes common knowledge that you have moved out of number 67, people will wonder why and who knows what else they might question."

"Sarah will never forgive me and—" He grimaced. "If I'm perfectly honest, I will never forgive her for not allowing Maria to die in number 67. It's unreasonable, I know because I would probably have done the same myself, but moving Maria hastened her death."

"Will told me Maria would never have regained consciousness."

"I know. It was just so unseemly – carrying her out onto the pavement on a makeshift stretcher."

"I could argue that it was unseemly for Maria to come to number 67 with the aim of provoking Sarah into striking her and hastening her death."

John nodded. "What do you suggest, then?"

"Number 67 is enormous. There is more than enough space for you and Sarah to live under the same roof but separately. That is if Sarah is willing to have you live under the same roof as her again, even independently. That is why we all need to sit down tomorrow evening and discuss it calmly."

"Will cannot seem to be calm."

"John, he is your son. He loves both you and Sarah and

he doesn't want to take sides. I won't take sides either, you are my parents-in-law, and I hold the two of you in equal high regard."

John lifted her hand and kissed it. "You are a remarkable young woman."

"I don't know about that," she said with a little shrug. "But I can see matters from both sides and I'm not afraid to speak my mind."

"If only I had spoken my mind thirty-six years ago."

"Be thankful for what you have now – a wife who also speaks her mind – a son to be proud of – a wonderful grandson – and another grandchild on the way. Please think about what I have suggested," she urged as the back door opened and Will carried young John down the steps and stood him on the lawn.

"John?" she called. "Come and say hello to your grandfather."

The little boy walked across the grass and stared at his namesake. "Hello, Grandfather," he said and Will's father's eyebrows shot up as the boy spoke.

"Hello, John," he replied. "I'm very pleased to meet you again."

"Do you like flowers?" young John asked and his grandfather pursed his lips for a moment.

"Yes, I suppose I do. Are there some you'd like to show me?"

"Yes."

"Well, lead the way." Taking his grandson's hand, John was led across the lawn to one of the flower beds.

She exchanged a smile with Will, who sat down in his father's place, leant over and kissed her lips.

Will got up from the sofa as his mother was shown into the morning room by Zaineb the following evening. She stared after the maid as the door was closed before turning to him.

"Florrie's replacement, I take it?"

"Yes. Her name is Zaineb and she is very satisfactory so far."

"Good. Well, where is he?" his mother asked briskly, glancing around the room.

"Father is with Isobel in the nursery saying goodnight to John and will be downstairs shortly. Sherry?"

"Perhaps, later," she said, sitting down in an armchair as the door opened and Isobel and his father came in.

"The wooden elephant?" his father was asking her as he shut the door.

"Yes," she replied. "He adores Mr Effalump Elephant. Hello, Sarah." Isobel sat on the sofa. "Thank you for coming. Please, take a seat, John."

Without acknowledging his wife, his father chose the other armchair and Will sat beside Isobel on the sofa. She gave him a little smile before turning to his mother.

"Do you wish to separate from John, Sarah?" she asked and his mother looked startled for a moment at such a blunt first question. "Because John has told me he cannot expect you to forgive him and that he will look for rooms."

"Rooms?" his mother exclaimed. "It would be impossible to keep our living separately a secret and—" Her shoulders slumped. "I would never be able to call upon anyone in Dublin ever again. People would question what I had done to drive John away. It would be viewed as my fault – it is always the wife's fault. Isobel, I simply don't know what to do. John and I cannot separate and we cannot live together any longer."

"That is not strictly true," Isobel replied. "As I have mentioned to John, number 67 is enormous. There is plenty of room for you both to live in the house – but separately."

"You have already discussed this with John?" his mother demanded.

"No, I have not," Isobel replied firmly. "I put it to him yesterday and I am putting it to you now. You would both be living under the same roof but entirely independent of one another. You could have the ground floor while John could have the first floor. Bedroom allocations would have to be discussed, as will the possible hiring of more servants, as this will mean a lot more work for your current servants – separate meals and more rooms to maintain every day – but the arrangement could work and it would mean that outwardly in your marriage, nothing has changed."

His mother sighed. "Will, I think I would like that sherry now, please."

"Of course." He got up and went to the decanters. "Lemonade, Isobel?"

"Yes, please."

"Whiskey, Father."

"Thank you, yes."

Will poured the drinks, passed the glasses around and sat on the sofa again. His mother was staring down into her glass, clearly deep in thought.

"Mother, you don't have to decide now," he said and she raised her head.

"I do, Will, because it is the only solution, isn't it?"

He gave her a sympathetic smile before glancing at his father, who nodded.

"Your mother is right. It is the only solution."

"Thank you for adjudicating, Isobel," his mother went on. "I'm sorry for raising my voice to you."

"Not at all, and if you and John would like to meet here again to discuss the arrangement, you are most welcome to."

"Thank you, Isobel. I'll go home now if you don't mind." His mother put her glass on a side table and got up. "Had I known our meeting would be so short, I would have asked the cabman who brought me here to wait. It's dark now, so could you ask your footman to find me another cab, please, Will?"

"I'll walk you home." He handed Isobel his glass, got to his feet and they went out to the hall. "It is a practical solution," he said, lifting his mother's black hat and cloak off the stand. "Number 67 is more than big enough to accommodate you and Father separately." He passed her the hat then draped the cloak around her shoulders and did up the buttons before putting on his overcoat and hat.

"Yes," she replied, positioning the hat at an angle on her head and pushing in a pin while he opened the front door. "For your father to take rooms somewhere was a ridiculous idea."

"Father assumed you wouldn't want him under the same roof as you," he said, as they left the house and went down the steps to the pavement.

"In an ideal world I wouldn't, but this isn't an ideal world, is it?"

"No, it isn't," he replied, putting on his hat and taking her arm.

"Was it a big funeral?" she asked.

"Yes, it was."

"Was anything said that I wasn't there?"

"No. The mourners were commenting instead on the fact Margaret Simpson didn't attend."

"Margaret didn't attend?" His mother shot him a sharp glance. "She should have made the effort for her mother-in-law."

"Perhaps, but I can understand why she didn't attend – it is so soon after Nicholas and Fred's deaths – it would have been awful for her."

In the hall at number 67, his mother passed her hat and cloak to Tess then reached up and kissed his cheek.

"Thank you for walking me home. Tomorrow, I will consider how the arrangement can work here. The sooner your father is out from under yours and Isobel's feet the better. Off you go now, it's getting late," she said and Tess opened the front door for him. "Goodnight."

Turning from Merrion Square South onto Fitzwilliam Street Lower, Will couldn't help but notice a man wearing a black three quarter length overcoat and carrying a hat in his left hand staggering along the pavement ahead of him. Continuing on along Fitzwilliam Street Upper and keeping a safe distance behind the man, Will heard him cough.

"I can't…" the man panted. "I just can't," he added before making a grab for some railings, missing, and falling to the ground.

Will approached him cautiously and kneeling down, he felt the man's neck for a pulse. It was rapid and the man was sweating profusely. Gently, Will turned him over and gasped. The face was battered and bruised but Will would recognise it anywhere. The man was Alfie Stevens.

"Alfie, can you hear me? It's Will – Will Fitzgerald."

There was no response and Will lifted both his eyelids.

Alfie's pupils reacted to the light of a nearby gas lamp – good. Will glanced up and down the street, wondering what to do. He wasn't able to carry him, but he had to get Alfie to number 30. If he turned up on Mrs Henderson's doorstep with Alfie the way his face was swelling, she'd have hysterics.

"You – help." Getting up, he ran out into the street, forcing a cab to stop. "I need help."

"Yeh feckin' eejit," the cabman roared at him. "Me horse could've trampled yeh."

"That man has been attacked." Will jabbed a forefinger towards the pavement. "I need to bring him to number 30 Fitzwilliam Square."

The cabman threw a cursory glance at Alfie before shaking his head. "You're not bringing him and the state he's in into my cab for a fare as short as that."

"I'm a doctor and I need to attend to him. Please?"

"Do you know how hard it is to clean blood off wood?"

"Yes, of course, I know – I'm a doctor. Do you know George Millar?"

The cabman laughed. "Everyone in Dublin knows George Millar."

"George Millar saved my life last year by bringing me in his cab from Cork Street to Merrion Square so I could have an operation. He didn't question the state I was in – and I was in a terrible state – I can tell you. So, will you help me or not?"

"Jaysis – all right." The cabman jumped down and reached back up to his seat for a woollen blanket. "Put this around him."

Between them, they wrapped Alfie in the blanket and lifted him into the cab. Will held him upright in a corner as the cabman turned the cab around and brought them to number 30.

"My father is inside," he said as the cabman opened the cab door. "His name is John Fitzgerald. Please ring the front doorbell and ask the maid to request that he—" Will hesitated and sighed. That he what? Join him in the garden for a breath of fresh air? In the dark? Isobel was no fool and she would wonder what the matter was. He grimaced. If she followed his father from the morning room, so be it. "Please tell the maid that Dr Fitzgerald wishes to speak to his father in the hall. When my father leaves the morning room, send him out here. This man is my wife's brother," he explained. "My wife is pregnant and I don't want to upset her."

The cabman nodded and a couple of minutes later, Will's father was following the cabman down the steps from the front door.

"Father?" he called from the cab. "This is Alfie Stevens. He collapsed on Fitzwilliam Street Upper. It looks like he's been given a savage beating. Please clear the table in the breakfast room."

His father nodded and went back inside.

"Please help me carry Alfie inside..?" he asked the cabman.

"John. John Hartley."

"Will Fitzgerald."

Slowly, they carried Alfie into the house, along the hall and into the breakfast room. Alfie was placed on the table and the blanket was passed back to the cabman. Alfie's face was almost unrecognisable. Both his eyes were now closed due to swelling, he had bruises on one cheek and a split lip.

"Thank you for your help, John. Go and get yourself a

cup of tea downstairs. Ask for Mrs Dillon, give her the blanket to be washed and get her to ask one of the maids to prepare the other guest bedroom."

The cabman took one last horrified glance at Alfie before he hurried from the room, pushing past Will's father in the doorway.

"Warm water and towels are being brought here."

"Thank you, Father," he said, undoing Alfie's tie and taking it and the collar off. "The skin doesn't seem to be broken anywhere apart from the lip – just this extreme swelling and bruising. His pulse is rapid but not excessive and his pupils react to light—" He halted, hearing a knock at the door and his father took a basin and towels from Mary. "Let's clean Alfie's face then bring him upstairs."

"Do you know where he was coming from?"

"I don't know. I think he was trying to get home but just couldn't walk any further. At first, I thought he was drunk. Is Isobel still in the morning room?" he asked and his father nodded.

"She fell asleep on the sofa shortly after you and your mother left."

"Good. Let's hope we don't wake her."

On opening the overcoat, morning coat, waistcoat and shirt, he saw that Alfie's chest was unbruised and a wallet was still in the morning coat's inside pocket. Reaching for a small towel, he dipped it in the basin of warm water, squeezed it and gently wiped the perspiration from Alfie's face.

"We're going to need cold water to ease the swelling," his father said. "I'll go and ask for some."

He went out, closed the door after him and Will felt Alfie jump and raise his hands to his face.

"Alfie – no." Dropping the towel, Will grabbed his hands. "It's me, Will Fitzgerald. You're at number 30 – you're safe."

"I can't open my eyes."

"You've been attacked. There's a lot of swelling. My father is here and has gone for some cold water which we'll use to reduce the swelling."

"Thank you."

"Alfie, what happened? Was David with you?" he asked but Alfie was unconscious again and he went out to the hall to look for his father and the cold water. Mrs Dillon, with his father behind her, was coming up the steps from the servants' hall carrying an ewer and basin and more towels.

"The bedroom is being prepared, Dr Fitzgerald," the housekeeper told him. "I'll bring the cold water up there now."

"Thank you. My father and I will carry Alfie—"

"What on earth is happening?" The morning room door had opened and Isobel stood in the doorway. "Will?"

"Come with me." Taking her arm, he brought her back into the morning room and closed the door. "It's Alfie," he said softly. "He's been attacked." She clapped her hands to her cheeks and he took them and kissed her fingers. "He has a split lip, his face is badly bruised and there is a lot of swelling but there doesn't seem to be any other injuries. I have cleaned his face, a bedroom is being prepared, and Mrs Dillon has some cold water which we'll use to bring down the swelling. Other than that he needs rest."

"Why was Alfie attacked?" she asked. "Was he robbed? Was David with him?" she added in a whisper.

"No, Alfie wasn't robbed, his wallet is still in his morning coat's inside pocket. I didn't see David."

"Oh, God, Will." Her eyes widened. "Do people know about them? We need to find David."

"I'll look for David," he promised. "In the meantime, Father and I need to carry Alfie upstairs."

"Yes," she whispered.

"Isobel, I must warn you that the bruising on Alfie's face is extensive. He can't open his eyes at present." She nodded and he kissed her forehead then opened the door for her. They went into the breakfast room where she gasped on seeing her brother lying on the table. "We will bring the swelling down," he assured her and she nodded again. She stood back as he and his father lifted Alfie off the table and carried him up the stairs to the second guest bedroom where Zaineb was on her knees at the hearth lighting a fire.

They placed Alfie in the double bed and Isobel pulled the bedcovers over him before going to the washstand and pouring some water from the ewer into the basin and placing it and a small towel on the bedside table.

Dipping the towel into the cold water, Will gave it a little squeeze then placed it over Alfie's eyes. The combination of cold and pain made Alfie moan and Will had to grab his hands again as he raised them.

"Alfie, it's Will. I have placed a towel dipped in cold water over your eyes to lessen the swelling. The towel will be dipped in the cold water and put back over your eyes every few minutes until the swelling subsides."

"Thank you."

"Good. Now, rest."

"I'll sit with Alfie and attend to him," his father announced and nodded towards Isobel. She was very pale and Will returned his nod. "If someone could please bring me a newspaper to read."

"Yes, of course. Isobel, let's leave Alfie to rest. We'll come back upstairs in about an hour," he added and led her from the bedroom as she opened her mouth to argue. "Alfie will be all right," he whispered on the landing, putting his arms around her.

"What if you hadn't come along?" she murmured into his chest.

"But I did, and he will be well again in no time."

"Mother will be expecting him home and," lowering her voice to a whisper again, she added, "David needs to be found."

"You go to number 55 and speak to your mother – simply tell her it was an attempted robbery – and I'll ask John Hartley to bring me to David's rooms."

"John Hartley?" Drawing back from him, she frowned.

"The cabman I had to bully into allowing me to bring Alfie into his cab," he explained. "He's in the servants' hall having a cup of tea. Oh, Zaineb?" He hailed the maid as she left the bedroom carrying an empty coal scuttle. "Please tell the cabman I need him for another fare."

"Yes, Dr Fitzgerald. Would you like some tea in the morning room?"

"Yes, please."

"Will, I don't need tea," Isobel protested. "I need to tell Mother now."

"You need a cup of tea first. You've had a shock and you're very pale. You're also pregnant, Mrs Fitzgerald, so," he kissed her forehead, "do as your doctor tells you."

John Hartley was standing beside the cab smoking a

cigarette as Will closed the front door behind him and put on his hat.

"Thanks for waiting, John. Could you bring me to Westland Row, please?"

"In you get, Dr Fitzgerald."

If David wasn't in his rooms, Will wondered as the cab turned onto Westland Row, where on earth could he be? Getting out of the cab, he checked his trouser pockets before pulling out all the coins and passing them to the cabman.

"The fare's not this much," Hartley protested.

"Call the rest an apology for shouting and bullying you into taking Alfie and me."

"Thank you, Dr Fitzgerald." Putting the coins in his overcoat pocket then raising his bowler hat to Will, the cabman clicked his tongue and the horse and cab left in the direction of the railway station.

Taking off his hat, Will stared up at the Georgian terraced house. David lived on the first floor but despite it being in darkness, Will banged the front door knocker and waited. Nothing. He banged the knocker again and continued until the door was flung open and a young blonde man in his shirtsleeves glared at him.

"What?"

"I'm here to see David Powell." Will pushed past him, ran up the stairs two at a time, along the landing and knocked on David's door. Again, there was no response and Will hammered on it with his fist. "David? It's Will Fitzgerald. If you're in there, open the door."

Slowly, the door opened and Will's jaw dropped. Despite the weak light from two gas lamps on the walls of the hall, he could see that David's face was almost as badly beaten as

Alfie's. One of David's eyes was almost swollen shut and his left hand was splayed over the right side of his ribcage.

"Where's Alfie?" he whispered.

"Safe at number 30," Will replied and David's face contorted in relief. "He's badly beaten but he's safe. Let me see to you," he added, stepping into the hall and closing the door.

"No, take me to Alfie."

"I can't. My father is there. Where's the washstand?" he asked and followed David along the narrow hall and into a large bedroom at the rear of the building. Turning up the gas lamps, Will went to the washstand in a corner of the room. A white flannel was floating in a basin full of water and Will reached for it, found the water cold, and squeezed it. "Hold this over your eye," he said and passed the flannel over. "Do you think your ribs are broken?"

"I don't think so." David winced as he held the flannel to his eye. "But they hurt like hell. Is Alfie really all right?"

"He will be. Both his eyes are swollen shut but my father is placing a towel soaked in cold water over them. What the hell happened?"

David sat on the edge of the double bed. "I had brought Alfie to a club—"

"A club – a club for..?" Will tailed off and David nodded wearily. "David, for God's sake," he cried before sighing. "I'm sorry, you don't need me to... Go on."

"As we were leaving, we were set upon by four men. I tried to protect Alfie but two of them started punching me in the ribs and I knew that if Alfie and I separated, they would, too, and we would have more of a chance of escaping. So I told Alfie to run one way and I would run the other way and that was the last I saw of him. I managed to lose the two men who were coming after me by hiding under the stairs in a tenement building, but I had no idea what happened to Alfie."

"Did you recognise any of the men?" Will asked and David shook his head. "Does anyone know of your sexual preference?" he added and David shook his head again. "What about Alfie?"

"No. And no-one knows we are lovers," he went on, much to Will's relief.

"Was this evening the first time you had visited that club?"

"No. But it was the first time I had brought Alfie. You needn't worry," he said, going to the washstand and dipping the flannel in the water, squeezing it, then returning it to his eye. "We won't be going back there now that its secret is out."

"Good," Will replied simply, lifting David's hand and the flannel away from David's eye. The eye was a little bloodshot. "How is your vision?"

David looked up, down, and from side to side. "It's fine. Where did you find Alfie?"

"On Fitzwilliam Street Upper. He collapsed and I had to bully a cabman into taking us back to number 30, but I got him there."

"And your father is with him?"

"Yes. Once we cleaned Alfie up and brought him to a guest bedroom, I came looking for you."

"Thank you, Will."

"Not at all. Isobel was worried about you, too. I'll take surgery tomorrow and Friday. We'll see how you look on

Sunday and decide whether I need to take Monday's surgery, as well."

"I'm sorry, Will," he said miserably. "It was just somewhere I wanted to take Alfie where we didn't have to pretend we're something we're not. We'll simply have to continue to pretend."

Will gave him a sympathetic smile. "Do you have enough food?"

"Yes, I do."

"Good. I'll call in the morning before surgery to see how you are and to tell you how Alfie is. Get that swelling down and then go to bed."

David nodded and they walked along the hall to the door to the landing. "I hope you can find a cab at this hour."

"It doesn't really matter." Will gave him a wry smile. "I gave all my change to the cabman who brought me here. He brought Alfie and me to number 30, so he earned it."

"Here." David delved into a trouser pocket and held out one shilling and sixpence. "Take this."

"No—"

"Take it, Will. I insist."

"Thank you." Will took the coins and put them in his trouser pocket. "I'll be back in the morning."

A cab stopped for him on Lincoln Place and he got out on Fitzwilliam Square two doors up from number 55.

"Alfie is asleep," he reassured Mrs Henderson as he was shown into the morning room and she anxiously got to her feet. "And Isobel needs her rest, too, so I have come to bring her home."

"Come over in the morning." Isobel kissed her mother's cheek.

"You will tell me if there is any change?"

"Yes, I promise," she said. "We'll see ourselves out. Well?" she demanded as soon as Will closed the front door. "Did you find David?"

"Come across the street." Taking her hand, he led her to the railings surrounding the square's gardens and to a dark area where they couldn't be seen. There, he told her, feeling her tense. "I will have to take David's surgery for the next two days and Father mustn't know, even though I will probably miss luncheon," he concluded.

"He won't know. For God's sake, Will, how could David have been so stupid?" she raged. "Both of them could have been killed."

"David won't be going back to the club."

"And is he sure no-one knows about them?"

"He's as sure as he can be." She didn't reply and he raised her hand to his lips. "Let's go home."

His father closed and folded a newspaper and put it on the bedside table as they went into the guest bedroom.

"What took so long?"

"Mother was upset," Isobel replied. "It took some time to persuade her it would be best to let Alfie rest and not to visit him until the morning."

"I see. Well, the swelling has subsided considerably and I think we should leave Alfie to sleep."

Will lifted the towel from Alfie's eyes and nodded before replacing it. "Thank you, Father," he said and followed them out of the room, leaving the door ajar.

Isobel lifted two packages containing ham sandwiches from Alfie's breakfast tray, went to the hall table and placed them in Will's medical bag before taking Alfie's breakfast tray from Zaineb.

"I'll take the tray up to him, thank you."

"Yes, Mrs Fitzgerald."

She climbed the stairs to the second floor, pushed the bedroom door open with her foot, then closed it with her behind. Setting the tray down on the bedside table, she went to the window and opened the curtains. Light flooded the room and Alfie groaned, shielding his bruised eyes.

"I'm sorry. Shall I close one of them?" she asked.

"No," he replied, heaving himself into a sitting position.

"First of all, David is safe," she said and Alfie raised a shaking hand to his forehead in clear relief. "Will went to Westland Row last night and David was in his rooms. He has one swollen eye, bruising to his face and bruised ribs. Will is taking his surgery today and tomorrow. Will's father doesn't know, so don't say anything."

"I won't."

"And I managed to stop Mother from coming straight over here last night," she continued. "She is probably on her way here now, so all she needs to know is this; You were the victim of an attempted robbery on Fitzwilliam Street Upper but you managed to fight them off. Will was returning home after seeing his mother back to Merrion Square and saw you collapse. Understood?"

"Yes," Alfie replied. "Will found me?"

"He was walking a little way behind you and saw you collapse. He managed to get you here by cab. Now," she added, lifting the breakfast tray off the bedside table and placing it on his lap. "Porridge, toast and marmalade, and coffee. Eat."

"Thank you," he whispered before his face contorted. "I thought they were going to kill us," he sobbed and she sat on the edge of the bed, clasped his hands and held them as he cried. "David told me to run one way and he would run the other and as I ran, I was sure I'd never see him again."

"David is safe," she assured him and Alfie nodded and wiped his eyes. "Will is calling on him before surgery," she said, adding milk and sugar to the porridge. "Eat."

"Why is Will's father staying here?" Alfie asked as he picked up the spoon and dipped it into the porridge. "I heard him speaking to Will on the landing earlier."

"Alfie, very few people know this, but Will's parents have been experiencing marital difficulties."

"Will's parents?" he echoed in disbelief.

She nodded. "John will be staying here until an arrangement is put in place that he and Sarah can live at number 67 entirely separately."

"Their marital difficulties are that serious?"

"Yes, they are. Please don't tell anyone," she begged. "They don't want it to become common knowledge."

"I won't say anything." He gave her a sad little smile. "Secrets, eh?"

"Yes," she replied quietly.

She sat with Alfie while he ate his breakfast and as she went downstairs with the tray, she heard her mother and Mary's voices in the hall. She passed the tray to Mary and escorted her mother to the second floor.

"Alfie has just eaten a huge breakfast," she said. "But I must warn you that, although the swelling has gone down, he has two black eyes."

Her mother gave a little cry when she saw Alfie's battered

face, rushed to the bed, and flung her arms around him.

"I need to go out," she said when her mother drew back and kissed both of Alfie's cheeks, making him squirm. "I won't be too long. Mother, if you would like some tea or coffee, ring for it."

Putting on her hat and coat, she walked to number 67, hoping Sarah wouldn't view the call as a tactic to hurry her into making a decision regarding the accommodation arrangement.

"Mrs Fitzgerald senior is in the drawing room, Mrs Fitzgerald," Tess told her as she admitted Isobel to the house.

"Thank you, Tess." She smiled at the maid, relieved she didn't have to use dubious means in order to lure Sarah upstairs. Now, she somehow had to sway Sarah into viewing her beautiful rooms dispassionately and then hand them over to John. "I'll join her there."

Opening the drawing room door, she found her mother-in-law standing in the middle of the floor with her hands on her hips.

"Sarah?"

"Oh, Isobel." Sarah turned, allowing her arms to drop helplessly to her sides. "I'm trying to decide how best to proceed but I'm not getting very far."

Isobel glanced around the large room. Like at number 30, it contained a sofa and two armchairs, three side tables and a bookcase, plus a writing desk and chair. Beyond it through double doors lay the dining room, containing a huge table – even bigger than hers and Will's – eight chairs, and a sideboard.

"Well," she began. "The dining room could be converted

into a bedroom and the furniture in here be re-arranged to accommodate the dining table, chairs and sideboard. John would have the entire floor to himself but the breakfast room would have to be used if you were to have any dinner guests. Alternatively, yourself and John could move to the bedrooms furthest away from each other, but you would still be sleeping on the same floor."

"Yes, and I did not want that. But I love these rooms. Oh." Sarah laughed forcibly. "You must think John and I are behaving ridiculously."

"No, not at all," she reassured her. "I wish my mother could have lived separately from my father, but the Glebe House, although one of the largest houses in the parish, simply wasn't big enough for her to do so. And Mother couldn't leave the Glebe House…" Tailing off, she shuddered, forcing from her mind the screams from the bedroom above the parlour as her father repeatedly struck her mother.

"Because your mother's parents had not wanted her to marry your father in the first place and wouldn't have taken her back with all the shame of a failed marriage," Sarah concluded. "Your mother did mention it to me."

"So," Isobel continued as cheerfully as she could. "John and yourself are very lucky to live in a house in which you have options."

"Which option would you choose?" Sarah asked eagerly and Isobel shook her head.

"I cannot decide for you," she said gently and Sarah's face fell. "You must discuss it with John."

"But, Isobel, I can hardly bear to look at him never mind discuss how to divide the living accommodation between us."

"Come and sit with me." Taking Sarah's arm, Isobel led her to the carved walnut sofa upholstered in cream silk satin and they sat down side by side. "When was the last time you and John had dinner guests?"

Sarah had to ponder the question. "It was the last time Edward was home," she said. "He came home for a week shortly before his wedding. We threw a huge dinner party to celebrate. That was five years ago and I haven't been at all inclined to throw one since. I've decided, haven't I, Isobel?" She exhaled a sad little sigh. "John can have these two rooms if he wants them. Would you mind very much putting it to him this evening, please?" Sarah asked hesitantly.

"Very well."

"Thank you. You'll be glad to know that Mr Ellison has looked over the will and the residency agreement and has found nothing problematic."

Isobel sucked in a breath as she felt a strong flutter from the baby. "It's the baby," she explained.

"Are you quite well?" Sarah asked anxiously, looking her up and down.

"Yes, thank you. The baby's flutters are getting stronger and stronger and will soon be kicks."

"He or she must take after Will. He kicked like nobody's business from early on."

"It's time Will and I sat down with young John and told him about the baby. I'm nervous about doing it, though," she admitted. "I don't know how he will react. The last thing I want is for him to hate the baby."

"Like he hates Edward."

"We will tell young John about his father when he is older," she promised. "And about his mother, even though we know little or nothing about her. You are most welcome to visit young John. I don't wish to limit you to a particular day and time, but when his grandfather is at the *Journal* would be best. I don't want any awkwardness, Sarah because I will be extending the same invitation to you both."

"Yes, of course."

"My father's parents died before I was born, and I have never met my mother's parents, so I really want young John to know his grandparents – and his Grandmamma Martha."

"And his soon-to-be Grandpapa James?" Sarah added with a smile.

"Mother has told you." Isobel returned her smile with relief. "I'm sorry, I didn't know if she had told anyone else."

"She is seizing the opportunity to be happy and I am absolutely delighted for her."

Will lifted two brown paper packages out of his medical bag, opened one and smiled. Leaving his surgery, he went downstairs to the office and passed the unopened package to Eva.

"From Mrs Dillon via my wife – ham sandwiches for a quick luncheon."

"Thank you, Dr Fitzgerald, how kind."

"Not at all. Well, I'd better get started, otherwise, we'll still be here at dinnertime."

Three and a half hours later, he advised the few remaining patients he would continue surgery in ten minutes, before going into the office and closing the door.

"Time for luncheon," he announced and Eva nodded. About to sit down, the front door banged shut and someone strode up the stairs. Quickly putting his sandwiches on Eva's desk, Will went upstairs to his surgery and found his father about to come looking for him. "Father?"

"Close the door."

"Why? What's wrong?"

"Just close the door."

Will did as he was told before turning to face his father. "What's the matter?"

"Where is David Powell?"

"He's ill. I'm seeing his patients today and—"

"A 'bad cold', is it?"

Will tensed. "What do you want, Father?"

"I want you to tell me Alfie Stevens and David Powell aren't lovers and that they weren't attacked outside a molly house last night."

"Lower your voice, for God's sake, there are patients downstairs," Will snapped.

"So, it is true, then?"

"I don't know what you're talking about."

"Do not lie to me, Will."

"I don't know what you're talking about," he repeated and his father glared at him, before pulling a scrap of newspaper from the inside pocket of his frock coat and handing it to Will.

It was an article torn from a newspaper detailing an attack on two men which had taken place outside what was rumoured to be a club and meeting place for sodomites. The two men had been singled out as they left the club and savagely beaten before they managed to escape in different directions.

"I don't know how – from this article – you can suggest such a thing." Will held the scrap of newspaper out to his father who silently took it from him and returned it to his pocket.

"Would the fact that Alfie called out for someone called David – twice – while I was sitting with him, suffice?"

Will closed his eyes for a moment. "It really is none of your business, Father."

"Does Isobel know? No." His father corrected himself with a humourless smile. "Of course she does. You tell her everything. Did she tell you to take David Powell on?"

"No, she did not," he shouted and heard someone running up the stairs and approaching the door. It opened and Eva looked in at them.

"Doctors, please, the patients can hear raised voices."

"I'm sorry, Eva," he said. "I won't be long." Eva nodded, the door closed and Will turned back to his father. "Isobel suggested David, that was all. Taking him on was entirely my decision. I have monitored him closely and he is a good doctor and he is good with patients."

"But he is a sodomite." His father almost spat out the word. "I do not want a sodomite working in this practice, Will, get rid of him."

"It isn't up to you anymore, Father. I run this practice now."

"What if it becomes common knowledge? This practice would be finished – this practice which has been in the Fitzgerald family for over a century."

"It won't become common knowledge because you will burn that article and go back to the *Journal* and forget we ever had this discussion."

"But David Powell is reckless. It is now common knowledge where there is a molly house in the city."

"David has assured me he will not be returning there – and I believe him."

"When did you speak to him?"

"Last night and first thing this morning. He will not be going back and this discussion is over Father," he said, walking to the door and opening it. "I have patients waiting for me."

His father glared at him again before leaving the surgery and going downstairs. A moment or two later, the front door slammed.

Will sat on the edge of his desk and ran a hand across his jaw. His father wouldn't give David and Alfie away for fear of damaging the reputation of the practice but this complication on top of all the recent events he really could have done without. His stomach rumbled, he got to his feet and went back down the stairs to the office. Eva glanced at him as she threw her sandwiches' brown wrapping paper into the wastepaper basket then brushed breadcrumbs from the skirt of her deep red dress.

"I'm sorry about that," he said, picking up one of his sandwiches and taking an enormous bite. He chewed and swallowed, took another bite, and shoved the rest inelegantly into his mouth.

"You'll give yourself indigestion, Dr Fitzgerald."

He nodded as he quickly chewed and swallowed. "My stomach was rumbling. Right. Who's next?"

Hearing voices in the hall at just after six o'clock, Isobel closed and folded the *Freeman's Journal* and put the newspaper on the arm of the sofa. About thirty tenants on the Loughry Estate in Co Tyrone had applied in the Land

Court the previous day for a reasonable reduction in their rent and Mr Parnell was in Paris where Victor Hugo held a reception in his honour. Either there had been little else of interest in the newspaper or she had too much on her mind. Getting up, she went out to the hall but, instead of Will, his father was passing his hat and overcoat to Zaineb.

"I need to speak to you, Isobel," he said shortly, following her into the morning room and closing the door.

"I need to speak to you, too."

"What I have to say is important," he added and she stiffened.

"So, is your future living accommodation, but do go on."

"Dr David Powell – you recommended him to Will – even though you knew he was a sodomite."

She opened her mouth to reply but nothing came out. How on earth had John found out?

"You need not bother trying to deny it," John continued. "Will told me himself."

"I suggested David – that is all – Will interviewed him and Will made the decision to take him on."

"My wife never interfered in the running of the practice."

"Will needed someone at very short notice to replace Fred and—"

"How dare you suggest that your brother's lover take over from Fred—"

"Fred had syphilis – he had to be replaced—"

"Not by a sodomite. I want you to tell Will to get rid of him."

"No," she replied emphatically. "No, I won't."

"Look." John pulled a scrap of newspaper from his frock coat's inside pocket and passed it to her. "Soon everyone will know about your brother and his lover and the reputation of the practice will be in the gutter."

The article detailed a violent assault on two men outside what was thought to be a club for sodomites but…

"No-one is named here – how do you know it is them?" she demanded.

"Your brother called out for his lover – twice – as I sat with him last night," he told her and her heart sank. "That, coupled with this article, led me to put two and two together."

"Neither Alfie nor David will be returning to that club."

"There will be others – molly houses are like brothels – when one closes another will open."

"Or any club," she added firmly. "They learned a hard lesson last night. They will not be going back. I will not tell Will to get rid of David, and the running of the practice is no longer your concern. It is Will's. Is that understood?"

"Your brother's lover," John snapped. "It is disgusting – both of them are disgusting – one is a doctor and one soon will be."

"Duncan Simpson was a surgeon and he loved a man – was he disgusting, too?"

"We never spoke of it."

That didn't surprise her. "You turned a blind eye to Duncan and yet you dare call Alfie and David disgusting. Well, Alfie stood between Mother, myself, and my father so many times I lost count. Alfie took beatings for us so we wouldn't have to. Father wanted Alfie to become a clergyman and when Alfie refused time and again he was beaten time and again – and you call him disgusting. Alfie deserves some happiness – he has found it with David – and

I insist you turn a blind eye to them, John."

"What is happening?" She jumped and turned around, not having heard the door open. Alfie stood in the doorway wearing his morning coat over the nightshirt Will had leant him. "I can hear you both shouting from upstairs."

"Have you not gone home to your mother, yet?" John asked and Alfie's eyebrows shot up.

"Go back upstairs, Alfie," she ordered.

"No, stay," John commanded. "Answer me this; whose idea was it to go to the molly house – yours or David Powell's?"

Alfie's brown eyes widened in horror but, to her relief, he didn't reply and left the room.

Isobel walked to the door then paused. "Sarah has offered you the entire first floor at number 67 as living accommodation," she said. "You are rapidly outstaying your welcome here so I would advise you to take it," she added before going out to the hall.

Alfie was sitting on the stairs, his head in his hands and his shoulders shaking.

"Come upstairs," she said softly.

"How did he find out?" Alfie mumbled as the front door opened, Will came inside and closed the door behind him.

Will placed his medical bag on the hall table, took off his hat and hung it on the stand, then frowned on seeing them at the stairs.

"What's the matter?" he asked immediately and Alfie raised his head.

"Your father knows about David and me."

"I'll speak to him."

"No, I will," she said, going to the morning room door

and opening it. "Bring Alfie upstairs, Will. I'll ask for his dinner be brought up to him on a tray."

John was standing at the window with his back to her when she went into the room.

"You insist I turn a blind eye to them," he said without turning around.

"Yes, I do," she replied, shutting the door. "You appear to be quite good at it when it suits you."

That made him turn around. "I have never been spoken to by a woman in the way you have spoken to me."

"Turn a blind eye, John, and accept the first-floor living arrangement at number 67."

"Did you propose it to Sarah?"

"No, she decided on it herself. The dining room would become your bedroom and the drawing room is big enough to serve as both drawing room and dining room."

"And if we were to hold a dinner party?"

"That is hardly likely given that your last was five years ago."

"The last time Edward was home," he said quietly.

"When my father threw me out and I came to Dublin, I thought I had lost my mother and Alfie forever. I pushed away everyone who tried to get close to me, not wanting to risk losing them, too. I am very lucky Will was so stubborn. John, don't push your family away. Accept the first-floor living arrangement."

"Will you bring my grandson to see me?" he asked, sounding a little tentative.

"I think it would be best for you to come here, John, at least until he is a little older. It wouldn't do for young John to tell anyone that his grandmother lives downstairs and he grandfather lives upstairs."

"Very well, I accept the arrangement."

"And you will turn a blind eye to Alfie and David as well?" she added and he turned back to the window.

"Tell me about Alfie."

"Alfie is a year older than I am and he has wanted to be a doctor for as long as I can remember. He never thought he would get this chance and now he has it, he is making the very most of it."

"Had you known about his preference for men?"

"No. I found out purely by accident."

"What do you know about David Powell?"

"David graduated in the top five in his year at Trinity," Will said and they both turned around as he shut the door, not having heard him come in. "Since he graduated, he has been doing locum work to gain experience. Isobel suggested him to me and we had a long chat and I decided to take him on."

"Will you get rid of him?" his father asked.

"No, I will not. He is still on trial but he has done nothing to bring the practice into disrepute and I will be keeping him on."

John pursed his lips before sighing. "You're stubborn."

"It is nothing to do with stubbornness, Father."

"Will you offer him a partnership?"

"It is far too soon for anything like that," Will replied and his father nodded.

"Please turn a blind eye?" she asked and John glanced at her.

"You are just as stubborn as your husband. Very well. But I want to meet them both. Perhaps some drinks here?"

"Yes." She fought to hide her relief. "Thank you, John."

"Will, your mother has offered me the entire first floor as living accommodation and I have accepted."

"Good," Will replied simply.

Before they went to the breakfast room for dinner, Isobel hurried upstairs. Alfie was sitting on the edge of the double bed but got his feet as she went into the guest bedroom.

"You called out for David twice yesterday evening," she explained and he swore under his breath. "But John has agreed to turn a blind eye."

"But will he?" Alfie demanded.

"I believe he will, yes. The not so good news is that he wishes to meet you and David," she added and Alfie's face contorted in dismay.

"Why?"

"You're my brother and Will is keeping David on at the practice. I'm afraid I lectured John a little on families and the two of you are part of his extended family now."

"Whether he likes it or not," Alfie finished.

"Be relieved he is turning a blind eye," she said, hearing a knock at the door. "That will be someone with your dinner. I thought it would be a little less awkward if you ate up here." Opening the door, she took the tray from Zaineb.

"Dinner is served downstairs, Mrs Fitzgerald."

"Thank you, Zaineb," she said and the maid closed the door. "Alfie, John is moving back to number 67 in the next couple of days," she went on, placing the tray on the bedside table. "It's entirely up to you when you want to go home and be fussed over by Mother."

"I'd like a few hours to myself so, perhaps, in the morning," he said and she was delighted to see him smile.

David Powell returned to work at the practice house the following Monday. Will's father went home to number 67 the same day and Will was more than relieved to see him go. Whether his parents' separate living arrangements could be sustained in the long run remained to be seen but the immediate crisis was over for now.

Whether he would ever come to terms with Fred's death, Will didn't know and as yet the loss of Fred was still too raw to evaluate. Jerry returned to London at the beginning of March and as the harsh winter gave way to spring, Will's life took on a predictable routine he was grateful for, both at the practice house and at home.

His mother came to number 30 for luncheon on Wednesdays, staying on to visit her grandson. His father visited his namesake on Saturday mornings before staying on for luncheon. Will took Isobel out for coffee on Saturday afternoons and John was brought to feed the ducks in St Stephen's Green after luncheon on Sundays.

At the end of April, James Ellison brought Will a letter from Lieutenant-General Beresford, the Commander-in-Chief of the Bombay Army. Like Edward had been, the Lieutenant-General was a poor correspondent. Apart from the welcome information that Major Fitzgerald had been buried with full military honours in the British Christian Cemetery at Deolali, the letter was full of banal platitudes and could have been written about anyone. But Will was thankful all the same that the Lieutenant-General had taken the time to sit down and write personally to his fellow officer's family.

After showing the letter to his parents and transcribing it so his mother could include the copy when she next wrote to Ruth, Will put it away with the photograph of Edward and Purnima for when John was old enough to be told about the father and mother he never knew.

Catching the little boy staring curiously at Isobel's belly one evening in early May, Will exchanged a glance with her and she nodded. Isobel was now seven months pregnant, and it simply couldn't be put off any longer. It was time to sit John down and tell him about the baby.

While Florrie went downstairs to the servants' hall for a cup of tea, Isobel sat at the nursery table with young John and Will, hoping the little boy would take the news well.

"You've noticed my tummy getting bigger, haven't you, John?" she began and he stared at her belly for a few moments before nodding.

"Yes."

"Isobel's tummy is getting bigger because there is a baby growing inside it," Will explained and the boy's eyes widened.

"A baby?"

"Yes. In two months' time, you'll be sharing the nursery with a cousin."

"A boy cousin?"

She smiled. "We don't know, it will be a surprise for all of us."

"Is Florrie going to look after the baby, too?"

"Yes," she replied. "And I will be helping as well."

"Will the baby cry?"

"It probably will at times," Will said. "Most probably when he or she is hungry. But before all that, Isobel's tummy will get bigger as the baby gets bigger, and when the baby has grown enough he or she will be born."

"In here?" John peered around the room.

"No, the baby will be born downstairs in our bedroom," she told the boy. "And you will be one of the first to see him or her. Is there anything you want to ask us?"

"Can I touch your tummy?" John asked, his gaze returning to her belly.

"Of course you can," she replied and he reached out and touched her belly with a forefinger. "Lay your hand flat against my tummy," she instructed softly and he did, sucking in an astonished breath as if on cue the baby kicked hard. "Can you feel that?" she asked and he nodded. "The baby's kicking."

"Does it hurt?"

"It can be a little uncomfortable but it doesn't hurt, no," she said and exchanged a grin with Will as John stroked her belly as if to calm the baby.

Despite Sarah mentioning how Will kicked like nobody's business from early on, it had worried her that the baby was so very active. Most nights she woke with a start as the baby wriggled and kicked her insides black and blue. Rubbing her belly to settle the baby, she would try her best not to wake Will, but it wasn't always possible, especially when he slept with an arm around her.

He always assured her it was nothing to be concerned about and when he examined her every few days, he would pass the stethoscope to her so she could listen to the baby's heartbeat. The first time she heard the strong heartbeat of the baby growing inside her – the baby she feared she would never carry – she had burst into tears of relief.

"Where will the baby sleep when it's born?" John asked.

"The baby will share your bedroom," Will replied.

"Isobel and I are going to buy a cradle and the baby will sleep in it. Then, when he or she gets too big for the cradle, we'll buy a bed like yours."

"I like my bed."

"Good. Shall we help you to get ready for bed?" he offered and the little boy nodded.

Ten minutes later, she sat on the bed on one side of John and Will on the other.

"If you have any more questions about the baby, just ask us, yes?"

"Yes."

"Good boy." Isobel gave him a hug and a kiss. "Goodnight."

"Goodnight." Will kissed John's cheek and the little boy snuggled down under the bedcovers.

Out in the nursery, Florrie was closing the door to the landing and gave them a questioning glance as they left John's bedroom.

"He wants a boy cousin," Will told her. "And he may ask you a hundred questions in the morning."

"But he took the news well?" the maid asked anxiously.

"Yes, very well, thank goodness. We'll try and answer his questions as best we can, taking his age into consideration."

"Yes, Dr Fitzgerald."

"Relieved that's over?" Isobel smiled as they went downstairs.

"Very," he replied. "I was dreading him asking how the baby got into your tummy."

"He might you that in the morning," she teased and he laughed.

"Well, I'm afraid my answer will have to wait a few years."

Chapter Nine

As June gave way to July and Isobel entered her ninth month of pregnancy, Will realised the weekend outings were becoming too much for her. She insisted on walking, but it had taken an age for them to reach the café on Grafton Street. He helped her to sit down at a corner table, she pulled the large black fringed shawl around her – used to conceal her now huge belly from disapproving eyes – and gave him a tired smile.

"Oh, my back aches." Extracting a handkerchief from the sleeve of her high-waisted silver-grey dress, she mopped her forehead. "Next Saturday, we'll have to come by cab."

"Do you want to go home?" he asked, sitting beside her and she shook her head.

"It's only four o'clock. I've managed to waddle here so I deserve a cup of coffee. I won't be able to waddle all the way home, though."

"That doesn't matter. You just tell me when to hail a cab." Turning to catch the attention of a waitress, he felt her grab his wrist.

"Will, don't."

"What is it?" Glancing back, he saw her brown eyes wide with shock.

"I've started," she whispered. "I feel wet."

Her waters had broken. Stay calm, he ordered himself. Stay calm and bring her home.

"I'll hail a cab."

"But it's too soon, Will," she said, her voice shaking. "The baby isn't due until the end of the month."

"We have an impatient baby," he said, mustering up as bright a smile as he could. Kissing her hand, he got up and went outside onto the street, holding up his hands to stop a cab. "My wife is in the early stages of labour," he explained to the startled cabman. "Are you willing to drive us to number 30 Fitzwilliam Square?"

"Course I am. Go and fetch her."

"Thank you." Will returned to the café and helped Isobel into the cab.

"It's too soon, Will," she whispered as the cab moved off.

"Try and stay calm," he said, as much to himself as to her.

When the cab turned into Fitzwilliam Square, Will spotted Alfie walking along the pavement and he thumped a fist on the ceiling. "Stop, please." The cab stopped and Will threw open the door. "Alfie?" he called and Alfie waved and crossed the street. "The baby's coming," Will told him before Alfie could speak and Alfie's jaw dropped as he peered into the cab at Isobel. "Follow us, then take this cab and find David," he added, closing the door and the cab carried on and stopped outside number 30.

"It's too soon, Will," Isobel said again as both he and Alfie helped her out.

"You have an impatient baby," Alfie told her with a smile.

"That's what Will said."

"And he's a doctor and I'm on my way to being one, so no worrying." Alfie kissed her cheek before looking up at the cabman. "Westland Row, please."

"Here." Will pulled half a crown out of his trouser pocket. "For this fare and the fares there and back. Take it," he insisted as Alfie hesitated. "Fetch David."

Alfie nodded and took the coin, got into the cab, and it pulled away.

"Let's get you inside," he said, helping Isobel up the steps and opening the front door." Mrs Dillon?" he roared, bringing Isobel into the hall and hanging his hat on the stand as Zaineb hurried out of the breakfast room. "Zaineb, please tell Mrs Dillon the baby is on its way."

"Yes, Dr Fitzgerald," she said and ran down the steps to the servants' hall.

Grabbing his medical bag from the hall table, they climbed the stairs, pausing on the first and second-floor landings before continuing on into their bedroom. He undressed Isobel and helped her into a nightdress before letting down and plaiting her hair. Lying her on the bed, she tensed and groaned.

"A contraction," he told her as he lit all the gas lamps. "It's perfectly normal."

"Dr Fitzgerald?"

Hearing a knock and Mrs Dillon's voice on the landing, he went out to her, leading the housekeeper away from the bedroom door so Isobel couldn't hear them.

"My wife is in labour. She is just under a month early. I've sent Alfie Stevens to Westland Row to fetch Dr David Powell and I'm going to need warm water, soap, and as many towels as you can find."

"Yes, Dr Fitzgerald."

"It might also be a good idea for Florrie to bring John across the square to Mrs Henderson as he may get upset hearing my wife in labour. Please ask Florrie to assure Mrs Henderson that there is nothing to worry about and the labour is progressing normally."

"But should we be worried that your wife is in labour so early?" Mrs Dillon asked quietly.

"I've delivered early babies before," he replied, pushing the seven-and-a-half-month girl he delivered in Weaver Square and who only lived for half an hour to the back of his mind. "There is no cause for concern."

"Yes, Dr Fitzgerald."

"Thank you, Mrs Dillon."

Returning to Isobel, he found her groaning again.

"I'm scared, Will, it's too soon."

"Look on the bright side," he said, shrugging off his frock coat and lying it on the back of the bedroom chair. "An early baby will be smaller than one which is full term."

"I suppose so," she replied and sucked in a breath before releasing it in a groan. "That one really hurt."

"You can shout and swear at me all you like," he added, undoing his cufflinks and putting them in the drawer of his bedside table.

"In front of David?" She spluttered a laugh. "I don't know about that."

"He'll get used to it."

"Why are you sending for him, Will?" she asked point blank and he rolled his shirtsleeves up then knelt on the floor beside the bed.

"I've delivered umpteen babies," he told her softly.

"Some well before their time. But none of them have been my own and none of the women in labour have been my wife. I like to think I'll keep a clear head but I don't know how I'll react so that is why I want David here – two heads are better than one – I didn't tell you before because I didn't want to worry you."

She nodded and he kissed her forehead. "Can I get up, Will? I'm very uncomfortable lying like this."

"Yes, of course, you can," he replied. "But wait until I've examined you."

"Dr Fitzgerald?" Hearing Mrs Dillon's voice again and another knock at the door, he got to his feet and opened it. The housekeeper and Zaineb were on the landing with towels draped over their arms and holding a basin and an ewer of water each. "Where would you like the water, Dr Fitzgerald?"

"On the washstand, please," he said, putting the towels on the dressing table. "Thank you." Closing the door after them, he washed and dried his hands before lifting Isobel's nightdress and examining her. "You're all but dilated already," he told her, trying to keep his voice neutral. How long had she been in labour for without realising it? "Our baby is in a hurry." Helping her off the bed, he held her hands while she bent her head as another contraction ripped through her. "Walk up and down if it helps."

"Yes." Holding tightly onto his hands, she walked to the end of the bed then let him go and gripped the brass bedstead. "Prepare the bed," she said. "I'll stand here."

Pulling back the bedcovers, he laid some of the larger towels in the bed and returned to her as she went to squat.

"Don't push just yet." Taking her arm, he walked her

around the room. "I'll tell you when it's time."

"But I need to push now," she cried, shaking off his arm and leaning heavily on the chest of drawers. "Oh, God, it hurts."

"Breathe deeply," he instructed. "In and out—"

"No, I need to push – I can feel the baby coming – it's coming now."

Grabbing two more towels, he placed them on the floor at the end of the bed and guided her onto them. She hitched the nightdress up around her waist before grasping the bedstead, her legs apart and screaming as she pushed. Dropping to his knees, he could see the baby's head.

"Another push for the head, Isobel," he instructed and she pushed down with a long groan. "Good." He held the head in his hands. "The head is out. Take some deep breaths and push again with the next contraction. With an agonising scream she squatted and pushed again and the baby all but fell out into his hands. "It's a boy," he said, hearing his voice shake. But a very small boy, he added silently, placing the baby on the towel as the boy began to wail. "And he has an excellent pair of lungs."

"Will?" she gasped. "I can feel something else."

"That will be the placenta."

"No, it feels heavy – I think it's another baby."

His heart somersaulted and he pulled his medical bag towards him and opened it. Reaching for a pair of scissors, he cut the umbilical cord before wrapping the baby boy in a towel he yanked down from the dressing table. Picking the baby up, he peered around the room before taking a pillow from the bed, laying the baby on the pillow and placing him on the dressing table beside the remaining towels.

Where the bloody hell is David, he raged to himself as he turned back to Isobel. And how the bloody hell had he not known it was twins?

"Let me get you onto the bed, Isobel. I need to examine you again."

Nodding, she shuffled to the side of the bed, sat down and lay back with her legs open. He got down on his knees but couldn't see a thing.

"Isobel, I'm going to have to do an internal examination."

Her only reply was a groan and he got up and went to the washstand. He scrubbed and rinsed his hands before soaping his right hand thoroughly and returning to her. Slipping his hand inside her, he felt her tense but he couldn't find anything. Pushing his hand further inside her, his fingers inadvertently broke the waters of a second twin and brushed against something firm. Lifting his fingers, they met skin.

"Isobel, it is another baby but I can't feel the head or the feet."

"Why not?" she demanded. "What's wrong with it?"

"It's my guess that this baby has been lying in a peculiar position in the womb all along – possibly partly under your rib cage. Now that his or her brother has been born, this baby has dropped down and is lying across the birth canal."

"Can you turn it around?"

"I'm going to try," he said, withdrawing his hand hearing a knock at the door.

"Will, it's David."

"Come in," he called and David came into the bedroom, closed the door, shrugged off his frock coat and threw it into a corner. "It's twins," he explained as the younger man undid his cufflinks, put them in his trouser pocket then rolled up his shirtsleeves. "A boy, born a few minutes ago over there on the pillow." He nodded to the dressing table. "The second baby is lying transverse," he added and David's eyes bulged momentarily. "I'm going to try and turn it. Please help me with Isobel." They lifted her a little further back onto the bed and he nodded. "Thank you. See to the boy."

Soaping his right hand again, he leant over Isobel. She was blinking furiously, trying not to cry.

"I'm scared, Will."

"I know, but there is the space the first baby was in and I will use that space to turn this baby. I can deliver the baby either head or feet first and one baby has already been born, so that will make it a little easier for this birth. I'm not going to lie to you and tell you it won't hurt because it will."

"Just do it."

He slowly eased his hand inside her once more. Isobel whimpered and he grimaced. This must be utterly excruciating for her. Feeling his way along the baby's body, he reached an arm and then a shoulder. Good, he told himself, you know which way the baby is lying. Gently, he moved his hand back along the baby's body, cupped the baby's bottom and pushed it upwards using his left hand to externally manipulate the head downwards. Isobel was whining with pain but he couldn't stop now. When he couldn't push any further upwards and the head was pressing against his wrist, he slowly withdrew his hand.

"Isobel, it's time for gravity to help you. I need you to stand up."

"I don't know if I can stand."

"David will hold you," he said, glancing across the room at him as David wiped the baby boy clean.

David put the towel down and, between them, they helped Isobel into the same standing position at the end of the bed she had assumed for the first baby.

"Hold the bed, hold me, or hold both," David told her and she nodded, gripping his shoulder with one hand and the bedstead with the other.

"Now, I need you to push with the next contraction," Will instructed and she pushed, screaming with effort. "Push harder, Isobel," he added and her scream descended into a long guttural howl. "Keep pushing – I can see the head – keep pushing – now stop," he ordered as the head emerged. "The head is out – now breathe, Isobel – breathe in and out – good. Now, with the next contraction, another hard push, Isobel."

This time, there was little more than a croak from her as David held her under the arms while she squatted and pushed. The baby slid out but Isobel passed out, her legs went from under her and David had to quickly lift her up and into his arms.

The baby was a girl and Will quickly cleared her airway. When she began to wail, he cut the umbilical cord before wrapping her in a towel. He took a pillow from the head of the bed and placed her on the dressing table beside her brother.

David laid Isobel down on the bed. Her face was the palest Will had ever seen it and shining with perspiration. Leaning over her, he forced himself to feel her neck for a pulse. It was pounding and he kissed her wet forehead, fighting back tears of relief.

David squeezed his shoulder, went to the door and opened it. Mrs Dillon and Zaineb were on the landing and darted forward.

"We need more water and more towels, please," David told them.

"And baby clothes and nappies from the nursery," Will added.

"How is Mrs Fitzgerald?" the housekeeper asked anxiously, peering past David.

"Exhausted."

"And the baby?"

"Babies," Will corrected her and she clapped a hand to her chest. "Isobel and I have twins – a boy and a girl. We don't have two of everything but please see what we do have. I need to stay with my wife."

"Yes, of course." Mrs Dillon nudged Zaineb, who was staring in horror at Isobel, and they hurried to the stairs.

Will stroked Isobel's damp hair but she woke with a jump and exhaled a groan as she tensed and pushed again.

"It's all right," he whispered. "It's definitely the placenta this time. Let me check it."

The placenta was complete and he wrapped it up in two towels and placed it on the floor beside the door. He then parted her legs and examined her, noting how she couldn't even raise her head to see what he was doing. Miraculously, she hadn't torn, and he covered her with her nightdress.

"How are the babies?" she murmured.

"We have a son and a daughter," he told her. "They are small but they are perfect. And you need to rest."

"I need to feed them," she said as someone knocked at the door. "Then, I'll rest."

David opened the door and took a large ewer from Zaineb, placing it on the floor beside the washstand.

"Mrs Dillon is upstairs in the nursery and will be here shortly, Dr Fitzgerald," Zaineb said. "I'll get some clean bed linen."

"Thank you, Zaineb," Will replied and the maid closed the door after her.

"Can I see the babies?" Isobel asked and Will sat on the bed. He lifted her and eased her back against him as David brought the babies to the bed, laying them side by side. "They're beautiful."

The girl had a fine covering of brown hair and stared solemnly at her parents with dark blue eyes. The boy had far less hair but opened his eyes and let out a wail.

"Dark blue eyes, too." Will said. "Which will probably be brown in time."

He watched as David dampened a towel and wiped the girl clean and when Mrs Dillon came in, he smiled as they dressed the two babies in nappies and white cotton smocks.

"Oh, aren't they just the loveliest little dotes." The housekeeper was almost in tears. "And two of them – such a surprise."

"Isobel is going to feed the babies and then she needs to sleep. Could you carry the cradle down here, please, David?"

"Yes, of course."

"Come with me, Dr Powell." Mrs Dillon opened the door. "I'll bring you to the nursery and I'll fetch some bed linen for the cradle."

When the door closed after them, Will helped Isobel take off her soiled nightdress, retrieved the pillows from the dressing table, and arranged them at her back. Sitting on the bed again and lifting up the baby girl, he held her to Isobel's left breast and they gazed in wonder as the baby sucked strongly on her nipple for a few minutes. Winding the baby, Will put her down on the bed and picked up her brother. The baby boy sucked on Isobel's right nipple far more noisily and Will felt Isobel smile. Winding the baby and placing him beside his sister, Will went to the chest of drawers and took out a clean nightdress. He dressed Isobel in it and lifted her up.

"Zaineb?" he called and the bedroom door opened and both Zaineb and Mary came in, Zaineb carrying bed linen and Mary carrying a laundry basket. After Zaineb fetched two more pillows from one of the guest bedrooms, she and Mary placed the babies on the pillows on the dressing table. The two maids then quickly stripped the towels and covers from the bed, put them in the basket and remade the bed. "Thank you," he said, laying Isobel down. She was asleep before he had even pulled the bedcovers over her and he kissed her forehead.

"Will Mrs Fitzgerald be all right, Dr Fitzgerald?" Zaineb asked anxiously.

"She's exhausted, but she'll regain her strength with rest and with nutritious food, as she'll be feeding the babies herself."

"What about the babies, Dr Fitzgerald?" Mary added and he turned to the dressing table.

"They're a boy and a girl. They're small – being twins and just under a month early – but they're healthy and feeding well, I'm relieved to say."

Zaineb opened the door and the three of them tidied the bedroom, bringing the basket, the towels from the floor, the ewers and the basins out onto the landing.

"Let me help, Dr Fitzgerald." Mrs Dillon was coming down the stairs from the nursery with bed linen for the cradle in her hands and David was behind her carrying the large mahogany cradle. "I'll get another basket for all the towels."

"Thank you, Mrs Dillon," he said, taking the bed linen from her. "David, if we can lay the babies feet to feet in the cradle until I acquire another one. Then, I need to tell Isobel's mother and brother and bring John and Florrie back here."

The bed linen was placed in the cradle, the babies laid down with a white cotton blanket covering them up to their chests and David gestured towards the bed.

"I'll sit with Isobel and the babies until you come back."

"Thank you. And thank you for coming, David. I'd never have managed without your help."

The younger man smiled. "Please don't take this the wrong way, Will, but I learned a lot today."

"We never stop learning. I had absolutely no idea it was twins, and I examined Isobel every few days. The baby girl must have been lying partly under Isobel's rib cage. No wonder she was so uncomfortable for the last few weeks."

"I thought you'd never get the baby girl turned but congratulations." David shook his hand warmly. "One of each."

Will nodded, feeling tears welling up. Grabbing his frock coat, he hurried from the room. He ran down the landing and into a guest bedroom, slamming the door and allowing great gasping sobs to overwhelm him. What if he hadn't been able to turn the baby girl? Would he have been able to perform a caesarean on his own wife? Would he have been able to watch David do it? Or even assist?

Throwing his frock coat onto the bed, he paced up and down the room until the tears subsided. He leant on his hands on the window sill, noting to his surprise that it was getting dark and lamps were lit in many of the houses around the square. Taking out his watch, his eyebrows shot up. It was five minutes to ten. Putting the watch back in his waistcoat pocket, he wiped his eyes, shrugged on his frock coat and opened the door.

An ewer of water, a basin, soap and a towel were on the floor to one side of the doorway. Picking them up, he brought them into the bedroom and over to the washstand. He washed and dried his face and hands before taking the ewer, basin, soap and towel back out onto the landing.

"Dr Fitzgerald?" Zaineb was waiting at the top of the stairs. "Shall I take those from you?"

"Thank you." He passed them to her. "And thank you for being so thoughtful."

"Shall I prepare the bedroom for Dr Powell?" she offered. "Or shall I send Gerald to find a cab to take him home?"

"Prepare the bedroom, please, Zaineb, and lend Dr Powell one of my nightshirts. Then, go to bed yourself."

"I will, Dr Fitzgerald. Goodnight."

Gorman admitted Will to number 55 and Will went straight to the morning room without waiting for the butler to show him in. John was fast asleep on the seat of an armchair under Alfie's morning coat. Alfie was sitting with his legs crossed in the other armchair and Mrs Henderson was seated on the sofa. On seeing him, Mrs Henderson and Alfie got to their feet, apprehension written across both their faces.

"Will?" His mother-in-law clasped his hands. "Tell me?"

"Isobel is well," he said and her mother clapped both hands to her cheeks in relief. "Exhausted, but well. We have twins."

"Twins?" Alfie echoed while Mrs Henderson simply stared at him in complete astonishment.

"It was a struggle, but they are both well, too."

"But… twins..?" Isobel's mother whispered.

"Yes. You have a grandson and a granddaughter."

"Oh, Will, twins…" His mother-in-law was clearly struggling to take the news in.

"Have a good night's sleep, then come over after breakfast to meet them."

"Do your parents know?"

"No, not yet. I'll go to number 67 tomorrow to tell them and ask if I can borrow the cradle Edward and I used."

Mrs Henderson frowned until the penny dropped. "Oh, of course, you've only got one of some items."

"Yes."

"Will, you're exhausted, too. Let me ring for Florrie and you can take John home." She kissed his cheek and pulled the rope. "He's been very good."

"Thank you for looking after him." Will picked him up and the little boy rested his head on Will's shoulder. "We'll see you in the morning."

Alfie followed them out to the hall and closed the morning room door. "Is David still over there?" he asked in a low voice.

"David is sitting with them and, as it's getting late, he's staying the night. Thanks for fetching him, Alfie, I really needed his help. Come over with your mother in the morning and meet your new nephew and niece," he added and Alfie showed them out.

"Well, Dr Fitzgerald?" Florrie asked eagerly, climbing the areaway steps to the pavement.

"It's twins," he said and smiled as her eyes bulged. "We're going to have to get you some help in the nursery."

He helped Florrie to put John to bed before going downstairs to his and Isobel's bedroom and beckoning David out onto the landing.

"You can't go home at this hour. Zaineb has prepared a bedroom for you, and Alfie and his mother will be here after breakfast."

"Thanks, Will."

"Not at all." He showed David to the guest bedroom and shook his hand again. "Let's all get a good night's sleep."

Returning to his and Isobel's bedroom, he closed the door and leant back against it. Both Isobel and the twins were fast asleep and he needed to be as well. Heaving himself away from the door, he got undressed and checked that the babies were warm enough. He lit the oil lamp and turned it down low before extinguishing the gas lamps and getting into bed. Leaning over Isobel, he kissed her lips then lay on his back and closed his eyes.

Something brought Isobel out of a deep sleep and she groaned. About to try and turn over, she realised what it was. Both babies were crying, wanting to be fed.

"Will?" she murmured but there was no response. "Will?" She tried again louder. "The babies…"

"Isobel?" He sat bolt upright and turned the oil lamp up. "What time is it?" he asked, more to himself than her and glanced at the clock on the mantelpiece. "Ten past four." He rubbed his eyes as the babies continued to cry. "The twins are hungry."

"Bring the boy first this time," she said, heaving herself into a sitting position while he got out of bed and went to the cradle. She lowered her nightdress, Will placed the baby in her arms and she guided her nipple into the tiny mouth. The baby sucked greedily and she smiled. "Thank you."

"What for?" he replied, both looking and sounding astonished.

"For being such a good doctor and being able to birth the second baby without having to perform a caesarean."

"I should have known it was twins."

"How could you know?" She tried to reason with him. "Especially if one baby was lying either in a peculiar position or in a peculiar place." He grimaced and she stroked his cheek. "It's over now and I'm worn out and I ache all over, but we have a son and a daughter and I'm so happy."

"I can't believe it. Especially as, for a time, you were carrying three."

"We'll give the babies three names each," she decided and Will nodded as he lifted the boy from her and rubbed his back to wind him. The baby burped loudly and Will laughed as he placed him in the cradle and picked up his sister. Isobel took the baby and pushed her other nipple into the girl's mouth. The baby sucked noisily and Isobel ran a hand over her head. "Can we weigh them?" she asked suddenly.

"Yes, of course, we can," he replied, sitting on the edge of the bed. "I'll ask Mrs Dillon for the scales in the morning. I'm curious to know myself how much they weigh, although the biggest twins I've dealt with were the two boys I delivered by caesarean while you were waiting for me in Brown Street."

"And I read half of *Wuthering Heights*."

"And I knew that I loved you," he whispered and broke down in tears.

"What is it?" Taking his chin in a hand, she tilted it up.

"When you collapsed and David laid you on the bed, I thought you were dead. I felt for a pulse——"

"Will, I would never have left you with two babies and a three-year-old to look after," she said softly and another tear trickled down his cheek into dark stubble. "For one thing, my nipples are much more useful than yours, Dr Fitzgerald."

That made him splutter a laugh and he leant over and kissed her lips. "I love you, Mrs Fitzgerald."

She fed the babies again four hours later. Will examined her and helped her to wash and put on a fresh nightdress before Mrs Dillon brought her breakfast in bed.

"Porridge, toast and marmalade, and coffee, Mrs Fitzgerald."

"Thank you. I'm starving, I had to miss dinner last night."

The housekeeper smiled and peered into the cradle. "Oh, just look at the two of them – they're beautiful."

"Mrs Dillon, I spoke to Florrie last night and I told her we would find some help for her in the nursery," Will said. "Would you look for a second nursery maid, please?"

"I will, Dr Fitzgerald. I've just shown Dr Powell into the breakfast room."

"Thank you, I'll be down shortly."

"Go downstairs to David," Isobel said as the housekeeper went out. "I'll eat this and have a few minutes peace and quiet before Mother and Alfie visit."

He nodded, kissed her forehead and left the bedroom, returning half an hour later with her mother and brother.

"Isobel." Her mother kissed her cheek before peering into the cradle beside the bed and bursting into tears. "Oh, they are beautiful."

Alfie gave her a hug and a kiss. "Going to name your son, Alfred, after his uncle?" he teased.

"Will and I had discussed some names but nothing had been finalised. We'll have another discussion after he's been to tell his parents."

"They will be so thrilled." Her mother bent and kissed each baby. "And how is young John? Has he been introduced to his cousins yet?"

"John is eating his breakfast," Will replied. "I'll fetch him in a few minutes and we'll try and explain that there are two babies and not one like we told him."

"Well, we'll leave you to your explanation." Alfie gave Will a grin and shook his hand. "Congratulations. And congratulations, Isobel. We'll see you all soon."

Her mother kissed her again and Will showed them out.

He put his head around the door a few minutes later. "I'll go and get John."

The little boy peered curiously at her leaning back against the pillows as Will carried him into the bedroom.

"Hello, John. Come and sit beside me." She patted the bed, Will sat John down and she kissed his cheek. "I'm so sorry Will and I couldn't come and help you to bed last night but do you remember what we told you about me having a baby?"

"Yes," John replied solemnly.

"Good. Well, last night I had two babies," she said and Will sat on the edge of the bed as they waited for a reaction.

"Two babies?" John asked.

"Yes. A little boy and a little girl. Would you like to see them?"

"Yes."

Will went to the cradle, lifted the babies out and laid them on the bed. John stared at them and she pointed.

"She is a baby girl and he is a baby boy. Will and I are going to discuss names for them. What do you think of your cousins?"

"Small."

She smiled. "That's because there are two of them. When you were born, you were probably the size of the two of them put together."

"What do they eat?"

"They are too small to eat yet," Will replied. "So, for a few months, they will drink a lot of milk."

"I like milk."

"Good. Milk is very good for you."

"They will live with you in the nursery," she said. "And there will be a lot for Florrie to do so we are going to find someone to help her."

"Who?" John asked.

"We don't know yet. We need to meet her – and you'll meet her, too – and we'll all make sure she's nice. What do you think?" she inquired and, to her relief, he nodded. "Good boy. I'll be up and about soon and I'll be spending a lot of time with the three of you."

"Why aren't you getting up now?" the little boy asked.

"Because having two babies was very hard work," Will

replied. "And Isobel is very tired. But she will rest today and get up tomorrow or the next day. So I will bring you down here this evening so she can kiss you goodnight and you can see the babies again."

John nodded, she kissed the top of his head and Will carried him out of the room.

"I'm going to sleep until the babies need feeding again," she said when he came back. "Go and tell your parents and they can come and visit after luncheon."

"I won't be too long," he replied, as she lay down and he pulled the covers up. He kissed her temple and she closed her eyes and slept.

The sun shone as Will walked to Merrion Square and he couldn't help but be grateful that the babies had been born in July. If Isobel had gone into labour during the January snow, Fred might have been unreachable and he may well have had to cope with only Mrs Dillon's assistance.

The thought of Fred made Will fight back yet more tears. They should both be fathers now and the word bittersweet sprang immediately to his mind this time. I'll tell your half-nephews and niece about you, Fred, he promised. You'll never be forgotten.

Tess admitted him to number 67 and he passed her his hat.

"Are both my parents at home?" he asked.

"Yes, they are, Dr Fitzgerald."

"Good. Could you ask my father to join myself and my mother in the morning room, please?"

Tess seemed a little hesitant but nodded, hung his hat on the stand, and went upstairs.

Will waited in the hall, not wanting to begin his announcement before his father joined him.

"Will?" His father came down the stairs with Tess following. "Is something wrong?"

"No, but I'd like you to come into the morning room," he said, opening the door. His mother was seated at the writing desk and twisted around in her chair as they went in. "Mother, I have asked Father to join us."

"I see," she replied crisply, putting her pen down. "Why? What's the matter?"

Will closed the door and turned to face them. "Yesterday evening, Isobel gave birth to twins."

There was a silence as they stared at him, his mother open-mouthed.

"Twins?" she echoed.

"Almost a month early," his father added. "Are they well? Is Isobel well?"

"I sent a cab for David Powell, and I'm glad I did as it was a struggle but, yes, they are all well. You have another grandson and a granddaughter."

"Oh, Will." His mother got up from her chair and threw her arms around him. "Oh, I am so delighted." She kissed his cheek then stood back as her husband held out a hand.

"Congratulations, Will."

"Thank you." He shook his father's hand. "They're small, which is to be expected, but they're feeding well."

"You said it was a struggle?"

"The boy was born first – all very straightforward – then Isobel told me there was a second baby. It was lying transverse and I had to turn it—"

"Turn it?" his mother exclaimed. "How?"

382

"Both internally and externally," he replied and she gasped. "Once the baby was turned, she was also born straightforwardly, but Isobel was exhausted and—" He breathed in and out, forcing Isobel lying unconscious on their bed from his mind. "For a moment, I thought I'd lost her."

"Oh, Will, how awful." His mother squeezed his hands. "How is she today?"

"Regaining her strength. She's just eaten a good breakfast, her mother and Alfie called for a few minutes, and we've just told John. She is sleeping now."

"You have a strong wife," his father said. "To have coped with all that."

"Yes, I have. I just—" He shook his head. "I just don't know how I didn't know it was twins – I should have known it was twins."

"It looked to me that she was carrying high."

"Yes, I've come to the conclusion that the baby girl was partly under Isobel's rib cage, which is why she remained undetected," he said, seeing his mother wince. "Does the *Journal* have any papers on unexpected or undetected multiple births?"

"Yes, lots. And most conclude – like you – that it is due to the positioning of the baby in the womb. Or it could also be that the undetected baby had died in the womb."

"But all's well that ends well," his mother interjected in a forcefully bright tone. "Have you thought about names?"

"Some. But we have decided that each baby will have three names - to remember the baby Isobel lost."

"She was originally carrying three babies." His mother gave a sad little sigh. "That is a lovely idea, Will."

"How did David Powell cope?" his father asked.

"Very well. I couldn't have managed without him. I also need to ask if we can borrow the cradle, please?"

"You can have the cradle, Will," his mother told him. "Apart from a layer of dust, there is not a thing wrong with it. I'll ask for it to be cleaned and polished and brought to number 30."

"And we'll see what else we can gather together and bring to you," his father said.

"Thank you."

"Twins." His mother kissed his cheek again. "I am so happy for you and Isobel."

"Thank you, Mother. I still can't quite believe it. You are both welcome to call after luncheon – together or separately – it is up to you."

He nodded to them then went out, leaving them together. If they would speak to each other, even if for only a few minutes, then all to the good.

Isobel was still sleeping when he returned to number 30 and the babies seemed content so, knowing John wouldn't get his walk to feed the ducks in St Stephen's Green that afternoon, he brought the little boy out into the garden instead.

"Isobel and the babies are asleep," he said as he lifted John onto the bench and sat down beside him. "Someone will take you to see the ducks next week, I promise."

"I like the ducks," John proclaimed. "Can we bring the babies, too?" he asked eagerly before his face fell. "But the noise of all the ducks quacking might wake them up."

"At the moment, while they are very young, they'll only wake up when they're hungry," Will told the boy. "But when we buy a perambulator, we'll all go out for walks."

"What's that?"

"A perambulator is a – well – I suppose you could call it a cradle on wheels and the person pushes it." Will laughed kindly as John gave him a puzzled frown. "You'll see when we buy one." Hearing a tapping, he glanced up and saw Isobel at their bedroom window. She smiled and waved and Will nudged the boy. "Isobel's waving at us," he said and John grinned up at her and waved back.

The two of them explored the mews, Will explaining that as he could walk to and from the practice house and to most house calls he didn't need a carriage, before carrying the little boy inside. Leaving John with Florrie in the nursery, Will went downstairs to his and Isobel's bedroom and found her placing the baby boy back in the cradle.

"Both fed," she said. "And we really need to give them names. I don't like calling them Baby Boy and Baby Girl."

"No." He helped her back into bed and sat on the edge. "So, our daughter?"

"Well, when Alfie and I were small, he used to call me Belle. Father didn't like it and insisted that I be called by my full name and Alfie by his but, for some reason, Alfie stuck and Belle went by the wayside. I don't like the practice of calling a child after his or her parents, though."

"What about Isabella, but we call her Belle?" he suggested and she nodded. "Isabella Sarah Martha?"

"Yes. Mother doesn't like her name but we can't not include it. Now our son? John is named after your father and Edward, so those names are out, and I know you want to include Frederick, but not as a first name."

"No," he murmured, racking his brains. "Benjamin," he

said suddenly. "Ben and Belle."

"Benjamin William Frederick?"

"Yes." He kissed her lips before smiling at the cradle. "Ben and Belle – our son and daughter."

After a luncheon on a tray of thick vegetable soup and soda bread, Isobel waited for Will's parents to arrive. Would they come together or separately, she wondered, and put her book down, hearing voices on the landing. The door opened and Will and his mother came into the bedroom. There was no sign of his father and she could see Will trying to hide his frustration.

"Isobel." Sarah rushed across the room and kissed her on both cheeks. "Congratulations. Oh." She exhaled a little gasp of delight as she leant over the cradle. "Oh, they are beautiful. Will tells me you have named them and weighed them."

"Yes, we have. Benjamin William Frederick." She saw her mother-in-law tense at the mention of Fred's name but continued; "He was just over five pounds in weight. And Isabella Sarah Martha, who was just under five pounds. Ben and Belle for short."

"Lovely names. And I know you aren't regular church-goers but you must decide on when and where to hold the christenings. And," Sarah went on hesitantly. "As we don't know if John was baptised, it would be lovely if all three could be christened together..?"

Isobel glanced at Will and he raised an eyebrow. She nodded and he smiled before turning back to his mother.

"We're going to need umpteen godparents."

"Alfie," Isobel said at once.

"Yes," he replied. "And Jerry and Lillian. I must send Jerry a telegram tomorrow."

"And David," she added and Sarah frowned.

"David Powell? But you hardly know him."

"I do know him, actually," she said, regretting mentioning him so soon. "I've met him on a number of occasions and I dread to think what might have happened yesterday evening if he hadn't been here to help us all."

"Well, when you put it like that," Sarah conceded. "But you'll need a godmother for Belle."

She exchanged another glance with Will, who shrugged, and she turned back to her mother-in-law. "I'm afraid we don't have many female friends, Sarah."

"There is always Margaret Simpson?"

"Margaret?" she repeated in surprise at Sarah mentioning Fred's widow.

"I know Will would have wanted Fred to be a godfather but—" Her mother-in-law grimaced. "Margaret may find the reminder of the loss of her own baby too painful – or she may jump at the chance to be a godmother – write to her."

Isobel exchanged yet another glance with Will. He seemed quite taken-aback but nodded and she smiled at Sarah.

"We shall."

Will's father arrived an hour later and kissed her cheek.

"You look very well considering what you went through yesterday."

"As I said to Sarah, I dread to think what might have happened if both Will and David hadn't been here to assist me. But Will and I have a beautiful son and daughter as a result."

John walked around the bed, crouched down at the cradle and chuckled in delight. "Which is which?"

"This is Isabella Sarah Martha." Will bent over and gently ran the back of his forefinger down his daughter's cheek. "And this is Benjamin William Frederick," he said, doing likewise to his son.

"Frederick?" John stood up abruptly and raised a shaking hand to his forehead. "What did your mother say to that?"

"Nothing. I think she knew we were going to use Fred's name somewhere."

"Thank you."

Will nodded. "Ben and Belle for short," he said and this time his father nodded.

"And Sarah has suggested Margaret Simpson as a godmother," she said and John stared at her in astonishment. "I will write and ask Margaret, but whether she feels she can accept is another matter."

"Yes," he replied quietly. "Well, I came by cab and I brought Edward and Will's cradle."

"Thank you, John."

Will saw his father out and she heard him run back up the stairs and along the landing.

"They could have made the effort to come together to see their new grandchildren for the first time," he raged as he closed the bedroom door.

"Did they speak to each other when you told them?" she asked and he shook his head.

"They barely acknowledged the other's presence."

"They will have to attend the christenings together. What they do at other times is up to them."

"Yes." Lying down on the bed beside her, he lifted her

hand and kissed it. "I just hoped they could be civil to each other. I was clearly expecting too much."

"Will, you'll just have to be content with the way they are now."

"You believe they will never change, don't you? That they will continue to live apart?"

"Yes," she replied softly, knowing she was dashing his hopes that the arrangement might change in time. "What each of them has done is simply too much for the other to forgive."

His face contorted and she lay down, kissing and stroking his hair as he wept into the pillow.

"I'm sorry," he sobbed. "I shouldn't be crying like this."

"It's relief over the twins."

"Yes."

"I was watching you with young John in the garden. You are a wonderful father-figure to him and you are going to be a wonderful father to Ben and Belle. This house – the house I didn't know if I would be able to live in – is now our family home – our happy family home. I will be strong enough to get up in the morning. Ben and Belle will be installed in the nursery with young John. You will take surgery and make house calls. And we will be happy – you and I – and our three children."

He kissed her lips then kissed them again. "I love you."

"And I love you. Do you think Mrs Bell would be willing to be a godmother to her almost namesake?" she asked and Will's face brightened.

"That's a wonderful idea. But—" He sighed. "I can't take a surgery in Pimlico – not now. I should have come to this decision a long time ago but my mind has been on you and

John, Fred and Edward, and my mother and father. I haven't spoken about Pimlico to David since we went there back in February and he stopped mentioning it as he knew my mind was concentrated elsewhere. Work-wise I've been focused on the practice these last few months, mainly to prove to my father that I am capable of running it competently and building up the patient lists. It's time to give notice on the two rooms, they shouldn't be lying empty."

"Speak to David tomorrow?" she suggested. "He was willing to take one surgery and one surgery per week is better than none. If you continue to pay the rent, you will still be contributing. Don't give notice on the two rooms in Pimlico just yet."

Chapter Ten

In the morning, Ben and Belle were placed in their cradles in the nursery bedroom they would now share with John. Will hated having to leave them all but he would be home for luncheon before one o'clock.

"How do you feel?" he asked Isobel as she came to the front door to see him off.

"I'm glad to be up and about again, albeit slowly and carefully. One day in bed was quite enough. Your hat, Dr Fitzgerald."

"Thank you," he said, taking it from her. "Don't do too much and I'll see you later." He kissed her lips, opened the door and went out.

Eva's face registered first shock and then delight when he hung his hat on the stand in the practice house office and told her.

"Twins?"

"A boy and a girl. Benjamin William Frederick and Isabella Sarah Martha. Ben and Belle for short."

"You gave your son Dr Simpson's name." Her eyes filled with tears. "We had our ups and downs but I still miss him."

"I do, too."

"They are lovely names, Dr Fitzgerald. Congratulations. And Dr Powell assisted, you tell me?"

"He did."

"He is a good doctor and I like him very much," she said as the front door closed and David himself came into the office, taking off his hat and hanging it on the stand beside Will's.

"Isobel and I have named the twins Ben and Belle," Will told him with a smile.

"Good names. How are they?"

"Thriving, and newly-installed in the nursery in a cradle each. They look rather lost in them, but they'll grow."

"They will."

"Come upstairs to my surgery, David, I need to ask you something. Please, excuse us, Eva." David followed him upstairs and closed the door. "After my house calls this afternoon, I'm going to register the twins' births and then call on Mrs Bell to tell her about Ben and Belle. I also need to tell her one way or another about the Pimlico surgery as the uncertainty has gone on long enough. David." He sighed. "I can't do it. I can't commit myself to a surgery on the other side of the city and I was foolish to think I ever could. Are you still willing to take one surgery there per week? I will continue to pay the rent on the two rooms and I would be more than happy to assist in any emergency but, for the most part, you would be on your own. If you'd rather not, I'd completely understand."

"I haven't changed my mind, Will," David replied immediately. "And I would be happy to take a surgery there."

Will gave him a relieved grin. "Thank you. We must

agree a day and a time and I'll bring you to Pimlico and introduce you to Mrs Bell and to Jimmy. One thing, though. Mrs Bell lives upstairs and Jimmy lives next door. They miss little or nothing. Pimlico is not somewhere you can bring Alfie."

"Because of the attack, we rarely go out together now, but I do understand."

"I also want to ask you if you would be willing to be a godparent to one of the twins?"

David's jaw dropped. "Me?"

"Isobel and I will also be asking Alfie but we would like you to be a godfather, too."

"I don't know what to say…"

"Yes?" Will suggested with a grin and David laughed.

"Yes, I would be honoured, thank you."

"No, thank you. Good. One down, eight to go."

"You need another eight?"

"John is being baptised, too, and each child needs three godparents. John and Ben, two males and a female. Belle, two females and a male. I'm hoping Mrs Bell will agree to be a godmother and possibly Margaret Simpson. We haven't asked Alfie yet, so…"

"I won't mention it until he does."

"Thank you. Well, we'd better get on with surgery."

At half past four that afternoon, he walked to Pimlico and knocked at the door of Mrs Bell's rooms, hoping she was at home. Feet approached the door and he took off his hat as it opened and his former housekeeper beamed at him in surprised delight.

"Oh, Dr Fitzgerald, I was thinking about you only the other day. Come in and sit down."

"Thank you." Pulling a chair out from the kitchen table, he waited for her to close the door and sit before sitting down himself. "I've called to give you some good news. Isobel and I have twins – a son and a daughter – born on Saturday evening."

"Jaysus, Dr Fitzgerald – twins?" she gasped and he nodded. "And they're both all right – the babbies – and Isobel, too?"

"They are all perfectly well. The boy is called Benjamin William Frederick and the girl is called Isabella Sarah Martha, but we'll be calling them Ben and Belle for short."

"Ben and Belle," Mrs Bell whispered. "Oh—" Getting up, she hurried around the table and kissed his cheek. "I'm so happy for you, Dr Fitzgerald."

"Thank you. I wanted to tell you as well, that I can't take a surgery here now. I'm sorry."

"I thought you mightn't be able to do it," she replied, returning to her seat, unable to keep the disappointment out of her voice. "You'll want to be with Isobel and your babbies as much as you can."

"Yes, but Dr David Powell has agreed to take the surgery instead and I will continue to pay the rent on the two rooms," he added, relieved to see her face brighten. "I've told David he can call on me to assist in any emergencies so I'd like to introduce him to both yourself and Jimmy."

"Yes, of course, you can. You bring Dr Powell here anytime and I'll send someone to fetch Jimmy."

"I will, thank you. David is about the same age I was when I came to Brown Street. But he's a lot less green around the edges than I was."

Mrs Bell smiled. "But now just look at you – married,

with two babbies and a little boy – and running that highfalutin medical practice."

Will laughed. "I think you'll find it's Eva, the secretary, who runs that highfalutin medical practice."

"But you're in charge of it all, Dr Fitzgerald."

"Yes, I am," he replied quietly. "I wish I could have kept my word about the surgery here and I'm ashamed for allowing the uncertainty to drag on for so long."

"Don't be ashamed, you've had a lot to cope with this year." Reaching across the table, she patted his hands. "We don't know what lies around the corner, do we?"

"No, we don't, so I want to ask you whether you would be willing to be one of Belle's godmothers?"

It was a long time since he had seen her so astonished. "Me, Dr Fitzgerald?"

"Yes, you, Mrs Bell."

"Oh, I would love to be a godmother, Dr Fitzgerald, thank you."

He gave her hand a relieved squeeze. "No, thank you, Mrs Bell."

"You're going to need a lot of godparents for two babbies."

"The two babies and John, so we need nine. But David has agreed, and Isobel and I will be asking her brother, Alfie, very soon. I've also just sent a telegram to a friend and his fiancée in London. So, if they all agree, we'll be over the halfway mark."

"When will the christenings be?"

"In a month or two. We haven't discussed where yet."

"You just tell me, Dr Fitzgerald, and I'll get out me new hat."

On returning to number 30, he found Isobel fast asleep on the sofa in the morning room with that day's *Freeman's Journal* on the floor beside her. Picking it up, he sat in an armchair and read an article on a meeting of the Ladies Land League in Co Leitrim attended by Mr Parnell's sister, Anna, then a report on a land meeting attended by many thousands in Co Wexford until Isobel stirred twenty minutes later.

"Oh, no, I fell asleep again," she murmured, rubbing her eyes then stretching. "You should have woken me."

"You're recovering from giving birth and you're feeding two babies. You need as much rest as possible."

"Yes, Dr Fitzgerald," she replied, lying back against the cushions and he smiled.

"I've registered Ben and Belle's births and Mrs Bell has agreed to be a godmother," he announced and Isobel clapped her hands in delight.

"Oh, good. I'm so glad. How did she take your news about the Pimlico surgery?"

"She was disappointed," he admitted. "But she's looking forward to meeting David."

"We need to ask Alfie to be a godparent."

"We'll go to number 55 straight after dinner this evening in case he's going out," he said and she nodded.

"Will, what do you think of my mother and James being two of young John's godparents?" she asked. "Mother is already his Grandmamma Martha but it would be lovely for her and James to be his godparents, too."

Giving her a grin, he put the newspaper on the arm of the chair, got up and went to the writing desk. "It's a fantastic idea. Who could be the other?"

"Well," she began, joining him at the desk. "Diana

Wingfield crossed my mind but the very thought of her would only anger your mother. So, I think it should be Harriett Harvey, even though it would mean he would have two godmothers instead of one."

"Mrs Harvey?" He pursed his lips as he opened the bottle of ink and picked up the pen. Pulling a sheet of notepaper towards him, he dipped the nib into the ink. "Yes," he nodded as he began to compile a list. "But just Mrs Harvey, not Jim. Jim is an ass."

John	_Ben_	_Belle_
Martha ?	_Alfie ?_	_Mrs Bell_
James ?	_Jerry ?_	_Margaret ?_
Mrs Harvey ?	_Lillian ?_	_David_

"We need to banish these question marks," he added, putting the pen down and slipping an arm around her waist. "But it's a start."

An hour later, they were shown into number 55's morning room and her mother and Alfie got to their feet.

"Isobel." Her mother kissed her on both cheeks. "How lovely to see you up and about again. How are the children?"

"Very well, thank you," she said as they sat down. "We've come to ask you both something."

"Oh?"

"Young John is going to be christened along with Ben and Belle and Will and I are hoping that you and James would be two of his godparents and Alfie one of Ben's?"

Alfie's face broke into a grin but surprise crossed her mother's face before emotion took over and she pulled a handkerchief from her left sleeve and blew her nose.

"We would be honoured. Thank you."

"It would be a pleasure," Alfie added. "How many more godparents do you need?"

Will's eyebrows rose and fell. "A lot," he replied. "But three less than an hour ago when Isobel and I were drawing up a list of possibilities."

"Will, I think it should be you who writes to Margaret," she said as they walked home. "I wouldn't want her to think any letter from me, telling her I have given birth to not just one but two babies, sounded boastful."

"I'll write to Margaret tomorrow. Now," he continued, opening the front door for her. "We will kiss John goodnight, you will feed Ben and Belle, and then we will lie on the sofa in the morning room."

The next evening, she curled up on the sofa with *The Irish Times* while Will sat down at the writing desk and picked up a sheet of notepaper. She didn't envy him, he would have to phrase this letter very carefully.

Twenty minutes later, he sat back in the chair and blew out his cheeks. He blotted the letter before getting up and passing it to her.

Dear Margaret,

I was sorry not to have had the opportunity to call on you before you left for Wicklow. I hope you are enjoying the country air.

I am now the father of twins. A boy named Benjamin William Frederick (Ben) and a girl

named Isabella Sarah Martha (Belle). Both they and
Isobel are well. Ben and Belle, along with John, who
is the son of my late brother, Edward, will be
christened in a month or two's time.

Isobel and I would like to invite you to be a
godmother to Belle. If you feel that you would rather
not, we will understand completely.

I miss Fred dreadfully and I hope by giving his
name to my son, it will be a way, albeit small, of
preserving Fred's memory.

I hope you are keeping well. If you need any
medical advice or would like me to recommend a
doctor to you, do not hesitate to ask.

Please call to number 30 if you are ever in
Dublin. Isobel and I will be delighted to see you.

Kindest regards,
Will Fitzgerald

"Very good," she said, handing it back to him. "Post it
first thing in the morning."

There was a surprisingly quick reply from Margaret the
following week, along with a letter postmarked London with
Jerry's handwriting on the envelope. Will opened both
letters and passed her Margaret's.

Dear Will,

Thank you for your most welcome letter.

I am absolutely overjoyed for you both and you have
my sincerest congratulations on the births of Ben and
Belle. I would be honoured to be one of Belle's
godmothers. Thank you for thinking of me and please

let me know when you have a date for the christenings.

I am enjoying a very quiet life here in Wicklow but Mother and I will return to live in Dublin soon. Probate of Fred's estate is almost complete and then I will find tenants for number 1 Ely Place Upper as it is unlikely that I will ever live there again. I am keeping well but I also miss Fred dreadfully and I cannot help but wonder what might have been if he and Nicholas were both alive today.

Thank you for your kind offer of a recommendation of a doctor. I will call to the practice house so we may discuss possibilities.

Maria's death was a terrible shock. I should have attended her funeral but, knowing she would be buried alongside Fred and Nicholas, and this sounds terribly selfish, it was too soon for me to attend another funeral and re-visit their graves. Diana Wingfield wrote and told me how kind you, Isobel, and your father were and you have my deepest gratitude.

I would be delighted to call on both you and Isobel when I return to Dublin and congratulations and thank you again for your kind invitations.

Kindest regards,
Margaret Simpson

"Oh, I'm so relieved – Margaret has agreed to be a godparent," she said.

"So have Jerry and Lillian," he replied, taking the letter from her. "As well as that, Jerry says Mrs Thompson's Home for Children underwent an unannounced inspection and has since been closed."

Her heart leapt. "Oh, that's wonderful. Isn't it?" she asked anxiously, as Will read the rest of Jerry's letter with a frown.

"The children in the home have been transferred to other homes. Unfortunately, Jerry says there is nothing to stop Mrs Thompson opening another children's home under an assumed name."

"Oh." This time, her heart sank.

"But John is safe with us," Will said softly. "We have brought him out of himself and he is now a happy little boy."

"Yes, he is, and we now have eight godparents. I'll call on Harriett Harvey after luncheon and if she accepts, we can make arrangements for the christenings."

Claire admitted Isobel to number 68 Merrion Square, the parlourmaid noting her lack of pregnancy belly, and showed her straight into the morning room.

"Mrs Fitzgerald, Mrs Harvey."

"Isobel, how lovely to see you." Harriett Harvey, wearing a gorgeous lavender-coloured day dress, got up from her chair at the large writing desk. "Some coffee, please, Claire."

"Yes, Mrs Harvey." Claire went out and closed the door behind her.

"Sarah told me about the twins. Congratulations. I am delighted for you and Will. Please, sit down."

"Thank you." Isobel sat on one of the leather sofas and Harriett sat beside her. "It certainly was a shock – a pleasant one – but a shock all the same."

"And Belle and Ben – beautiful names. When will you hold the christenings?"

"In a month or so's time. It's the christenings I came to speak to you about, Mrs – Harriett. You see, we are having young John christened as well, and Will and I would like you to be one of his godparents."

Harriett's eyes widened but her face broke into a broad smile. "Me?"

"Yes. When I came here, I was very lost and you were so very kind to me and—"

"Jim and I dismissed you, Isobel," Harriett reminded her gently.

"You had every right to. I had become pregnant. But that is in the past now, and what I am trying – badly – to say is that you are the person who could be just as kind to young John." Her shoulders slumped. "Does that make any sense whatsoever?"

Harriett laughed kindly. "Yes, it does. And I am very touched that you would think of me and I would be delighted to be young John's godmother."

"Thank you, Harriett. You must call to number 30 and meet him and the twins."

"I shall. I must admit that Sarah did tell me about the boy and how you and Will have performed miracles with him."

"He speaks now and that was a huge step. We still can't mention Edward as young John believes his father didn't want a bastard, as he put it, and abandoned him in the children's home. When he is older, we will try and set the record straight."

Harriett's face crumpled in sympathy as she nodded. "And his mother is dead also?"

"Yes. We have a photograph of her with Edward. She was beautiful and young John has her eyes but Will says everything else is Edward."

"You never met Edward, did you?" Harriett asked.

"No, I didn't. I wish I had. I've heard so much about him and I'll never be able to judge for myself whether any of it is true and—" She broke off as the door opened and Claire came in with their coffee and set the tray down on a side table.

"Thank you, Claire." Harriett reached for the coffee pot, poured them a cup each, then added milk and sugar. "Young John is a very lucky little boy to have a home with yourself and Will and now two little cousins. You have a busy nursery now."

"Yes, we do. Mrs Dillon, our housekeeper, has found another nursery maid she thinks is suitable. The girl is coming to number 30 in the next few days so Will and I can meet her."

"You and Will do almost everything together, don't you?" Harriett asked and Isobel flushed. "No, don't be embarrassed, Isobel, I think it's wonderful. Jim has almost always left the servants to me and it's the same with John and Sarah – well – it was," she corrected herself with a little grimace.

"Thank you again for turning this house over to us that day. If you hadn't said yes…"

"Jim still doesn't know that Maria was brought here to die," Harriett told her quietly. "He believes what was put about – that Maria collapsed when she called here after Tess told her Sarah was unwell and was not receiving visitors. Isobel, I would prefer for Jim never to know what really happened that day."

"Of course. So Mr Harvey doesn't know John and Sarah are living separately?"

"No. And, as far as I can ascertain, no-one knows."

"My mother knows now, but I don't think John has told any of his acquaintances."

"Do you think the arrangement is permanent?" Harriett asked. "Sarah never refers to John anymore, so I don't like to mention him."

"Yes, it is. Will was hoping that at some point in the future they might reconsider, but they won't. And it is for the best, however sad. Sarah will never forgive John for all the years of deceit and John will never forgive Sarah for not allowing Maria to die in number 67. Too much has been said and done, so this is the way things will be."

"They will have to attend the christenings together for the sake of appearance."

"I know." Isobel sighed. "And I hope they manage to put on a convincing act."

The following Saturday afternoon, Will introduced David to Mrs Bell and Jimmy and they all went to inspect the surgery and waiting room. Two oil lamps, a lockable cupboard for medicines, a desk, two chairs and an examination couch had been purchased from a second-hand furniture warehouse and the waiting room contained twenty dining chairs and two stools. He and David had stocked the medicine cupboard, marking each item on a list as it went onto the shelf. Will had to admit David was off to a much better start in Pimlico than he had been in Brown Street.

"I'm impressed." He grinned at David. "It looks very well."

"And everyone knows it's just one surgery a week," Mrs Bell confirmed.

"Well." Will kissed Mrs Bell's cheek and ruffled Jimmy's hair before shaking David's hand. "I'll leave you to it."

He went out onto the street, put on his hat and smiled at the freshly-painted sign hanging on a nail on the wall beside the door.

David Powell M.D.
Surgery Weds 5 pm – 7 pm

Straightening the sign, Will gave it a bittersweet nod before walking away without looking back.

At number 30, Isobel came out to the hall as he hung his hat on the stand. Taking his hand, she led him into the morning room, closed the door then kissed his lips.

"Did anyone go with you when you went to Brown Street for the first time?" she asked and he shook his head.

"No. Because I knew no-one would approve."

"Then, David is very lucky to have had your help – and Mrs Bell's and Jimmy's help from now on," she said, kissing him again. "Mrs Dillon has just told me that Bridget, the prospective nursery maid, will be here at seven o'clock this evening."

Bridget was tall, dark-haired and in her early twenties. She sat down in one of the armchairs in the morning room and stared nervously at him, seated beside Isobel on the sofa, clearly not used to being interviewed by both prospective employers.

"Mrs Dillon told me your previous employers emigrated to Boston," Isobel began.

"Yes, Mrs Fitzgerald," Bridget replied, pulling a sheet of notepaper from an envelope, unfolding it and handing it to her.

He and Isobel read the glowing character reference and he noted that the Cornell family had four children – twin girls aged three, and two boys aged five and seven.

"Had you attended to the twin girls from their birth?" Will asked.

"Yes, Dr Fitzgerald."

"Were there two of you in the nursery?" Isobel asked and Bridget nodded.

"Yes, Mrs Fitzgerald. Myself and a second nursery nurse."

"Well, as Mrs Dillon has probably told you, we have twins – a boy and a girl – and John, who is my husband's three-year-old nephew. Up to some months ago, John lived in a children's home, was treated very cruelly, and was traumatised by his experience. We have managed to bring him out of himself and, although he appears to be a happy little boy, we still all need to have patience with him."

"Yes, Mrs Fitzgerald, Mrs Dillon did mention Master John and I do understand."

"Do you have any brothers or sisters?" Will asked and she giggled before clapping a hand to her cheek in horror.

"Oh, I'm sorry, Dr Fitzgerald. Yes, I'm one of twenty."

"Twenty?" Will's jaw dropped. "Good grief."

"We're the biggest family in the parish. I'm the twelfth. I have five sisters and fourteen brothers. Eight of them are still living at home."

"Which is where?" Isobel asked.

"Near Salthill in Co Galway," Bridget replied and Isobel smiled.

"I was born in Ballybeg."

"No?" Bridget's eyes bulged. "Kathleen – she's the

fourteenth – she has just started as a maid of all work in the Protestant Glebe House there. Do you know of it at all, Mrs Fitzgerald?"

"I do," Isobel replied. "I was born and brought up there."

"No? The previous people there were called Stevens."

"That's right. My family."

"Good gracious me, who'd have thought?" Bridget proclaimed before clapping a hand to her cheek again. "Oh, dear, I am sorry."

"Not at all." Isobel laughed and the three of them got to their feet. "We'll show you the nursery and you can meet Florrie, John, Belle and Ben."

Will went to the door and opened it, extending a hand out to the hall. "After you, Bridget."

"Thank you, Dr Fitzgerald," Bridget said as she went past him.

Catching Isobel's eye, he gave her a little smile and she smiled and nodded in reply.

The marriage between Martha Henderson and James Ellison was to take place on the morning of Saturday 10th December at St Peter's Church on Aungier Street. Invitations would be sent out once the engagement was announced in *The Irish Times* but Isobel knew her mother assumed the christenings would be held there, too.

"The trouble is," she told Will. "I still associate that church with funerals and sadness. And it's not as if we attend service there every Sunday either. Alfie told me Mother considers us both lapsed Church of Ireland. I do wish the wedding was taking place there first, but I know it can't."

"We got married in Trinity College Chapel. Shall we see

if our children can be baptised there, too?" he suggested and laughed as she threw her arms around his neck. "I think I'll take that as a yes."

Following a meeting with the Trinity College chaplain, a date was set for the christenings – Saturday 20th August. They then went straight to a stationer's and ordered invitation cards. Isobel collected the cards two days later and sat down at the writing desk that evening.

"It probably seems silly to post them," she said, picking up the pen as Will lay down on the sofa with his hands behind his head. "Especially Mother and Alfie's, but I think it's lovely to receive an invitation through the post."

"How many guests did your mother and James decide on in the end?" Will asked.

"Twenty. And many of them are James' brothers and acquaintances. London has been decided upon for the honeymoon."

Margaret Simpson was one of the first to reply and within a fortnight all the godparents had replied confirming their attendance.

The day before the christenings, Isobel and Mrs Dillon went upstairs to the drawing room. The double doors were open and Mary and Zaineb were covering the dining room table with a huge white linen tablecloth. The last time the two rooms had been used was the unfortunate evening with Fred and Margaret. How long ago that seemed now.

"The rooms will look wonderful," the housekeeper assured her. "There is absolutely nothing for you to worry about, Mrs Fitzgerald. I haven't cooked a luncheon for such a large party in a long time and I am very much looking forward to it."

The next morning, Isobel went into the drawing room and smiled before continuing on into the dining room. Every piece of furniture and each ornament, every item of silver plated cutlery and each crystal glass was polished and gleaming.

"Well, Mrs Fitzgerald." Will was standing in the double doorway buttoning up his frock coat then smoothing down a silver-grey cravat. "Will our family home impress our guests?"

"Mrs Dillon, Mary and Zaineb have worked wonders so, yes, it will. You look very handsome, Dr Fitzgerald."

Taking her hands, he stood back to admire the square-necked cream dress she'd had made especially for the occasion.

"You look so very beautiful, Mrs Fitzgerald." Pulling her gently towards him, he bent his head and kissed her. "Shall we go? We have a lot of introductions to make before the service begins."

Belle, dressed in the christening gown her mother and uncle had been baptised in, slept in Isobel's arms all the way through the service. Ben, dressed in the Fitzgerald christening gown, kicked and screamed in Will's arms. John, being held and strategically placed on his namesake's left hip so the little boy was in-between his grandparents, made everyone laugh by exhaling an exaggerated sigh and rolling his eyes at his cousin's bad behaviour.

"May I help put the children to bed?" Margaret asked, sounding hesitant, as they all returned to number 30 and went into the hall. "And I think Lillian wishes to help, too."

"Of course you may," Isobel replied. "Would you like to hold Belle?" she added tentatively and Margaret's face lit up.

"I would love to."

She placed Belle in Margaret's arms and tears began to spill down Margaret's cheeks.

"Take her to the morning room, Isobel," Sarah told her quietly. "I will bring Mrs Bell, the Harveys' and Will's father upstairs to the drawing room."

"Thank you. Where has Will gone?"

"To the garden, I think."

Isobel nodded and guided Margaret out of the hall.

"Sit down on the sofa," she instructed softly.

"But Ben..?"

"Will has Ben."

Margaret sat down as Lillian followed them into the morning room. On seeing Margaret's distress, she went to discreetly leave.

"No, Lillian, please stay." Margaret gave her a wobbly smile and Lillian closed the door. "I'm just being silly."

"No, you are not." Isobel sat beside her and squeezed her arm. "I know today must be very difficult for you."

"It is, but I wanted to come. I should be holding my own baby now, you see," Margaret explained and Lillian's face crumpled in sympathy. "And I cannot have another, so having a godchild means the world to me."

"And you are welcome to visit Belle – and Ben and young John – whenever you are in Dublin," Isobel told her.

"Thank you. I'm so glad we have all met at last – Fred's widow, Will's wife and Jerry's fiancée – I was beginning to think we never would."

"I like Dublin and Jerry and I hope to visit regularly," Lillian said. "And it would be lovely if we could all meet for tea or coffee."

"I would like that very much." Margaret looked down as Belle opened her dark blue eyes and yawned. "It has been a tiring morning, hasn't it?" she asked the baby softly. "Why don't you go back to sleep? I think you should," she added and Belle yawned again before closing her eyes.

"Why don't we have a breath of air in the garden before luncheon?" Isobel suggested and Margaret nodded before attempting to pass Belle back to her. "I think Lillian would like to hold Belle."

"Oh, I would, thank you." Lillian took the baby and kissed Belle's forehead.

In the garden, they found Will and Jerry – with Ben in his arms – standing beside the bench looking up at the back of the house. David and Alfie were at a rose bush with young John, who was squealing with laughter at something Alfie was telling him.

Lillian went straight to Jerry and they began to compare the twins. Will came to her, kissed her hand and they watched as Margaret made a beeline for young John. The little boy gave her a grin, pointed to the rose bush, and she bent and sniffed the yellow flower.

"Where are my parents?" Will asked.

"Margaret was a little upset so she and Belle, Lillian and I went into the morning room while your mother brought the Harveys', Mrs Bell and your father upstairs," she replied.

"I hope he and Mother behave," he murmured, glancing up at the house again and she followed his gaze.

John Fitzgerald was standing at a window surveying them all. On seeing them both look up at him, John immediately moved away from the window and she turned back to Will with a comical shrug.

"They have so far and I've seated them opposite and not beside each other at the dining table. Your father is in between my mother and Harriett and your mother is in between James and Mr Harvey. Enjoy the day, Will. With both Mother and Harriett on their guard, there is nothing to worry about," she concluded and Will nodded, slipping an arm around her waist.

"Thank you. And thank you for everything – oh, dear," he added as both babies began to cry. "I think they've had enough of being the centre of attention."

"They want to be out of their christening gowns and in their cradles," she explained as Lillian and Jerry turned to them with helpless expressions. "We'll bring them upstairs," she said as she took Belle from Lillian and Jerry passed Ben to Will. "We're bringing the twins to the nursery to change their clothes and put them in their cradles," she called to the others.

"Can we all come and help, Isobel?" Margaret asked.

"Yes, of course," she replied with a smile. "Then, we'll join everyone in the drawing room."

"Come along, John." Will put Ben in the crook of his left arm then held out his right hand. The little boy clasped it and they all walked across the lawn towards the house. "Your cousins need their sleep."

THE END

Other Books by Lorna Peel

The Fitzgeralds of Dublin Series

A Scarlet Woman: The Fitzgeralds of Dublin Book 1
Dublin, Ireland, 1880. Tired of treating rich hypochondriacs, Dr Will Fitzgerald left his father's medical practice and his home on Merrion Square to live and practise medicine in the Liberties. His parents were appalled and his fiancée broke off their engagement. But when Will spends a night in a brothel on the eve of his best friend's wedding, little does he know that the scarred and disgraced young woman he meets there will alter the course of his life.

Isobel Stevens was schooled to be a lady, but a seduction put an end to all her father's hopes for her. Disowned, she left Co Galway for Dublin and fell into prostitution. On the advice of a handsome young doctor, she leaves the brothel and enters domestic service. But can Isobel escape her past and adapt to life and the chance of love on Merrion Square? Or will she always be seen as a scarlet woman?

A Suitable Wife: The Fitzgeralds of Dublin Book 2

Dublin, Ireland, 1881. Will and Isobel Fitzgerald settle into number 30 Fitzwilliam Square, a home they could once only have dreamed of. A baby is on the way, Will takes over the Merrion Street Upper medical practice from his father and they are financially secure. But when Will is handed a letter from his elder brother, Edward, stationed with the army in India, the revelations it contains only serves to further alienate Will from his father.

Isobel is eager to adapt to married life on Fitzwilliam Square but soon realises her past can never be laid to rest. The night she met Will in a brothel on the eve of his best friend's wedding has devastating and far-reaching consequences which will change the lives of the Fitzgerald family forever.

A Discarded Son: The Fitzgeralds of Dublin Book 3

Dublin, Ireland, December 1881. Isobel Fitzgerald's mother, Martha, marries solicitor James Ellison but an unexpected guest overshadows their wedding day. Martha's father is dying and he is determined to clear his conscience before it is too late. Lewis Greene's confession ensures the Ellisons' expectation of a quiet married life is gone and that Isobel's brother, Alfie Stevens, will be the recipient of an unwelcome inheritance.

When a bewildering engagement notice is published in The Irish Times, the name of one of the persons concerned sends Will and Isobel on a race against time across Dublin and forces them to break a promise and reveal a closely guarded secret.

A Forlorn Hope: The Fitzgeralds of Dublin Book 4
Dublin, Ireland, September 1883. The rift between the Fitzgeralds deepens when Will's father threatens legal action to gain visiting rights to his three grandchildren. But Will, Isobel and John are brought unexpectedly together by Will's mother when Sarah's increasingly erratic behaviour spirals beyond their control.

Isobel is reunited with a ghost from her past unearthing memories she would rather have kept buried while the fragile marriage of convenience orchestrated by John becomes more and more brittle before it snaps with horrifying consequences.

A Cruel Mischief: The Fitzgeralds of Dublin Book 5
Dublin, Ireland, October 1885. The fragile peace within the Fitzgerald family is threatened when Dr Jacob Smythe becomes one of Will's patients, angering his mother. But in attending to the elderly gentleman's needs, Will inadvertently reunites Sarah with an old adversary and Isobel discovers she and Dr Smythe have an unexpected and tragic connection.

When Alfie receives a card on his twenty-ninth birthday, the recognisable handwriting and cryptic message shatters his hard-won personal contentment. Has a figure hoped long gone from his life returned to Dublin to wreak a cruel mischief on all those who banished him? Is Alfie's ambition of becoming a doctor about to be derailed when he has less than a year left at Trinity College?

A Hidden Motive: The Fitzgeralds of Dublin Book 6
Dublin, Ireland, September 1886. Will is reacquainted with his former fiancée when his father's close friend Dr Ken Wilson dies suddenly. On finding they have received the only invitation to the Wilson residence after the funeral, the Fitzgeralds witness the tensions between Cecilia, her mother and her in-laws and discover her hidden motive for wanting them present.

When Isobel is reunited with an old friend from Ballybeg, his shame at what he has done to survive hampers her attempts to bring him and Alfie together again. With an empty life and low expectations, can Peter regain his self-respect or are he and Alfie destined to be alone?

The Fitzgeralds of Dublin Series: Books 1-3 Box Set
This Kindle box set contains the novels *A Scarlet Woman, A Suitable Wife* and *A Discarded Son*.

Historical Romance

Into The Unknown
London on 3 September 1939 is in upheaval. War is inevitable. Into this turmoil steps Kate Sheridan, newly arrived from Ireland to live with her aunt and uncle and look for work. When she meets Flight Lieutenant Charlie Butler sparks fly, but he is a notorious womaniser. Should she ignore all the warnings and get involved with a ladies man whose life will be in daily danger?

Charlie Butler has no intention of getting involved with a woman. But when he meets Kate his resolve is shattered.

Should he allow his heart to rule his head and fall for a nineteen-year-old Irish girl while there is a war to fight?

Private conflicts and personal doubts are soon overshadowed. Will Kate and Charlie's love survive separation, parental disapproval and loss?

Brotherly Love: A 19th Century Irish Romanc

Ireland, 1835. Faction fighting has left the parish of Doon divided between the followers of the Bradys and the Donnellans. Caitriona Brady is the widow of John, the Brady champion, killed two years ago. Matched with John aged eighteen, Caitriona didn't love him and can't mourn him. Now John's mother is dead, too, and Caitriona is free to marry again.

Michael Warner is handsome, loves her, and he hasn't allied himself with either faction. But what secret is he keeping from her? Is he too good to be true?

Mystery Romance

A Summer of Secrets

Sophia Nelson returns to her hometown in Yorkshire, England to begin a new job as tour guide at Heaton Abbey House. There, she meets the reclusive Thomas, Baron Heaton, a lonely workaholic.

Despite having a rule never to become involved with her boss, Sophia can't deny how she finds him incredibly attractive.

When she overhears the secret surrounding his parentage, she is torn. But is it her attraction to him or the fear of opening a Pandora's box that makes her keep quiet about it?

How long can Sophia stay at Heaton Abbey knowing what she does?

My Name Is Rachel

Rachel Harris was abandoned as a baby on the steps of a church-run children's home, fostered and later adopted. Who was her birth mother and what were the circumstances which led her to give up her baby?

Searching for someone who doesn't want to be found seems a hopeless task until Rachel meets Matthew Williams, a Church of England clergyman.

Then the anonymous and increasingly frightening attempts to end their relationship begin. Are these actions connected to the mysterious events surrounding Rachel's birth?

Only You

Jane Hollinger is divorced and the wrong side of thirty – as she puts it. Her friends are pressuring her to dive back into London's dating pool, but she's content with her quiet life teaching family history evening classes.

Robert Armstrong is every woman's fantasy: handsome, charming, rich and famous. When he asks her to meet him, she convinces herself it's because he needs her help with a mystery in his family tree. Soon she realises he's interested in more than her genealogy expertise. Now the paparazzi want a piece of Jane too.

Can Jane handle living – and loving – in the spotlight?

About The Author

Lorna Peel is an author of historical fiction and mystery romance novels set in the UK and Ireland. Lorna was born in England and lived in North Wales until her family moved to Ireland to become farmers, which is a book in itself! She lives in rural Ireland, where she writes, researches her family history, and grows fruit and vegetables. She also keeps chickens and guinea hens.

Contact Information

Website - http://lornapeel.com
Blog - https://lornapeel.com/blog
Newsletter - http://eepurl.com/ciL8ab
Twitter - https://twitter.com/PeelLorna
MeWe - https://mewe.com/i/lornapeel
Pinterest - http://www.pinterest.com/lornapeel
Goodreads - http://www.goodreads.com/LornaPeel
Facebook - http://www.facebook.com/LornaPeelAuthor
Instagram - https://www.instagram.com/lornapeelauthor

Printed in Great Britain
by Amazon